RADULF CUPPED HER CHEEK, HIS THUMB BRUSHING HER BOTTOM LIP.

Lily felt the earth shift and tremble beneath her, or was it only her own legs that shook? Radulf's other arm curled about her hips and drew her slowly against him.

Lily looked into his eyes. "My lord? What are you doing?"

"I am doing what I wanted to do the first moment I saw you," he murmured. He lifted the long strands of her hair, winding his fingers in them, gently drawing her face closer to his.

Lily felt his warm breath on her lips. She could see her own reflection in his black eyes, and for a moment didn't recognize herself. She looked flushed, her lips moist and parted, her gray eyes half closed. She looked seductive. She looked as if she wanted to be kissed.

Radulf's mouth closed on hers, then his tongue slid inside. Lily opened her mouth to him, unable to resist, no longer sure she wanted to. In a moment she was lost . . .

SARA BENNETT

The Lily and The Sword

AVON BOOKS

An Imprint of HarperCollinsPublishers

This is a work of fiction. Names, characters, places, and incidents are products of the author's imagination or are used fictitiously and are not to be construed as real. Any resemblance to actual events, locales, organizations, or persons, living or dead, is entirely coincidental.

AVON BOOKS
An Imprint of HarperCollins*Publishers*
10 East 53rd Street
New York, New York 10022-5299

Copyright © 2002 by Sara Bennett
ISBN: 0-06-000269-7
www.avonromance.com

First Avon Books paperback printing: March 2002

Avon Trademark Reg. U.S. Pat. Off. and in Other Countries, Marca Registrada, Hecho en U.S.A.
HarperCollins® is a trademark of HarperCollins Publishers Inc.

Printed in the U.S.A.

10 9 8 7 6 5 4 3 2

To Robin, Emma and Alex,
who made this book possible

Prologue

Northumbria, the North of England
1070

"**I** have seen him!" Rona hissed.

"Where?" Lily moved closer to the fire, her breath stirring the steam above the kettle of thin stew her old nurse tended.

"Careful, my lady!" But the glance the white-haired old woman gave her was gentle. "I saw him and his men ride through these woods on Hew's trail. They stopped a moment by the stream to water their horses. I was watching from the trees."

"What is he like?" Lily whispered, trying to still a tremor. Radulf was her enemy, the man who wished to conquer her.

"Big. Powerful. A man to be feared." Rona looked up at her, slanting green eyes watchful.

Chilled, Lily turned her face away from the old

1

woman's piercing gaze. "I must escape."

"Yes—tonight." The shadows in the smoky hut were growing longer; night was coming on swift feet through the forest. "Your husband Vorgen is dead, your kinsman Hew has fled north, and this Radulf will come for you. They say he is not one to give up."

"If I surrender, I fear he will give me to his master, King William—who will crush me in his fist like a butterfly."

Lily shuddered. She had seen enough of what William and his men had done to the north; for the past four years there had been nothing but war.

Rona urged, "Follow Hew over the border to Scotland; find sanctuary there."

"Run like a hare, you mean?" Lily's answer was bitter.

"Hew has run."

"I am not Hew."

No, thought Rona, *you are not*. Gentle Lily had sought peace even while her father Olwayn, husband Vorgen, and kinsman Hew were intent on making war. Now Olwayn and Vorgen were dead, and Hew gone, and Lily was left to bear the full brunt of William of Normandy's anger.

And William had sent Radulf to find her.

"My lady," Rona spoke firmly, "we cannot change the past, but the future is yet to be made."

"I feel as if I have no future."

Lily closed her eyes, long lashes dark against her pale cheeks. Her hair, moonlight silver, was concealed beneath the hood of her green cloak, though wisps curled free at her temples.

She was so weary, so alone.

Radulf—it was a name to strike terror into the

hearts of all Englishmen. They called him the King's Sword, because he was an extension of William's strong arm. Yet what was he but a greedy mercenary come to plunder England and murder the rightful rulers? His reputation was bloody and fearsome, but he was still only a landless, lowborn Norman. Lily's father had been an English nobleman and her mother a daughter of a Viking king.

She would not humble herself to Radulf.

At last, Lily opened her eyes. They were gray, a dark, stormy gray. "If I leave England I will never be able to return."

But if she stayed she would die, and her death would be merely one more meaningless episode in a world where men had run mad with bloodlust. Better she hang on to her life in the hope she could still do some good for her people.

"If only I were a man," Lily muttered. "I would stay and face Radulf."

"A woman has weapons, too, my lady, and sometimes they are stronger than any sword," Rona said.

Lily frowned, not understanding.

"You must go now," Rona insisted. "Quickly, before it is too late. Already Radulf may be turning his eyes in our direction. He is very strong, a formidable enemy."

Lily's hand rested a moment on Rona's stooped, bony shoulder. "Yes, it is time to go. Farewell, Rona."

"Farewell, my lady. May God keep you from harm."

After Lily's slender form had melted into the dark forest, Rona turned back to her kettle. When she had seen Radulf and his men, the King's Sword had stood alone, big and intimidating. Frightened and yet fascinated, Rona had crept closer, trying to see his face. Her foot had slipped on the leaf mold and made a soft sound.

Radulf had turned to look.

Dark eyes were narrowed in a harsh face, strong and manly. He had stared for a long time and Rona had held her breath, terrified. When Radulf turned away, relief had made her dizzy. After the Normans climbed back upon their horses and left, she had crept back to her hut.

Rona could only pray that her Lily would safely escape—for the King's Sword would have no mercy if he found her.

Chapter 1

Lily stood perfectly still, listening.

She had ridden for many days, skirting isolated farms and villages, holding her breath at the edge of a wood when a group of men-at-arms rode past. There was no route north that was safe, and she had zigzagged across the country, doubling back again and again, until she was exhausted.

Grimswade was directly in her path, and Lily had felt as if it had been meant that she come here. Her father was buried in this church, her mother beside him. If Lily was to be forever exiled from England, this would be her final goodbye. Determinedly, she made her way toward the western door.

Before her loomed the familiar blunt tower of the church, while faint candlelight caressed the arched windows. Was Father Luc here, she wondered, his blue eyes bright with kindness? The Grimswade priest was sympathetic to the rebels, hating the king's wanton destruction. Father Luc would hide Lily . . . help her.

The smell of woodsmoke drifted from the village beyond the rise, and with it the occasional bark of a dog. Lily's anxious gaze swept over the stony fields, and the narrow road that ran between what remained of the corn. Her mare was hidden among some wind-bent trees, a few yards from the church.

The door opened to her touch.

Inside the church, tallow candles spat and smoked. Lily paused, expecting any moment to see Father Luc bustling toward her. The hem of her cloak brushed the floor, stirring a faint scent of rosemary. Lily's clothes were stained with travel, and the inside lining of the cloak had been torn during her sojourn in the woods. A small jeweled dagger, her only weapon, was strapped high on her thigh beneath her red wool gown and linen chemise. A bundle containing a few personal things was fastened to her mare outside—all that was left of her previous life.

Lily took another step into the nave and felt the empty silence about her. She was alone. Her slim shoulders slumped. The priest wasn't there. There would be no warm greeting, no offers of safety and gentle remembrances of times long past, when life was good. Before the light was snuffed out on her world.

Disappointment formed a lump in Lily's throat, but she gulped it down with the cold air. This was no time for her courage to fail her. So she was alone? She had been alone before. So she was tired? She had been tired before. When she was safe over the border in Scotland, she could rest. Lily knew now that she should have gone when Vorgen was killed. She should have realized then that all was lost, that her lands would never be hers again. But she had thought, hoped, that as long as she stayed in England, she would have a chance of righting her evil husband's wrongs. That she could offer King William her allegiance through Radulf, and he would listen to her tale of betrayal—how Vorgen had betrayed William, then killed her father to gain her lands. She'd hoped he would then leave her in peace to rule her lands.

Foolishness!

Why had she thought Radulf would be different from Vorgen or Hew? Radulf would never allow her to regain what was hers! And he would never believe she could maintain peace in the north. She was a woman, to be used and treated as if of no account, while Radulf made war on her land, on her people.

Lily paused before the altar, where her parents were buried. Once she had thought to make a proper monument there, extolling their virtues, but Vorgen had refused his permission and so there was nothing to mark their passing. Yet another reason for Lily to hate him.

Forcing her chaotic thoughts to the back of her mind, Lily prepared to pray. She had just bowed her head when, from outside the church, came the thud and rattle of horses. The clatter of armored men.

Radulf?

Gray eyes wide, Lily ran to one of the arched windows. Stretching up onto her toes, she peered out into the darkness just as a shape galloped past. And then another. A boy ran with a flaring torch.

Its flame lit up a nightmare scene of Norman foot soldiers and men on horseback, the gleam reflecting on their chain mail, shields, and weapons.

She fell back, her blood pounding. Radulf! He had come for her! She had heard the stories. He was a giant with a hideous face and blood dripping from his sword. Children screamed at the sound of his name. He would be worse than Vorgen, much worse! A barely human monster . . .

Lily tried to calm herself. Her hands clenched and unclenched in her wool cloak. How did she know it was Radulf? There were many Normans in Northumbria; small bands of them had systematically destroyed large areas of it. She must be brave and cunning. These men would not know she was Vorgen's wife, how should they? Lily might be any woman. A Norman lady, perhaps, fleeing the English even as Lily was fleeing the Normans.

And she could easily play the part of a Norman lady. For two years she had been Vorgen's wife. She had sat at a Norman table and watched how they lived and ate and thought. She could speak French; these men would not guess she was the woman they hunted.

The western door banged open.

Lily scrambled sideways and pinched out the nearest of the betraying candles, then slid down behind one of the pillars. If she was lucky, they would not find her, but if they did . . . A fleeing Norman lady encountering a group of armed men would naturally conceal herself.

A foot soldier came running up the nave, breath wheezing, feet shuffling. Behind him came another man, this one holding a torch, the flames rearing up to show a young, clean-shaven face and short-cropped brown hair. A Norman face. A boy's face.

Lily stared, frozen like a wild, hunted thing. When the boy shouted Lily jumped, clutching her cloak about her tightly, as if trying to vanish into it. Her eyes stung with lack of sleep, for she had lain awake many nights now.

"Priest! Where are you?" The boy's voice wavered up and down, as if it were not properly broken yet. "Priest, my lord wishes words with you!"

Lily blinked, hard. *My lord*?

The cold was seeping through her thick wool cloak, numbing her flesh, but her senses were sharp as needles. Where *was* Father Luc? Perhaps he had known the soldiers were coming. Father Luc might be a priest, but the Normans were a treacherous lot, and Lily could understand the kindly priest not wishing to be caught up in the fighting. More importantly, he might give away Lily's identity—so it was better that he was absent.

The soldier and the boy with the torch had reached the altar. The flame's red glow reared up the walls of the choir, glinting in the windows of colored glass. The boy turned, looking back down the nave toward the door, and his voice echoed in the shadows.

"My lord, he's fled!"

Slowly, afraid any movement might betray her hiding place, Lily leaned a fraction out from the pillar and looked back to the doorway. A dark shape filled it. A man. Behind him, more torches flared as more men ran past, but the dark shape did not move, his very stillness both menacing and compelling.

The boy was hurrying back down the nave, and

his torch shone out toward the man, slowly revealing him. Lily's eyes grew rounder.

Such a tall man, with such a breadth of chest and shoulder. Rona's word *powerful* slipped into Lily's head. Chain mail, a dull silver, covered his body from neck to knees. On his head he wore a conical helmet with a broad nose guard, so that his face was hidden by metal and shadows, except for the pale line of mouth and chin.

"He's gone, my lord," the boy repeated dully, revealing his disappointment.

"Gone for now," the man replied in a deep, husky voice that gave the impression of anger. He moved as if to shrug his shoulders and then caught his breath in a sharp hiss of pain.

"You're hurt, my lord?"

The knight shook his head impatiently. "Go and fetch my horse. We will have to ride north without the priest."

"Perhaps," the boy ventured, "he has gone already. Perhaps he is persuading Vorgen's wife to surrender to us. Perhaps she has had enough bloodshed, my lord."

A low laugh was his answer. "They are dull-witted, these English," the man growled. "They must be shown the error of their ways. Now fetch my horse, boy!"

"Aye, Lord Radulf."

Lily gasped as her worst fears were realized. The man and the boy didn't hear her, but the dog did. Until then, Lily had not even noticed it was present, but now it ran forward with a growl, the soldier behind it. Lily tried to scuttle out of the way, but the dog followed, barking with a sharp, high-pitched sound.

"Here, sir!" the soldier cried excitedly. " 'Tis the priest hiding!"

The boy thrust the torch toward her. The heat of it made Lily's eyes blink, and then rough hands closed on her arms, dragging her forth into the nave and dumping her unceremoniously at the feet of her enemy.

The dog was still snuffling around her, and the soldier pulled it away and led it outside. Lily, her heart leaping in her chest, slumped, frozen and waiting.

The silence seemed to stretch interminably.

"What is this? Have the priests in Northumbria taken to wearing women's gowns?"

The husky voice was full of a wry humor that surprised Lily more than if he had struck her with his fist.

"No, my lord." The boy didn't seem to notice his master's amusement, and took his words at face value. " 'Tis a woman in truth."

Radulf did not answer him, speaking instead to Lily, at his feet. "Lift your face, woman, and let me see you."

It was an order. Lily might be gentle, but she was no coward, and she had never yet shown her fear to the Norman conquerors. To them, her reticence appeared as frigid hauteur.

Straightening her slim shoulders, Lily slowly lifted her head.

The man towered over her, all brawn and bulk. Iron spurs decorated the heels of his leather boots, and dark breeches molded his strong legs, the cloth firmed by leather cross garters. One big hand rested on the hilt of his sword in its scabbard, and Lily noted a scabbed cut across his knuckles. His tunic of chain mail, or hauberk, was dull and stained from the day's fighting, and there was a rent at his broad shoulder.

Beneath his conical helmet Lily was able to make out his clean-shaven chin and his mouth, full-lipped despite being so rigidly held. To her consternation, her interest remained fixed on that mouth, only slowly lifting to his eyes, which glowed darkly either side of the metal nasal. They stared deep into hers, and there was a quick intelligence in them that once again surprised her.

Perhaps something of her thoughts showed on her face, for the gleam was abruptly doused, the dark eyes narrowed suspiciously, and Radulf demanded, "Who are you? *What* are you?"

Lily glanced down at her hands to give herself time to concoct a believable story. Her fingers were clasped tightly at her waist, and on her thumb something gleamed gold in the torchlight. A ring.

Her father's gold ring! Given to him by Lily's mother, and which Vorgen had taken from his dead finger, and which in turn had been taken from Vorgen's finger when he was killed. Lily had worn it ever since, for it rightly belonged to her. It was a ring like no other, a symbol of leadership. Her father's device, a hawk, was chased on a black niello background, the hawk's eye set with a bloodred ruby. Around the hawk design an inscription was engraved, the words also filled with black enamel or niello: "I give thee my heart."

Appreciating the value of symbols, Vorgen had taken the hawk as his own when he killed Lily's father, and it had flown on flags and banners over every battlefield on which he had fought.

Radulf would recognize it.

Lily lifted her gaze and fixed it on Radulf, not knowing what she would say, only that her life depended on it. Beneath the cover of her cloak her fingers were busy tugging at the one thing that might give her secret away. Her voice tumbled out, breathless.

"My lord, I have been staying with my cousins over the border, in Scotland, during this trouble in Northumbria. When we heard Vorgen was dead, I was sent home with a group of men-at-arms. My father, Edwin of Rennoc, is a vassal of the Earl of Morcar, and lives ten leagues south of Grimswade. We had reached the forest just north of here when we were attacked by outlaws. I managed to escape on my horse. I don't know what happened to the men."

The English Earl of Morcar had been King William's man and had refused to join Vorgen in the rebellion. So any vassal of Morcar's would also be William's man, and Lily knew Edwin of Rennoc had a young, fair-haired daughter.

"I was weary and afraid and took shelter in this church. I hoped to find sanctuary. There is so much warring in the north, I did not know who was friend and who was foe."

" 'Tis true 'tis sometimes hard to tell one from the other," Radulf agreed softly. *More humor*? Lily had no time to ponder Radulf's strange manner, for his voice curtly demanded, "Do you know who I am, lady?"

She nodded. Beneath her cloak, the ring popped off her thumb, and she nearly dropped it.

"Then you know I am the king's man. If you are indeed who you say you are, you are safe with me."

"Yes, my lord."

Could he believe her so easily? Lily gripped the
ring tightly in her slippery palm as Radulf leaned
over her, his dark eyes holding a twin image of the
boy's fiery torch. Steadying her fingers, Lily
slipped the hawk ring neatly through the tear in
the lining of her cloak.

None too soon. Radulf was holding out his
hand, palm up, and with the sensation of placing
her head in a wolf's jaws, Lily gave him her shaking fingers. His skin was very warm, and callused
where he gripped his sword. As he raised her to
her feet, his gaze ran over her face, taking note of
her features as if he were making an inventory,
she thought in frightened anger. Lily was well
aware of what he would see; her face was no mystery to her.

Widely set gray eyes framed by thick, dark
lashes and above them arching dark brows. An
oval face with high cheekbones, a straight nose
perhaps a little long for true beauty, and a stubborn chin. Skin like pearl, growing flushed now
from his intense perusal. Once a bard had come to
her father's manor and sung songs in praise of her
beauty and of how he wished to melt her heart.
Hers was a cold beauty, and strangers assumed
her heart was equally cold.

Lily only wished it were so. In truth her heart
was soft and tender, and she had had to guard it
all the more diligently to prevent it shattering. The
defense came naturally now; she had lost the ability to be open.

Carefully, as if he were afraid of startling her,
Radulf reached to slip the hood of her wool cloak
from her hair. The pale silk, neatly plaited when

she had left Rona's, was now a wild mass of escaping curls. The sudden flash of heat in Radulf's dark eyes told Lily more than any words what he was feeling.

"The moon has come down from the sky to light our way," he murmured. "What say you to that, Stephen?"

The boy laughed nervously.

Radulf lifted a strand of her hair and allowed it to slide through his brown, battle-scarred fingers. Lily's breath caught in her throat, and warmth crept into her cheeks. The sight of her hair against his skin was disturbing in a way she didn't understand. This was Radulf, she reminded herself, the man who would hunt her down and destroy her.

Slowly, Radulf's hand cupped her face, his roughened fingers sliding over her skin as though he sought to imprint it in his memory. A tingle ran through her from the point of his contact, down her throat, spreading across her breasts and arrowing into her belly. He made a wordless sound, but she did not look at him, too caught up in her own sensations. It was as if she were a pale candle and he were the brand that had set her alight. And now she was burning. Slowly, languorously burning.

"You have not told me your name," he reminded her, his deep voice gentle, and tilted her head back so that she was looking far into his eyes. He wanted to kiss her—Lily read it in those dark depths. And she wanted him to. Lightheaded, Lily found her gaze shifting again to that sensuous mouth. Watched it curve up ever so slightly at the corners.

"Your name?" he whispered.

"My name is Lily." Instantly, she cursed her wandering wits. Then she remembered that to the Normans, Vorgen's wife was known as Wilfreda. It was only her father who had called her Lily—*my cool, beautiful lily*.

"Lily," he repeated, warming the name on his tongue. "Aye, it suits your cool beauty."

His thumb smoothed the jut of her chin and, as Lily's breath sighed softly between her parted lips, boldly brushed her full lower lip. She trembled, sliding deeper into a situation of which she had little experience. Suddenly his mouth was so close that Lily could feel his warm breath, smell the male scent of him.

She knew then that this was not fantasy, this was not a dream. He really did mean to kiss her, right there, in Grimswade church. And if he kissed her, Lily feared she would melt into a puddle at his feet, would be his to command. An even more dangerous situation than the one she was now in.

Lily jumped away, like a startled mare.

The boy grunted a curse as her elbow connected with his midriff, and then muttered an apology to his lord. Lily felt her cheeks warming again as betraying color flooded her pale skin. Never in her life had she behaved in such a wanton manner! *And never in your life have you wanted to.*

Radulf had stepped back. He was smiling, but all humor had vanished from his face. It was as if Lily's fear of his kiss had broken whatever strange, hot spell they had been under, reminding him of who and what he was. This time when Radulf leaned toward her, his voice was soft with menace rather than desire.

"Yes, I am to be feared, lady. You do well to remember it. You tell me you are loyal to King William, but why should I believe you? For all I know, your loyalty may lie with Vorgen or his she-devil of a wife."

Lily shook her head firmly, trying to still the savage beating of her heart. *She-devil!* He dared call her so, when all she had ever cared for was the welfare of her people! And yet how could Radulf or King William know her truly, when Vorgen had ruled her lands and made war in her name?

"My lord," she said, "truthfully, I am no 'she-devil.'"

But the eyes that had gazed into hers so warmly were cold and unfeeling; the mouth that had promised her such pleasure had become a thin, hard line. The change in him was frightening, and yet it was also a relief. *This* was how she had always imagined Radulf, not that other man with his melting dark eyes and delectable mouth. She could hate *this* man.

Radulf had turned away from her, speaking to the boy, Stephen, as if Lily no longer existed. "Take the lady to my tent and guard her there. When I return from Vorgen's keep I will question her again."

Lily gasped at his high-handedness. She had expected to face some suspicion as to the truth of her identity, but she had still hoped Radulf would give her the benefit of the doubt and send her on her way. She should have realized a man like Radulf would be overcautious. How else had one as hated as he lived so long?

He was watching her again, absently rubbing his shoulder where the chain mail had been cut. Lily saw that blood the color of rust had seeped through his under tunic.

Her heart gave a hard, solitary thump.

"You are wounded, my lord Radulf."

The words came out of her mouth involuntarily. As Vorgen's wife, Lily had learned to scheme and dissemble, to be what she was not—it had been necessary to enable her to survive. But this time the notion that displaying womanly sympathy might be wise only occurred to her after she had spoken.

" 'Tis nothing." Gruffly, Radulf shrugged off her concern.

" 'Tis not 'nothing' if you are hurt, my lord."

He narrowed his eyes at her. Lily felt his suspicion like a stone wall between them. "What would you do about it then, Lady Lily?"

Lily swallowed. His gaze was so intense, as if he were watching her for some sign . . . but of what? "I . . . I would tend you, my lord."

"Ah, 'tend me,' " he murmured. His body relaxed. His mouth twitched. "Do you think that wise, lady?"

Lily's brow wrinkled in a frown. "My lord?"

Radulf stepped closer, and Lily's body went rigid as she fought a sudden, mad desire to sway into his arms. "I may ask you to tend more than my shoulder," he murmured, his breath stirring tendrils of her hair.

Instinctively Lily's eyes lifted to his, reading the truth there. Radulf desired her . . . as had Vorgen. Fear trickled in icy drops down her spine, but this was not fear of Radulf her enemy. This was a fear Vorgen had planted in her, a dark skein of dread, and within that dread were woven myriad strands of doubt and shame.

"Lady?"

He spoke sharply and Lily blinked. The present refocused. She was in Grimswade church with Radulf, and, strangely, relief was now her uppermost emotion. Lily tightened her cloak about her, attempting to regain her composure.

Radulf sighed; he seemed disappointed. Lily realized too late that again he had read her fear and thought it was of him. "Take her to the camp," he commanded Stephen. "Now!" And turning abruptly, he strode on long legs outside into the darkness.

Stephen took her arm in a strong grip. "Come, my lady," he said cheerily, in his boy-man voice. "Lord Radulf has spoken."

Outside, dawn's cold light was gathering on the eastern horizon. The air was sharp, filled with the smells of burning torches and sweating horses, but most of the hurrying soldiers had now moved northward across the cornfields, toward Vorgen's stronghold.

Toward Lily's home, two leagues away.

Her eyes glittered with tears. They would find nothing there but a burned, black shell. After Lily had fled, her people had burned what remained, so that never again could the Normans use the buildings to shelter their soldiers.

Stephen gripped her arm tighter and tugged her along. Lily shook him off, losing some of her assumed meekness. Whatever spell Radulf's presence had spun, it was dispersing with his going.

"I have a mare hidden in the trees over there," she said, pointing at the small thicket. "If I leave her, she will be stolen."

Stephen eyed her cautiously, but must have thought she spoke good sense, because he sent off another boy to fetch the mare.

"Why does Radulf go to Vorgen's keep?" Lily asked, more of herself than the boy.

Stephen hesitated, but youth and excitement loosened his tongue. "He thinks Vorgen's wife hides there. He plans to capture her and take her to the king."

And what then? Instinctively, Lily assumed an expression of icy disdain, concealing her thoughts and emotions. Such precautions were second nature to her now, as necessary as breathing in keeping her alive.

A soldier hovered nearby, and Lily realized she was to have a guard. So Radulf feared "Edwin of Rennoc's daughter" might escape? Perhaps she would have tried it, were she not so tired. But even if she did escape, where would she go? Strange as it seemed, Radulf's tent was probably the safest place to hide just now. No one would be looking for the *she-devil* there.

"I am weary." She spoke at last. "It has been a long and perilous night. Is your lord's tent far . . . Stephen, is it?"

Stephen gave her a shy smile. "Aye, I am called Stephen. I am Lord Radulf's squire. And it is not far. Our army is camped just beyond the village of Grimswade."

Lily nodded and made certain to pull her hood back over her hair, tying it close so that her face was half hidden. If she remained in the Norman camp she would not be recognized by anyone in Grimswade village, but she could not take any chances.

Her life depended upon it.

Chapter 2

Radulf ignored the pain in his shoulder and the soft, constant drizzle that fell from the iron-gray sky, soaking him right through to the skin. He wished he were elsewhere, preferably in the lady Lily's bed. The memory of her pale beauty in the gloomy church and the feel of her silken hair slipping through his fingers caused a hot, aching jolt that had nothing to do with his wounded shoulder.

He tried to remember how long it was since he had had a woman. There had been that plump, compliant merchant's wife in York, and before that . . . ? His mouth turned grim; it was longer than he had thought. And very long indeed since he had wanted one particular woman. Radulf shifted uncomfortably in his saddle, trying to concentrate his mind above his waist.

The chilly light of dawn had long ago given way to day as Radulf had led his men north to

Vorgen's stronghold. He had paused at the church only because he'd thought the priest might speak to Vorgen's wife, and beg her to see reason. She could not win. If Radulf did not open her hiding place like a dagger tip in an oyster shell, then William would. Either way, Vorgen's wife was doomed.

Ahead lay a series of green hills swathed in white mist, and upon the tallest one, what was left of Vorgen's stronghold. It stood dark above them, straddling the gloomy sky. The keep had been constructed of wood and rose high upon a man-made mound of earth and rock. A deep ditch was the outer defense, and inside this a tall wooden fence or palisade further enclosed Vorgen's stronghold.

Someone had set out to burn it, and done a reasonable job.

Radulf frowned. It was like a hundred other scenes he had witnessed in a hundred other places. He doubted anyone was still living there, especially not a highborn bitch like Lady Wilfreda.

Radulf released his pent-up breath with an irritable hiss. He and his men had come from his estates in the south many months ago, and Radulf wanted nothing more than to go home.

He was tired of war.

The feeling had been growing, making it increasingly difficult for him to obey the king's orders with his old enthusiasm. And yet he had marched back and forth across England, putting down rebellions, ordering the building of more keeps and fortifications, enforcing the king's laws. Once Radulf had been as keen as any man to take up his sword and do what he knew he did best. Now, more and more often he thought of Crevitch, and the stone castle he was building and the crops he was growing. He dreamed of stripping off his chain mail and riding across his land with the sun on his bare head, breathing deeply of the ripening wheat and the wildflowers in the meadows.

"Like an old stallion put out to pasture," he muttered scornfully to himself.

But it was true. He was tired of death.

Angrily, Radulf quickened his destrier's pace. The great, feathery hooves kicked up clods of sodden earth. His men struggled to keep up with him. Probably they thought him eager to put as many men, women, and children to the sword as he could find. His reputation had long since eclipsed the reality. Now it was so dire, often he had only to appear before an opposing army or demand a besieged castle open its gates to him, and the deed was done.

All well and good, but there was a darker side to the coin. When he laughed, when he was gentle, people thought it a trap, to trick them into trusting him so that he could pounce. Only those who knew him well saw the real Radulf, and they were few enough.

The face of the woman in the church crept back into his thoughts, and he scowled so blackly his men feared for their lives. Radulf didn't even notice them. As a youth he had sworn never to love any woman, be she common wench or highborn lady. His own father's plight had been too bitter. When Radulf grew up and became a man, he realized that even had he wished to be loved by a woman, it was unlikely one could be found to love the King's Sword.

Why was it, then, that lately he had felt a terrible yearning to love and be loved? He had never been one to harbor foolish fancies. A man in his position should be satisfied with fighting and killing, increasing his wealth and power, and swearing fealty to his king. And he *had* been satisfied, until recently. But as his taste for war decreased, this other need increased—maybe it had been there all along, bubbling and roiling beneath the surface, until it could no longer be ignored.

Radulf shifted uncomfortably in his saddle. Was he like his father after all? Did he, too, long for that all-consuming passion, half madness, that had gripped the old man and blinded him to the truth about his second wife? Was Radulf also destined to be brought to ruin by his own weakness?

Radulf's face turned grimmer. Women were creatures to be used and discarded, and certainly never trusted—it was as well his reputation frightened them away! And he was wise to refuse King William's repeated requests for him to marry and sire an heir to his huge estates. A wife was a dangerous appendage. The idea of one living at Crevitch gave him a twitch between his shoulder blades, as if a knife were pricking him.

Better to leave well enough alone.

"My lord!"

Radulf started, then drew his mount to a stop. He had reached the place where the gate had once stood, and the blackened stronghold rose before him. Quickly his men rode up to surround him, their faces flushed and sweating, their horses huffing and blowing. All about was the smell of wet ash and devastation.

"My lord?" Radulf's captain, Jervois, eyed him warily. "This place looks empty."

Radulf frowned. "Aye. But if Vorgen's wife *is* here, we will find her. Who will lead the search?"

There were a dozen volunteers for the task. Once he, too, would have gladly risked his life for the honor of fulfilling such a request. Now he risked his life every day and every day expected to die, and for what? One day he *would* die, but his legend would live on. Was that a blessing or a curse?

Radulf watched his men walk their horses down into the ditch and up again, cautiously exploring the deserted bailey and burned-out ruins of Vorgen's keep. Where was she, this she-devil who kept him in the wild north when he longed for home?

Had she gone to Scotland, to beg safety from the wily Malcolm? Or was she even now trying to gather another army to drive William from this place? Did she not comprehend the fruitlessness of such an effort? William had subdued the rebels and laid waste to the land, and if the people didn't starve this year, they would next.

She-devil indeed!

She was certainly too dangerous for William to allow her to remain free in the north. He would have her killed. Radulf could understand his king's thinking. William had been inclined to leniency in the beginning, willing to leave certain Englishmen in charge of their own estates. However, too many of them had failed him, particularly in the north, so now he ensured their loyalty by force rather than diplomacy.

What was the life of one woman against the peace of the whole realm?

Radulf had known Vorgen when the Normans invaded England; they had fought together at Hastings. Vorgen had been loyal and tough, a white-haired man with a face lined by hardship. Radulf was certain the Vorgen he had known then could not, alone, have caused such turmoil here in the north.

It was Vorgen's wife who had worked on him, convinced him to rebel against William. 'Twas said she was the Norse king Harald Hardraada's granddaughter, and a Viking temptress. She had turned faithful Vorgen into a traitor, with her silken tongue and witchy ways. Some women had the devil in them, and all their lovely smiles and sweet kisses were but lures to destruction.

Like Anna.

How different the girl in the church! Her pale, ethereal beauty, her great gray eyes, the soft tremble of her lips. Radulf had been shot through with a lust as deadly as any spear, but he had also felt a compelling urge to protect her, and to prevent any further harm or fright from coming to her. And then she had remembered who he was and she had trembled again, only this time not from fear of her situation but from fear of him! Angry and frustrated, Radulf had turned from her.

Must it always be so? Must his name for brutality always overshadow the real man?

Radulf recalled the story she had told him of her journey from the border and subsequent escape from unknown attackers. He knew the Earl of Morcar, and had heard of Edwin of Rennoc— they were both, for now at least, the king's men.

He had no reason to disbelieve her, although it was in his nature to be suspicious. Yet there was something . . . He would divert his men on the return journey; the wood Lady Lily had spoken of was only slightly out of their way. If what she had said of the battle between her men and their attackers was true, there should be some clear sign of it.

An entire day had passed since Stephen had brought Lily to Radulf's tent, a day in which she had paced and worried, and paced again. Although she was probably safe just now, that could not last. She must escape as soon as possible, or persuade Radulf to let her go.

Eventually, as the light began to fade, Lily wore herself out and flung herself down upon the bed. It was Radulf's bed, there was no doubt of that. The wool covers and animal skins reminded her of him; they had his body scent. The acknowledgment made her want to leap up again, but Lily forced herself to be still. *It is important not to be afraid of him*, she told herself firmly. *He is just a man, like Vorgen or . . . or Hew.*

Is he? mocked her inner voice. Lily shivered and wondered how a man with such sensuous lips and intelligent eyes could be as cruel and frightening as was generally believed. She had thought she was adept at reading a man's mind and character—such tricks had been necessary to keep her alive—but Radulf was a puzzle. The man who had touched her in Grimswade church was not the same man whose legend was spoken of in hushed tones. Lily would stake her lands on it—if she still had any. He had desired her, and to

Lily's surprise, she had desired him. Her surprise at her own feelings wasn't because Radulf was undesirable—such a big, masculine man must always be attractive—but because of Vorgen.

There had been no love between Lily and her husband. In fact Lily had hated him, and at first Vorgen had seen her as nothing more than the means to his domination of the north. He had not pretended otherwise, and anyway, how could Lily love the man who had murdered her father and turned her comfortable, ordered existence into hell?

In the beginning, when they were first married, Vorgen had tried repeatedly to consummate their marriage. He had pressed and pummeled her, hurting her when he failed. As time passed his attempts became fewer, but were still as frantic and frightening. Lily had imagined his impotence was due to his age, for he was nearly as old as her father. But with each failed attempt, Vorgen's need to have her grew. He roared at her that it was all her fault, that she was a frozen bitch, and it was her coldness that had made him incapable.

"Then I am glad. Glad!" she had screamed back at him, and earned herself a bruised cheek. But she had been glad he could not take from her what she had always considered hers alone to give. Still, his cruel words had hurt as much as his hands. And he began to say them so often and with such venom, Lily could not help but believe them.

Occasionally Vorgen would threaten her with other men. He told her that he would force her to mate with them, for Vorgen needed an heir to consolidate his position. His subjects thought of him as a foreigner, but they would accept a half-Norman, half-English child and give it their allegiance.

Yet the threats had been just that. And then Vorgen was dead, and she was his widow without ever having been his wife.

The coming of night had been something to dread, in case he visited her chamber. She did not think she would have dreaded the nights if Radulf had been her husband, but Vorgen had left behind a legacy of doubt. Would Radulf, too, find her cold and undesirable? Would he kiss her with passion, only to find that heat chill and shrivel to naught?

He is my enemy! her weary brain reminded her. But that only further confused her; it felt as if her mind and her body were playing tug-of-war.

But Radulf's bed was soft and warm, and Lily's body rested in a comfortable hollow. The past weeks, the past few years, had been like living on a knife edge, and it was a very long time since Lily had been so peaceful or so relaxed.

Finally, she succumbed to exhaustion.

Her sleep was so deep, she did not hear the sounds of the army camp settling for the night, or Stephen coming to light the candles, or an owl calling outside. She slept on, dreamless, her silver hair spread about her.

"My lord?"

The last lingering effects of sleep dissipated abruptly, and Lily held her breath. Stephen's soft voice had come from the direction of the tent door, but it was not Stephen who had awakened her so abruptly.

There was someone standing over her. She

could feel him, smell him—a combination of sweat, damp wool, and man.

Radulf.

Beneath the folds of her gown, Lily's hand closed hard, her nails digging into her palm.

"My lord?" Stephen repeated, his puzzlement evident.

Now all of Lily's senses were awake and quivering. There was a movement nearby as heavy wool—a cloak?—swirled, brushing against her cheek. The contact caused her to flinch, but Radulf had already turned away, his footsteps retreating. Very carefully, Lily opened one eye and peered through her lashes.

Her enemy had his back to her, and by the tilt of his head was drinking from a goblet. Stephen stood beside him, waiting until Radulf had finished, and then refilling the goblet from a beaten metal jug. Radulf grunted his thanks.

Lily noted that Radulf had removed his hauberk and helmet, and now wore a green, short-sleeved tunic over a white linen shirt and breeches of a muddy brown. A thick, dark-colored cloak was thrown loosely over one shoulder. The chain mail had taken with it some of his bulk, but he was still enormous, wide of back and shoulders, his body as strongly muscled as any large fighting animal. *Powerful.* Again Rona's word seemed to encompass all that was Radulf.

"My lord Radulf," Stephen spoke. "Will I dress your wounds?"

Radulf paused, the goblet once more lifted. His hair was very dark and cut short over his skull, shorter even than the Norman fashion.

"No," Radulf answered his squire. "My lady offered to do so," and he nodded in Lily's direction.

She tried to make herself smaller on the bed. Dressing a knight's wounds was the province of a lady, but Lily was wary of touching that warm skin.

"Did you search Vorgen's stronghold, lord?"

"Aye. Empty."

"So there was no battle, my lord?" Stephen sounded disappointed.

Radulf gave a snort of disgust. "No, there was not." He flexed his shoulder, easing the ache.

"So the she-devil is still free?" Stephen looked uneasy at the idea of anyone defying his lord.

"She is. There would be less bloodshed if she yielded now instead of cooking up more plots, but it matters not. I will have her sooner or later."

Lily bit her lip, cold fear crawling over her skin. What if he were to find out that the woman he held safe in his tent was the very woman he sought? Surely he would kill her?

"Women are weak creatures, meant to be confined," Stephen was saying knowledgeably, more like a swaggering knave than an untried boy. "'Tis not right they should be allowed the freedom to lead men and make war. 'Tis not right they should cause such pandemonium about the land!"

"Calm yourself, boy."

Radulf was laughing, Lily could tell by his voice. How could Radulf, the bloody warrior, the putter-down of rebellions, be laughing? The men Lily had recently known in her life did not laugh very often, and when they did their humor was coarse and violent. This Radulf was a puzzle, and

Lily could no longer keep still. She opened her eyes and sat up.

Stephen, facing her, frowned and glanced quickly at his lord. Radulf turned, the goblet in his hand and dying laughter in his eyes. Lily's breath slipped out of her open mouth.

The church last night had been dark, the light poor. Although she had had an impression of size and strength, and a sensation of dangerous dark eyes and a sensuous mouth, she had not really seen him. Now Lily saw Radulf as he truly was, and her heart tumbled over and over, like a small water wheel in a raging millpond.

Why did his face stir her so? It was by no means handsome in the usual way, not at all like the blond perfection of Hew. Radulf's nose had been broken and was a little crooked, and there was a deep scar that ran across one cheekbone and up into his hairline, just missing his left eye. Strong and masculine, it was the face of a man who had lived and seen much. His eyes, dark and deep set, were watchful and older than his years. And his mouth . . . Lily felt weak at the thought of pressing her own against it, of feeling those full lips moving over hers.

Her thoughts careering out of control, Lily's gaze flew wildly to Radulf's as she wondered whether he could read her mind. And then, horrified, whether he would need to. Surely women threw themselves at him every moment of every day? Such a man must be a honeypot for all womankind. With a mixture of uneasy fascination and horrified expectation, Lily watched Radulf approach her.

An angry spark flared in eyes that had a moment before been laughing and warm, and there was a hint of cruelty in the curl of his lips. He looked cross—had he discovered the truth already? No, if he knew the truth he would be *furious*. Lily held her breath as Radulf came to a halt beside the bed.

"You do well to fear me, lady," he said in his deepest, most menacing voice. "You are the lamb to my wolf. I could tear out your throat."

Lily gazed up at him, her eyes held prisoner by his. Oh yes, this was indeed her feared enemy, just as she had always imagined him. The terror of the north, the King's bloody Sword! A shudder of fright ran through her body . . . and then faded. Lily's frozen mind thawed and began to work. Why, if Radulf was so alarming, if his face was as hard and cold as his sword, was the expression in his eyes so achingly weary? As if his own infamy were a burden he could hardly bear.

"I am not afraid of you." Lily heard the quiet certainty in her voice.

Surprise flickered in those dark depths. Slowly the cruel smile faded and became genuine. "No, lady?" He shrugged, winced, and dropped his deep voice to a husky rumble. "Then methinks you are very foolish. *Everyone* is afraid of me." Radulf held her gaze a heartbeat longer before turning away, back toward Stephen. His next words were offhand, a deceptively negligent challenge. "However, if you speak the truth, and are brave enough, you may tend my wounds. Stephen usually does so, but his hands are more used to the serving of meat than the repairing of it."

Radulf turned again to look at her, while Stephen appeared suitably shamefaced.

Lily slowly rose to her feet, smoothing the red gown where it had wrinkled over her hips. She could not help but notice how Radulf's eyes followed her movements, their expression reminding her of a hungry wolf suddenly confronted by a plump lamb. Lily trembled as she used the same analogy as he, but in a very different context. She could not mistake such a look, and her need for self-preservation should send her fleeing from Radulf, and yet . . .

Lily raised her chin.

He was watching her keenly, searchingly, and her proud gesture made him smile. He bowed his head to hide it, but Lily saw the tug at the corners of his mouth.

Did he find her so amusing? Briefly, anger flared within her, but she could not afford to be angry.

"You do not frighten me, my lord Radulf," she repeated firmly, "though for some reason you try. Besides, you forget, I am in your debt."

"My debt?" If he had forgotten the circumstances of their meeting, she had not.

"For granting me your protection."

"A damsel in distress," he murmured, and once again amusement warmed his eyes. Lily waited patiently while he catalogued her features as thoroughly as before. She was not nearly as calm as she pretended. Inside she was asking herself what she hoped to accomplish by her acceptance of his challenge. His trust? Or was there more to it— some secret reason that made her heart flutter and her body weak? Perhaps tending him was just an excuse to touch that hard body and let her thoughts linger on impossible dreams.

When Radulf nodded his consent, Lily didn't know whether to be glad or sorry.

"Very well, lady. Stephen, fetch what needs to be fetched. And bring food. I am hungry, and the lady will eat with me before you take her to Gudren's tent."

When Stephen had hurried out, Lily dared a question. "You were hurt today?"

Radulf gave her one of his unreadable looks. "No, lady. I was hurt yesterday when we fought what was left of Vorgen's army. An arrow pierced my chain mail. 'Twas a slighting blow, not serious. I could ride out and fight now, if need be, without any difficulty."

Lily was sure he could. Such a man as he appeared indestructible—part of Radulf's legend stated he was unable to be slain—but Lily had begun to unpick that mythical tapestry.

Stephen returned with a bowl of warmed water, some cleaning cloths, and strips of linen for binding the wound. He also removed an earthenware pot of salve from a small chest in the corner, and placed it upon the trestle table with the rest. At a nod from Radulf he bowed and slipped back out of the tent, leaving them once more alone.

Radulf eased himself down onto a stool and gave Lily a faint, mocking smile over one shoulder. "You say you are not afraid of me, lady. Prove it."

Lily shrugged in pretended disdain. He turned away from her, and she was left facing a broad and unfriendly expanse of back. She sensed he was waiting; she also sensed his tension—it was a brave man who turned his back on a stranger in Northumbria. He was testing her. Lily took a step closer, and then another, until she stood directly behind him.

His big body gave off such warmth. It attracted her, an irresistible pull. Her inner voice was still protesting but Lily took no notice. There was something very strange happening to her, and Radulf was at its core. Her fingers trembled as she lifted them, and carefully rested her hands on his broad shoulders. Lily felt his muscles tense beneath her touch, and he shifted restlessly on his stool.

"Am I hurting you, my lord?"

He laughed wryly. "Aye, I hurt, lady." Radulf glanced up at her and, seeing her incomprehension, sighed. "Tend me then, Lily. You are not hurting me."

With infinite care, Lily began to remove Radulf's tunic and undershirt. The cloth was fine and well made, as befitted a great lord. Radulf lifted his arms to help her, and first the tunic and then the shirt slipped up over his head. Lily folded them neatly, placing them to one side before turning again to Radulf.

She bit her lips.

Her mother, before she died when Lily was a child, had told her wondrous stories of Valhalla, the Norse heaven, peopled with gods like Odin and Thor and Freyr. Thor was Lily's favorite. He was the strongest, a giant, but he was clever, too, and according to Lily's mother, of such manly beauty a maiden might fall instantly under his spell. Lily had listened to those stories, her gray eyes wide, dreaming that one day she might behold such a creature.

And now she had.

Radulf's back was broad and brown, with well-defined muscles roped beneath his skin. Lily was tempted to run her hands over his shoulder blades and down his spine, smoothing her palms over that firm, healthy body. And as for his arms, why, she would need two hands to measure their upper circumference, and even then her fingers would not meet! Hew had been slim and golden, while Vorgen had been old and sinewy. Not like this. Never like this.

Stop it. Are you losing your wits? Remember who this is, remember what he could do to you.

The wound—she must tend the wound.

It was but a shallow gouge in his flesh, just beyond the ridge of his shoulder. Lily could see where the arrow had sliced through his skin, luckily not piercing it too deeply. There had been some bleeding, though that had stopped, and there was now only a slight leaking of watery fluid. Still it looked red and sore, and must hurt him quite a bit.

"Does this hurt you?" She pressed the edge of the wound, gentle but firm. It was best to know now if there was any swelling or poison. Lily had seen men die of something so small it was hardly noticed by them, and yet they sickened and, within a short time, died in great agony.

"No," he said, his deep voice husky. "Your hands are gentle, lady. 'Tis long since I have had such tender care."

Lily suddenly became very brisk, bathing away the dried blood, careful not to inflict further pain or hurt. Radulf sat as a statue, never flinching or crying out as Vorgen had always done. During her ministrations Stephen returned with food and more wine, setting both silently upon the table and once more leaving them alone. When Lily finally lifted the earthenware pot and opened the stopper, she held it up to her nose and sniffed sharply.

Radulf turned his head to look up at her. A glint of amusement shone deep in his eyes. "Do you mean to anoint me with it, lady, or eat it?"

She ignored him. "I know it," she murmured with relief. " 'Tis from the marigold plant. A goodly potion for healing wounds such as yours."

"You are a healer?" he asked sharply, still watching her.

Lily laughed, genuinely amused. "No, my lord, I am no healer. I have learned only a little. But enough," she added. There was no need to tell him too much; she must not give her secrets away.

Radulf seemed satisfied and nodded, turning back to his contemplation of the food on the table. It must be growing cold and he was hungry, yet he hadn't spoken angrily to her, he hadn't lifted his hand to strike her. He had sat still and patient and allowed her her way with him.

What sort of Norman was this?

"Have I time to see to your hand?" she asked quickly and a little breathlessly.

Radulf lifted his hand in surprise, as if noticing the cut on it for the first time. Had he not felt the discomfort? Was he so used to these things that they were normal for him? And, now that she thought on it, his shirt had been damp and his breeches were definitely so.

"As you will, my lady," he was saying, and watched her curiously as she gave his hand her attention.

To distract herself, Lily clucked her tongue and

instructed him. "You should see that your servant keeps you dry and warm. The north of England is different from the south, my lord. Here the cold creeps into your bones and lies there, making them ache. You will become ill if you do not change into warm, dry clothing."

He laughed, but he sounded pleased. "Enough," he said, still smiling. "We will eat first, and then you can strip me and rub me dry." One eyebrow lifted slowly, suggestively. "If you wish."

Lily knew the color was rising in her cheeks again. "My lord," she began breathlessly in denial, but the thought was between them, vivid as if it were already a fact. She could not seem to look away from his eyes, and he appeared to be in similar difficulty.

"You must be hungry, my lord," Lily managed to say through the constriction in her throat.

Radulf lifted his hand and cupped her cheek, his thumb brushing her bottom lip, as it had in the church. Lily felt the earth beneath her shift and tremble, or was it only her own legs that shook? Radulf's other arm curled about her hips and drew her slowly against him.

Lily looked down into his eyes. "My lord? What are you doing?"

"I am doing what I wanted to do the first moment I saw you," Radulf murmured. He lifted the long strands of her hair, winding his fingers in them, gently drawing her face closer to his. Lily felt his warm breath on her lips. His eyes really were black, she realized. She could see her own reflection in them, and for a moment didn't recognize herself. She looked flushed, her lips moist and parted, her gray eyes half closed. She looked seductive. She looked as if she wanted to be kissed.

Lily wasn't surprised when Radulf did kiss her. What *did* surprise her were the sensations that went with such a simple act. Her mouth throbbed, her breasts tingled, and the place between her legs felt achy. The tip of Radulf's tongue followed the outline of her lips, and then slid inside. Lily opened her mouth to him, quite unable to resist, no longer sure she wanted to. In another moment she would have been lost . . .

The clearing of a throat sent her stumbling backward, the heat draining from her body like wine from a ruptured barrel.

"My lord?"

Stephen's voice seemed unnaturally loud, and he stomped his feet as he entered the tent, looking everywhere but at them. Lily figured he must have already seen them, left the tent, and re-entered. She put a shaking hand to her mouth, as if to hide the evidence of their kiss.

"What is it, boy?" Radulf sounded annoyed at the interruption, his eyes on Lily. She felt them boring into her back, but refused to turn and meet them. She felt flustered and confused. How Vorgen would have laughed! There had been nothing cold about her a moment ago in Radulf's arms. Had she lost her mind, to allow her enemy such power over her?

But Stephen's next words swept all self-recriminations from Lily's mind.

"We have found the priest, my lord!"

Chapter 3

The priest!

Lily's heart stopped, and started again. Father Luc! Here was danger in full measure. She had always liked Father Luc, and she thought he liked her. She prayed desperately that he had his wits about him and would not give her away.

"Must I see him now?" Radulf sounded weary as well as annoyed.

"You've been seeking him, Lord Radulf; don't you want to speak with him?"

Stephen seemed puzzled by Radulf's resistance, and at any other time Lily might have found it amusing. As it was, she watched in tense silence as Radulf reached for his shirt.

"Very well," he growled, "but he'd best be quick. I'm hungry."

Stephen's gaze skimmed over Lily but didn't linger. He bowed and gestured to someone beyond the entrance to Radulf's tent. "Come," he said, the authority in his voice somewhat marred by its tendency to waver up and down the scale. "My lord will do you the honor of speaking with you."

"He'll do me the honor, will he?"

Lily stepped back into the shadows and stayed there unmoving as Father Luc waddled into the candlelight. A small, rotund man in a coarse brown gown, his bald melon head was pink with anger, his eyes a vivid blue. Before the Normans came, Father Luc had had a wife and children— the English church saw no harm in its priests marrying. Afterward, Lily heard that the wife and children were sent away to safety, and Father Luc took on a solitary existence more in line with the Norman idea of piety.

"My lord," he puffed now, "your men are rough and uncouth. What mean you by this disrespect?"

"What mean *you*?" Radulf growled softly, long legs splayed out before him. He did not bother to get up. "You have been well hidden, priest. I have been seeking you."

"There have been many people seeking me since you came north, my lord," Father Luc replied tartly. "Plows and farming tools have been broken, and crops burned in the fields. Animals have been slaughtered. The people are starving. They turn to me and God, and I give them what help I can."

"I want you to help me, priest."

Father Luc frowned, trying to read Radulf's face. "In what way, my lord?"

"I am looking for Vorgen's wife. Do you know her?"

The priest nodded cautiously, his eyes still

fixed on Radulf, but Lily had the distinct impression he was very well aware she was there. "You seek the Lady Wilfreda?"

"Have you seen her recently?"

"She fled, Lord Radulf. Fled when she heard the King's Sword was coming. Your name is a powerful one. Only a fool would stand and fight."

Radulf snorted. "Vorgen fought."

"Aye, lord, and he was a fool."

"And you take me for one, too, old man?" Radulf leaned forward threateningly. "I've heard too many rumors that Lady Wilfreda is still in Northumbria. I don't believe she's gone north."

Father Luc shrugged.

"Perhaps you could be persuaded, priest?" Radulf sneered. "The men of God I know are always short of gold."

Father Luc's amiable face seemed to pinch upon itself. "She has fled. Best you resign her to her fate and go home. Go home, my lord, and take your gold with you."

He was brave, thought Lily, but foolish to antagonize Radulf. She glanced quickly toward the Norman, expecting him to show his anger, but Radulf appeared unmoved by the priest's words.

"When I have found Wilfreda I will go home," Radulf replied mildly. "Until then I will hunt."

The priest's rosebud mouth tightened, but his eyes remained steady.

"However, you may be able to help me in another matter," Radulf added. He turned and stared over to where Lily stood. "This lady was hiding in your church. She says she is Edwin of Rennoc's daughter, returning home from the border. Do you know her?"

Father Luc allowed his eyes to flick briefly to Lily and away again. Lily's heart squeezed within her chest. He must recognize her, must have recognized her as soon as he entered the tent, and yet there was nothing whatsoever in his face to show it. "I do not know Edwin of Rennoc's daughter, my lord."

"And yet the villagers know of her."

"Ah, that is a different matter, my lord. I know he *has* a daughter, fair-headed and fair of face, but I have never met her. And you say this is she?" The priest nodded in Lily's direction. "She looks weary. Have you hurt her?" he asked with a frown. "Her father is the Earl of Morcar's vassal, and Morcar is the king's man. Surely the king would be angry if he knew his Sword was striking at his friends as well as his enemies."

Radulf stiffened, and Lily held her breath. Father Luc had questioned Radulf's integrity. If this had been Vorgen, the priest would be dead by now, and she had no reason to think Radulf was any different. But before she allowed such a fate to befall the little man, she would speak the truth. She would not allow another to suffer in her stead; there had been enough suffering.

To her astonished relief, Radulf's shoulders eased back and the frown smoothed from his brow. Contrarily, the sense of strength and power that surrounded him increased rather than diminished. Lily knew then that a man like Radulf did not need to kill and maim to build on his consequence, and admiration mingled with her relief.

"You are a brave man, priest, but take care with your tongue." Amusement curled Radulf's lips, but there was a warning in his dark eyes.

The priest gave him an innocent smile.

"Boy!" Stephen hurried to obey his master's call, eyes wide as he looked from the priest to his lord. "Let him go. He's of no use to me after all."

"Thank you, my lord." Father Luc straightened his gown, smoothing its sleeves and shaking the mud from its hem. His face remained impassive, but his blue eyes twinkled as he turned to Lily. "Be of good cheer, my lady of Rennoc," he told her gently. "You will soon be among friends."

Lily stared after him as he left, wondering what he had meant, and if, indeed, the words had contained any meaning beyond the need to comfort.

"A priest who cannot be bought or bribed," Radulf said with a shake of his head. "A rarity."

Lily frowned, moving slowly forward until she faced him across the table of uneaten food. "You are cynical, my lord."

"I have grown so, Lily." That look was in his eyes again, as if beneath the battle-hardened warrior lay a wounded soul.

"Perhaps it is the company you keep."

Radulf laughed briefly. "Perhaps it is. Come sit down, my lady. We will eat, and this time there will be no interruptions."

His eyes promised much more than food, but Lily avoided his gaze. "I find I am weary rather than hungry, my lord. I would sleep now."

The silence grew heavy, but still Lily refused to look up. She heard Radulf sigh.

"Very well, lady. I will have Stephen take you to Gudren's tent."

Lily's stiff bearing eased with relief, and yet there was a traitorous sense of disappointment. She had liked it when Radulf kissed her, liked it

very much indeed. She would not mind if he
kissed her again. But kisses would lead to other
things, and Lily was not sure she had the strength
to resist. Radulf might be her enemy, but he held
an attraction for her that was well-nigh irresistible.

Radulf swallowed the last of a chunk of mut-
ton, and reached for more. His body was burning,
but this was no ordinary fever. He gulped down
half a goblet of wine, refilling it immediately, as if
the sour red liquid might somehow quench the
fire Lily had started in him. He forced himself to
chew more of the meat, then bit into the hard
brown bread. Radulf wondered wildly if he
should send his squire to bring him one of the
whores who were a permanent part of any soldiers' camp. But he didn't want a whore.

He wanted Lily.

He had wanted her as soon as he walked into
the tent and saw her lying asleep on his bed, her
pale hair spread across the covers, her mouth
curved in a secret smile. If Stephen hadn't been
there, he might have been tempted to caress her to
wakefulness, to befuddle her with kisses so that
she would not remember who and what he was.
Until it was too late.

Instead he had ordered her to tend his wound,
suffering agonies of lust as her scent teased his
nostrils and she touched him with her gentle fingers, each brush of her skin another twig upon the
pyre of his need.

Radulf sighed, impatient with himself. He was
a fool. He had seen the terror in those gray eyes
when she woke and saw him. What woman could
fail to fear him? And yet she had tended his

wound and met his eyes straightly when she spoke to him. She had courage. Perhaps her gratitude would overcome her fright long enough for him to make her forget he was Radulf.

He remembered his mouth on hers, the sweetness of it, the heat as she opened her lips to his tongue, and clenched his jaw on a groan. She had been in his arms, her lashes dark crescents against her pale skin, her long, fair hair curling in wild tendrils about her back and shoulders. Her breasts had swelled beneath the red wool of her gown, rising and falling quickly with each breath—already he knew their size and shape, as if God had made them precisely to fit into his hand.

Radulf gave up trying to eat.

He knew he should have questioned her further about Morcar and Rennoc. He should have questioned her in regard to her journey from the border. He should have asked her about the ambush in the wood and how she alone had escaped the attackers. And why three of his men, sent to investigate that same wood, had found no sign of any fighting.

Was she a liar?

He didn't care.

Nothing seemed to matter anymore but the heat in his groin and satisfying it with her.

Radulf did not know how long he sat, staring at nothing, before the sounds penetrated his mind.

The clash of swords and the shouts of men, the unmistakable noise of battle.

Gudren's tent was roomy, although a fire just outside combined with a brisk breeze to send frequent gusts of smoke within. Once Lily had adjusted to the gloom and the pungent odor of woodsmoke, she found the tent warm and clean. Gudren, ignoring her protests, supplied her with an ample supper of bread and goat's cheese, as well as ale to wash it down.

Gudren was a woman of middle age, her body comfortably plump, her pale eyes wrinkle-wrapped and watchful. She preferred to keep her silence, as Lily discovered when she had spoken several times and received nothing but smiling nods in reply.

After she had eaten her fill, Lily set about combing her tangled hair with an antler comb, and plaiting it into one long braid. Gudren seemed to be dozing, eyes half closed. The fluttering tallow candle smoothed the age from her face and bleached the gray from her hair. They might have been anywhere, anyone . . . two women taking respite after a busy, task-filled day.

Outside in the Norman camp, all was quiet as the soldiers huddled in sleep around their fires or in their tents. Lily felt oddly secure, like a child again, in the safety of her father's hall. She even heard his voice.

You carry the blood of warriors and kings in your veins, Lily. But 'tis possible that you may be forced to bow your head one day, for the sake of your lands and your people, to lesser men. Be proud and remember, your altruism and your ability to compromise does not make you weak, rather it strengthens you.

Had he known even then that war was inevitable? Perhaps he had felt the cold wind from across the channel, the stirring of the Norman conquerors. Perhaps he had stood at his gate to greet those same conquerors, and seen the greed in Vorgen's eyes. What would he think of Radulf? Would he see only that here was another Norman, or would he see past the outer trappings to the man within, as Lily was beginning to?

A rustle beyond the tent startled Lily, bringing her back to her surroundings. Peering through the smoky gloom, she made out the shape of a soldier standing at attention before the entrance. As she watched, he shuffled his feet again, and his sword scabbard clinked dully against his chain mail.

Lily was Radulf's prisoner. How could she imagine anything else?

She closed her eyes again, trying to recapture her previous mood, but the warm contentment had vanished.

"You are tired, my pretty one?"

"A little, mother."

Lily answered before she thought. Dismay washed over her, and she opened her eyes slowly as she straightened. Gudren had just spoken in the Norse tongue, and Lily had answered her.

Gudren was grinning, a cunning gleam in her pale eyes. Lily saw then that it was not silence Gudren craved, 'twas only that she was a foreigner who spoke French badly, if at all. No wonder she was smiling with delight! How many Norman ladies could claim to know such a language?

Gudren leaned closer, bringing with her the combined aromas of herbs and goat. " 'Tis long since I heard any other than my husband speak the sweet sounds of our own country. Are you from Norway, lady?"

Lily shook her head. It was pointless now to

prevaricate. "No, Northumbria is my home. What do you in Grimswade, mother?"

Gudren sighed. "I follow my husband, Olaf. He came to England as a mercenary with William of Normandy, and now he is armorer to Lord Radulf."

Lily's gray eyes widened. "That must be a mighty job!"

Gudren laughed heartily at that, her round stomach jiggling. "You are right, 'tis difficult to cover such a big man, but Lord Radulf rewards his armorer well. Olaf makes swords, too, as fine as any in England. They fit to the hand as if they were born there, and sing with joy as they slice through flesh and bone."

Lily felt her face lose some of its color. She was not squeamish; she had learned to face the truth about war—but there had been so much killing. Why must the Normans see every petty squabble as a chance to test their battle skills?

"You have come from Radulf's estates?" Lily asked quickly.

Gudren nodded. "Aye, from Crevitch. We have been away for many months now. 'Tis soft country," she added, with a trace of scorn. "Gentle hills and valleys, long green grass, and marshy flats. Lord Radulf longs for home, although"—she grinned knowingly—"he will never say so."

Lily tried to imagine Radulf longing for something, anything. The Radulf of legend liked nothing better than to slay his enemies, eat heartily, and slay some more. Nowhere in the story did it mention yearning to go home.

Gudren poured herself more ale. "You seem curious about Lord Radulf. I will tell you the story of his life," she announced, settling back in her chair.

There was a scuffle beyond the tent entrance, followed by a cry, and then a man the size of a mountain forced his way past the guard and into the smoky interior.

Lily screamed.

Wild white hair, a face tanned almost black, and eyes as blue as the sky. He crouched double as he came toward her, his fist clenched around a lethal-looking axe.

"Olaf?" Gudren's voice was mildly scolding. "Why do you frighten the lady?"

Olaf gave her a hideous scowl. "We are attacked, woman! Cannot you hear the fighting further up the hill? Bah, your tongue clacks too loud for you to hear anything! Come"—he reached out one meaty hand to Lily—"I am to take you to my lord. He would see you safe."

Now that the pounding of her heart had slowed, Lily *could* hear the sound of battle. Dull thuds and men's shouts and the screams of the wounded. They were being attacked, but by whom? If they were enemies of the Normans, then surely they must be Lily's friends?

Briefly, she considered pushing by Olaf and running.

But Olaf was enormous, and dangerous. She wouldn't make it, and then she would have to explain her actions to Radulf. Meekly, Lily gave him her hand.

"She speaks the language of the far north," Gudren informed him with pleasure, as if there were nothing wrong.

Olaf's scowl remained, but his wife's unflap-

pable calm brought an appreciative gleam to his
eyes. "Stay here, Gudren. I have set men to guard
the women's tents." His voice dropped and became almost gentle. "I would not have anything
happen to you."

Gudren smiled serenely. "I know you wouldn't,
husband."

For a moment their love for each other was like
a fire, the sensation so strong that Lily was certain
that if she reached out her hands, she would feel
the warmth of it. A wave of loss and longing came
over her as she thought of her terrible marriage to
Vorgen and her childhood sweetheart Hew's betrayal. Why couldn't she have a love like Gudren
and Olaf? Why must she always be frightened
and alone?

"Come," ordered Olaf.

Outside, the darkness was lightened by an almost full moon, which far outshone the feeble
fires of the campsite. The fighting seemed to be
beyond the horses' enclosure, the sounds of battle
waxing and waning on the chill breeze. Olaf's
tight hold on Lily tugged her onward between the
tents and past grim, running men. The clatter of
swords and shields made her head ache.

Olaf grunted. "We will slaughter them like
pigs."

Lily swallowed, and found her voice. "Who are
they?" she managed, hoisting her skirts higher so
that the wool cloth no longer impeded her
progress—Olaf did not believe in taking ladylike
steps.

"What is left of Vorgen's rebels. They have been
watching us and they crept too close. I do not be-

lieve they wanted to fight, but they were discovered by our scouts. Now they are dying."

Were those poor souls the "friends" Father Luc meant? Lily hoped not. She did not want men to die for her, for a war already lost. If only she could speak to her people, to make them understand that further fighting would gain them nothing but more misery, and that their only hope now lay in Lily's making peace with William of Normandy.

And Radulf.

They reached Radulf's tent and Olaf unceremoniously pulled her inside. "Stay," he barked at her, and was gone. Lily was left, disheveled and panting, in the place she had so recently escaped.

"My lady!" Stephen, big-eyed with excitement, suddenly looked very young. "My—my lord asked that I stay here with you until he comes. Do you wish for wine? I have wine."

He obviously needed something to do. Lily nodded and allowed him to pour her a goblet. The sounds of fighting were growing sparser as the rebels escaped or were slain. Lily shivered, lifting the goblet and spilling some droplets in her haste. The wine slid down her throat, warmed her, and gave her back her courage. Her mind began searching for some hope to hold to, a spell against despair. More and more, she was beginning to believe she was Northumbria's only chance of avoiding total devastation.

Suddenly her legs felt weak with the responsibility. Lily sank down onto one of the stools, the goblet still grasped between her fingers.

"My lady, you are ill?" Stephen asked from his place by the door.

Lily shook her head. Silence fell, and so they stayed for some time.

Until the heavy tread of men drew nearer.

Lily lifted her head, listening. Voices called. She heard Radulf, his husky tones too low to be understood. Others answered him. A horse snorted and stomped. A man laughed—Olaf? And then Stephen straightened his back, like a soldier, and Radulf entered the tent.

Chapter 4

Radulf was an imposing figure in his hauberk and helmet. To see him so gave Lily a tingling shock. It was as if they were back in Grimswade church, at the very beginning, and strangers.

They did not feel like strangers now.

Lily comprehended this with some surprise, for they were barely more. Besides, he was her enemy, and furthermore an enemy she must persuade to her point of view if she was to regain her lands and save her people.

Radulf removed his helmet, and Lily's agitated thoughts came to a halt. His dark gaze was fixed on her, and suddenly it was as if nothing else mattered but being here with him. The moment was broken as Stephen hurried to assist his lord in unbuckling his sword and removing his hauberk. When Radulf sat once more in only his linen shirt and breeches, the boy carried away the chain mail, staggering under the enormous weight of it.

Radulf ran a hand through his short black hair, flexing his shoulders, and lifted the goblet of wine Stephen had poured him. He did not appear to be cut or bruised, and the only sign Lily could see of the recent fighting was the reopening of the scab across his knuckles. She tried to view him dispassionately, telling herself it was the other men who deserved her concern, the pitiful remnants of Vorgen's rebel army.

But her heart told her she lied.

Lily found her voice. "Have you taken any prisoners?"

Radulf shook his head. "The leader and half the band escaped before my men could surround them. The rest of them preferred to fight. No one surrendered, they all fought to kill, and so did we. Brave men, if misguided."

"Who were they?"

Radulf shrugged, and then winced when it hurt his wounded shoulder. "Vorgen's men. Outlaws. Maybe both."

Stephen poured more wine and asked in a murmur if his lord was hungry. Radulf shook his head. "Go to bed, boy. I will return this lady to Gudren's tent myself."

When the squire had gone, Radulf gulped down the rest of his wine. The quiet of the tent seeped into him, and outside his camp returned to slumber. The attack had been countered and won, and he was whole and safe, and once more alone with *her.*

The elation of battle had passed and left him, as always, light-headed with weariness. In such a state, he might have expected the lust to have died. It hadn't; if anything it was worse than ever. And it was not that familiar lusty longing for a woman, any woman . . . no, this was different.

For why had he sent for her? She had been safe enough in Gudren's tent; Olaf would have seen to that. There had been a suspicion that her presence in the camp and the rebel attack were connected, but Radulf didn't really believe that. He had thought only of having her close, protecting her.

The acknowledgment was like an ache in his chest and memories of his father clamored for his attention. That worn, hard face the last time Radulf had seen him, twisted with a pain so vast there was no escaping it. He had died, they said, of a broken heart. Radulf had felt as if he, too, had died that day.

He had vowed, after that, that never again would he allow any woman to penetrate his wounded heart. Love was for fools.

Now he searched blindly for the well-worn phrases and reminders that had always worked before, on the few occasions he was tempted to forget.

He could not find them.

All of that was suddenly unimportant. He was lost in a foreign land, alone and confused and frightened. A land he had visited but once before, with disastrous consequences. Dare he try again?

Slowly, Radulf lowered his goblet and let his gaze settle on Lily.

He forced his mind to be cold, objective. She was only a woman . . . *Only a woman* . . .

She was standing near the wall of the tent, her fair hair neatly plaited, her hands clasped at her waist. He wondered how old she was, and then dismissed the thought—she was old enough. He let his gaze run over her breasts, where the curves were clearly outlined beneath the red gown. Her waist was so trim he could span it with his hands, and her hips were rounded despite her slenderness. The long line of her thighs was clearly visible, and before he could prevent the thought, Radulf was wondering if the curls nestling between those thighs were as wondrous fair as her hair, or as dark as her lashes and brows.

She was only a woman.

Beads of sweat stood out on his broad brow. Slowly his eyes lifted to Lily's, the banked fires in their depths alight and burning out of control. She would run now, he thought. Run screaming from his tent.

"My lord?" Lily managed. He realized, in shocked surprise, that her voice was as constricted as his. Could she possibly be feeling something of what he was feeling? He didn't know and in another moment wouldn't care. One thing was certain: she was not running, and if she did not run soon, then he would have her.

She was only a woman and he was the King's Sword. Had he not the right to take what he wanted?

"You are wondrous fair, Lady Lily," he whispered, his voice deeper even than usual. He watched her lashes flicker, her breath quickening between her lips. Could she . . . was it possible that she was caught up in the heat of a passion just as great as his?

The thought gave him just enough strength to control the powerful urge coursing through him. He would not grab her and take her like a wild animal. Instead he would woo her, turn her willingness into submission. He knew—that damned ache in his chest again!—that he wanted her to want him. To take her and afterward see nothing but fear and loathing on her face would be worse than dying.

"Come here, Lily."

He held out his hand and she stared at it as if she didn't understand what he meant.

"Please?" he murmured thickly. His fingers flicked softly, beckoning. The great Radulf, begging! Yet in this moment he was no more than a man, and she was only a woman.

It was the *please* that drew Lily to him. Hesitantly she gave him her fingers. Slowly and with infinite care, Radulf drew her forward until she stood in the space between his knees. Lily's eyes half closed until they were nothing but a silver-gray gleam through her thick lashes. Her breath quickened.

But she did not move away.

Radulf leaned closer and lifted his other hand, again so slowly that Lily had more than ample time to tell him no, or to run away. His hand trembled. Again she waited, her breasts rising and falling as though each breath were a labor. At last his fingers brushed her lips, hardly a touch at all, and then slid quickly down over her throat, fingertips callused against her softness, and closed over her left breast.

Lily gasped, her body stiffening, a heat rising in her such as she had never experienced before. In the befuddlement of her mind she wondered at the power Radulf had over her. His touch was certainly magic. Her breast seemed to swell in his hand, the nipple growing taut. He brushed his thumb against it. The movement caused a new rush of hotness, and Lily's skin felt flushed all over, from her head to her toes.

With a groan, Radulf swept her off her feet and onto his lap. His arms closed about her, encircling her in a warm, safe cave of flesh and muscle. Yet Lily knew the feeling of safety was an illusion.

Halfheartedly she pushed her hands against his chest, thinking he would ignore her feeble attempts at self-preservation, not really wanting him to stop. But Radulf stopped as if she had struck him with his own sword. There was a moment of heavy breathing silence, and then he lifted her chin and searched her eyes with his own. His face was taut with desire, his mouth a thin, hard line.

"Lily?" The question was a husky rasp.

Lily sighed languidly. Her body felt warm and liquid, awakening to sensations so new and exciting, she did not want him to stop. She hardly recalled the reason she was there. Whatever happened later, she would savor this moment.

He must have read her answer in her eyes, because abruptly, as if he had lost his slender grip on self-control, Radulf bent his head and claimed her mouth in a deep, passionate kiss. Lily heard her own soft groan.

She ran her hands blindly over his face, tracing the scar across his cheek, and then up into his hair, tugging him closer. Beneath her thighs his hard muscles tightened, while his manhood jutted boldly against her hip.

And still the kiss went on, as if it would never end.

Lily allowed Radulf to open her mouth with his, to taste of her as if she were his goblet of wine. His tongue slid inside to tangle with hers, and brought with it a vivid impression of her body catching fire from his. And burning.

When at last he drew away, he looked dazed, as dazed as she. "It is too late to run now. You are mine," he breathed against her throat. His mouth began to move downward in soft, quick kisses, seeking the sweet flesh beneath the neckline of her chemise, while his hand reached up to once more encircle each breast. The feeling of his hot mouth closing over her nipple catapulted Lily to a place she had never known before. How could she have imagined such sensations were possible? How could she have known from Vorgen's frustrated, angry fumbling, or Hew's boyish kisses, that passion such as this existed? Radulf reached a place inside her that she hadn't even acknowledged was there.

It frightened her. If Radulf could so easily turn her from the woman she had always been, how could she stand against him? How could she leave him?

Lily pushed at his head, as if to force him away from her breasts, but, contrarily, when he lifted his gaze to hers, she felt the loss of him. He was watching her again, his tanned cheeks flushed. What was he always seeking in her face?

Worried and afraid, Lily tried to stand, saying in her most censorious voice, "No, Radulf. Is this how a knight cares for a lady under his protection?"

Radulf grinned. He stood up, following her cat-footed as she backed toward the bed. "If the lady is willing, yes."

"What if the lady is wed?" she burst out.

That stopped him. He frowned at her, tension in every line of him. "Are you wed, Lily?"

Reluctantly, the truth was forced out of her. "No. Not any longer. He is dead."

A smile curled his lips once more. A victor's smile. "Then come to me, *mignonne*," he murmured, and drew her to him. Lily gasped as his hands smoothed over her back and hips, closing on her buttocks, pressing her firmly against him. She felt the hard length of him, and hot visions of her touching him, holding him, opening to him, took hold of her fevered mind. There was a terrible yearning ache in the pit of her stomach, and the need to satisfy it overshadowed all other considerations. If there had ever been a time to draw back, it was now gone.

"Radulf," Lily gasped.

He was peeling off her red gown and then her chemise, his hands unintentionally rough against her bare, smooth skin. She was naked from the waist up. Lily cried out softly when he found her breasts and began to knead the full warm flesh. He made a low sound in his throat and bent his head, his mouth fastening on a swollen bud.

Lily's head fell back, her long plait spearing over her arched spine. Only Radulf's arm about her shoulders prevented her from falling. Her body had lost all strength, had turned molten. She groaned again, her hands creeping blindly beneath his shirt and running over the hard, curving muscles of his chest. There were scars there, too, and she smoothed them with her fingertips, as if her touch would heal all past hurts.

Perhaps, she thought dizzily, they could heal each other.

Radulf finished with one breast and turned his attention to the other. Lily swayed, offering her flesh to his hands and lips. Still it wasn't enough. As if he sensed as much, Radulf swung her up into his arms and in one fluid movement laid her upon his bed. Lily opened her mouth to protest, dazed gray eyes turning to him, and stopped in wonder.

Radulf was stripping off his clothing, tearing at the cloth in his haste. Lily's awestruck gaze wandered over his broad chest, down to his flat stomach and narrow hips and rampant masculinity. Vorgen had never been so . . . so big, so hard. Lily had not known that a man's body could become so proudly arrogant, and yet so beautiful.

She reached out as if to touch, and then stopped as Vorgen's words echoed in her mind. He had called her cold and unfeeling; he had said her flesh leaked poison and prevented him from being a man when he was with her. He boasted of his conquests with other women, swearing that his impotence was for Lily alone.

Radulf had seen her movement, and her withdrawal, but thought it only womanly modesty. He bent now and slipped her clothing from her hips, tossing it aside, and turned to gaze avidly upon her nakedness.

"Blond, like your hair," he murmured, fingers grazing the curls at the juncture of her thighs. His gaze dropped to the jeweled dagger that was still strapped to her upper thigh. He ran his fingers over her creamy flesh, over the leather strap and sheath, until they rested on the green and red stones adorning the dagger's hilt.

"What is this?" he asked her, his voice a husky rumble. "My Lily has a thorn?"

" 'Tis . . . protection."

Their eyes met, and for a moment Lily thought he would pull back from her. Instead he gave a reckless laugh, unbuckled the leather strap, and tossed the dagger to the floor, before burying his face in the fair curls between her thighs.

Lily gasped his name, clutching wildly at his hair as his tongue found her moist core. Never had she thought . . . never had she imagined . . . A desperate trembling seized her body; the beginnings of a hot and urgent need rose within her. Lily arched and pressed closer to that wonderful mouth and closed her eyes, climbing the wave, savoring these new sensations. But just as she was sure she was about to reach some strange and marvelous peak, Radulf moved away.

Lily cried out in dismay, and then her eyes opened wide as she felt Radulf's big body sink down upon hers, all that hard flesh and sinew, all that power, completely covering her. His dark eyes were narrowed, gazing deep into hers, and she felt him reach his hand down between her legs, his fingers sliding into the slick heat he had stirred there. Lily moved against him, and he smiled with a slight, satisfied curve of his mouth. Gently he parted her thighs and settled between them. Radulf sighed with contentment, as if this was where he had wanted to be all his life.

"Are you ready for me?" His voice seared her. Lily had a frightening yet comforting sense of great strength held in check, awaiting her answer.

But what did he mean? She had not understood women, like men, could be prepared for the act of mating. She had believed it was a woman's duty to endure, as she had endured Vorgen. Now, with her body hot and aching, she knew better.

She gasped, involuntarily lifting her hips against him, her body giving him her answer without words.

He entered her with a single deep thrust—he was so big, he had always found swiftness the best way. Time enough once he was inside to gentle matters. In a haze of pleasure he heard her soft scream, felt her body convulsing. There was an exquisitely tight, almost untried resistance. He checked, wishing he had not been so hasty. She was young; he had not realized she had been so long a widow.

But Lily was more than ready, her discomfort already fading. She moaned as her body stretched to take all of him, welcoming him. Radulf's mouth closed on hers, his tongue diverting her while she adjusted to his size. His skin, beneath her palms, was as hot as fever.

"Are you ready for me, lady?" He asked it again, his breath against her ear making her shiver, and this time she understood his meaning.

"I am," she panted, and then gasped as he began to move.

Long, slow thrusts at first, then quickly increasing in speed and strength, teaching her with his hands and body to match his rhythm. Lily learned quickly, eager to be the mistress of her own pleasure.

And then Radulf began to lose his control. His mighty arms shook, and he bent to suck on her breasts, groan her name. It didn't matter. Lily was more than willing to follow him, wherever he was taking her.

In some far corner of his mind, where his wits were residing, Radulf remembered to see to Lily's pleasure before he took his own. He slid his hand down between their slippery bodies, stroking firmly on that swollen nub. She went rigid with surprise—he almost laughed aloud at the amazement in her gray eyes—and then she was convulsing and crying out as if she had never reached that peak before. She was still gasping and clinging to him as he thrust deeply into her, once, twice, and with a harsh groan, followed her over the mountain.

Lily felt as if her soul had left her body and drifted away to some brighter place. She lay snug and warm in Radulf's arms, her shoulder to his chest, her hip against his belly. What had passed between them was beyond words. She only knew that she had made a wondrous discovery, one she had every intention of revisiting with Radulf as soon and as often as possible.

Lily smiled at the pledge and opened her eyes. Radulf was looking down at her, his warrior's face alert and watchful. Again the directness of his gaze startled her, but only momentarily, and then she reached up and stroked his cheek, gently tracing the puckered skin of the old scar.

"How came you by this, my lord?" she whispered.

He shuddered, as if her touch were hurting him, but when she, remembering again Vorgen's cruel taunts, would have withdrawn, he turned his face and gently nibbled at her fingers. "A fight with a brave man," he murmured. "I deserved what he gave me, and much more." He began to kiss her palm, his mouth hot and hungry.

Lily watched him, holding her breath. This was Radulf, her great enemy, the man she had been fleeing. This was Radulf, the terror of the north. And he was hers.

A great relief filled her, and with it an incredible tenderness for the man beside her. He was hers, and Lily had learned to fiercely protect what belonged to her, be it flesh and blood or sticks and mortar.

She lifted herself on her elbow, stretching to meet his lips with her own. Radulf's tongue delved into her mouth. His hand still clasped hers, and now he drew it down to his groin. She stiffened, trying to pull back, but he laughed and held her tighter. His manhood was already hard again, and he seemed proud of the fact. "My lord," she gasped, as he rolled her over onto her back, straddling her. He raised her hands above her head, pinning them there with a satisfied smile, so that she was powerless to stop his kisses even had she wanted to.

She didn't.

"I feel besieged," she whispered.

He laughed arrogantly. "The castles I besiege always surrender to me. They open their gates"— he slid his thighs between hers, opening them— "and surrender." His manhood prodded her entrance. "Do you open to me, lady?" he teased huskily. "Do you surrender yourself into my care?"

And Lily, afire again, could only gasp her assent.

It was not until they had caught their breaths once more that Radulf moved to pull the covers over them both. Lily felt him tense. The warm tenderness turned chill. He turned his dark eyes on her, and although they were blank and unreadable, Lily sensed his growing anger. She was reminded with a sharp, prickling awareness that although Radulf was her lover, he was still Radulf.

"Lady, you have lied to me." His voice was as quiet as an assassin.

Lily stared back at him, gray eyes huge, wondering what he had discovered, and how.

His soft voice went on. "You told me you were married and that your husband was dead."

"I *was* married, and my husband *is* dead," she managed, her throat dry.

Radulf held up his fingers, and by the light of the smoking candles Lily could see the dark smears of blood. "You were virgin," he stated angrily.

Lily refused to look away. " 'Tis true," she managed through the lump in her throat. "I was wed, but he was . . . was unable. I was a wife in name only."

Radulf continued to stare at her, as if trying to see beyond her words, to see inside her head. "Why did you not take another?" he demanded. "Why wait until now, until me?"

Lily did not answer him. After a moment, when she could bear his gaze no longer, she leaned forward to rest her cheek against his chest. His heart beat strongly beneath the wall of flesh and muscle.

"I was waiting for you," she whispered, and acknowledged as she spoke that the words were truth.

Radulf laughed in disbelief.

Lily, her hand trembling, touched his skin, exploring the rough dark hair on his chest, rubbing her fingers over it. He did not move, and she sensed his aloofness, his resistance. He thought she had lied to him, and now he distrusted her even more.

And yet he did not push her away, or move from the bed. Lily continued to caress him, her fingertips finding his nipple, and remembering what Radulf had done to her, she covered him with her mouth. Radulf took a ragged breath, his hands capturing her head and holding her still. "Lady, tell me again how you came to Grimswade church?"

Lily smiled against his chest. "I was seeking sanctuary," she whispered, "and I have found it."

He tilted her face so that she had no choice but to meet his eyes. "I sent my men to the wood you spoke of," he told her harshly. "They searched and found naught of any battle between your soldiers and their attackers."

Lily said nothing, gazing back into his eyes. In a nervous gesture, she licked her lips.

Radulf moaned deep in his throat. He wound his hands through the long strands of her hair, pressing his face to them, kissing the silken locks. "Ah, Lily, Lily," he groaned. "*Mignonne*, you are foolish if you think your gift will soften me if you lie."

His yielding emboldened Lily. She pressed her palms to his shoulders, urging him back. When he lay among the blankets and skins, she leaned over him. The tips of her breasts brushed across his chest, and her hair made a cave about their faces.

"I will take that chance," she told him softly. "I do not think you will hurt me, my lord."

Radulf hesitated a moment, as if he were tempted to disillusion her, and then he was pulling her down to drink from her mouth, and all conversation was forgotten.

Chapter 5

Lily woke to the dawn, with Stephen creeping about the tent, tidying and laying out platters of food, careful not to disturb his master. She lay still until the boy had gone and then, easing her tangled hair out from beneath the heavy weight of Radulf's arm, sat up.

Was it truly only two nights ago that she had made her way to the church? Then she had been frightened and alone, at the end of her tether. Now she felt changed. Not just in body, though her limbs ached pleasurably and her mouth was swollen from Radulf's kisses. But in mind and heart, too.

The dark, painful memories of her time with Vorgen seemed to have faded just a little. Radulf had undergone no difficulty; did that mean Vorgen had been wrong? That Lily was not a woman who sapped a man's vigor with her touch? That maybe the fault had been with Vorgen alone?

Hope seeded itself in her heart. Suddenly she wished that the story she had told Radulf were the truth. How much simpler it would be now, were she really Edwin of Rennoc's daughter! Maybe, if she were to wake Radulf, tell him who she was? Explain . . . ?

A cold whisper of warning halted her hot rush of impetuousness. Radulf was a Norman lord, and she knew the high price such men placed upon their honor and their allegiance to their king. In his greed Vorgen had turned his back on both, and had hated himself for it even as he was powerless to stop himself. Lily knew instinctively that Radulf was not the kind of man to compromise his honor, nor would he betray his king. If she were to tell him her secret, that she was the Lady Wilfreda, he would give her up to King William.

You are foolish if you think your gift will soften me to you if you lie.

Radulf's words echoed in her head, and Lily shivered in the chill light of morning. So she would be damned if she lied, and damned if she didn't.

Very uneasy now, last night's exhilaration completely faded, Lily glanced down at the sleeping man at her side, almost expecting him to have grown horns and a tail.

He lay sprawled across the bed, beautiful in a stark, masculine way, his big body still and yet alert even now. His short dark hair was disordered by sleep and Lily's fingers, his face relaxed, the lines about his eyes smoothed out and his firm lips slightly open. Lily longed to stroke the scar on his cheek and kiss him awake.

She did neither.

He had made love to her as thoroughly as any man could, and yet he had been aware of her needs, too. Lily remembered, with a rich coloring of her cheeks, how he had brought her to her pleasure time and time again before he took his own.

Would Vorgen have caressed her, lifted her to such heights, made her forget her very reason for being? Assuming, of course, he had been capable of it! Lily shuddered at the idea of swapping Radulf for Vorgen. Vorgen was as different from Radulf as rain from sun. And Hew—what of Hew? Once, long ago, Hew had begged her to allow him to visit her in the night, and Lily had been young enough and flattered enough to agree. Luckily, her father had guessed what was afoot and prevented any harm from coming to his precious daughter.

At the time, Lily had raged and wept with a mixture of shame and regret. She had been spoiled and headstrong—the only child, and her mother dead. Now she was glad her father had stopped Hew that night.

So Radulf is a fine lover.

Lily's inner voice invaded her mind, scattering her thoughts.

Will his kisses keep you safe, if he discovers the truth?

No, of course they would not! Radulf cared nothing for her—how could he? He didn't even know her. He thought her a widowed Norman lady, grateful for his protection.

I do not think you will hurt me.

Lily had meant what she said in the tingling warmth of Radulf's embrace, but now . . . Fright caught like fingers at her throat, quickening her breath.

Lily had had her night of love, and she knew she would never forget it. But now, she must go. She did not think of *where* she would go. The dread of Radulf's discovery was driving her, and that had little to do with common sense.

Cautiously, fearful of waking him, Lily crept out of Radulf's bed. Shivering from the cold and her somber thoughts, she found her clothing and dressed hurriedly. The jeweled dagger lay on the ground, and she strapped it around her thigh. Breathlessly she caught up her cloak and, with one eye on Radulf, felt for the ring in its lining. The rounded shape had lodged into one corner. Lily slipped her hand into the tear to remove it, and hesitated. Where else would she hide it? It was safe enough where it was; best to leave it for now.

Moving noiselessly across the tent, Lily noticed that, as well as some cold meats, Stephen had brought water for washing, a knob of sweet-scented soap, and a drying cloth. Hastily she availed herself of all these things, then wavered over the wild tangle of her hair. At some point during the night Radulf had freed the silver strands from her braid, running his hands through them as if through gleaming water.

Impatiently Lily cast the memory aside. There was no time now to tidy her hair. She thrust it down inside her cloak and pulled up the hood. Yet even as she set her mind to the task ahead, she turned once more to face the bed.

Radulf slept on, his long brown legs and strongly muscled torso framed by the dark furs, his face turned from her into the shadows. Lily took a sharp breath, swamped by regret for what might have been. In another time, another place, she and Radulf could have met and loved.

Lifting her chin, her back stiffening with determination, Lily turned and made her way on soft feet to the tent opening. There were several slices of dark bread on a platter on the table, and she picked one up as she passed, nibbling at the coarse crust.

Lily peeped outside into the steely morning.

She saw the camp, hazy with smoke. Soldiers were setting about their daily tasks. A woman laughed, a horse stamped, voices were raised in mild dispute. And two guards in chain mail stood just beyond the entrance to Radulf's tent.

Lily jumped back like someone bitten.

Of course there were guards—and whether they were there to keep her in or others out made little difference.

She was a prisoner.

There would be no escape this morning.

A flutter of relief somewhere in the region of her heart caught her by surprise. By God, she must stop this madness!

"Is he up, Stephen?" came a voice from outside.

Lily peeped out again, more cautiously this time. A thickset man of medium height was walking toward the tent, his gleaming chain mail and the decorated hilt of his sword proclaiming him a knight as surely as his confident manner. The squire hurried forth to meet him, looking rather like an eager, half-grown puppy.

As Lily watched, Stephen gave Radulf's tent a nervous glance. "No, he's not awake yet, Lord Henry. Think you I should wake him? He said we would search to the south this morning, and his men are already waiting. Will he be angry if I wake him?"

The knight laughed, tipping back a mop of short chestnut curls. He was almost as handsome as Hew. "Angrier if you do not! Come, boy, let me do the deed for you. I am used to his scowls."

Lily stepped back swiftly, the piece of bread dangling from her fingers.

She came up against something very large and hard and warm . . . and naked. She froze. Radulf! Thank God she had not been able to attempt her escape, he would have caught her as easily as a hound a rabbit.

"Careful, wench," his voice rumbled in his chest. Bending his head, he began to nibble at the soft, sensitive flesh between her ear and neck.

"My lord!" Lily gasped as her willing senses were aroused all over again. "You have a visitor."

At that very moment the visitor in question appeared in the tent doorway. Radulf's hands closed over Lily's shoulders and, startled, she looked up at him. Radulf blinked in the sudden shaft of light from beyond the door, and then he smiled broadly. Lily stared in amazement as his hard face was transformed into that of a younger, more carefree man.

Her heart seemed to dive like a hunting falcon, so fast it made her giddy.

"Henry!" he cried, releasing Lily with one arm, and slipping her behind him with the other. Puzzled, Lily stood in the shelter of his big body, hidden from view. Was he embarrassed by her? Ashamed of her presence? Then, as he glanced over his shoulder and gave her a questioning look, she decided Radulf was too arrogant to care what others thought of him or his actions.

"Your boy here tells me you're riding south, Radulf?" Henry peered sideways around the other man, trying to catch a glimpse of Lily, but Radulf moved to block his view. The fact that he was stark naked didn't seem to bother Radulf as much as Lily's fully clothed presence.

"That vixen, Vorgen's wife, still eludes me."

" 'Tis a pity that, with the north more or less peaceful once more, you cannot return home to Crevitch."

Radulf shrugged. "I've left behind enough men-at-arms to guard my lands from greedy eyes. I can do no more than that. The king needs me here and here I stay."

"And this, my friend?" Henry lifted his chin in the direction of the invisible presence beyond Radulf's broad shoulder. "Does she help to make your exile from Crevitch the sweeter?"

Radulf tensed and shot his friend a dark look. "All the wenches fall for your cherubic looks, Henry. This one is mine. Stephen!" he shouted.

Lily stilled. *Mine?* Was she really *his*? Was that why he had tucked her away behind him so possessively?

"They may fall for me, Radulf, but they gaze at you as if they had been lightning-struck. If you would learn to scowl less and smile more, you could have your pick."

Henry was grinning, his blue eyes crinkled at the corners. Lily decided he did look rather like a cherub, albeit a wicked one. Then his eyes fell to Lily and he sobered.

Radulf had grunted in disbelief, but seeing the

new direction of Henry's curious gaze, he half turned and drew Lily firmly into his embrace. With an irritable frown, he shoved down the hood of her cloak and freed her long hair, and with it the scent of flowers and spring rain. Lily felt her face turn a fiery red before Lord Henry's bold stare.

"Perhaps the lady can tell you the truth of what I say, Radulf," he said smoothly. "What think you of Lord Radulf, lady? Is he not a handsome and virile man?"

Henry was jesting, but still she felt Radulf's arms tighten, felt him hold his breath as he waited for her answer. She should say something light and amusing in return, but Lily had led a life too fraught with danger to easily manage either. As Vorgen's wife her simplest pronouncement was inspected, dissected, and suspected. There was no room for levity, for funning. Lily had lost the ability.

"He is neither, my lord," she answered at last, her voice soft and husky. "He is a god."

Henry's eyes widened and laughter flushed his face until Lily thought he would burst with holding it in. Radulf released his own breath in a sharp hiss. He chuckled softly and squeezed her tighter. His breath tickled her hair as he bent over her, and his hand slid up to cup her jaw, lifting her face so that she was forced to meet his dark eyes.

The watchful expression was back, and with it some new, indefinable gleam. Lily knew she had pleased him, even as his next words reduced hers to insignificance. "The lady has difficulty telling the truth about anything; why should I believe her in this?"

Lily opened her mouth to argue, just as Stephen arrived at last.

"My lord, I beg pardon, I was—"

Radulf didn't waste time with excuses. "Take the lady to Gudren's tent," he said gruffly. "Now!"

Lily found herself given firmly into the squire's care, hurried past Henry's amused and admiring gaze, and out into the brightening day.

The air struck her chilly, warm as she had been in Radulf's arms, and she blinked about her at the camp.

Tents blended into the hillside, the unmoving veil of smoke giving further camouflage. Women were grouped about a cart from which one Grimswade entrepreneur was selling freshly baked bread, while men practiced their fighting skills in a meadow close by. Radulf's huge black destrier was being saddled and readied for its master.

Lily wondered anxiously how long Radulf intended to be away, and what would happen to her. Would she be safe? And then she smiled. If his jealous care of her just now was anything to go by, she was very safe indeed.

Her smile faded.

With Radulf gone, she could escape. Yes, she told herself, ignoring the shiver of regret that came from a well deep inside her being, *that* was what she would do.

"Come, lady." Stephen gave her an impatient glance and led the way, trudging down the muddy track. Lily followed, sniffing the unsettling mixture of animal manure, woodsmoke, and bread. Her stomach alternately lurched and rumbled. She hoped Gudren had something to eat; she had barely taken a bite of the food in Radulf's tent before Lord Henry arrived.

And if the opportunity came to escape today, she preferred to do so on a full belly.

Radulf pulled on a clean pair of breeches and another shirt, while Henry sat down at the table and began to partake heartily of his friend's breakfast. Radulf eyed him with fond disgust. Fonder than the disgust in which he held himself. Henry had been amused by his behavior with Lily, but Radulf hadn't been able to help himself. As soon as he'd seen Henry's eyes fix on Lily, he'd experienced such a bolt of jealousy he was sure the soles of his feet were sizzling.

"And that lady is under your protection?" Henry repeated after Radulf's brief explanation. "That being so, should you have . . . uhmm . . . taken advantage of her undeniable charms?"

Radulf splashed the now lukewarm water over his head and picked up the cloth to dry himself. Lily's scent was on it, and desire gripped him with hot, urgent fingers.

Her words were still ringing in his ears. Although he knew she must have been playing up to Henry's teasing, she had not smiled when she said them. And she had spoken as if what she said was what she believed.

Radulf shivered.

Women had been known to lie. Anna had lied and lied again. It was wiser not to believe them, wiser not to become involved . . . no matter how much he yearned to.

"Radulf? Are you still asleep? Or are your wits addled?"

"She was hiding in the church," Radulf said quickly, avoiding Henry's knowing gaze. "I have been looking into her story."

"Oh, 'looking into her story,' " Henry echoed, nodding solemnly.

Radulf ignored the jibe and sat down, piling food high on one of the silver plates and pouring a generous quantity of ale into his mug. "She is the daughter of one of the Earl of Morcar's vassals, Edwin of Rennoc. She had been visiting in Scotland, and when they heard that Vorgen's rebellion had ended, she was sent home with some men-at-arms. They were attacked in the wood north of Grimswade. She fled and took shelter in the church, which is where I found her. That is what she says."

Henry paused in his eating, eyeing Radulf curiously. "You sound as if you doubt her story."

"Because I do. I sent some men to search the wood and they found nothing."

"Is it a big wood?"

"Not particularly. There should have been something to prove her story. Where are the bodies, the signs of battle? Could they have been hidden so cleverly, and if so, for what purpose?"

"For fear of your reprisals?" Henry replied promptly. Radulf only grunted. "Other than the question of the wood, she appears to be what she says? A vassal's daughter? Come, Radulf, you are used to reading people! What do you see when you look at this lady?"

Radulf hesitated. When he looked at Lily his

thoughts were more erotic than analytical. How could he explain to Henry the joy he had found last night in Lily's arms? The deep, gut-wrenching satisfaction he had experienced every time he entered her, made her his? When he felt her tremble beneath him, and heard her soft cries of pleasure—

Radulf shook his head sharply, angrily, clearing his mind. Henry was right—his wits were addled. Too many lives depended on Radulf's decisions; it was time to unscramble them.

"She is a lady," he said. "Gently reared. Yet I have learned to mistrust appearances, and there is something about this girl that knocks a sharp warning."

"What is this 'something,' Radulf? Come, tell me."

Again Radulf hesitated. He had sensed a restlessness about Lily, a fear she was eager, nay, desperate, to disguise. Yet that fear could well be of Radulf himself. Most feared him; he had come to expect it. Why not her, too? And yet . . . and yet . . .

"She is proud for a mere vassal's daughter," he admitted at last, "but I have known many proud ladies with little to back their high opinions of themselves."

Henry guffawed.

"I have questioned some of the villagers here at Grimswade, and they tell me that Edwin of Rennoc has a fair-haired daughter, young and pretty."

"Ah, then, it cannot be she! This girl is beautiful!"

Radulf ignored him. "They did not mention Rennoc's daughter had been wed, but Lily tells me her husband is dead, so perhaps it was not well known."

He was making excuses for her now, inventing reasons to believe her.

"She had only one small bundle on her horse, and her clothing is serviceable rather than richly made," he continued.

"A sensible girl would not dress in her best for such a journey, and perhaps she had more belongings on another horse which was taken in the wood. Have you asked her these questions?" Henry asked.

Radulf frowned, avoiding his friend's eyes. He had not asked because he was wary of the answers. "What does it matter? I will hold her tightly until I know the truth."

"And while you hold her, you will enjoy her?" Henry took a swallow of his ale.

Radulf shrugged as if the subject no longer interested him. "She is comely."

Henry grinned, and Radulf knew that his pretended indifference wasn't fooling his friend. Henry had known him far too long. Since they were boys, and Henry had come to Radulf's father's house in Normandy to be trained as a knight. Now, as if homing in on his deepest troubles, the secrets Radulf kept hidden, Henry said, "I saw my Lord of Kenton on my way north."

Radulf froze.

"He was present at the king's table in York, where I stayed while traveling to you. He is an odd fish. Smiling with his mouth while his eyes stay cold. He hangs over his new wife like a lovesick boy."

Radulf, barely aware of the scorn in Henry's voice, forced himself to continue with his meal, biting into a slice of apple. He made himself ask the question. "And how does his wife?"

Henry hesitated, eyeing Radulf's shuttered face. So the pain is still as great, he thought. Would Radulf ever forgive himself, or would his bitterness and self-reproach continue to corrode that possibility?

Henry shrugged. "His wife is in York with him. She is still fair, and she is still adept at drawing a veil over her true nature when she is in the company of others." He glanced at Radulf's blank face, and then said swiftly, "She asked after you. She said she wished to be remembered to you. She told me so twice, so she must have meant it."

Radulf gave a savage laugh. "The woman's vanity knows no bounds!" For a moment he saw her face, beautiful, beneath him, and watched as her amber eyes widened, shifted beyond his shoulder . . . Then disgust filled him for himself and her, and he shut the door on his memories.

"I have heard enough of bad tidings, Henry. Tell me instead why the king has sent you."

"To reinforce you. Perhaps he thinks his Sword is weary." Henry smiled to take some of the weight from his words. "I am to take up stewardship of Vorgen's lands until William decides who will have them."

" 'Tis poor, wild country," Radulf muttered. "The people struggle to grow their crops and feed their beasts. Such hardship breeds discontent; Vorgen would not have found it difficult to draw supporters for rebellion. They are so far from London here, they think William's long arm cannot reach."

Henry yawned. "The country is all very well, my friend, but I prefer to spend my time at court."

Radulf shook his head. "You fight battles with your tongue, Henry, while I use my right arm. That is the difference between us."

"The difference is that I was up while you were still abed!" Henry retorted, and watched Radulf smile.

His eyes narrowed with sudden interest.

Radulf had a sated look to him that Henry had not seen for a long time. The lines about his eyes had smoothed out, and the rigid set of his mouth was softer. Perhaps this mystery woman was what Radulf needed. He deserved some happiness. If she was what she claimed to be, Radulf could keep her by him.

And if she was not . . . ?

Quite suddenly, Henry understood the reason that Radulf had not pursued the matter further. His friend was afraid of what he might find! And yet was not the truth, however hurtful, better than living a lie? Radulf had seen his father suffer in a fool's paradise; did Radulf intend to take the same misguided path?

"You say you are riding south today," Henry said thoughtfully. "How far are Morcar's lands? Twenty . . . twenty-five leagues? Two . . . three days' riding? Why not take the lady and return her to her doting father? Rennoc is probably worried; you will be doing him a favor. Then, if she is as she says, you may continue your dalliance. There is not a man in England who would dare withhold his daughter from Radulf, the King's Sword."

Radulf grunted.

"Come, Radulf, it is a good scheme. I will continue your hunt for Vorgen's wife and guard her lands. It will take only two days to get to Rennoc, and your mind will be set at ease."

He was right, Radulf knew. Best to discover once and for all the truth about Lily. Then why this sense of deep reluctance? As if he knew the truth might not be something he wished to hear? Just as the truth had been something his father had refused to acknowledge . . . Nay! he could not go down that road.

A feeling of calm settled over him. Lily might well be any number of things: a liar, a straying wife, an English spy, a follower of Vorgen's wife. There was a myriad of unpleasant possibilities. But whatever she was, Radulf had two days—three or four if he took his time—in which to enjoy her before they reached Rennoc.

Curtly he nodded his agreement, but Henry noted the tension had returned to his face.

Back once more in Gudren's tent, Lily reacquainted herself with the smell of smoke and the taste of goat's cheese. Gudren appeared pleased to see her, chattering away in her own language. Lily had only to nod occasionally to keep the conversation going.

In truth, she was too caught up in her own thoughts to pay Gudren much attention.

He is a god.

Why had she said such a thing? Though they had thought her jesting, the words remained to Lily a betrayal of the depth of her feelings. And she knew Radulf had sensed their truth, just as he sensed her lies.

Soon he would be gone, soon she could plot her escape. There would not be another chance like this. Once Radulf returned, he would send for her again. And with each moment the leaving would grow more difficult, and the danger more intense.

She could not risk it.

"You are far away, my pretty one."

Gudren was watching her with pale eyes, her round face made even broader by her smile.

"There are things to be considered, mother."

Gudren nodded wisely, as if she understood. "Lord Radulf has a fiercesome reputation, lady, but you should not believe all you hear."

Lily smiled despite herself. "Is he a lamb then, to follow meekly? I think not."

"That would depend on who called," Gudren retorted.

"They say," Lily began thoughtfully, "he is without a heart or a soul, that he kills to feed the lust within himself. That he knows nothing else, except the authority of his king. That he is as cold and hard as the sword he wields."

"The legends would have it so. He is a great warrior, 'tis true, but he is also a wise and just lord. I cannot speak for others, but I know that my Olaf is well paid for his work, and has a dry, comfortable place to live and sleep, and that our table groans with food. At Crevitch, the people do not talk of his lack of heart. Their bellies are full and their bones are warm, and they cheer him when he rides home."

Lily shifted uneasily. "You almost make me believe him to be a great man, mother."

"And so he is, lady. So he is. He is also a fine lover . . . so I have heard."

Color flooded Lily's cheeks.

Did everyone in the camp know of last night? Life here was close-knit, necessarily so. The Normans were strangers in a foreign land and clung together for safety as well as the familiarity of their own kind. They would know if their lord coughed, and why. They must know about Radulf and Lily.

"You do not under—" Lily began, when a deep voice from outside interrupted her.

"Lily?"

Her gray eyes widened on Gudren's. Briefly she considered remaining silent, pretending she was not there, but dismissed the idea as cowardly and foolish.

Radulf would simply come in and drag her out.

She nodded stiffly in Gudren's direction. "Thank you once again, mother. I will not forget your kindness."

Gudren watched her go, a knowing smile in her eyes.

Radulf stood outside, a giant in chain mail, his dark hair damp and sleek to his skull, his face cleanly shaven. A tightness gathered in Lily's chest, a breathlessness. Truly, it was just as well that he was leaving. He was more dangerous to her than all the Normans in the land.

"I have come for you, lady," he said, and held out his hand.

Without thinking, Lily gave him hers, and felt his hard fingers close tightly. A tingle of anticipation ran up her arm. He felt it, too, she was certain of it. She could see those fires, banked now, in his dark eyes. She resisted the urge to sway against his body like a feeble sapling, forcing herself to remain aloof.

"Olaf says you speak the language of the far north." Radulf's frowning eyes searched hers.

She blinked back at him, her eyes stinging from the smoke and the cold clear air.

"How do you speak that tongue?" he went on. "Where did you learn it?" His voice was hard now, and demanding.

You could tell him the truth, the treacherous voice whispered in Lily's head. *Remember what Gudren said? He is a wise and just lord. He will listen to you; he will understand. Tell him now. Now!*

Angrily, she shook her head.

Radulf thought she shook it at him. "Lady," he groaned in exasperation. "You try me too hard. I will have answers."

Above them, on the rise near Radulf's tent, preparations to leave were almost complete. Lily noticed that her own mare was saddled and waiting, her small bundle of possessions strapped in place. She turned in wide-eyed astonishment to the man scowling down at her.

"Why are you taking me with you?"

"Give me your answer."

Lily's eyes searched his dark ones, but could not read them. She sighed, surrendering. "I had a servant who spoke the language and she taught me."

It was only partially a lie. Lily *had* had a Norse servant, but she had learned the language from her mother.

Radulf was still frowning, unconsciously rubbing his sore shoulder. Lily refused to allow the possibility of his pain to distract her.

"I am taking you home to your father," he told her at last, and watched as she stilled, her pale skin turning a shade paler. But the next moment she was smiling as if she had never heard better news, and he convinced himself he had mistaken her pleasure for shock.

"He will be glad to see me," she murmured prettily. "It has been long." A strand of hair blew across her cheek.

Radulf reached out and secured it, smoothing the soft tress behind her ear.

"My blood burns for you, lady," he said harshly. "Even now I can only think of when next I can have you in my bed."

Lily knew he expected her to complain of his manners, or run like a frightened doe.

Her fingers lightly brushed the back of his hand, tracing a thin white scar on the brown skin.

"I, too, burn, my lord."

Radulf's hand turned and gripped hers fiercely, his face tight with desire. "Then God help us if you lie, lady. God help us both!"

Chapter 6

The horses stamped restlessly. Lily, flanked by two of Radulf's men, waited as the group of soldiers prepared to leave. They were traveling light; Radulf was leaving most of his army at Grimswade, awaiting his return. In the meantime, Lord Henry would begin his stewardship of Vorgen's lands.

My lands, Lily thought bitterly.

She pretended at a light heart. Her stomach roiled and churned like a stormy sea, but the Normans must not know it. Lily knew she had to effect her escape before she reached Rennoc, but how? Radulf watched her as if he knew her secret already, and when he was not watching, his men were.

Still, there must surely come a time when they would be distracted. A moment would do. There were hills and woods and streams aplenty between Grimswade and Rennoc, time for plotting and planning and taking advantage of any opportunity that might present itself. Lily would be ready.

"My lord!"

Lily glanced up as two soldiers appeared, huffing and puffing. They were carrying something between them, and as Lily watched in horror, they tossed the body of a man to the ground before Radulf.

The man's long brown hair was tangled, his tunic torn and trousers mud-splattered. A stained and blood-soaked bandage bound one arm. He was obviously dead.

"My lord." One of the soldiers had caught his breath enough to speak. "We found this rat in a hut in the village. I'm certain he was one of the rebels who attacked us last night. He had a Viking axe, and nearly shaved off my ear. I sliced him with my sword, but I didn't see him fall."

"Must have crawled off to die." It was Jervois, Radulf's captain, who commented.

"Scum!" One of the soldiers spat noisily.

Radulf raised an eyebrow, flicking his gaze to Lily, and the man mumbled an apology. Radulf urged his horse closer, the huge feathery feet surprisingly graceful. "Turn him over."

Lily watched as the two soldiers rolled the body onto its back. A jolt went through her, causing her fingers to tighten involuntarily on the reins. Her mare shifted edgily.

Radulf glanced at her, but Lily kept her eyes down and her face expressionless. She felt that dark gaze move over her, warm like sunlight, probing at her secrets. The color heightened in her cheeks, while the air between them seemed to hum with secrets. *I burn for you, lady*, he had said earlier. Would he still burn if he knew the truth? Or would anger take the place of passion?

At last he looked away, and a soft sigh of relief escaped Lily's lips. Once again she furtively inspected the dead man. Yes, she had been correct. He was one of Hew's men. And if, as Radulf's soldier claimed, he had been involved in the skirmish last night . . .

Lily's shoulders tensed, and the muscles in her neck ached as she worked on unraveling the tangle of thoughts in her weary brain. Hew's man being in Grimswade made no sense, for when Vorgen was killed, Hew and his men had fled across the border into Scotland to reassess their future.

Hew had come to her the day after Vorgen died, at dawn.

Hew brushed aside Lily's ladies, stumbling as he entered her chamber. The clumsiness was uncharacteristic, he was always so graceful. And then Lily looked to his handsome face and saw that it had turned old and white with exhaustion and failure. He had betrayed her father, thrown in his lot with Vorgen, and now it was over.

He knelt before her, his head bowed, long golden hair matted with sweat and blood. Lily stood like a cold statue, wrapped in the smoking candlelight and the thick cloak thrown hastily about her shoulders to cover her near nakedness.

Hew rose at last, staggering wearily to his feet, and taking her trembling hand, pressed something small and heavy and familiar into her palm. Lily looked down, knowing what she would see.

The gold ring was still warm from Hew's grip. Warmer than her chill flesh, when she realized that the return of her father's ring could only mean Vorgen was dead.

Hew was telling her in a hoarse voice that the battle, and possibly the rebellion, were lost. Radulf, he said bitterly, had won. But Lily was thinking, *I am free!* Her soul, so long held captive, soared, only to plummet once more to hard earth when she met the desolation in Hew's eyes. Vorgen was dead, but with the end of his greedy dreams came a new and perhaps more terrible threat.

As Vorgen's wife, she had been able to cling to the remnants of the old ways. Now they would be swept to oblivion. Radulf would take her lands, maybe even her life.

Blindly, Lily was aware of Hew's arms about her, his mustache tickling her cheek, the cloying, clinging smells of death and battle. "I am for the border," he was saying. "Come with me, Lily, before it is too late."

Yes, yes, she thought.

"King Malcolm was your grandfather's friend; he will give us sanctuary until we can rally. This is not the end, Lily! We will raise another army, and return to send the Normans fleeing!"

He was fierce, angry, and for a moment he sounded like the boy she had once loved and believed she would wed. But when Lily looked into his eyes she recognized that his emotion was but pretense. Hew was beaten; they were all beaten.

Slowly, Lily lifted her head, looking around her. People had gathered at the edges of the candlelight, with fearful faces, and scared eyes. They were watching her, their hopes, their futures pinned on her actions. If she fled, what would happen to them? She was all they had, all that stood between them and total destruction. They had not asked for Vorgen's war, just as she had not asked to be Vorgen's wife. They could not turn tail and run for the border. They could not leave their homes and crops and families.

Perhaps . . . maybe Lily could secure some sort of peace for them?

But she could not do that if she was hiding in Scotland.

Slowly, Lily shook her head. "I cannot go with you, Hew. I am needed here."

Pain twisted his face. "They will kill me if I stay!" he cried. "You too!"

She drew herself up. "So be it."

That had been the last time she saw him.

This new possibility, that some of Hew's men had remained in Northumbria, caused a flurry of unanswered questions that Lily didn't have time to explore. Radulf's voice, cutting through the past, reminded her of where she was and of the precariousness of her position.

The Normans were still gazing down at the pitiful body.

"Did anyone in the village know him? Did they claim him?"

Head shakings were the only response to Radulf's questions.

The soldier who spat looked as if he meant to do it again, then changed his mind when he met his lord's narrowed eyes. "No, Lord Radulf. Those we spoke to said they'd never seen him afore. Said the hut he was in was an empty one."

"They're afraid." Jervois leaned closer to Radulf. "If they support Vorgen's rebels, you will punish them, and if they support you, the rebels with punish them."

Radulf grunted in agreement. "When we return from Rennoc, we must make it more profitable for them to support us. Lord Henry always says gold coin will win a war, when hot heads are cooling."

Jervois nodded. "Aye, lord. Lord Henry has the right of it."

Radulf glanced at his captain. Jervois was the son of a Norman mercenary and had been with Radulf since 1066, when King William granted his Sword the extensive estates at Crevitch in gratitude for his support at Hastings.

Crevitch had been a joy, but it had also brought problems. Plenty of greedy eyes had turned in Radulf's direction. He had needed good, loyal men to help him guard his good fortune. Jervois had proved himself both loyal and intelligent, an immensely useful captain. And unlike Henry, he did not seem overly ambitious.

Radulf had once been just like Jervois. Wielding a sword had made him feel unstoppable, invincible, but now even that was stale. Again Radulf found his thoughts drifting to Crevitch. Perhaps at thirty-three he had grown too old, too tired. He wanted to feel the warm breeze across the wheat field, smell the scents of summer, but now the dream had grown. He no longer wished to be alone in his paradise. He saw a woman riding crossways on the horse before him, her warm body melded to his, her pale hair streaming over his shoulder, her face flushed and smiling as she gazed up at him . . .

"Perhaps I should remain here at the camp. Hunt them down." Jervois was speaking again. There was a frown in his green eyes that told Radulf he was fully aware of his master's distraction.

Radulf mentally shook himself, and cold fear doused him. *Stop it! Put her from your mind!* He had known men to die from a brief moment's lack of concentration; he had known battles to be lost through wandering wits. If Jervois sensed the extent of Radulf's self-indulgence he would begin to think of turning elsewhere, of finding a more dependable master, one who would not get him killed. And Radulf would not blame him.

"No," he said sharply, frowning as if he had been considering this question all along. "Leave that to Lord Henry. We'll deal with what's left when we get back. 'Tis only a couple of days' ride to Rennoc, after all."

As the little band rode out, a wiry man in one of Father Luc's brown gowns watched from the shelter of the trees, his hands clenched at his sides, his gaze fixed on Lily's bent head.

The sun shone between showers. Lily wasn't sure which was worse, the dripping dampness of her cloak or the steaming warmth. Each clip of her mare's hooves took her farther away from her lands, and her mind was filled with one wild scheme after another.

What did the discovery of Hew's man mean? Was he part of a last pocket of resistance, a leaderless rabble who had decided to sacrifice themselves in a final attempt to drive the Normans from the north?

Lily rejected that explanation. Olaf had said the rebels were watching the camp, and had been seen and then trapped by the Normans.

Had they been watching for her?

Lily stilled, her mare slowing, until one of her guards edged close. "Lady? You must keep up."

How could they be watching for her? Lily urged her mare forward once more. They did not even know she was at the camp unless Father Luc had told them. Was that what he had meant when he'd assured her she would soon be among friends again? Were these men attempting to rescue her from the Normans so they could use her as their own figurehead?

The idea was frightening. She had no intention of being the leader of another futile rebellion that would only further harm her people. Lily wanted peace, and the only way to find it was to talk with the conquering Normans, to win their trust, to work with them.

You've made a good start then, the voice sneered in her head. *Does sleeping with their leader count?*

That just . . . happened. I would never do such a thing in an attempt to win Radulf's trust!

Trust? the voice mocked. *How can you speak of trust, when your every word to him is a lie?*

And the alternative? Lily demanded. If she had told Radulf the truth, he would have taken her captive and delivered her to the king! She stared blindly ahead. If Hew's men had been trying to rescue her from the Normans, to prop her up as the head of their depleted rebel band in the hope more recruits might swell their ranks, then her escape became even more imperative.

Lily began to listen closely to the soldiers' conversations, hoping to hear something to her advantage. At first the men appeared stilted and uneasy, but as the journey dragged on and Lily's presence among them became more familiar, they tossed comments among themselves. Nothing extraordinary, just normal concerns—the chafe of their chain mail, the rub of a boot, the suitability of the country they were passing through for hunting or an ambush, their longing for the women who might or might not be waiting for them at home.

As the hours passed, Lily noticed that Radulf's captain, Jervois, was also keeping an eye on her. He would ask if she was thirsty or hungry, if she was weary and might prefer to ride before him. Lily did not know whether he was acting under Radulf's orders, or whether he was making her comfort his concern for other reasons. Maybe he thought to gain her favor, and therefore Radulf's. So it had been when she was Vorgen's wife— Vorgen's men vying for her notice, until they understood how little power she had to wield on their behalf.

Probably it was Radulf's orders, for several times Jervois rode up to speak with his master, and occasionally he would ride into the surrounding country, always reporting back to Radulf.

Radulf rode in front of his men. Sometimes he would turn to look back, his face a blur beneath his helmet, his gaze sweeping over them, checking each detail. Once he ordered the soldiers nearest her—her "guard"—be changed, but he didn't seem to notice Lily in particular. She was just another task, another detail to be dealt with.

Perhaps he had already forgotten the night they shared, and his words of that morning. The warm generosity of his lovemaking had turned, in an instant, to cold calculation. Did he have the ability, like Vorgen and Hew and even her father, to shut off his emotions when the situation demanded it? His tall helmeted figure, bulky with armor, astride the huge destrier, was every inch that of a cold, heartless warrior. A fighting machine.

Radulf, the King's Sword.

He was well named.

Lily shivered. She found it almost impossible to understand such behavior. Her own emotions were too much a part of her to switch them on and off. She had never been able to make decisions in such an emotionless manner, no matter how she tried. Her heart ruled her, sometimes tempered by her head, but if there was ever a conflict between the two, it was her heart that triumphed.

If women ruled the world, she told herself fiercely, there would be no bloodshed, there would be no wars. Women understood better the importance of life, for it was women who brought it into the world and then tended and cared for it. What could Radulf know of the suffering of the children? What did he care?

So deep in her bitter thoughts was she, Lily did not notice the terrain changing about her. The rocky outcrops and uneven ground had given way to gentler hills and a forest of tall beeches. Soon they were making a steady descent into a valley. She was surprised when she heard the cry to halt. As the command passed swiftly down the line, Lily craned her head to see up ahead.

A narrow stream, water flashing silver as it trickled over smooth stones. Moss-mottled tree branches overhung one side, while the ground was grassy and more open on the other.

Radulf threw out his orders, but everyone knew what to do. They had done it often, up and down the width and breadth of England, as the King's Sword subdued the English and forced them to assume the Norman yoke.

Fires were soon lit and cook pots started. Men sprawled about, eating and drinking, taking their ease as if it were a holy day. But the relaxed air was deceptive. Lily noted the watches Radulf had set on the higher ground about them, and the weapons close to every man's hand.

She sat in the middle of the camp, on a flat-topped rock beside a rowan tree. She had already eaten the bread and cheese brought to her by Radulf's captain, and now sipped from a cup of cold stream water. Jervois sat close by, his old-young face tense and alert beneath his flopping fringe of yellow hair. Lily wondered a little at his diligence—she was surrounded by soldiers, after all. How could she escape? Only a fool would attempt it.

She removed her heavy cloak, took up her antler comb, and prepared to coax the knots and tangles from her hair. It was in an even worse state than it had been when she awoke in Radulf's arms that morning. She had to comb each section several times, laying the gleaming silver strands over her back and shoulders, while shorter tendrils curled about her face. On the few occasions she happened to glance up, the men about her appeared to be studiously avoiding looking at her.

Apart from Radulf. He was looking, and frowning. Lily refused to let him intimidate her, turning back to her grooming.

A linnet sang in the rowan tree, competing with the blackbirds in the beeches to be the sweetest songster. Lily smiled as she listened, and stopped to finish sipping her water. The sun warmed her back, and although gray clouds hovered, the showers had eased. It seemed briefly as if everything that had happened to her during the past four years had faded, become a dream. Lily felt lighthearted, and young. For so long, she had been forced to carry a burden far beyond her years. Now, she remembered with surprise that she *was* young, barely twenty.

A faint chill breeze stirred her silken cloak, sending several gossamer threads across her face. As Lily lifted a hand to smooth them back, she became aware of Radulf once more. He had removed his hauberk and his tunic, and a breath of air flattened his sweat-dampened shirt against the hard, curving muscles of his broad chest, while his tightly cut breeches clung to his lean hips and thick, strong legs.

He was standing by one of the resting groups of men, but as Lily watched through her lashes he moved on, pausing here and there for a word, leaning down to listen with a frown to a complaint or with a smile to a joke. She had known his men were in awe of him, but now she saw that, more importantly, they loved him. Each and every soldier he spoke to lifted his chin higher and made his back straighter.

They would fight to the death for him. Gudren had been right: Radulf was loved just as much as he was feared.

Lily's head cleared abruptly when Radulf glanced up, catching her watching him. He held her briefly but fiercely with the dark spear of his gaze, before continuing among his men as if nothing had happened.

But something *had* happened.

Lily held her breath, and released it very slowly. Her heart began to pound. Radulf might pretend he was randomly seeking out this man and then that one, but each and every step brought him nearer to Lily. Her heart told her it was she who was his true objective.

Why had she suddenly drawn his attention? He had barely noticed her except to order the guard on her tightened. Now, as he circled her, weaving among his men, stealthily, closer and closer, she thought she knew how a hunted animal might feel. Stalked, cornered . . . devoured.

A shudder ran through her as another eddy fanned her skin. The long gleaming strands of her hair stirred and she reached up with trembling fingers to straighten them, gather them, and begin to plait . . .

He was behind her. She knew it even before Jervois rose to his feet. Tiny prickles of awareness lifted the flesh on the back of her neck. His hand closed on hers, stilling her movements. "No," he said softly, and in two steps was standing before her.

Instantly her dark lashes swept down to veil her eyes, afraid he would read the emotions he stirred in her. Her heart was drumming so fast she thought he must hear it, as she remembered what they had done last night in Radulf's bed.

He stood before her, a dark giant against the threatening sky. Radulf, warrior of legend, whose name would be forever remembered. But it was not that Radulf Lily yearned for. She wanted the Radulf who had held her tenderly in his arms, lavishing his body upon hers until she no longer belonged to herself, only to him.

"My lord?" Jervois was looking from one to the other, uncertain what was required of him.

"Go and change the watches," Radulf said quietly.

His captain went without argument.

Lily blinked, trying to collect her wandering wits. He was so close. She could smell the clean, masculine scent of him. She could see the hard satin and the dark silk of his chest where the shirt gaped at his throat. Her eyes were drawn inexorably down, over his flat stomach, to the ties at the waist of his breeches, and finally to linger on the bulge between his thighs. His manhood appeared to grow under her attention, and in direct response Lily's breasts swelled, the nipples tightening, until they were outlined clearly against the wool cloth of her gown.

Shocked by her body's betrayal, Lily glanced swiftly up at Radulf, color staining her cheeks, praying he hadn't noticed.

He had.

His dark gaze was fixed on her jutting nipples,

and when he lifted his eyes to hers, she was scorched by the smoldering fires in their depths.

She did not know that the sight of her combing her hair, the unbound glory of it, had heated his blood beyond bearing.

He had found himself drawn to her as a swimmer caught in a tidal pull tries for the shore. Struggle though he might, his eyes kept returning to Lily as she combed that wondrous hair, the sweet curve of her neck and cheek, the swell of her breast. His groin throbbed and burned. He wanted to run his hands through that silver wave, press his mouth to it, hold it fast as he thrust his body into hers.

Two days, maybe three, and Lily would be at Rennoc with her father. The future beyond that was uncertain. He had so little time to be with her. She was the moon to his ocean, drawing him with a subtle yet irresistible pull.

He knew he had lost his struggle when he had stood up earlier, telling himself he must see to his men.

Now Radulf had lost even the will to pretend.

"Come!" He held out his hand.

Lily blinked. "My lord?"

But Radulf couldn't wait for explanations. He grabbed her hand and jerked her to her feet, spilling the cup of water. Lily cried out softly, stumbling after him. "My lord," she gasped. "There is no need— My lord!"

His men scuttled out of his way, openmouthed.

They think he means to kill me, thought Lily in fright, *and perhaps he does.* Radulf kept walking, pulling her behind him. Across the slippery stones in the shallow stream, between the moss-clothed trees, until the twisted branches above them filtered the sunlight into a swirl of green.

"Radulf!" Lily gasped, pulling her gown free from yet another bush of thorns. Her shoes were thin, and stones and twigs dug through the soft leather, bruising the soles of her feet. Her hair, which she had spent so much time tidying, was snarled again, blinding her.

Radulf spun her around and pulled her hard against him, his mouth coming down on hers with barely controlled savagery. His hands clasped her buttocks, pressing her against him, and leaving her in no doubt as to his urgent need.

Lily gasped, and then softened against him as the reason for his roughness suddenly became very clear to her. He was not angry; he wanted her! Wanted her with a desperate, unstoppable urgency.

Just as she wanted him.

Her response startled him. It was as if he expected her to struggle, to cry out for help, to be afraid. But Lily wound her arms about his neck and clung instead, her mouth opening to his, her tongue as wild to taste him as he was her.

Radulf groaned and caught her about the waist, dropping them both down onto their knees in the soft, thick carpet of leaves. Above them the linnet sang again, and the beeches rustled softly in the cool breeze.

Their mouths parted and for a moment they remained motionless, breathing quickly. As if, thought Radulf, they were at prayer. The ridiculousness of the situation struck him forcibly. He almost laughed. What must his men think of the terrible Radulf now, dragging this girl into the woods because he could not control his lust for her?

He was making a fool of himself, just like his father.

The thought turned him so cold he nearly pulled back. And then Lily put her hands, light as butterflies, upon his shoulders, and leaned against him, her soft mouth lifted invitingly to his. Desire roared through him again, and with a groan he bent to kiss her. She pressed still closer, her breasts soft through his shirt, her nipples still hard.

Radulf lifted his hand to cup one firm mound and felt her tremble, her gasp softly erotic against his lips. If he didn't get inside her soon he would burst. He sprawled onto the ground, uncaring of the damp soil and damper leaves, and his back came to rest against the trunk of a tree.

He could take her now, quick and hard. The thought was tempting, very tempting, but he wanted her to enjoy the act as much as he. And he wanted to make it last.

Grasping Lily's waist, he pulled her down onto his lap so that her legs straddled his thighs. Slowly, purposefully, his warm, strong hands slid under the hem of her chemise, gliding over satin skin, following the curves and hollows of her body.

Lily sighed in bliss and reached for him. Radulf grasped her hips and held her still. "No," he said. "You are impatient, lady. You will have your turn."

Radulf's hands kneaded and stroked and caressed until Lily gasped and swayed, beyond thought. And then his fingers slid into the curls between her thighs, dipping and sliding in the moisture there.

It was too much. Lily swayed closer, her lips parted. He was watching her, dark eyes gleaming through his lashes, his face tense with the battle to control his desire.

Her mouth was his undoing.

Lily reached up and pressed her lips to his, and felt him shudder. The kiss deepened at the same moment as Radulf's finger thrust itself further into her heat. Lily gasped and trembled like a shot bird, dizzy with the sensations he was drawing from her. His finger stroked boldly, mimicking his tongue in her mouth.

Lily peaked with a cry, shuddering and clutching at his chest. He waited while she calmed, soothing her with gentle caresses over her back and shoulders. Then he lifted the gown and chemise from her, leaning forward to kiss her breasts, his tongue lathing the sensitive nipples. Lily moaned, her fingers clutching his head to bind him closer.

Gently, but firmly, he pulled away. Dazed gray eyes met heated dark ones. Radulf smiled. "Now it's your turn," he murmured.

Delicate color flooded her face as she grasped his meaning. For a moment Vorgen, and all the bitterness and doubt he had heaped upon her, swam through her mind. Her touch was poison, vile . . . And yet she wanted dearly to touch him.

Slowly, tentatively, Lily ran her hands up under Radulf's shirt, raising it to his shoulders. The hard muscles of his chest rippled under brown skin. She leaned forward to press her lips against him, the strands of dark hair tickling her nose. Her tongue flicked over his nipples, then down his breastbone, to his hard, flat stomach. Radulf groaned, and Lily stopped.

Uncertainly, her gaze lifted to his.

Her own blood was on fire from simply touching him, and she was amazed to see that Radulf, too, was burning. From her touch, her kisses! The realization gave her courage. Her fingers found the ties.

She was slow at first, clumsy, but as Radulf leaned forward to press hot little kisses over her face and down the line of her throat, she quickened, tugging eagerly at the laces.

The waist of his breeches loosened suddenly as the knot came free. Quickly Lily pushed them down so that she could see . . . She sighed. Ah, this was what Vorgen had lacked. She hadn't then understood what could happen to a man who desired a woman. Radulf pulled back slightly and Lily hesitated, her fingers cool against his stomach. Again she remembered Vorgen—she couldn't help it.

"Go on, lady." Radulf's voice was husky, sending deep tremors through her. "Touch me."

Lily's hand slid down, and tentatively, wonderingly, she closed around the hard length of him. He was so smooth, so big. Velvet-covered iron. At the tightening of her grip, Radulf groaned again, closing his eyes. Lily instantly relaxed her fingers, moving to withdraw, but his own hand closed over hers, giving her back her courage.

"I want you so much. Touch me, *mignonne*, feel me. This is all for you. I am yours."

Flushed, her eyes bright, Lily obliged. "You like me to do this, my lord?" she whispered.

Radulf heard the surprise in her voice, and dismissed it as a virgin's qualms. "Aye, Lily," he managed, with a half laugh, half groan. "I like it very much. But we have not finished yet."

If she kept on with her petting and stroking, Radulf knew he would explode. Gently, he took her hands in his, placing them about his neck. He leaned forward to kiss her, and at the same time clasped his hands about her waist. He lifted her up from her cozy spot on his lap.

Lily gave a startled squeal, clinging to his shoulders. He smiled into her uncertain eyes, his own like a night sky in July, so hot. Slowly, slowly he lowered her, until the tip of his manhood just nudged the blond curls between her thighs. Looking down, Lily held her breath. He lifted her again, then lowered her, and then again, each time sliding deeper into the welcoming sheath.

Radulf's mouth found her breasts, pulling at the nipples, sucking hard. Lily gasped and arched them toward him, head thrown back, hair spilling about her. As he settled himself deeply and entirely within her, Lily leaned forward, brushing frantic butterfly kisses over his face and throat. Radulf gripped her hips more firmly, then thrust up deeply. Lily's palms slid over his chest. She trembled, gasping, as he seemed to reach the very core of her being. The pleasure pooled between them, heavy and hot. Lily dug her fingers into his shoulders, holding on tightly, fearing she might be torn apart and flung to the four winds. When the convulsing climax took them, Radulf's dark eyes stared into hers.

He spoke no words, yet it was as if Lily heard

his vow: *Whatever happens after, in this moment you are mine.*

The strength went out of her body and she collapsed against Radulf, her cheek on his shoulder, his breath warm in her hair. "Whatever happens after," she murmured.

Chapter 7

⌒◟◞◟◞⌒

Lily lifted her face to the sun, easing her aching back and legs. The constant riding was tiring, and she had discovered sore spots in surprising places all over her body. Although, she thought, hiding a smile, there could be other reasons for her tenderness.

Last night they had camped on a sheltered hillside. Radulf had taken Lily to his tent, his arms all the warmth she needed as they lay together in the darkness. He treated her as if she were as necessary to him as food and water. Already her body had learned his so well that merely standing close to him caused a tremor of anticipation, her nipples hardening, warm moisture pooling between her thighs.

And Radulf felt it, too, she was certain of that.

She looked up now, sensing his eyes upon her, and noticed that he had indeed turned his head to seek her out. His expression might be deeply shadowed beneath his helmet, but she knew the emotion that would shape it.

Desire. Need.

Radulf wanted her.

Lily understood completely, for she wanted him, too.

She sighed and shifted uneasily in her saddle. How could she have allowed the Norman into her blood? It was madness to want such a man! It was not safe to want *any* man. Lily's beloved father had died making war. Her childhood sweetheart had betrayed her for his own ambition. In her albeit limited experience, she had found men such as Radulf were not to be relied upon. Not to be trusted. Certainly she had never meant to get this close to one of them.

Especially not an enemy!

Radulf was a man of pride and honor, a Norman lord sworn to obey his king. Yet he was also a man of contrasts, light and dark, much more complex than the tales about him had led her to believe. Intellectually and emotionally, Lily found the combination of strength and vulnerability, of mastery and humor, irresistible. Physically, her body craved his as parched ground craved water.

She was caught in a terrible bind. She was tied by the fiery ropes of desire to a man who, if he knew her true identity, would be required to hand her over to his king. Already two days had passed, and with each hour that crept by, they drew closer to Rennoc.

And to discovery.

* * *

Radulf had slowed their pace after the first day. They dawdled, stopping often, enjoying the fine weather. When Lily asked Radulf why he was in no hurry to reach Rennoc, he laughed and bent closer, his warm breath sending tingles over her skin.

"Need you ask, lady? Or do you look for flattery?"

Lily lifted her chin proudly. "If I did not need to ask, my lord, I would not."

His finger brushed her cheek. Her pride seemed to amuse him. " 'Tis you who keeps me from my duty, *mignonne*."

Lily's gray eyes had searched his, discovering the truth of what he said. Pleasure warmed her. Her lips curved into a teasing smile, but her words contained more than a hint of tartness.

"And how many days have you set aside for this distraction, my lord? And will you put me from your mind when they are passed?"

They were questions Radulf had been asking himself, and still he did not know the answers. "That depends, Lily," he murmured, and made himself return her smile. "You are pensive today."

Lily turned away, watching a hawk, solitary above a rocky crag. "I am thinking of Rennoc," she said.

He rode beside her in silence, his eyes on the perfection of her profile, the soft wisps of fair hair that had escaped their braid to dance about her face. She was like no other woman he had ever known. Such beauty should mean a certain vanity, an expectation of men's besottedness, but Lily acted as if she was unaware of her looks. There was no coyness about her, nothing flirtatious.

If he had met her anywhere else but hiding in

Grimswade church, Radulf would have been tempted to trust her. But the circumstances of their meeting and his instant attraction, as well as his past experience, made him suspicious and wary. It was only when they lay together that he was able to abandon such suspicions.

"Tell me of your father."

The suddenness of his question surprised Lily, but she didn't let it show. The hawk had dived, vanishing behind some scrubby trees, but she kept watch for its return.

"Edwin of Rennoc is kind but firm, a good father and a good vassal."

"And are you a good daughter?"

Lily smiled. "Of course."

"Obedient?"

"Yes."

"Loving?"

"Yes."

"Truthful?"

Lily glanced at him, still smiling. "Why do you question me, my lord? Do you intend listing my shortcomings to him?"

Radulf frowned. "I would not dare, lady. It is you who should list my shortcomings. I have treated you with far less honor than you deserve."

Surprised, Lily saw repentance in his eyes, but a certain arrogance, too. "Do you mean you are sorry for taking me to your bed, or sorry for the way in which it happened?"

"You were a maid."

"I was widowed, so how could you know I was still a maid?"

"I should have known it." His look was wry. "Truth to tell, Lily, I was too hot for you even then.

And no, I am not sorry for taking you to my bed, only sorry that it was done so rashly."

"Nay," she whispered, reaching out to rest her hand lightly against his thigh. "There was a fire between us, and neither of us could have doused it in any other manner."

He looked down at her hand, and Lily felt his already hard muscles tense. She had spoken in the past tense but they both knew the fire had not been doused. The flames were as bright as ever.

"What will happen when we reach . . . when I am home?" she asked softly, and then wondered why she asked. She knew what would happen. Radulf would end it. But she wanted to pretend a little longer, fool herself that she really was Edwin of Rennoc's daughter, and Radulf was taking her home. Then she could ask herself if his desire was strong enough for him to consider keeping her by him. Or would he visit her, when his duties permitted, riding swiftly to Rennoc to bed her and leaving an hour later?

Lily shivered. She did not want that. If she were to complete her fantasy as she really wished, then Radulf would be with her always.

But that was madness. An impossibility. A child might believe in such things, but Lily was no child. She desired Radulf, yes, but she must not give in to it, for if she did he would destroy her.

"What will happen when we reach Rennoc?" Radulf repeated her question, and answered it. "I know not, Lily."

"My lord!"

Radulf turned as Jervois pulled his mount to a rattling halt. The animal looked as if it had been ridden hard, and the young captain reined in closely beside Radulf to murmur his news. The two men spoke a moment, their expressions serious.

Lily watched them curiously.

Radulf was now gazing between his horse's ears, frowning, deep in his own thoughts. Jervois had dropped back. When Radulf had still not spoken after several minutes, Lily ventured curiously, "Something concerns you, my lord?"

Radulf shot her an impenetrable look. "There is always a need for concern, Lily. And caution. In all things."

A tingle ran down her spine. Was he giving her a warning? He was suddenly so distant. What had Jervois told him?

Lily twisted around to look at the other man, but his face was also closed, no more readable than Radulf's. Lily turned in time to see Radulf's broad back as he spurred his horse into a gallop, riding up the line to the front of the column. As if by some prearranged signal, Jervois moved to take his place.

"Has something happened?" Lily asked him, not expecting a proper answer. "You have been away." She had noticed Jervois's absence since yesterday but had not thought to ask where he was— Would they have told her anyway?

"My lady?" Jervois raised his blond eyebrows in surprise. "I have been . . . solving a puzzle, but now everything is going as planned."

"You are not afraid of attack?"

Jervois considered her. "It would be foolish indeed to attack such a well-prepared band of men, lady."

"Nevertheless, Lord Radulf does not relax his vigilance?"

Jervois smiled, the tension smoothing from his face until he looked suddenly very young. Almost as young as Lily herself. "No, lady, he does not relax. That is what makes him such a good soldier. He trusts nothing and no one."

Another warning?

Lily had come to believe suspicion was part of Radulf's nature, and not just in the execution of his duties. Radulf was not a man who gave of himself easily; he guarded his emotions as closely as he guarded her.

And yet he had made love to her as if he were starving.

But none of this altered the fact that she must escape before they reached Rennoc. The truth would be out as soon as she rode through Rennoc's gate.

The soldiers guarding her had increased their watchfulness. For every step Lily's mare took, there were now several soldiers right beside her. Grim-faced and eagle-eyed, they did not allow her out of their sight. How could she possibly elude so many men? Lily's tension increased, her neck and shoulders beginning to ache. Her gray eyes were underlined with faint shadows of tiredness as she constantly searched the surrounding countryside for a way out.

They stopped again at midday, but this time when Radulf sought her out it was not to drag her off into the woods and make love to her. Instead he caught her chin in his fingers, turning her face for his perusal, a frown that might have terrified any other woman drawing down his dark brows.

"You should have told me no last night," he murmured. "You needed your rest."

Lily laughed shakily. "My lord, I did not wish to tell you no," she mocked.

Radulf smiled, his thumb stroking her jaw, while between their bodies and beneath her cloak, hidden from the men, his hand slipped down to gently cup her breast. Lily drew a ragged breath, knowing she should pull away but unable to do so. He caressed her until her eyes were half closed and her lips parted and her legs trembled.

And then, when she was dazed and willing, he leaned even nearer and said, "We are close to Rennoc, lady. You are almost home."

He was watching her, judging her reaction. Lily swallowed and managed to nod calmly, while her heartbeat quickened with fear and anger. Had he touched her only to put her off her guard? Was he really so devious, so cruel?

"We could ride hard and be there by nightfall," Radulf went on, his voice soft in her ear, "but I fear you are weary. Trier Monastery is a short ride east of here. We will rest there tonight and you will have a proper bed, and tomorrow you can return home to your father."

A reprieve.

Did he see the flicker of relief in her eyes?

"Thank you, my lord."

Radulf nodded, and Lily watched him walk away, calling out for his men to remount. The monastery was her last chance. Radulf would only increase his watchfulness tomorrow on the ride to Rennoc.

"Lady?" One of the soldiers was holding her mare, waiting for her to remount. Lily placed her foot into his palm, springing neatly into the saddle, then she sat waiting for the others, her eyes blind to the busy scene about her. Tonight she must escape and never see Radulf again.

He would hate her for her deception. He would think she had used him. And there was nothing Lily could do about it, for how could she state her case if she were gone? She did not regret what had happened between them; she was only sorry she would not be able to make him understand that it was an entirely separate thing from her allegiance. Those tender moments had been like a sheltered island in a vast, cold sea, but now she must turn her face once more to the storms.

They reached Trier in the late afternoon. It was a poor, ramshackle construction of wood and stone. The buildings appeared to be sinking, rather than nestling, in a dip in the surrounding hills. The abbot, himself a recent Norman replacement, was more than willing to give Radulf and his men shelter.

Lily learned that they were Benedictines, the so-called Black Monks, the most populous order in England. As with most other religious houses, the monks of Trier grew their own food and made their own bread, but these monks also produced their own cheese from a small herd of cows, and wine from a precious, tiny vineyard on the sheltered side of a hill.

She was able to sample the wine for herself as she sat down to dinner with Radulf and the abbot. The abbot, though very old and stern-faced, spoke of his home in Normandy with all the longing of a child for its mother.

His reflections on Northumbria were stark and brutal.

"This is a most uncivilized land. The people are pagans. Savages!" He spat out the word like a sour plum. "King William must be strict with them, Lord Radulf, if he is to humble them. They are like defiant children in need of discipline."

"Surely, Your Grace, even defiant children would respond to kindness rather than discipline, if they were given the choice?" Lily said.

The abbot peered shortsightedly at her, and she almost wished she had bitten her tongue as she had done so often at Vorgen's table. But when the old man replied, it was with puzzlement rather than anger.

"You sympathize with these rebels, Lady Lily?"

Lily smiled her sweetest smile, while inside a new and dangerous sense of freedom began to blossom. "I neither sympathize with war, nor with those who make it. I believe . . ." She hesitated as both the abbot and Radulf gave her their full attention, one curiously, the other with a frown of disapproval. And yet, she asked herself defiantly, why shouldn't she say what she truly thought? She was no longer Vorgen's wife, afraid that the least hint of spirit might gain her a blow from Vorgen's fist or a vicious tirade from his tongue.

The words came out in a rush.

"I believe the north has seen enough bloodshed. We could have peace, if the king would allow it."

Radulf grunted, unimpressed. "If you imagine King William is a warmonger you are mistaken, lady. He wants peace, just as you do. His coffers and his temper suffer when he cannot rest one day in his kingdom without fearing a rebellion. You think him harsh, perhaps, but it is a harshness brought on by the people themselves."

"Discipline them, like children!" The abbot nodded his hoary head.

"Maybe that was so in the past." Lily leaned toward Radulf, as if she spoke to him alone. "But now cannot the harshness stop? There are rebels willing to listen . . . at least, I believe it is so. Can the English and the Normans not live in peace together?"

Radulf narrowed his dark eyes. "There will be no peace while Vorgen's wife stirs the pot."

"Lady Wilfreda?"

The name shocked Lily to frozen silence.

But the abbot didn't notice, easing his bony buttocks upon the hard wooden seat. "I have heard appalling stories of her cruelty, Lord Radulf. I have heard her likened to a she-wolf eating her own young!"

Radulf turned to him. His voice was soft. "You know her?"

The abbot, startled by his guest's intent stare, hurriedly shook his head. "I don't know her, no, but I can see into her heart."

Radulf shrugged and lost interest. "Everyone has heard of her, but no one knows her," he growled. "I begin to think she is a witch who can vanish and appear at will!"

The abbot's eyes widened and he crossed himself.

"I have heard," Lily began, dizzy from her own daring, "that Vorgen kept her locked away from the world. His prize and his prisoner."

Radulf sipped his wine.

Emboldened by his silence, she went on. "Everybody speaks of Wilfreda as if she were a devil's daughter, but as you so rightly said, my lord, not one of these rumor bearers has seen her or spoken to her. Lord Radulf, you know what it is to be a tall tale. Perhaps she is not nearly so terrible as the stories would have us believe. Perhaps she, too, is weary of war."

Now Radulf's eyes were riveted to hers. Lily forced herself to remain calm while his dark gaze delved deep, deep into her heart, until she became light-headed. At last, when she was sure he must know all her secrets, he shrugged, and returned to his wine.

"You mean well," he allowed, "but you know not what you say. I knew Vorgen, I fought with him at Hastings. He was a loyal soldier. It was his wife who turned him into a traitor."

Lily blinked, amazed by his willful blindness. Anger bubbled inside her, and with it a swirl of memories of her life with Vorgen. The pain and humiliation, the damage to her body and mind. But somehow she forced all emotion down, using her cooler mind to subdue her eager heart.

Remember that Radulf could not have known Vorgen as he really was, or he would not speak so. Vorgen must have changed, or he had hidden his true self well. Or was it just that Radulf, being a Norman, could not denigrate another Norman when there was an Englishwoman handy to take the blame?

For her sake as well as his, she must try to make him see, wake him from his sleep. It was foolish, perhaps, but when she was gone she wanted Radulf to understand.

"I understand what you say," she said gently, "but men change. Perhaps the Vorgen you knew changed. Greed is like an illness that can afflict any man. Vorgen came north on the king's busi-

ness and saw he, too, could be a king. At least . . .
that is what I have heard."

"We must all be vigilant against the sin of
greed," the abbot murmured perfunctorily. He
was losing interest, his head nodding.

Radulf played with the stem of his goblet. He
preferred to believe Wilfreda had caught Vorgen
in her spell like an evil, alluring spider might
catch a helpless fly. He had a picture of her in his
mind: raven-haired, amber-eyed, smiling into
men's eyes and saying one thing while she meant
another. Wilfreda had become Anna, and he
hated her.

"Who have you heard speak on this matter?"
he demanded, a growing anger coloring his deep
voice. "Does your father indulge in treason,
lady?"

Lily shook her head, startled at the expression
in his eyes—black and furious, like the storms
that boiled over the hills near Vorgen's keep.

"But you plead Wilfreda's case?" he went on,
leaning toward her, crowding her.

Again Lily shook her head, refusing to be intim-
idated. "Nay, Lord Radulf. I merely offer you my
thoughts. Are women not allowed to have opinions under King William's rule? I had heard he is
very fond of his wife, and listens to her advice.

"Matilda is different—"

"And how is that?" Lily searched his face, very
aware of this new tension between them. And the
danger in his eyes. A combination of desperation
and determination drove her on. "Matilda is a
woman, the same as Wilfreda, the same as I am.
Should a woman not be given the same fair and
just treatment as you have given Vorgen?"

Radulf's frown grew blacker. "You know not of what you speak, lady. These are men's matters. Stay with what you understand, Lily. I have made my judgment. Vorgen's wife is a scourge upon the north and will be captured and brought before the king for just punishment."

A chill ran through Lily, freezing any reply she may have made.

Radulf's voice had wakened the old abbot from his doze. He sounded quite hearty but clearly had heard nothing of their conversation.

"I knew your father, my lord! A fine man. He was most generous to our order. I heard he requested prayers be said for him after his death, to shorten his stay in Purgatory. Aye, a fine man. You must be proud to tread in his footsteps!"

Radulf turned and looked at him. Whatever the abbot saw in his face startled him so that he jerked back, his lips working.

"My lord . . ." he muttered. "My lord, I meant no offense."

Radulf had already turned away, and a heavy silence ensued while the abbot struggled to regain his composure.

Radulf's anger dissipated slowly, and with it went the red mist from his eyes. He reminded himself that the old abbot could not know of the rift between him and his father. He should apologize, make all right, but he found the words difficult. The wound inside him had still not healed; perhaps it never would. But it was his wound and he did not share his pain with many. Over the years, the hurt had become an old, familiar companion.

No, it was Lily's quiet argument that had really infuriated him. All but accusing him of lacking

fairness in his decisions, instructing him on how
to deal with the rebels! No woman had ever dared
meddle like that before, and he would not allow it
now. He might desire Lily with a raging, insa-
tiable hunger, but she was a woman.

He could not start trusting her now, especially
not after what Jervois had discovered.

And what if she is right?

The voice in his head was very like Henry's.
Teasing, questioning, the devil's advocate. Radulf
stiffened. How could she be right? he argued
silently. He had known Vorgen; he did not know
Wilfreda. Should he slander the man he believed
loyal for a rebellious, treacherous woman?

So you are not biased in your thinking?

Of course not!

Then . . . why did Lady Wilfreda resemble
Anna in his thoughts? Had he allowed his hatred
for the one to cloud his judgment of the other?

He tried to remember Vorgen more clearly,
pushing past the knightly bravado and comrade-
ship they had shared at Hastings.

A memory came to him, sharp and somewhat
unpleasant.

Vorgen had won a sword. It was a handsome
thing, the handle decorated with emeralds and
rubies and gold filigree, the blade as sharp as a
scold's tongue. Vorgen claimed he had won it fair,
but Roger, the man who had lost the sword,
claimed foul play. He had complained loud and
long to any who would listen. Until he had died at
Hastings—not in the main battle, but in a minor
skirmish elsewhere.

Afterward, the mutterings of Roger's friends
had not gone away. They said that Roger hadn't

died at the hands of Harold Godwineson's troops, but by his own sword, held in Vorgen's greedy grip. Their accusations had continued on so long, Radulf had heard of them and investigated. In the end, his ears ringing with Vorgen's strenuous denials, he had dismissed the matter. And indeed, there had been no proof.

Only now he remembered the incident, and wondered.

Radulf shifted in his chair, flicking a restless glance toward the abbot. The old man was asleep again, mouth agape, wrinkled face slack. Radulf's lips twitched as he turned to his other side.

Lily was watching him, her gray eyes wary, as though he were a stranger again. The mighty and fearsome Radulf, who ate English children for his dinner.

Radulf's heart contracted.

Tomorrow they would reach Rennoc, and tonight . . . well, tonight was already in hand. He could not call a halt to his plans, even had he wished to.

What would be, would be.

Whatever tonight's outcome, this might well be the last time he sat with her, looked upon her—apart from in his dreams. He could not lie with her in his arms, here. Lust was another sin the abbot would frown upon. *Perhaps that is to be my punishment for bringing her to the monastery and weaving my deceit. I can look, but I cannot touch.*

He lifted her hand, which rested beside her goblet, and kissed her fingers, then turning it, pressed his lips into the soft hollow of her palm.

His eyes were dark and intent, his voice an intimate, husky murmur. "Tomorrow I deliver you safe to your father."

Lily kept her eyes on his, not daring to speak. Her throat was thick with tears.

"My lady." He clasped her fragile hand in his large one, leaning even closer. She saw her reflection in his dark eyes, a pale ghost compared to his earthy solidity. "My lady, I know you have secrets."

Still she refused to speak, gray eyes wide in the flare of the candles.

"Lily, will you not trust me?"

It was foolish to ask it. He knew that as soon as the words were spoken. How could she trust him, when he had just shown himself incapable of listening to her without turning on her in fury? Yet he *wanted* her to trust him. His pride demanded it! His heart yearned for it.

For a long moment dark eyes gazed into gray, and then Lily gave a breathless laugh. She reached up with her free hand, hesitated, and then stroked his temple, smoothing back a lock of short dark hair.

"My lord, I *have* trusted you. More than you know."

Her lips trembled as she smiled. It required all of Radulf's self-control not to lean forward and taste them, to lose himself in the sweetness of her mouth. A terrible ache filled his chest.

This was more than want.

Madness, whispered the bitter skeptic inside him, but Radulf didn't care. At that moment he would gladly have drowned himself in Lily's eyes.

The abbot cleared his throat loudly.

With a sigh, Radulf leaned back to put some

space between them, although he retained her hand. Lily's eyes sparkled with tears.

"The hospitaler has come to take you to your room, lady," the abbot said coolly. "You must be weary after your journey and in need of sleep. I have set aside a private room in my house for your use."

"Thank you." Lily glanced sideways at Radulf.

"The guest quarters will be our billet," he answered her unspoken question.

Lily bowed her head and spoke calmly, only the slightest tremor betraying the depth of her feelings. "I am very tired. I would be glad to retire now."

As she rose, Radulf also stood. He brought her hand to his lips with a murmured, "Sleep well, *mignonne*."

Lily gasped at the feel of his warm mouth once more against her skin. The gleam in his eyes spoke of desire and possession, and of longing. This might be the last time she ever saw him, and the tears filling her eyes threatened to spill over her lashes and fall. His face blurred, and she blinked to clear her vision before she replied huskily.

"And you, my lord."

As the hospitaler led her away, she did not turn. *Trust me*, Radulf had said. And the strange thing was, she had almost been prepared to do so. Until his anger, his inflexible stance on Vorgen, had made her see the danger of such an action. Like a game of chance, she would not know the outcome until it was too late.

And Lily could not afford to dice with her freedom, or mayhap her life.

Chapter 8

Bells rang from the church calling the monks to Compline, the last prayers of the day, as the hospitaler led Lily through a small court-yard. She paused, breathing deeply to calm herself. The dark vault of the sky above her was ablaze with stars, but tonight their beauty appeared cold and distant to Lily.

She shook her head, forcing back the urge to weep. When he knew the truth, Radulf would be glad that she had gone. He would hate her. But if she had deceived him, then she was being pun-ished for it.

Lily took another gasping breath. Time enough later to grieve. She forced herself to concentrate, to look about properly for the first time.

There were several open archways leading from the little courtyard. In the moonlight beyond one she could see a walled herb garden, and through another the dark, angular shape of the gatehouse.

Her way out.

"My lady?"

The monk, a black shadow, was waiting patiently beside a wooden doorway. Lily hastened to follow.

Her room was narrow and plain, and contained a bed, a crucifix, and a fat candle. After some of her recent sleeping places, it seemed like a palace. When the hospitaler had gone, she sank down wearily on the pallet. She was very tired, but must not fall asleep. She would wait until everyone else slept and then she would find her mare in the stables, and ride away from here.

Away from Radulf.

Her heart ached, but what choice had she? The arguments, the questions kept running through her head, but there was only one answer. She must leave tonight and never see Radulf again.

Time passed slowly. Eventually the monastery grew very still. Lily imagined the Norman soldiers sleeping, Radulf too, his hard face made vulnerable. Once again tears swelled, only this time she allowed them to trickle down her cheeks. Their salt stung her lips, and with shaking fingers, Lily lifted one corner of her cloak to wipe them away. Something round and hard made a ridge in the lining.

The ring.

With difficulty, Lily tipped the golden circle into her palm. The hawk seemed to stare back at her from its black background, the red eye glinting in the candlelight. " 'I give thee my heart,' " she whispered.

In Lily's eyes the ring had always stood for fairness and a just ruler, as well as the love her Viking mother bore her English father. Vorgen had stolen it for a time and subverted it into something mean and avaricious, but now it was Lily's.

She had hoped that, through her, the ruby-eyed hawk would one day be seen again as the mark of a fair and just ruler. And that she would be that ruler. Could such dreams still come true, or was she doomed to run and hide for the rest of her life?

Lily turned the ring over in her fingers, testing the familiar weight of it. With a fatalistic flourish, she slipped it onto her thumb.

The time for subterfuge had passed. Whether she was captured now, trying to escape the monastery, or tomorrow when they reached Rennoc, Lily was lost. At least she would be herself: the Lady Wilfreda, daughter of an English nobleman and a Viking princess, and rightful ruler of her father's Northumbrian lands.

Her eyes dry, her mind clear, Lily rose to her feet. As she moved toward the door, she hesitated, then removed her jeweled dagger from its sheath, slipping it under her girdle. She did not expect to use it, but the threat might be enough if the situation required it. Carefully, trying not to breathe, Lily cracked open her door.

The abbot's house was dark and empty. Lily's hand crept to her dagger anyway. She had expected one of Radulf's soldiers to appear before her and demand to know where she was going. Icy droplets of fear on her skin made her shiver as she tried to pierce the shadows. There was no one. In some corner of her mind it occurred to her that Radulf had been strangely remiss in not posting his usual guard, but she was so relieved by his oversight that she let her doubts slip away.

Lily's shaking fingers uncurled from the dagger and she slowly eased out of her room, closing the door behind her.

There were no guards outside the abbot's house, either, and it was a simple matter to slip into the small courtyard. Breathing fast, heart thudding, Lily pulled the hood of her cloak over her bright hair and ran beneath the archway in the direction of the stables.

Everything was so still.

The monastery buildings were dark, silent shapes, which Lily's imagination peopled with dozens of watching eyes. The stables were situated near the gatehouse, and the stable door easily creaked open to her touch. The smells of horse and hay were released from within, comforting in their familiarity.

Lily peeped inside.

A torch flared on one wall, which struck her as providential rather than strange. There was no sign of Radulf's men or any of the monks. A ladder ran up into a hayloft, and after holding her breath and listening, Lily decided that, too, was empty.

Her mare gave a soft whicker of greeting, and several of the other animals moved restlessly. Radulf's great destrier eyed her solemnly, as if questioning her right to be there. Like its master, the war horse filled Lily with a sense of awe . . . and regret.

No time for that now!

She hurried forward, the hem of her cloak brushing softly over the straw-littered floor. Her mare thrust a soft nose over the length of wood that served as a gate. "Hush, my beauty," Lily whispered. "Hush now. I'll have you out of there in a moment. And then we must fly, silent and swift as night owls."

Her fingers closed on the wooden bar, clumsy in her haste. It fell with a dull thud to the earth floor.

"Lily?"

The word was a whisper, but it may as well have been a thunderbolt. Lily jerked around, searching blindly for the dagger tucked into her girdle.

"Lily!"

Lily wrenched the dagger free, color draining from her face, her breath catching harshly in her throat. The torch threw monstrous shadows, turning the slender man into a giant.

"Stay back!" she ordered harshly. The horses, sensing her fear, began to shift nervously in their stalls.

The man ignored her command. As he strode forward, his long hair and mustache caught the torchlight with a glow like gold. The smile on his handsome face was achingly familiar.

Lily's dagger fell from her nerveless fingers. She started toward him. "Hew? Hew! How can you be here?"

He caught her, his breath warm in her hair. His arms held her tight with a wiry strength. "Hush, Lily! 'Tis not safe. We must go quickly, before the Norman bastards wake."

Lily shuddered. "Yes, of course, but—" Suddenly she pulled away. In her excitement she had forgotten so many things, and thought only of her sunny childhood when Hew had been a boy and she a girl. Now she remembered again the man he had become: ambitious, ruthless, and untrustworthy.

"Why are you here, Hew? I thought you long gone across the border into Scotland."

He reached out to stroke her cheek, his handsome face softening. He was so familiar it was almost as if her father had returned to life. Once he had been almost as close to her as a brother, and Lily struggled against her instinctive need to believe in him.

"I have been in Malcolm's lands, Lily, but now I've returned to raise an army in your name. And to do that, I need you."

The warm sense of intimacy fell from her at last. Lily stared back at him, too numb to reply.

Hew smiled the devastating smile he had always used to such good effect. Now it left Lily cold.

"King Malcolm is willing to send us men, but must be cautious since he swore fealty to William the Bastard. Once he sends us his men, Lily, I can gather more. They'll flock to us—but first you have to come to Scotland and promise Malcolm you'll lead our army. That was Malcolm's condition—and even if it were not his, I would have made it mine."

Lily could speak now, and she did so forcibly.

"You're lying, Hew. You would never agree to me giving you orders."

He grinned, not the least bit ashamed of his deceit. "You're probably right. I need you to look beautiful and tragic—Lady Wilfreda, her husband murdered, her proper place usurped by the invading Normans! You can look tragic, can't you, Lily? You can smile and promise Malcolm whatever he asks? I'll do the rest."

No. The rejection was instant. *No, I will never allow my people to be drawn into another war.*

But Hew, she had learned from experience, was not very receptive to *no.* She could refuse him now, and be dragged out of here and forced into compliance. Or she could agree, escape with Hew, and then make her own plans once she reached Scotland. King Malcolm might listen; he was a clever man. So clever, she wondered he had allowed himself to be persuaded to back Hew in yet another rebellion.

Of course, Hew could be very persuasive.

"Yes, Hew, I will come with you," she said, with as much assurance as she could master. In case he should see the lie in her eyes, she turned and walked back toward her mare. Her dagger lay on the ground where she had dropped it, and she bent to collect it, slipping it back into her girdle. Hew followed her, soft-footed and alert. When he touched her shoulder, his fingers caressing, Lily tried not to stiffen. It was probable Hew wanted more than a platonic partnership. Could she pretend an attraction for him she no longer felt?

Maybe she could have done it once . . . before she knew Radulf.

Lily shuddered, and disguised it by drawing her cloak more tightly about her body as if she were cold. Once she had thought she loved Hew, that she desired nothing more than to be his wife and lie in his arms. Now she knew how shallow and foolish her youthful feelings had been. She had never loved Hew. Her time with Radulf had given her a taste of what real love must be; a fiery dragon that set your blood ablaze. What she had felt for Hew was pitiable in comparison.

Lily glanced up and found Hew watching her, his blue eyes smiling but strangely cool, as if the good humor were but a façade behind which his devious mind was plotting. She forced herself to smile back, to pretend all was well.

"How did you find me?"

"The priest, Father Luc, sent word to me. He was always fond of you, Lily. We have been following you since Grimswade, hoping for an opportunity to free you, but Radulf kept you too close. How came you to fall into his hands?"

Lily patted the mare's soft nose to gain time. The truth seemed safe enough. "I was hiding in the church and he found me."

Behind her, Hew was silent. Lily stroked the mare, pretending to be unaware. All the lessons learned from being Vorgen's wife were returning. The knowledge stirred a bitterness inside her. Tonight, when she sat at the abbot's table, she had felt as if she was at last beginning to throw off the restrictions being Vorgen's wife had placed upon her. At last she had felt able to say what she really felt instead of what Vorgen wanted her to say. Now, because of Hew, she must assume her hateful disguise again. Become once more the cold, Norman wife who measured her words as carefully as the spices she kept locked up in a box.

"What were you doing in Grimswade church, Lily?"

She glanced at him, and this time did not try to hide her surprise. "My father and mother are buried there, Hew. I went to say goodbye."

He had forgotten. She saw the flash of remembrance in his eyes, though he nodded as if he had known it all along.

"So," Lily found her saddle, "it was your men who were watching the camp?"

"Aye. They were careless and the Norman bastards killed half of them. The rest of us got away, but they were lives I can ill-spare until Malcolm sends me more." He cocked an eyebrow. "But I saw enough to know you were not the usual sort of prisoner. Are you consorting with the enemy, Lily? Or are you more devious than I thought?"

Lily lifted her chin, color flooding her face. "Perhaps you don't know me as well as you think, Hew."

Hew laughed without humor. "Oh, I think I do. I think I know you very well indeed. You would not give that lovely body to a Norman unless you could gain something from it. You are cold and calculating, just as Vorgen said. You bewitched him, and now you've bewitched Radulf."

Lily wondered at his stupidity. Vorgen had known her not at all, and if he had been bewitched it was through no fault of hers. And yet Hew believed him, and did not see the suffering behind Lily's eyes. Radulf, too, had believed Vorgen. A mixture of frustration and anger filled Lily, but she thrust the volatile emotions down.

Now was not a good time to allow her heart to rule her head.

"I was watching you the morning you left the camp at Grimswade," Hew went on. "I saw Radulf's tender demeanor. You have played a fine joke on him, Lily. He will have to explain himself to William the Bastard, explain why he has been riding about the countryside with the very woman he was sent to capture. I think you have made certain his star will very soon be setting!"

Lily managed to shrug as if she didn't care one way or the other, as if she were really as cold and calculating as he seemed to believe. Hew's eyes gleamed with respect, and she wondered at a man who would admire a woman who lied and cheated and used others to further her own ambition.

He was far worse than she had ever imagined.

"Will you help me saddle the mare?" she asked coolly, neither her voice nor her manner betraying her sick heart.

Hew smiled and complied. "If you hadn't arrived when you did, I would have come to fetch you," he said, hands busy with straps and buckles. "What's left of my men are waiting beyond the crest of the hill. I did not trust them, not after Grimswade. They are fools. Not like us, Lily."

They led the mare toward the door, Lily whispering soothing words as the animal whickered nervously. Outside, the darkness was as still as ever and the monastery slept on. Hew threw Lily up into the saddle and took the reins, walking the mare toward the gatehouse, a black and bulky silhouette against the cold, starry sky.

"I persuaded one of the lay brothers to open the gate for me," he murmured, unable to help boasting of his own cleverness. "I told him I was your husband and Radulf had stolen you from me. He believed me. He would have believed far worse of a man with Radulf's reputation."

"And you always were a good liar."

Hew laughed softly, taking her words as a compliment. "Well, maybe it isn't really a lie. I mean to marry you, Lily. Together we would be an unbeatable force. Better than you and Vorgen—he knew nothing of our people."

"I remember my father telling you that, just before you betrayed him."

Hew looked up at her, his face silvered by the starlight. She could tell he did not like what she had said; he did not like to be reminded of his perfidy. It had been foolish to let him know she remembered.

Quite suddenly, Lily was afraid of him.

She had never thought to be afraid before. He had always been Hew, whom she had once loved and now hated, but still Hew, whom she had known all her life. Now, in a flash, she saw that Hew was also a dangerous man, and no friend to her. At present he needed her because of Malcolm's decree that she head their army, but once Hew had his men . . .

The gatehouse rose directly before them. Hew led his own mount from where it had been hidden in the shadows by the wall, and climbed quickly into the saddle. He retained his hold on Lily's reins, sending her an enigmatic look. He did not trust her, either.

Maybe, she thought bitterly, when you had betrayed as many people as Hew had, it was difficult to trust anybody.

"We will ride to the coast," he told her calmly, as they passed into the deeper shadows beneath the gatehouse. "Find a boat. We can sail north to Malcolm. 'Tis safer and quicker than going overland."

"As you say." Lily was empty. She felt as if she were leaving her future behind. With Radulf.

Why had she not trusted him when she had the

chance? If she had, she would not now be in this dangerous situation. Though he was her enemy, Lily had never felt as if her life was at risk when she was with Radulf.

Hew was a different matter.

As if he had read the name in her mind, Hew muttered, "I wish I had more men. I would have killed Radulf, taken him in the throat with your dagger, while he slept." He turned and grinned at her, sharing his evil joke. "Or I would have woken him first, and let him see your face so that he could understand the trick we had played upon him, before he died."

Lily closed her eyes. She saw Radulf, too, but not as Hew described him. He stood before her, dark eyes warm and shining, sensuous lips smiling. She took a shaking breath.

All at once there was a clink of metal; the soft scrape of a sword being drawn from its scabbard.

Hew moved sharply, pulling his horse around to face the danger.

And the night split apart.

Men came running at them from all sides, voices roaring. Moonlight glinted on armor and sharp edges.

Hew yelled, "Lily! Run!" and slapped the flank of her mare. But instead of bolting, the mare screamed in fear and outrage, and rose up on her hind legs. Lily had no time to cling on. She was thrown into the chaos about her, and hit the ground hard.

The impact took her breath away. She lay in a tangled heap of wool and linen, her cheek sunk in mud. Somewhere to her right Hew whipped his terrified horse back, through the gateway, toward the monastery buildings. A furious gaggle of Norman soldiers pursued him into the darkness.

Two big, hard hands fastened about Lily's waist, hauling her to her feet. She swayed, and was steadied.

Slowly, feeling as if this were a bad dream, Lily raised her head to confront her captor.

He was well suited to bad dreams. He towered over her, his big body made bigger by his hauberk, his massive chest rising and falling with each harsh breath. She couldn't see his face properly because of the helmet, only the glint of his eyes.

She was profoundly glad for that.

"He was right," growled a deep, familiar voice. "You should have run."

Lily said nothing. Her body was bruised and winded, her head ached, and the cold fear of her capture had numbed her until even her breath was no longer warm enough to cloud the night air.

"My scouts noticed that the rebels had been following us since Grimswade," said Radulf. "I wondered why."

"And now you know."

"Now I know."

"My lord!" One of Radulf's men had returned, his shoulders bowed with defeat. "We lost him."

Radulf's eyes remained fixed on Lily. "Keep looking." He stepped forward and gripped her arms, pulling her hard against him. Lily was instantly aware of his body heat and his great strength. They were no longer comforting.

"You are no Norman lady." His voice was low and menacing. "You were never traveling home from the border to Rennoc. I sent Jervois ahead to speak with Edwin and he returned yesterday. Edwin's daughter Alice is safe at Rennoc. I knew about your lies, lady, before we set out for Trier. I asked you for the truth and you would not give it—"

"I could not," Lily whispered, pushing her hands against the chain mail. "Do not punish Alice for any of this. She knows nothing of it."

"Who are you?" Radulf demanded, and his fingers gripped her own so angrily that the hawk ring cut into her flesh. Lily cried out.

He stilled. She had worn no rings before.

"What is this?"

Radulf lifted her hand, catching the glint of the gold. He shouted for light. Another of his men ran with a torch and, at Radulf's instruction, held it above their joined hands. The stinging smoke made Lily's eyes water but she did not try to pull away. She was almost glad. No more lies, no more pretense. There was an inevitability about this moment.

Radulf bent close, and the red eye of the hawk winked up at him. He went very still.

"Lady Wilfreda isn't in hiding, is she?" he said, trembling with his fury. "She's here. With me."

"Yes."

He looked up then, and she was sure he would strike her. His voice ate into her with its bitterness. "What did you plan to do, lady? Murder me? Was that why you carried a dagger, to plunge it into my heart? It must have amused you to have Radulf in your snare."

Lily shook her head. Whatever he thought of her, she could disabuse him of that. "No, Radulf, I never meant to trick you. You cannot believe—"

He leaned closer, his breath hot on her face. His eyes glittered like onyx. His voice shook as he spoke, betraying the enormous self-restraint he was exercising upon himself. "I may have been a fool, lady, but you made me a fine whore!"

Lily flinched, and swayed. Could he not see the truth in her eyes? It seemed he could not . . . *would* not see. "I am no whore," she answered dully. "You of all men know that."

He dropped her hand as if it burned him. "No, you're right. Whoring would be too honest a profession for one with your treacherous soul."

Anger bit into her. Pain and fear and hurt all meshed together in a great, hard ball in her stomach, where the fire of fury consumed them. Why had she ever thought him kind? How could she have imagined there was anything soft between them? This was Radulf, her enemy. He hated her! And she hated him.

Blinded by her anger, Lily fumbled at her girdle, finding her dagger. She would kill him, stab him through the heart—if he had one! She drew the dagger and struck at him, but Radulf grabbed for it and the blade sliced into his thumb rather than glancing off his mailed chest.

Warm blood dripped onto her gown and Radulf laughed in his fury. "Aye, here is the real Lily!" he declared, his eyes blazing.

Lily went even whiter, instantly releasing the weapon into his keeping. She felt sick and dizzy, as shocked by her action as by its result. Radulf slipped the dagger into his own belt, ignoring the shallow cut to his thumb, his eyes never leaving hers.

"No, my lady liar," he mocked. "I am not ready

to die yet. First, you will have your reckoning. Just as I promised."

She opened her mouth, but there were no words left in her.

Radulf had already turned away. "Secure her!" he roared. "In the morning we ride to York—to King William!"

Chapter 9

⤜⤚◦⤙⤛

Radulf was in the grip of an anger such as he had never experienced before. It tore at his flesh, churned his stomach, and shot molten arrows into his brain. He rode for hours turned inside himself, burning with the rage which had dug its talons into him at Trier.

That he had known she was lying, even before his man returned from Rennoc, did not help. Nor did the fact that he had deliberately set a trap for her to fall into. He had wanted, desperately wanted, to be wrong! As he had waited with his men outside the gatehouse, Radulf had prayed to suffer nothing more than lack of sleep. He had told himself, over and over, there must be an innocent explanation for all of this, and soon he would know it.

What an idiot he had been!

How Henry would laugh at him!

Radulf, the King's Fool!

Smitten by the she-devil, Vorgen's wife. The very woman he had been pursuing all over the north . . .

Radulf ground his teeth. His men edged away from him, but he didn't notice. He was remembering how she had cried out beneath him, how her body had trembled, the tenderness in her eyes . . . She must be a witch indeed to wind such a charm about him.

What madness had possessed him, that he had trusted her despite all the warning signs? What madness possessed him still, that he wished she had trusted him enough to tell him the truth?

And what would you have done? Let her go? So that she could rejoin her lover, rejoin this . . . this Hew?

Radulf had sent Jervois to Lily to discover the escaped man's name and identity—he had not dared go himself.

He had been too crazy with hurt and fury.

When Jervois had returned somberly from his bidding, it was to tell Radulf that Hew, Lily's cousin, had come to rescue her.

"She did not try to hide it," Jervois had informed him nervously, eyes watchful in case his lord finally lost that iron hold he had clamped on his temper. "She said to tell you that she wished with all her heart he had succeeded."

Now Radulf's eyes narrowed and his jaw clenched. No doubt she was wishing she was with her lover at this very moment! Well, Radulf would make certain she never saw him again. He would kill her first, or . . . or lock her away at Crevitch forever. Ah yes, that idea held appeal. As his prisoner, she would be at his mercy. Better still, he could continue with his enjoyment of her body. Keep her for himself alone, far from her lover.

Only he isn't her lover.

The cold thought pierced his hot madness.

Radulf frowned, and finally some of his rage fell from him. His wits, which had been writhing like snakes in his head, began to calm. He asked himself whether, in the heat of his passion, he could have imagined her maidenhead. No, he had not been mistaken. Even now he recalled the resistance when he broke it asunder, and how she had explained her virgin state.

My husband was old.

Vorgen *was* old.

He was unable.

Radulf recalled there had been rumors, even before Hastings, that Vorgen was impotent.

She had not lied in everything, then.

His frown deepened. If she had told some truths, was it possible that she had told the truth when she said she burned for him? Burned for him as much as he burned for her?

Radulf shrugged his shoulders angrily. What did it matter? Why was he splitting hairs? She was the Lady Wilfreda, *that* was the important point. He had been ordered by his king to find her and bring her before him.

He was happy to obey. Ecstatic!

At that moment, Jervois bumped against him and earned himself a look that would have turned a lesser man to jelly. "My lord," he began, his voice strained, "I beg your pardon, but the lady will not eat or drink. She is making herself unwell. I fear by the time we reach the king at York, she will be no more than a wraith . . ."

But Radulf wasn't listening to his captain. After that brief glare, his restless gaze had traveled past Jervois, over the tired and dirty faces of his soldiers, and settled on the author of his troubles.

Lily rode hemmed in by heavily armed guards. *Lady Wilfreda*, Radulf corrected himself. May her soul rot for making such an idiot out of him. For tempting him to open wide his sore, wounded heart, only to have her stab him with her lies. She was an evil conniving bitch. Just like Anna. She was—

"My lord?" repeated the long-suffering Jervois.

Lily had begun to sway in her saddle. Her face had turned chalk-white, and her silver-fair hair was tangled and dulled. There was a mark on her cheek, caused by her fall from her mare during the escape attempt.

The woebegone sight of her did not soften Radulf's heart. Instead his fury returned, a different sort of fury and hotter than ever. Like a spurred devil, it rode him, raking him. Giving him no rest. Suddenly he could bear it no more.

"Stop!"

At his bellow, his men did stop. They pulled up so sharply their horses danced, and their swords grated in their scabbards as they prepared for certain attack.

"Be easy," Radulf ordered gruffly, when he saw what he had done. He looked about him at the weary, exhausted faces, as if seeing them for the first time. "We will rest here awhile."

He could not miss the exchange of grateful glances, but no one said anything as they dismounted. Radulf swung down to the ground and strode back toward Lily, still atop her mare, every movement he made proclaiming his anger.

Lily stiffened, watching him approach. Her eyes were reddened and gritty from lack of sleep, while apprehension had drained her face of all color. But she refused to let him see her weakness, gripping the reins tightly to hide the trembling of her hands, reminding herself of who she was. She had gone from misery to hatred so many times, she no longer knew what she felt.

Radulf barely paused as he reached her, lifting her abruptly from the saddle. Her hands were tied before her, so she was unable to prevent him, but she made her body rigid and unhelpful. As Radulf set her down, however, her breasts brushed his chest. That, and his hard hands at her waist, almost shredded her carefully constructed defenses, and she had to exert all her strength to prevent herself from melting against him. Focused so hard on being strong, she didn't notice how very gently he set her on her feet.

Dark eyes looked down, gray eyes lifted. Fury and ice clashed and collided. Perhaps it was the proud coldness in her eyes, so at odds with her bedraggled state, but suddenly Radulf found his anger unraveling. When he spoke to Jervois, his voice was almost mild. "Has she had aught to eat and drink?"

Jervois had hurried along in his lord's wake, and sounded breathless. "No, my lord. She will take neither."

Radulf grunted. He lifted Lily's hands, checking on the tightness of the rope, and saw at once the red marks where the coarse fibers had rubbed her tender skin. Something twisted inside him, a truth he had tried to keep buried until now. She let him inspect a bruise on her wrist and a torn fingernail, pretending haughty indifference. She was like a queen, only far more regal than any queen Radulf had ever known. He felt a wild urge to pull her into his arms and hold her fast until this proud stranger was vanquished, and all that remained was his sweet, beautiful Lily, the girl from Grimswade Church.

Instantly he stifled it.

This was no time to loose his grip. The part of him that was his father's son might want nothing more than to throw all caution to the four winds, but Radulf the warrior knew better. Still, the sheer madness of such a thought at such a time brought a gleam of appreciative humor to his dark eyes.

Lily recognized it, and her own eyes widened.

Radulf had pulled her jeweled dagger from his belt and was slicing through her bonds. When he lifted his face again, it was once more a stony mask, and his eyes were as bleak as winter.

"Now, eat!" he ordered, and turned and walked away.

Lily watched him go.

Her body ached, her head ached, but most of all her heart ached. And although she had known what would happen if he ever learned the truth, in some small corner of her being, she had hoped that somehow he would understand and forgive.

How could she have been so blind?

This was a Norman lord, to whom duty would always come first. He would take her to his king and sacrifice her at the altar of his own pride.

Better you had gone with Hew.

Lily shook her head. No, she could never go back to being the consort of such a man. And now Hew had escaped. Lily didn't know whether to be glad or sorry about that; a little of both, maybe. She was glad that Hew had thwarted Radulf, but sorry that someone with Hew's evil intent was again free in the north.

"Come, lady, you heard what Lord Radulf said," a voice murmured bracingly at her side. "You must eat and drink; you must stay strong."

A cup of water was pressed into her hands, and Lily sipped it without thinking. She allowed Jervois to lead her to a flat rock, and press her down onto the makeshift seat. A chill wind tugged at her cloak and her hair, stinging her eyes. Jervois removed the cup and replaced it with food. Lily chewed slowly, gazing at nothing.

"Good." Jervois nodded, and eyed her a moment more before turning in Radulf's direction. His lord and master stood stiff-backed, pretending an inordinate amount of interest in the surrounding countryside. Jervois shifted his shoulders, as if there was an invisible weight upon them. In truth, the situation he now found himself in was more wearisome and worrisome than any battle he had ever encountered.

He had been with Lord Radulf for nearly four years, and he had seen him angry before. But never this mindlessly, boilingly angry. And all over a woman! She was pretty, yes, but Jervois was never very comfortable in the company of women. He rested his green eyes once more on the lady. At least she was looking less white and strained, less like she might collapse. Radulf had been forcing the pace, riding as if the devil were on his back, but it would not do for her to collapse before they reached the king at York. Jervois had the uneasy feeling that despite Radulf's own thoughtless haste, the man would have Jervois's head if the lady suffered.

It made no sense, but then Jervois had found that when it came to the fair sex, sense went out the door. Give him a good battle any day! Man pitted against man. He was far more at home at war than faced with a lady's smile.

And yet . . . a very pretty picture of golden hair and bright blue eyes leaped into his mind. Alice of Rennoc. He had seen her, spoken with her, during his short visit. His head had naturally been full of Radulf's orders and Lily's lies, but still he had retained the look of the girl and the scent of her skin.

"I am sure my lady Lily had good reason for her actions," she had declared, when questioned.

Jervois admired loyalty. He had found himself remembering her words, and the inflections of her voice, ever since.

While Jervois puzzled over life's inconsistencies, Lily was berating herself for being dim-witted. For one so used to living in the constant danger of Vorgen's keep, she had been very lax. The fact that Radulf had not set a guard at her door should have alerted her at once to his trap. Like a cunning wolf, he had been watching her, waiting, and when the time was right he had pounced.

Lily doubted Radulf had been born to a flesh-and-blood mother, rather he had been created by Olaf the armorer, wrought in fire and fashioned in iron.

He had no heart.

The glint of ironic laughter she had seen in his

eyes just before he cut her ropes only went to prove her point. No sane man would find humor in such a situation.

Tears threatened, but again Lily held them back. She had lost everything and she trusted no one. She was all alone again, just when she had begun to allow herself to feel safe. Perhaps she would always be alone; perhaps it was meant to be.

Lily knew she should be using these moments to plot what she would say when she came face to face with King William. She did not fear that she would break down and sob for clemency; she had shown courage enough before when Vorgen had threatened her, and William could be no worse.

But she was numb, and the words would not come to her.

The sturdy wooden walls of York glowed warmly in the late afternoon sunshine, while roofs and spires appeared tipped with gold. The city had been fortunate in that none of its many occupying forces had sacked and burned it.

The Romans had long come and gone. The Vikings and Danes had known the city as Jorvic, and made it prosperous with their trade and their ships. Then York had been the capital of the Anglican kingdom of Northumbria. Now the Normans were here, and William had proclaimed York his center in the north, the second city in England after London.

The rivers Ouse and Fos enclosed York, their watery arms a silver sparkle. The Ouse was the larger, its banks crowded with ships loading and unloading, and seamen, merchants, and their minions conducting business. King William's castle, a wooden tower raised high upon an earthen mound, reared up beyond the walls. He was in the process of building a second castle on the opposite bank of the Ouse, the unrest in the north having made extra fortifications necessary.

As Radulf's band of soldiers drew nearer to the city, Lily could see an iron chain barring their approach. It was strung across the road, several yards in front of the gate through the city walls. Guards were prominent at the bar, as well as on the walls behind it.

Lily sighed and managed to stretch her aching muscles without whimpering out loud. Compared to their previous manic pace, their travel over the past few days had been slow. Lily had overheard some of the soldiers muttering their relief that at last their lord had outrun his anger.

Lily disagreed.

Radulf's anger had just seeped inside, where it would gather and ferment. Apart from his sense of betrayal, Lily had made him look a fool, and no Norman took well to that.

No, his anger was with him still, and Lily would suffer for it.

After Radulf had cut her ropes, he had left her untied and, as if by a silent and mutual consent, Lily had no longer refused food or water. Radulf's reason for freeing her was not kindness; she knew that. He wanted her alive and alert when he brought her before William. He wanted her to see and hear and feel every bit of her punishment. If she had not eaten, she was sure he would have forced her.

The things he had said to her that night at Trier! And the arrogant way in which he had refused to listen to her explanations . . .

With difficulty, Lily swallowed down her grief and anger before they choked her.

She should have told Radulf the truth at the very beginning, from the moment he found her in Grimswade church. Then she would never have seen that glimpse of paradise, and would not now be suffering.

The soldiers bunched together as they passed beyond the bar and Bootham Gate. A tattered group of alms seekers watched them clatter down Petergate, one of York's main thoroughfares. As the armed band passed by wooden houses and shops and a stone church, the smells of the city alternately attracted and repelled. At any moment, Lily expected to be faced with the grim bulk of William's castle, but instead Radulf led them down a narrower street. The soldiers necessarily pressed even closer about Lily, their sweat competing with wafts of ale and pastries coming from the building directly before them. Above the noise of the horses' hooves, she heard Radulf call a halt.

The weary band shuffled to a less than precise stop, horses blowing and puffing, the soldiers' tired faces stoic beneath the grime of their journey.

Lily looked about her in bewilderment. Instead of the castle, they were stopped before an inn.

Radulf had summoned Jervois to his side. His captain was listening carefully, and there was an air of tension about them. Radulf's black war horse seemed to sense it too, edging away, ill-tempered, from Jervois's mount, its huge feet stamping, its head tossing.

Radulf spoke again, urgently, and Jervois nodded slowly. Seemingly against his better judgment. The expression on the younger man's face proclaimed him more than a little dumbfounded by his orders. Then the two men turned, Radulf stony-faced, Jervois with reluctance, and looked straight at Lily.

She held her breath. Something momentous was about to happen. Oh God, why did Radulf look so stern? He spurred his destrier toward her. Lily refused to flinch, although her heart was thundering inside her chest and each breath was a struggle and she wanted to turn and flee . . . Radulf reached her, pulling his irritable horse up at the last moment. His gaze was fastened on hers, and it took a few seconds for her to realize his words were not addressed to her, but to his men.

"Secure this inn. We will stay here tonight, and we want the whole house."

Relief. A great, howling gale of relief. It threatened to demolish the flimsy walls of courage and pride Lily had constructed about her. She might have broken down completely, if Radulf had not been watching her. Instead she stared challengingly back at him.

"This is an inn, lady," he said, with a hint of mockery. "The only thing to be anxious for in this place is the state of the bedding and the cleanliness of the kitchen."

He would have turned to leave, but Lily spoke quickly. "My lord, when am I to go before King William? I want a chance to speak to him."

Radulf examined her face with the intensity she had come to expect. Suddenly she thought: *He will deny me, because he can. He will smile and say no, just as it once pleased Vorgen to refuse the smallest of my requests.*

Until now, Lily had not realized how much she

was relying on a face-to-face meeting with the king.

Radulf must have seen her thoughts in her eyes, or perhaps he could read her mind. He smiled. "No, Lady Wilfreda," he said in a soft, low growl. "I am neither a monster nor a tyrant. You will see King William soon enough."

He paused as if expecting her to thank him, but Lily could say nothing.

"I will leave you with Jervois, whom I trust like a brother. Be assured he will keep you from harm."

She was so close to tears that she chose sarcasm to mask her weakness. "Harm from whom, my lord? I am alone and friendless. Hardly any great danger to you or your king."

He leaned closer. "Ah, but you *are* a danger to me, lady."

Lily could not help but catch his meaning; his lust for her burned in his eyes. Her own gray ones widened, but Radulf had moved back, scowling black enough to terrify any lesser woman, as though his feelings infuriated him as much as they confused her.

"Do as Jervois tells you, Lily, and you will be safe."

Her emotions were now so jumbled Lily doubted she would ever disentangle them. What did he mean? How could she possibly be safe with Radulf and his men?

He was her enemy!

Wasn't he?

Radulf spurred his horse faster, ignoring the narrow, cluttered street and the shout of a man attempting to cross it. The man fell backward, rolling in the mud, cursing Radulf. Radulf was cursing himself. He was a fool, and he knew it. Yet he could no more stop himself than spread his arms and fly.

Radulf snorted in self-disgust. He had not forgiven her; he was not *that* much of a fool! The memory of her perfidy would live long in his unforgiving heart. But for now he had to put all that aside.

In obeying his king, Radulf had placed Lily in danger. And if he handed her over to the king, he would lose her.

William would imprison her.

And then he would either forget her, or marry her to some greedy lord in return for her lands—someone like Alan de Courcy perhaps, with his big belly and soft mouth, or Robert Pearmaine with his reputation for hurting women but leaving no mark . . .

Radulf shuddered violently; everything in him revolted. *No!* He could not bear that. What she had done to him was a secondary issue, a separate issue. Her safety, her life was his first concern now. He could not bear to see even a single scratch on her, and he certainly would not be able to bear losing her to another man. She was his, he thought fiercely, and if any punishment was due to her, then he would be the judge of it and provide the method!

Radulf rode on, staring blindly. How was he to convince William to let her go? Even if he declared her innocent of the rebellion made in her name—which he himself was yet to be convinced of—Lily remained a danger to the peace and stability of the north. She was a figurehead for others, and William would see her removal and subjugation as a priority.

Radulf growled in frustration. If he were Henry, he would use smooth words to cajole and convince, but he was Radulf—and it was ever his way to speak his thoughts plainly, without flowery phrases.

Radulf shifted uncomfortably.

There *was* a way to save Lily. If, God help him, he had the courage to take it. The idea had come to him on the journey. At first he had dismissed it, amazed by his own lunacy, but it had returned again and again, like a prickle in his boot, until he had taken a serious look at what seemed utter madness. And he'd grasped this was the perfect answer. Indeed, it was the only way to keep Lily safe and under his watchful eye, and completely his.

Radulf's grip tightened on his horse's reins.

He would do it! He would put the whole matter before his king, and hope good sense and the firm ties of a long friendship would prevail.

Of course, he would not tell William that he had already given Jervois certain instructions. The amazed expression in Jervois's eyes showed he'd thought Radulf had lost his mind, but Radulf knew that if the message came from the castle that he had failed in his bid to sway the king, then his trusty captain would take Lily to immediate safety.

Unfortunately, Radulf would then have to face the consequences of his actions.

He was prepared for that.

He would give his life, or more probably his title and his lands, for her safety.

Radulf scowled, frightening several small children. He didn't notice. Who would have thought the day would come when the King's Sword would be willing to give up everything for a woman!

Truly, he was his father's son.

Chapter 10

Lily woke to half darkness and the sound of movement beyond her door. There was laughter, and voices rising and falling. She knew most of those voices; she had traveled with these men for many days now. She felt comfortable with them, which was odd since they were her enemies.

Where was Radulf?

The question spurred her to turn her head, examining the room. She had seen little of it last night. After she arrived at the small chamber, tears, so long restrained, had filled her eyes and run down her cheeks. Alone at last, all hope gone, she had cried herself to sleep.

Voices again, closer now, murmuring at her door. Lily thought one of them was female, probably the innkeeper's young, shy-eyed daughter. Last evening, while Lily sat by the fire in the steamy warmth of the main room of the inn, the girl had served her ale and a pie straight from the oven. The other guests had been sent packing by Radulf's soldiers, some of them ejected quite violently with their belongings tumbling after them. Their loud complaints faded only when Jervois handed out coins from the leather purse at his belt.

It was the Norman way to take what they wanted, Lily thought bitterly. Although, she admitted grudgingly, Vorgen would not have bothered to appease them with money . . .

A hard knock on the door, and then again.

Lily sat up—she hadn't dared to undress—and pushed back untidy hair that badly needed washing and brushing. Her skin was still gritty from the journey, and her clothing stiff with dust. It was long since she had bathed at her leisure and dressed in fine clothes. Another place, another life. All gone now.

"Who is it?" she called out in a voice hoarse from disuse.

"My lady, 'tis Jervois!"

Lily got up and opened the door. The morning sun was glinting through the open door of the inn, while the smells of bread and ale lingered, mixed with pungent woodsmoke.

It was obvious from Jervois's pallor and dark-circled eyes that he hadn't slept much. Yesterday, while she ate her pie and drank her ale, Lily had noticed how the captain's green gaze had ranged continually about the inn, cataloguing its strengths and weak points.

Lily wondered if there was more to his orders than she perceived—she had assumed from what Radulf said that Jervois was to keep her safe. Maybe her assumptions were wrong.

As if he had read her thoughts, Jervois said, "Lord Radulf has sent word, lady. You are to accompany me and the men to the castle as soon as may be."

"Rather a large escort for one woman, Jervois. There is no need; I do not intend to run away. I want my audience with the king."

Jervois looked uncomfortable. "You must ask Lord Radulf those questions, lady. I am his captain, that is all."

"I think you are more than that, Jervois. He has told me he trusts you like a brother."

Jervois's tanned cheeks flushed a dull red at the compliment Radulf had paid him.

Lily shot a glance past him into the smoky room. "Where *is* Radulf?"

"He is still at the castle, lady. But before you join him there, he has instructed me to have water brought for your bath and . . . and your other matters attended to." He flushed again at Lily's wide-eyed look, and added in a voice made prim from discomfort, "Lord Radulf orders you to look your best for the king."

Lily continued to stare in astonishment. Look her best? Vorgen would have dragged her before William bleeding and in rags. "I see," she managed, but saw not at all. Yet did it matter whether she understood? She was very likely about to be imprisoned for the rest of her life. This might be the last bath she ever had.

Jervois was waiting for her reply, respectful and attentive as always. She managed a smile. "I want to thank you, Jervois. You have been kind to me."

He did not smile back; there was a flicker of unease in his eyes. "I only obey my orders, lady. 'Tis Lord Radulf you should thank."

Lily raised her eyebrows in disbelief.

Jervois hesitated, as if struggling with some unfamiliar emotion. He cleared his throat. "It is not my place to speak of such matters, lady, but . . . you wrong Lord Radulf if you think him the brutish warrior of legend. Aye, he is a powerful man, with much wealth and large estates. This . . . this bounty makes him more wary than most, and indeed he has many enemies. But beneath the fable, he is a man like any other. Do not believe the tales that are spun of him."

Surprised by his words and the earnestness with which they were delivered, Lily replied, "I do not believe them. Well"—when Jervois in turn raised his eyebrows at her vehemence—"not now, I don't. But what have those stories to do with aught?" She swallowed the lump in her throat. "Radulf hates me."

For a moment her haughty demeanor fractured, and she sounded young and unsure. The proud ice princess sounded like a frightened maid, struggling in desire's sticky toils.

Jervois shook his head and almost laughed aloud. Of course he did no such thing, but an uncharacteristic glimmer of humor filled his eyes. Ever since Radulf had given him his orders, he had been beside himself. He well understood what his lord was risking, but for what? A woman! Beautiful, yes, but still a woman, and a rebel at that. Now, suddenly, Jervois saw Lily through new eyes.

"Nay, lady," he said quietly, "Lord Radulf does not hate you."

"Please, Jervois, do not take me for a fool! I understand your loyalty to your lord, but Radulf and I are enemies."

The look on his face infuriated her—as if he knew a secret and was not about to tell. Her gratitude forgotten, Lily dismissed him, and when he had gone, she dismissed his words, too.

I betrayed Radulf, and a man like him will never forgive such a transgression. He will take me to his king and be rid of me without having to soil his own hands further.

Chilled, she played out the scene in her mind. The king calling for guards, their brutal grip on her arms as they dragged her away. She would not sob or cry out, she vowed. No, she would maintain her pride to the last. And Radulf would stand, his face a cold and indifferent mask, watching her go . . .

Angrily, Lily shook her head. No, that was not how it would be! She would not be taken like a lamb to the slaughter. She must fight, and her tongue would be her weapon. She had words to speak to the Norman king, words that might well move him . . . bend him. Lily would not beg; such lack of pride was abhorrent to her, and she knew it would draw William's scorn rather than his pity. Instead she would argue her case, reminding him she was still useful to him if he truly wished for a lasting truce in the north.

Lily did not fool herself into imagining he would be compassionate. And it was said William had a strong sense of justice, of right and wrong. He would look upon her first and foremost as Vorgen's wife, remembering that Vorgen had been a traitor who caused him endless trouble. Now

Hew, her cousin, was set to stir more rebellion, and all in her name. William would consider her a danger to himself and his new realm.

He would want her gone.

Somehow she must persuade him otherwise. Impress him with her genuine desire for peace, show him she was willing to live and work with the Normans to bring that peace about. She must be eloquent. Radulf had claims on William that Lily could not possibly match, but perhaps she could sway him with her calm good sense.

She must try, and memories of Radulf would not stand in her way. For that was all they were, she told herself sternly, memories—that part of her life was over.

While Lily's mind was busy delving for the right words to sway a king, Una, the innkeeper's daughter, arrived to supervise her bath.

Lily soaked in the steaming scented luxury, lathering herself with a knob of soap while Una washed her hair. By the time Lily climbed dripping from the bath, she had decided the direction her speech would take. Her only remaining doubt concerned Radulf.

He had planned her downfall, and her mind accepted that. Her heart was another matter. Her heart had a tendency to soften and sigh, like a lovestruck maiden. *You are mine and I am yours!* it cried.

Her heart, she decided coldly, was a traitor. Her heart was in league with her flesh, which was prone to grow heated and achy every time Radulf drew near. Both required careful guarding, needed reminding that Radulf was her enemy and could never be anything else.

"Such fine hair. Like silver thread." Una's reverent voice broke in on Lily's anguished thoughts.

The girl was combing Lily's hair, while Lily sat wrapped in a drying cloth. Her clothing had been hastily sponged and brushed, but was still a sad sight. Lily would have preferred to present herself before the king in rich cloth, weighed heavy with jewelry. The Normans respected show. Would they see this poorly dressed young woman as the rightful ruler of much of Northumbria, someone deserving of their respect? Or would they see her as a weak pawn in a man's game?

Lily made herself smile. "My hair has not had care such as this for many a long week, Una."

Una grinned back shyly. "Thank you, lady. Do you think I'd make a good lady's maid?"

"Indeed, you would. I am only sorry I cannot offer you such employment."

Una's smile faded into a frown, and her eyes grew sly. "They say . . . the soldiers say that you are the Lady Wilfreda, the rebel Vorgen's wife."

"I am," Lily replied softly, "but remember, I am also a woman, just as you. I will not hurt you."

Una looked puzzled and then she laughed. "Oh, lady, I am not afraid of you! 'Tis him that scares me. The King's Sword. Such a big, grim man. Are you not afraid of him?"

Lily looked at her in surprise. Then, remembering the night at Trier, she said, "Only sometimes."

By the time Lily was ready, Jervois had the mare saddled and waiting in front of the inn, along with most of the soldiers. Lily mounted stiffly, silent in her anxiety and her mask of icy pride. The small band rode through the streets of

York toward the castle, Radulf's men clustered close about Lily, with Jervois at their head.

Lily twisted her father's ring upon her finger, and the red hawk's eye flashed fire. For some reason Radulf had left her the ring, the symbol of her lost power. Had he done that on purpose, or had he been careless? No, she would not be led down that path again. She would never again believe that Radulf acted with anything other than the most careful deliberation.

The thought of him opened again the hollow cave inside her, a place echoing with sorrow and longing. Those brief days and nights she had spent with him seemed dreamlike, a fantasy woven out of foolish dreams.

Now she must return to her cold cage, to become again the icy woman who had lived as Vorgen's wife. How else could she survive this latest ordeal?

Jervois led them through the outer bailey of William's new castle, picking his way around the workers who were still finishing the structure. He informed her in a colorless voice that it usually took the king two weeks to complete a wooden keep, while stone took a good deal longer.

Before she knew it, Lily was dismounting, all but smothered by her zealous guard as they bundled her through the castle door. Dazed, frightened, she could take in little. A large dark hall, the smells of smoke, roasting food and clean rushes, men's voices, and hounds snuffling and barking. Then Radulf's men stepped back, and Lily was alone, apart from the tenuous comfort of Jervois's hand on her arm.

Faces and finery blurred about her. Stern-looking men-of-war, a number of William's barons, and ladies in soft gowns and fine wimples, their fingers heavy with jewels. Feeling dowdy and insignificant, Lily raised her chin.

And saw Radulf.

He stood directly before her, a giant in his ruby-red tunic and dark breeches. Without even trying, he claimed her full attention.

He was frowning at her. It seemed his temper had not improved. As he strode forward Lily quailed inwardly, while her outer demeanor grew even more glacial. At his lord's nod Jervois stepped back, and Radulf replaced his captain at her side. His grasp on her hand surprised her with its warmth and strength, and it would have been comforting had it not been tainted with disturbing memories of hot kisses and hard flesh. Radulf bent his head, and Lily's unwilling eyes rose to meet his. She knew her own were cloudy with remembered passion, for her skin tingled and ached with longing, but she hoped he would think she was suffering from rage.

"Come and curtsy to the king." His voice was low and husky, his lover's voice.

Did he, too, have an all but irresistible urge to throw himself into her embrace? Lily drew a ragged breath. She must fight it. For her life, she must fight her body's betrayal!

His fingers tightened. His dark eyes narrowed. "Do it, by God, or I'll hold you down by the scruff of your neck."

Unafraid, Lily glared back at him and finally noticed how his skin was tinged gray with weariness and his eyes were hollow and bloodshot. The smell of ale clung about him, and his hair was damp, as if he'd lately poured water over it. Evidently while Lily had been locked in her small dark room at the inn, worried sick, Radulf had spent the night carousing at the castle.

Anger built on the storm already brewing inside her. Her gray eyes darkened like thunderclouds about to burst. She opened her mouth.

He bent his head and kissed her.

In front of the king, his court, his men-at-arms, everyone. His wonderful mouth closed on hers in a kiss. It was not a gentle kiss, rather it was demanding, forcing Lily to respond whether or not she wanted to. It was the sort of kiss a man might give if he was starving for the woman in his arms.

The heat melted Lily's treacherous bones. She wanted to moan with pleasure and scream with rage, both at the same time. Cheers and laughter swirled through the great hall, but Lily cared only for Radulf's powerful arms and his hot, unrestrained mouth.

He released her as abruptly as he'd seized her.

Lily gasped, face flaming, and only just managed to hold herself upright. As she twisted her face away from Radulf, she had a brief, vivid glimpse of a woman with golden eyes and a face white with shock, then Radulf reclaimed her full attention.

"That's better," he murmured in her ear, the rumble of his voice sending tremors down her spine. "Now, come and curtsy to the king, lady."

The king! She had forgotten the king!

Anger, pain, fear, and confusion . . . the wild tangle of emotions ran through her. Lily murdered Radulf with her eyes, even as she stepped

forward and gave the curtsy he ordered. Radulf
released a muffled sigh of relief, surprising Lily.
Why was it so important to him that she appear
compliant, obedient? And why had he kissed her?
To show that he could! her mind replied furiously.
Her heart was less sure.

"Lady Wilfreda!"

Lily froze. The king! Slowly, gathering her
pride about her like a tattered cloak, Lily rose
from her curtsy. She moved closer to the dais, her
fingers tightening unconsciously on Radulf's.
William, even seated, had an extraordinary presence. Strong of body and long of limb, he radiated
restless energy, as if he'd much rather be riding
and hunting than sitting there playing king.

"Radulf has spoken of your fair beauty. At
length." His voice was harsh and amused. "Does
he always greet you so familiarly?"

There was general laughter. Radulf shifted impatiently, while Lily kept her gaze on the king. She
waited until the sound died before answering.

"Always, Your Majesty."

A hum of amusement and consternation.
William's eyebrows rose. "Do you deal with all
your prisoners in like manner, Radulf?"

A few more chuckles greeted this. Radulf
laughed himself. "Only Lady Wilfreda, sire."

William's smile faded. "He has not ill-treated
you, lady? I do not like to see women ill-treated."

Lily bit her lip. Here was her chance to damage
Radulf's reputation. She felt him stiffen beside
her—he expected the worst—but she could not do
it; she was not naturally vindictive. There had been
no rape; Lily had been Radulf's willing partner.

"No, sire," she answered with a touch of regret,

"he has never ill-treated me." And had the satisfaction of coolly returning Radulf's nonplussed stare.

William was nodding, a satisfied smile on his face, his bright gaze flicking between Radulf and Lily. "Very well. Let us move on. Radulf has brought you before me to answer a charge of inciting rebellion in the north. What say you to that, lady?"

Lily took a breath, preparing herself. "I say those charges are false, sire. Vorgen took up his sword against you. I did not."

"And yet your father married you to Vorgen. Vorgen made war in your name, beneath your banner." The energy fairly crackled from him now. Lily expected him at any moment to leap from his chair and shake the truth out of her. She retained her cool composure with difficulty.

"Vorgen may have fought beneath my banner, but he stole that along with everything else. My father did not agree to our marriage. Vorgen killed my father and married me over his dead body. I never asked him to make war upon the Normans, or upon anyone else. I want peace in the north— and I ask that you allow me to rule my lands in peace. Please, sire, allow me to show my people how to live in peace with the Normans rather than die under them!"

Had she spoken too presumptuously?

William was frowning. "What do you say to this, Radulf?" he asked in his rough voice.

Radulf gave Lily another glance, but she did not trust it, or understand the reason for it. How could she, when he had never shared his thoughts with her?

He drew himself up to his full impressive height. "Sire. You may well believe what the lady says, and mayhap she believes it herself. Tales have been told of the Lady Wilfreda, that she is a sorceress, an icy Viking murderess..." He shrugged disdainfully. "I do not listen to rumor. I have too long been the subject of such tales, and I know their worth. Here before you is a flesh-and-blood woman, young and beautiful, but powerless. I believe Vorgen used her. Other men will use her. I have fought hard to bring the north to its knees, and I do not see a lone woman being able to keep it there, whatever her good intentions."

Lily felt as if Radulf had taken a knife and severed her only lifeline. Her fine words had been discounted as nothing more than a woman's weak and meaningless prattle. What hope was there for her now? Her sense of betrayal nearly overwhelmed her, and she had to blink furiously to refocus.

William was scratching his chest. "Aye, Radulf," he said, "you have the right of it. 'Twould not be wise to set a woman to rule over those lands. A stronger hand than yours is needed, Lady Wilfreda, even could we trust your promises."

"Sire, Lord Henry has a strong arm," Radulf began, ignoring Lily, frozen at his side. "And a diplomatic tongue."

William appeared to consider it. "No," he said, and struck the carved chair arm hard with his hand. "I have a better man in mind: you, Lord Radulf! You have spent much sweat and blood bringing peace to Northumbria. You shall have Lady Wilfreda's lands. I make a gift of them, and order you to oversee the building of a strong stone castle. A good Norman castle, Radulf! What say you to that?"

Radulf felt as if the floor had dropped away beneath his feet.

He and William had spoken at length last night, but Lily's lands had never been part of that conversation. Now that the king had made his generous gift, Radulf knew he was expected to be humbly grateful, but all he felt was dismay. What of his home? He had been longing to return, and now he must go north again and begin building yet another castle. The fact that it was *his* castle seemed immaterial.

Lily's fingers, stiff and frozen, tightened their grip on his.

Radulf went still. In all the worry about saving her, he had forgotten that these were *her* lands and *her* people he and William were disposing of. She must love them just as much as he loved Crevitch. How did Lily feel, hearing them pass from hand to hand so cavalierly? And if he did not accept this gift, this ... burden, then another, lesser man might. He must take on the mantle of protector of the north—if not for himself, then for the sake of the woman at his side.

He bowed low. "You are very generous, sire. I accept."

William nodded, satisfied. "Now!" The king leaned forward. "That leaves the question of the Lady Wilfreda herself."

Lily's face turned even paler but she held his gaze, her own unflinching. A ripple of admiration traveled through the great hall. There were words she should say, words she had planned to say, but her throat seemed to close up. The king had just given her birthright away as if it were a counter in a child's game. Why should he value her life? A curious humming sound filled her ears, so that she had to strain to hear.

"Radulf? What say you? We cannot set the lady free, for fear she fall prey to rebellious elements. Should we shackle her?"

Inwardly Radulf groaned. William was amusing himself. The king's playful, oftimes violent sense of humor was famous, and rightly feared.

"I agree she should be shackled, sire," he replied, refusing to meet Lily's stricken gray eyes, although he felt their power like a spear in his belly.

William shifted eagerly in his ornately carved chair. "And what should we use to shackle her, my friend?"

Radulf pretended to be thoughtful. "For such a woman as this we must use a mighty restraint, sire. Shackles she cannot possibly escape, shackles which will hold her prisoner all her life."

The great hall was hushed, anticipation rubbing against horror until the atmosphere was raw.

"Yes." William drew the word out thoughtfully. "Mighty shackles. I think I know what will hold Lady Wilfreda securely, Radulf. You will marry her, and without delay!"

The hall erupted in a cacophony of sound. William reduced it to a murmur with a single glare.

Lily swayed as the hum in her head turned into a roar.

Marry him? Was this a jest? A cruel game, designed to add to her suffering?

Oh God, this was even worse than she had imagined!

"Well, Radulf?" the king demanded. "I have ordered you to marry this lady. What say you?"

Radulf bowed low. When he spoke, his voice was loud enough to fill the silence. "I will humbly obey my king, sire."

"Are you sure your lady is willing, Radulf? She appears to be about to faint."

Radulf slipped an iron arm about Lily's trim waist. "She's overcome with joy, sire."

William snorted. "Mayhap she still mourns her last husband, the rebel Vorgen," he jested, but there was a hint of steel in his voice, as if he were having second thoughts.

Radulf laughed coarsely. "After Vorgen's limp dagger, 'twill be a fine pleasure for the lady to have the King's Sword between her thighs!"

William grinned at the ribald jest, his good humor restored.

Shame and fury burned Lily's fair skin. She struggled, pushing at his hands, but Radulf held her easily, pinioning her to his side.

"Patience, lady," he mocked. "I will bed you soon enough."

Gales of laughter greeted this sally, William's voice loudest of them all. When it had eased, he spoke again, a grin still splitting his face.

"I have ordered you to marry her, to protect her from those who would use her in their traitorous schemes. Make an heir on her—a child of your blood and hers. Norman and English. You will conquer the north by breeding the treachery out of it, Radulf! Aye, let every one of your men who is unwed marry a girl of English or Viking blood!

We shall win these people over by means far more pleasurable than making war on them!"

William rose to his feet and dealt Radulf a hearty blow on the shoulder that would have felled a lesser man.

"We'll see you wed here on the morrow. I order a feast to be prepared! I'm only sorry the queen will not witness it—she has so long despaired of seeing you marry, Radulf."

There was a note of sadness in his voice. Happily married and deeply in love, William would never risk his wife, so he had returned Matilda to Normandy.

Radulf bowed and led Lily away, pretending not to notice her struggles.

"You have chosen a wildcat to take to wife, Radulf."

The voice was sweet and melodious, and despite her own tumultuous feelings, Lily sensed Radulf's shock on hearing it. Instinctively she turned toward the speaker, and found that it was the same golden-eyed woman she had noticed earlier. The lady stood, a half smile on her wide mouth, very secure in her fine velvet gown. A smooth strand of dark hair curled at her brow, the remainder covered with a gossamer veil. Not in her first youth, she was nevertheless breathtakingly beautiful.

"Radulf?" she queried with a laugh when he did not answer her, but Lily sensed a touch of pique.

Radulf bowed, a brief tilt of his dark head. His movements, always so graceful despite his size, seemed suddenly clumsy. "Lady Anna."

The golden eyes slid over him, devouring him.

"You have not changed," she said, but Radulf had already turned away.

Taking long strides toward the door, he pulled the now subdued Lily along behind him. As they passed into the outer chamber, Lily finally managed to free herself. She spun to face him, stiff and white.

With a resigned and heartfelt sigh, Radulf prepared himself for the onslaught. He felt physically and mentally drained, and now Anna was there to complicate matters. But he had expected Lily to be angry, and after what had been said about her and done to her, it was natural she would want her say.

"I will never marry you!" Her voice was trembling uncontrollably. "All Normans are greedy land-grabbing monsters! I had thought Vorgen bad enough, but now I see that you are worse!" She swung her arm, aiming blindly.

Radulf easily caught the blow in his palm, folding her shaking hand into his. He lifted an eyebrow and replied mildly, "You know that is not true. I have lands enough, and no love for your northern wilds. I agreed to take them because I feared what would happen to them if I did not. And as for marriage . . . if you do not marry me, lady, then you will be imprisoned for the rest of your life. Tell me, would you prefer to be shackled by a vow, or by irons?"

"Irons!" Her voice bit, stirring his own anger despite his determination to listen to her complaints with patience. "I was wed to one Norman, and I'd rather die than be wed to another!"

"Lady—" he warned.

"No! Take me back! I will speak again with your king. I am the granddaughter of Harald

Hardraada, the king of Norway! I am the daughter of an English earl—"

He grasped her shoulders and shook her, until her voice faltered and stopped.

"The king has ordered that we marry, and you will marry me tomorrow and smile and pretend you like it. Just as I will. I have your lands now, and the ruling of your precious people. If you argue with me, if you disobey me, I will take my vengeance out on *them*."

He did not mean it. He had never been a man who vented his spleen on the defenseless, but Lily could not know that. Her gray eyes glittered silver with tears.

"Why?" she gasped. "Why marry a woman you hate . . . who hates you? Is it to punish me? I do not understand," she wailed, "why could you not have refused!"

He looked down at her a moment longer. "If I had refused then William would have found you another Norman, one less amenable then I."

She made a most unladylike sound.

He smiled coldly. "It was *my* pride you dented with your tricks and your lies, not some other Norman's. I will have my revenge on you *my* way. And what better revenge than to have you as my wife, in my power, forever?"

Lily flushed again with what he assumed was anger, but was actually horror. Her heart was thumping like a muffled drum, and for a long moment she thought she really might faint. She knew very well the fate that lay before her as the wife of a man who hated her.

"And if I do not wed you, you will ravage my lands?" she whispered.

"Aye," he blustered.

She said nothing, giving him a wild look.

"But there is something apart from all that, lady. Another consideration."

"Oh?" She managed through her aching throat.

"Aye, and it was this that swayed me most in favor of the king's order." She stiffened only slightly as he bent close to whisper in her ear. "I find great pleasure in your body. I enjoy touching you, kissing you . . . I enjoy being inside you and hearing you cry out. I think I will enjoy making an heir on you, lady. Planting my seed and seeing you swell."

She had gone very still. He watched her eyes dilate, her breasts begin to rise and fall very rapidly. "You . . . you will?" she managed to croak.

"Yes, I will. And do not think to deny me once that heir has been born. I will have as many children on you as I can while we are both able!"

It was a monstrous thing to say, he knew it as soon as the words were past his lips, but it was too late to pull them back. Besides, he wanted her and it was best she know it. He stepped closer, grasping her shoulders and pulling her up against the hard wall of his chest until her breasts were flattened against him. Her nipples, he noticed with interest, had gone hard.

His voice was a husky whisper. "I will lay with you every day of my life, *mignonne*, and still it will not be enough to rid me of the spell you have cast upon me."

There was such a shimmer of heat in Radulf's dark eyes that Lily's lips fell open; her breath caught in her throat. Her skin was still flushed and hot, but now something very different from anger was heating it. The truth was well-nigh unbearable to her pride. Oh God, she *wanted* him to wed her! She *wanted* to lie in his bed every day, just as he said. She *wanted* to bear his children! Large, black-haired, brawling boys!

He read the need in her eyes, and his wonderful mouth tugged up at the corners. "Do you want that, too, lady? Do you?" His fingers slid across her cheek, playing with the soft fleshy part of her ear. His breath heated her lips.

He gave a short, humorless laugh. "We are both caught in the spell then, with no way out. William has forced us into marriage and we will make the most of it."

Lily swallowed and closed her eyes against the wicked temptation in his. "Never!" she gasped, but it was a lie and he knew it.

He laughed again, and with Lily folded within one powerful arm, led her from the castle.

Radulf passed, unseeing, through the castle guard. His smile had gone, and beneath his grim exterior his feelings were careering as wildly out of control as Lily's. He had come to William yesterday with the express purpose of begging his king to grant him leave to make Lily his wife.

After a long night, much talk, and more to drink, William had finally agreed to Radulf's request. Only now that Radulf had had his wish granted, he saw it was not so simple.

She hated him, and he could not trust her!

And he had certainly not made himself any more palatable to her with his coarse playacting in the king's hall.

The one thing Radulf felt reasonably certain of was the power he exerted over her body. Their kiss had shown him that, and he had reaffirmed it moments ago, when she all but swooned in his arms at the thought of the marriage bed. By God, she wanted him; she burned for him as hotly as he burned for her! Perhaps if they spent every moment together in bed, they could find some measure of rosy happiness among the thorns of distrust and lies . . .

Jervois had the horses ready. As Radulf threw Lily up into her saddle, he fancied for a moment that he saw sheer anguish beneath the furious mask of her face. The impression was gone in a flash and she was glaring at him once more like an icy wildcat.

Aye, he had been granted his wish. Lily was to be his wife.

Pray God he did not live to regret it.

Chapter 11

Lily rode back to the inn in even more of a daze than she had left it. The afternoon was fading, night closing over the city like a dark lid. Gray smoke drifted across thatched roofs, and shadows gathered in narrow streets while mist, like ghostly fingers, plucked at the surface of the Ouse.

When they reached the inn, Lily slipped quickly off her mare, ignoring any helping hands, and marched inside without a word. By the time Radulf had followed her, she was in her room with the door shut. Alone with her thoughts.

They were chaotic.

Primarily, there was the frightening but indisputable fact that her emotions and her body were in direct opposition to her mind. Despite everything Radulf had said and done, as soon as he touched her . . . as soon as he looked at her *in that way*, sensible and considered behavior lost all meaning.

Radulf had admitted he would use her lands and people against her if she disobeyed him, that he did not trust her and meant to punish her in his own way and in his own time for the damage she had done to his pride.

And still she wanted to tumble blithely into his strong arms!

Lily sank down on her bed and stared at the wall. It was no use wishing things might have been different. It would be oh so easy to sink into his embrace and allow him to do with her as he willed. Then she would be his prisoner indeed! He knew she burned for him, she could not hide that, but that was all it would ever be—lust. And lust could be controlled, held on a tight rein, maybe even worn out.

One thing Lily swore to herself: Radulf must never conquer her.

"Lady?"

Una's gentle voice was accompanied by a tap on the door.

"I've your supper here. Are you not hungry?"

Lily hesitated, but the rumbling in her stomach convinced her not to take the martyr's path. Best to continue to eat well, so that she had the strength to resist Radulf.

When she opened the door she knew she had made the right decision. Una beamed at her over a bowl of mouthwatering stew, thick slices of buttered bread, and a mug of ale.

"Lord Radulf said to be sure you eat it all," she announced as she set out the food. Her open countenance took on a speculative quality. "The soldiers are saying you are to wed Lord Radulf, lady. Upon the morrow!"

Lily took a bite of the bread and nodded soberly. " 'Tis true, Una. I am to marry him. The king has ordered it."

Una gave a dramatic shiver. "Oh, lady! Are you not afeard? Such a great big man will crush your bones when you lie with him!"

Lily choked on her ale. Una didn't appear to notice.

" 'Tis times like this," she went on thoughtfully, "I'm glad I'm free and lowborn. No king will ever be interested enough in me to order me to wed."

"Lucky indeed," Lily assured her with a wistful smile.

Una's mouth pursed. "You will need a fine wedding gown, lady."

Dismayed, Lily looked down at the stained and threadbare gown she wore. "This is all I have, Una. Mayhap I can borrow one of yours?"

It was said in jest, but Una blushed rosy red. "Oh no, lady," she breathed, "it wouldn't be fitting! You must ask your lord. They say he is almost as rich as the king. He could buy you furs and jewels enough to fill a room!"

"No doubt he could," Lily replied dryly, but she would not ask. Call it stubborn pride, but she would much prefer to wed Radulf in her travel-stained rags than beg him for new clothes. Still, she continued to brood on her lack of suitable adornments. After Una had gone and Lily retired to her bed, she stayed awake wondering what would become of her.

Although she doubted she could have slept anyway, with Radulf and his men celebrating.

Probably tallying up his new estates, she told

herself bleakly. Well, she hoped he had a very sore head in the morning.

Radulf, unaware of his wife-to-be's ill-wishing, was laughing at his men's sallies and playing the bridegroom. He had what he wanted, why not enjoy it? Let all his doubts and troubles wait until the morrow.

Still, his eyes slid often in the direction of Lily's closed door. Behind that stout wooden barrier lay the woman who had turned his life upside down. He pictured her, one arm outflung, pale hair twisting about her like a silver rope, lips slightly apart, soft and sweet on the outside, so hot and welcoming on the inside.

Would she welcome him now, if he came knocking? Radulf did not think so. More likely she would fly at him, nails crooked like claws, screaming her fury like a banshee.

He shuddered.

"What will you name your first son, my lord?" some wit demanded, drink slopping down his chin. "Eric Bloodaxe?"

Radulf snorted, ridding himself of his gloomy thoughts. "Nay, he will be Radulf! A good Norman name."

Jervois raised his goblet high. "To Radulf, son of Radulf!"

Radulf smiled, his gaze resting on his trusted captain. He had put the other man in a difficult position earlier on, asking him to obey his lord's orders above the king's. If it had become necessary to take Lily into hiding, Jervois would have been risking his life. Such loyalty was to be valued highly. Aye, he would reward Jervois, reward him well!

"My lord?" His captain leaned closer, green eyes glazed, his head bobbing with drunken wisdom. "What do you in . . . intend to give Lady Lily . . . that is, Wilfreda, for a bride gift?"

Radulf blinked at him, his mind gone suddenly blank.

"Our host . . . host's daughter told me that 'tis customary," Jervois went on, slurring his words badly, "to give your bride a gift on her wedding day."

Radulf stared back at him. How could he have been so dim-witted as not to comprehend he needed a bauble to present to his wife-to-be? Women, as he was well aware, were very fond of baubles. His father's money had soon dribbled away on the purchasing of jewels and pretty things for his second wife, and all the while, eyes gleaming, she had demanded more.

The memory caused Radulf's expression to harden. No, he decided stubbornly, there would be no bride gift. She was getting the rich and powerful Lord Radulf, wasn't she? She should be content with that!

He said so aloud, ignoring Jervois's disapproving tut-tuts.

"Sh . . . she won't see it that way. She'll feel sl . . . slighted. Women always feel sl . . . slighted over the little things."

Radulf scowled. "Whether she feels slighted or not is a matter of complete indifference to me."

Jervois tried to focus his eyes. "Make you miserable," he said at last. "No talk, no smiles, no bed."

Radulf's scowl deepened.

Defeated, his captain walked away, weaving slightly from side to side. "Both as st . . . stubborn as mules," he muttered darkly to himself. "God grant I never have a wife!"

When the morning came, and Una told Lily there was a gift for her, her heart soared.

The idea that, after all that had passed between them, the breach could be healed with a mere bauble was ridiculous. And yet Lily's spirits lifted with her heart. The gift must be a gesture of truce.

The next moment, Una dashed all her eager hopes.

"A manservant brought it, my lady. It comes from Lady Kenton and is a gift, her man says, for you to wear at your wedding."

When a disconsolate Lily had unraveled the carefully wrapped bundle, she found inside the most beautiful gown. She could not help her gasp of wonder. Cut from heavy silk cloth, the gown was a sumptuous golden color and embroidered all over with fine gold and silver threads. The accompanying chemise and veil were as fine as a spider's web on a spring morn. A pair of pointy-toed shoes, the same golden color as the gown, completed the outfit.

It was a dress fit for a queen—or at least a Viking princess's daughter. Speechless, Lily touched the cloth with trembling fingers. Una had no such trepidation, and lifted the dress up against her mistress. She gave a deep, heartfelt sigh. "Oh, lady, you will be an angel!"

Lily smiled, but her eyes were no longer dreamy. "This Lady Kenton is most generous, Una, but perhaps it would be best if I sent back her dress. Lord Radulf has not given me permission to wear another's clothes. I can only think he wishes me to wear the clothes I have."

Una narrowed her eyes, hearing the note of disappointment in Lily's voice. She had become fond of Lily, admiring her courage and even more admiring her kindness to those of lesser standing than herself—in short, girls like Una. Her father, the innkeeper, said Lily was proud and cold, but Una did not believe that was so. It was all pretense, just as Una sometimes pretended to be what she was not.

She did not want to see Lily unhappy on her wedding day just because that surly giant Radulf had failed to buy her something nice for a bride gift. Last night Una had tried planting the thought in his captain's thick ear, but to no avail. Now she must use more direct methods. "Send it back and insult her?" Her shrill cry at least gained her Lily's full attention. "No, lady," she went on more softly, "you must wear it."

"Must I?"

"Oh yes. And you will see, Lord Radulf will not mind. Why, he will not be able to say a word, for he will be struck dumb at the sight of you!"

Una watched a glimmer of speculation light up Lily's gray eyes. That Lily should care for such a frightening man amazed her, but it was obviously so. He would not be Una's choice, goodness me, no! There was a boy in the next street who sold fish . . . but there was no time for such daydreams now. Una had decided Lily would be happy on her wedding day, and happy she would be!

Lily did not argue as Una helped her to don the gown. The thought of Radulf struck dumb by the sight of his bride was a temptation too great for her to resist. When she was dressed, Una combed out her hair so that it hung loose about her in a veil finer and fairer than any cloth. The gold brought a warmth to Lily's pale skin, and with a touch of red at her lips, it was easy enough to overlook the shadows under her eyes.

Una stepped back to peruse her handiwork. "You are a wondrous fair bride, lady," she breathed reverently.

" 'Tis the dress," Lily murmured. "Such a gown would turn any woman into a beauty."

She hardly heard Una's protests. Now that it was time to appear before her bridegroom, Lily was very nervous. She knew she must pretend at haughtiness, enclose herself once more in the ice cage, but such pretense was difficult on her marriage day.

Radulf had released her from the cage, but it seemed that he still held the key.

"Lady?" Una was at the door, eyes bright, eager to show her off.

Lily gathered the stiff, heavy folds of her skirt in her hands, lifting the hem above her matching shoes so that she did not trip. *You have faced Vorgen*, she reminded herself, *and you have faced King William. There is no need to be afraid of Radulf.*

Radulf and his men had celebrated long into the night, and the common room was still smoky and untidy, and reeked of ale and wine. Lily stood in the doorway, noting one man holding his head and another green-faced in the light from the door. She could not at first see Radulf, and as she stood there, searching, one by one the soldiers' voices fell silent.

Lily ignored their stares. She had found who she was looking for. He was such a tall and commanding presence, Lily did not know how she had missed him. He was standing by the fireplace, one booted foot resting against the hearth, a tankard in his hand, a smile on his mouth as he bent his head to converse with the innkeeper.

"My lady!" Jervois spoke the words softly, reverently, from his place by his lord.

Radulf turned, the amusement dying in his eyes. Despite the smoky gloom, Lily caught the flash of heat in that dark gaze. It was like sunlight, melting her flesh and bones, dazzling her so that for a brief moment she could not think at all. Then Una slipped an unobtrusive arm about her waist, fearing perhaps that she was about to faint. When Lily had regained her composure the heated look had gone, and Radulf's eyes were unreadable.

He looked well, she admitted grudgingly. The tunic he wore was Lincoln green in color, and a short, dark, fur-lined cloak was flung across one shoulder and fastened with an ornate brooch. It swirled about his muscular legs as he turned to murmur some instruction to Jervois. A heavy gold chain shone dully across his breast, indicative of his position. Oh yes, he looked very well indeed.

Today they would be joined together as husband and wife, as close a union as was possible between man and woman. The knowledge sent prickles of fright and excitement across Lily's skin.

Radulf was striding toward her, setting his tankard down on a bench as he passed. By the time he halted, he was too close. Why did he always stand too close? Lily longed to take a step back and create space between them, but he would consider it a sign of weakness.

"We ride to the castle within the hour," he said in a formal voice. "Will you take some wine with me before we go to celebrate our marriage?"

The men stood silent and waiting, while Una held her breath at Lily's back. That she didn't slap his face, Lily told herself, was more for their sake than her own. Radulf threw a glance at the innkeeper, and the man hastened to pour wine into two of the finest goblets.

"It is a pleasure, my lady," he began, but Radulf silenced him with a single glance.

"To the lady Lily!" Radulf declared. As the wine reached his lips, an uncomfortable thought occurred to him. "Or should I call you Lady Wilfreda now?"

Lily refused to look away from those dark questioning eyes. "It is my name, my lord," she replied just as formally.

He drank half the wine. His men raised a ragged and subdued cheer, obviously afraid their heads would crumble if they yelled too loudly. "So who is Lily?" asked Radulf, his brows drawn together.

"My father called me Lily. It is the name I am called by those who love me," she said very coldly, so he would know he was not one of them.

He stared down at her a moment longer, then shrugged indifferently. "Then I will call you Wilfreda, or perhaps vixen, for you have been as cunning as one." He swallowed the remainder of the wine. "Drink up, lady! You will be tired and thirsty ere this day is done. The king tends to wring every drop of amusement out of these occasions."

He did not speak to her again, but turned to

thank his men and receive more of their congratulations. Making them, thought Lily crossly, even more his slaves than they already were. *Vixen*, indeed!

Lily swiftly drank down her goblet of wine, to help dull her fears. When it came time to mount her mare and ride to the castle, she was able to do so quite regally and with very little nerves.

"You do us proud, lady," Jervois complimented her, as he assisted her into the saddle. "The King's Sword could not have found a more ravishing bride."

Honeyed words were rare from Radulf's captain, and Lily wondered if he had spoken them because Radulf had not. Apart from that one burning look, Radulf had said nothing at all about the golden gown. But then, why should he? They were only marrying because the king had ordered it, and despite what he had said about revenge and enjoying her body, Radulf must be feeling angry and resentful.

She hardly knew what she herself was feeling. Confusion, pain, anger . . . and other, darker emotions she didn't want to examine too closely.

Lily's mare shifted nervously, perhaps sensing her mistress's shift in feelings. When Radulf moved in beside her, his destrier frightened the mare even more. As she tossed her head and sidestepped, he reached over and took her reins from Lily's fingers, wrapping them firmly about his big hand.

"My lord," Lily gasped, shocked by his highhanded behavior, "please return my horse to me!"

He ignored her, calling something to the innkeeper who was hovering in the doorway.

Her father had determined her life when she was young, then Vorgen had controlled her, and Hew had tried to. Men seemed always to be telling her what to do.

"My lord!" Lily hissed under her breath. "I asked that you return me my reins. I will not be led behind you like a child."

Radulf turned and looked at her then, eyebrows raised. "You wish to be thrown, lady?"

"My mare is afraid of your destrier, Lord Radulf, but I can manage her."

There was a note of pride in the statement.

Radulf did not appear to care one way or the other, for he shrugged and said indifferently, "As you wish, lady. Let us go."

Lily took control of her mount once more, settling her heavy skirts about her. It wasn't much, perhaps, but it was a start.

They rode through the narrow streets, Radulf's banner carried snapping before them—a fist with a sword held upright on a field of azure. There were plenty of people to cheer for them. William had been busy, Radulf informed Lily, noticing her bewilderment. The king had ordered York to rejoice in the joining of Norman and English, in the coming of a new age of peace and prosperity to the north.

Flower petals settled about them like perfumed rain. The blossoms were sweet and heady, and those who threw them were smiling, enjoying the moment as much as Lily was not.

"They have denuded the gardens," Radulf murmured close to her ear, humor tugging at his mouth.

The surge of longing in her heart frightened

Lily, and made her voice sharp and shrewish. "The king has ordered it. Who would dare disobey?"

Radulf sat back, disinterested again. "Not I, lady."

He grasped her hand, raising it high in his, and the crowd cheered.

"Smile," he told her. "I order it."

Lily smiled, her face stiff and frozen, her heart leaden. It was all so beautiful, but it was all wrong.

Radulf glanced sideways at his bride-to-be. She was beautiful, even the normally taciturn Jervois thought so. And yet she seemed as brittle as eggshell. He had taken her mare's reins because he was afraid for her, and then she had demanded them back. She could not even allow him that small courtesy, her pride was so monstrous.

Radulf irritably brushed a petal off his nose.

If he could get this business over with, take her back to the inn, there might be a chance of melting that icy hauteur. But that was hours and hours away; William's feasts were never brief. Radulf sighed and settled himself for the long wait.

The castle yard was crowded with servants and musicians, welcoming them and announcing their arrival. Inside, the great hall was resplendent with green twining leaves and more flowers, until it seemed more like a forest than a manmade structure. The sweet smells of herbs and blossoms almost but didn't quite overpower those of stale sweat and hunting dogs—the more typical aromas of a Norman keep. Cooks and servants dashed about, while William's guests drank enormous qualities of wine.

The Normans were great fighters and hunters, but they were also great eaters and drinkers. They indulged their senses with passion. Why then, when it came to matters of the heart, were they so reserved and cautious?

Lily remembered her father's manor when she was young, and the laughter and merriment to be found there. Her father had honored her mother with his smile and his gaze, loving her deeply and not caring who saw it. There was nothing wrong in loving someone. Love, she decided, did not depend upon land or wealth; rather it was the connection between two hearts.

And what of lust, which was what she felt for Radulf? Certainly in their case lust had nothing to do with land or wealth, or even which side of the battlefield they stood on. Like being struck by a bolt of lightning, it was beyond explanation.

The priest was waiting in the small chapel. Radulf and Lily were led toward him, and guests crammed in behind them. Foolishly, Lily had hoped for someone like Father Luc. This priest was almost cadaverous, with sunken cheeks and hooded eyes. Lily stood, her chin up and her outer demeanor cold, while the words were spoken and the replies given. Beneath the surface pomp and glitter, beneath her regal pose, she was frightened by what was happening. And yet, at the same time, she felt a strange elation.

For better or worse, they were joined together.

As she thought it, Radulf swooped down and set his lips to hers in a quick, hard kiss. And then William was slapping his back and other voices were shouting congratulations. The noisy, colorful crowd moved back into the hall to begin the eating and drinking, and the king himself took Lily's hand and led her to the high table on the dais, to the place of honor by his side.

"Your hand is cool, Lady Wilfreda," he said, when she was seated. "Does that mean your heart is warm?" But he seemed to doubt it; his sharp eyes held little of the friendship he shared with Radulf.

My heart is broken.

"Will you be a loyal wife to my Sword?" he went on, not waiting for an answer. "I would not like to see him unable to rest in his own chamber, fearing a dagger in his back."

William, Lily recalled, was himself happily married and, it was rumored, had never been tempted to stray. Perhaps some Normans understood love after all.

"I wish only to see my lands ruled well and wisely, sire, and will do everything in my power to bring that wish about. Does that make me a loyal wife?"

"No, lady. Loyalty is not a cloak to wear when it suits you. Radulf deserves better than that."

"I do not intend to betray my husband," Lily said quietly.

William frowned at her, opened his mouth to say more. Just then an enormous plate was carried in, topped by a roasted boar crouched upon a bed of vine leaves and surrounded by honeyed vegetables. A murmur of appreciation arose from the guests, and William rubbed his hands together in anticipation. Lily watched in dismay as he piled her plate high and then ordered her jeweled goblet filled to the brim with the heady spiced wine.

"You will celebrate your wedding, Lady Wilfreda," he commanded, "whether you willed it or not. Now eat up!"

"Yes, sire." She modestly lowered her eyes to hide her anger. When the king's suffocating attention had moved on, she dared a glance at Radulf on her other side. He caught it, reading it correctly as his dark gaze swept over her piled plate. The corner of his mouth tugged up.

"You are clearly ravenous, lady."

"No," spluttered Lily, "I am not!"

He made his mouth serious, though a gleam still lit his dark eyes. "You are thin, wife. A little more flesh could not hurt."

Lily sighed in exasperation. "If I eat this, I will be as round as a bladder."

He threw back his head and laughed, the tension smoothing from his face as if by magic. She had never seen him laugh like that. He looked so handsome and so carefree, not like the King's Sword at all! It caught at her, confused her, like a hand squeezing her heart. Then someone else claimed his attention and Lily was left with a view of his back.

It was, she decided, a very nice back. Broad, straight, shoulders wide . . . She took a small piece of meat and began to chew. She felt absurdly pleased with herself for making him laugh. Somehow their byplay had lightened the mood, and even sitting beside a king who did not like her very much didn't seem quite so bad.

Lily glanced at Radulf again, secretly examining him. The ice within her melted still further as she allowed herself a brief daydream. Radulf's arms around her, his mouth on hers . . . Loud and discordant music brought her to her senses, luckily before she could melt completely into a warm puddle of lust.

A group of players capered about the hall, singing and playing their instruments until Lily's ears rang with their racket. When they had done, a harpist played and sang some plaintive songs, but was soon ousted in favor of acrobats and then some actors, who performed a play based on Lily's own recent capture and wedding.

Surprised and dismayed, Lily recognized herself in a lithesome lad with a long, fair wig and a disdainful air. He glided about, swinging his hips and tossing his locks, while glancing coquettishly in the direction of the player who was meant to be Radulf.

If Lily had found her own portrayal embarrassing, Radulf's was worse. He was depicted as a fool, blundering about the hall, tripping over feet and dogs, cursing and shaking his fist, and all the time making much of his "sword." Bawdy laughter followed every jest.

Radulf, leaning back in his chair beside Lily, gave the occasional snort of laughter, but like her he was embarrassed that his personal affairs had become fodder for William and his gossip-hungry court. He was more used to inspiring fear than laughter.

As the play came to an end and the "bride" and "groom" were entwined in a clinch more like a wrestling match than an embrace, Radulf breathed a deep sigh of relief. He glanced sideways and noted Lily's bowed head and the flush of color in her cheeks. Had this nonsense upset her? She glanced up, just a quick flicker of her long lashes, and he was gazing directly into a pair of dark gray eyes.

" 'Tis only silliness," he assured her in a murmur, his voice low and gentle.

Lily's pupils were huge and dark and she shivered, but when he asked her if she was chilled, she shook her head. "No, it is only . . . no, it is nothing, my lord."

He wanted to ask her to tell him what she really felt; he wanted to take her aside and hear her voice close to his ear, her breath warming his skin. For suddenly it seemed as though the iron shield she held so rigidly before her had been lowered. But in a moment it was back up again, her chin raised, her gaze haughty.

Radulf nodded and turned away, back to the conversation of the man to his right. Yet he remained intensely aware of Lily, as if her every movement was imprinted on his skin. Was it his fevered imagination, or had he seen invitation in her gray eyes? Was it possible his wedding night was going to be more than sitting with his men getting drunk?

Nerves jumped in Radulf's belly. He felt like a boy with his first girl. It was ridiculous, demeaning, but he couldn't help it. He wanted Lily, he needed her, and tonight that was all that mattered.

Chapter 12

The trestle tables were being cleared, but whether the feast was over or they were simply waiting on more courses, Lily wasn't sure. The need to relieve herself was an excuse to slip out of the hall. She was glad of a moment alone, for the strain had been considerable. And she had almost made a fool of herself, swaying toward Radulf like a besotted maid, trembling with the need to have his arms about her.

Such things could not be. Real life was not a play. Radulf had stated his reasons for marrying her, and because she was his wife there would always be parts of her life which were completely in his power. She must never allow him to discover he heated her blood to such an extent that she was his willing captive. No, that would never do.

When Lily returned to the hall, she paused a moment in the doorway, watching the guests. Dress, both male and female, varied from the elaborate to the shabby. Fashions did not change much from year to year, but there were subtle differences. London styles, Lily supposed.

When someone tapped her arm she turned with a start, and found herself facing the same golden-eyed woman she remembered from yesterday's audience with King William.

"Lady Wilfreda." The woman's voice was alluring, her clothing exquisite. She wore a wine-colored gown glittering with gold thread and tiny pearls. Upon her dark, curling hair sat a circlet of gold studded with rubies. Her beauty transcended the tiny lines about her eyes and mouth, the inevitable signs of her age.

"You do not know me?" she asked, disappointment in the lift of her dark brows. "I am Lady Anna Kenton. I sent your bridal gown."

Lily gasped, flushing with embarrassment. "Lady Anna, I did not know . . . I am most grateful for your kindness. The gown is beautiful. I had brought little with me from . . . from home, and such a gift was most welcome."

Anna smiled, satisfied with her reply. "I knew that Radulf would not think of your wardrobe, or lack of. He is never interested in women's affairs."

There was something behind the smile, something unpleasant. As though Anna were laughing at Lily in the guise of kindness. Surprised, she took a step back.

"You know Lord Radulf, Lady Kenton?"

Anna laughed softly. "Oh yes. I know him. I know him well. Has he not spoken of me? Ah well"—with a shrug—"there are some things which cannot be shared with outsiders. I hold a part of him, my dear, that you will never have, no matter how you strive to win it. Do you know what that is?"

Lily shook her head, bemused.

Anna's golden eyes lit up. "It is his heart, lady."

A bolt of jealousy drove through Lily, filling her instantly with suspicion and envy and all manner of emotions she had never felt before. Who was this woman, and what did she mean by saying such things? How could she make such a claim, and what was she to Radulf?

But there was no time to ask the questions blistering her tongue. The next moment she sensed a familiar warmth at her back, and then Lady Anna's gaze had lifted to someone above and behind her.

"Radulf," Lady Anna murmured, her mouth curling up in a smile. "I have been telling your wife how well I know you. No one knows you as well as I do, or as . . . thoroughly."

Radulf gripped Lily's arm so roughly she flinched, beginning to protest. Only to stop abruptly after one glance at his face.

His sensual mouth was white and pinched at the corners, his eyes black as pits of tar. Lily had never seen him look so, not even when he had caught her trying to escape with Hew.

"Come," he said in a voice that had no strength. "We will take our leave of the king."

"Radulf . . . ?" she began in instinctive protest.

Anna laughed, more softly now, taunting and triumphant. "Yes, run away," she mocked. "But you know you will never outrun the memories, Radulf. And those memories can be more than cold, dead things. We can bring them back to life. I have been thinking of that ever since you left me."

" 'I left you'?" he repeated blankly, as if he couldn't comprehend her meaning.

Lily felt sick. This was not Radulf! When had he ever been so drained, so drawn? Whatever Lady Anna had been to him, the very sight of her was leaching out his will to live.

"What think you of your new wife's gown, Radulf?" the woman went on, still smiling. " 'Tis mine. I have been a part of your marriage, you see. I have stood between you and her"—with a dismissive wave at Lily. "I knew you would not notice the dress, would not question it. You never did notice the outer coverings, always so eager to get to what lay underneath."

Radulf took a shaky breath. "You drew me into your chamber to help with your gown," he said, his voice not his own. "And sometimes you wore no gown."

"I wanted you, Radulf, even then. I want you still. There is no one else for me."

With what seemed a tremendous effort, Radulf turned and walked away. Lily, after one more glance at that lovely smiling face, turned and followed. He was taking such big strides she had to run to catch up to him. Lily glanced over her shoulder, but the other woman was soon swallowed up in the crowd.

"Radulf, what—"

"No!" he roared, and then, controlling himself, "no. You will return that gown tonight. You should never have worn it."

Lily frowned up at his rigid profile, her heart thumping with fright and confusion. "I had nothing else to wear," she said, lowering her voice. "You did not think to supply me with a gown."

Radulf turned and glared at her. "You did not ask!"

"I did not know I could!"

He halted, and Lily gave a sigh of relief. The expression on his face was more familiar now, though still pale. He was cross and he was frowning. "You can make any reasonable request, lady. I am your husband and bound to consider it."

Lily laughed angrily. "Vorgen never did! Why should you be different? You have told me you are marrying me to punish me, and now you say I have only to ask for a thing and you will grant my wish. Forgive me if I find it difficult to reconcile those two statements, my lord."

"Nevertheless, it is true," he replied in a voice more like a snarl.

"Radulf."

They both looked up, startled by the interruption. A slight man in a fur-trimmed tunic stood before them, a quizzical smile upon his thin lips. His hands were encrusted with rings, a sign of considerable wealth.

"You look pale for a bridegroom, Radulf," he went on. "And this is your wife? Lady, you are fair indeed. I can see why Radulf is keen to tame you to our Norman ways."

Lily flushed, sensing the subtle barb behind his polite words. "I am already well acquainted with Norman ways, sir!" she retorted sharply.

He laughed. "You are more robust than you look, lady. You will need to be so if you are married to Radulf. I know of these things. I am Lord Kenton."

Lily flicked a surprised glance at Radulf, who was stony-faced and seemingly unmoved. "I am glad to meet you," she ventured. "I have met your wife."

Kenton's pale eyes were curious and strangely sympathetic, as if he felt a kinship with her. The light brown hair, though creeping back from his high forehead, was yet luxuriant about his ears. He was older than Radulf and very different. Lily felt oddly repelled.

"Do you stay in York long?" Radulf's soft voice broke in on her thoughts. He had mastered whatever emotions had overtaken him when he came face to face with Lady Anna, but Lily caught a glitter of banked fires in those eyes.

Lord Kenton smiled and shrugged. "I leave that to my wife. She was very insistent we come to York, and now she wants to remain a little longer. There are people she particularly wants to see."

Radulf grunted a noncommittal reply.

To Lily's mind Lady Anna and her husband seemed a mismatched couple, the lady so tall and beautiful, the man so slight and strange. Perhaps the amount of precious stones upon his hands explained their wedding.

Lord Kenton seemed to read her thoughts upon her face, and a smug little smile pulled at his mouth. "Lady Anna is very beautiful, is she not, lady? Such a woman needs a man who can display her in the correct setting."

Radulf grimaced. "You speak in riddles as usual, Kenton."

"Not at all, Radulf. It is just that you are a plain-spoken man. So I will speak plainly to you. My wife is my property and I will never release her."

Lily felt a jolt down her spine, but Radulf appeared unmoved. He settled himself more easily upon his strong legs, folding his arms across his broad chest.

"Aye, that is direct. This shuffling about an issue tires me far more than a good battle. I like to see a man's eyes over a sharp blade; then I can tell what truly lies in his heart.

"I have great respect for other men's property, Kenton. As you can see, I am only lately married myself."

Lord Kenton gave Lily his little smile. "And she is beautiful . . . in her way. Have you used your sorcery on her yet? Once he does, lady, you will never be free of him. I am one who knows. Radulf has had a way with women since he was a boy. That is so, is it not, my lord?"

The undercurrents between the two men rippled and swirled, and Lily wondered where this odd conversation would end.

"Someone has led you astray on this matter," Radulf said at last, his face thoughtful, his words almost tentative. "It is not for me to advise you in these things, Kenton, but do not believe all that you hear. I have been down that road before—"

"No." He did not raise his voice, and yet that single word had enough strength in it to stop Radulf in midsentence. "I will hear no more on this. You should take your wife and go home to your marriage bed."

Radulf bowed his head in farewell. "I intend to do so."

As Lily moved to pass him, Kenton leaned forward, his breath hot in her ear. "Do not love him, lady, whatever you do." Then, when Lily jerked back, "Lady, it has been a pleasure to meet one so fair. Lord Radulf is indeed a lucky man to have acquired you with your northern lands. It seems that brutality has its place."

"He is very peculiar," Lily murmured, when they were far enough away so that Lord Kenton could not overhear.

"What did he say to you?"

Do not love him, lady. "I didn't hear it."

Radulf gave her a frowning look. "Aye, he is peculiar, and slippery as an eel. He has lands not far from York, which he got through the use of his tongue rather than his sword arm. If he wants to fight, he hires mercenaries to die for him." Radulf's eyes were hard and cold. "I do not like him, lady. I do not trust him. You should take care if you are ever again in his company."

"That is odd," she retorted. "He said the same thing about you."

His eyes flashed, and Lily was reminded that the fire of his anger was only banked, not yet quenched. She wondered if it was Lord Kenton himself that Radulf disliked, or the fact that he was Lady Anna's husband.

"For a Norman he appeared harmless enough," she went on, as if unaware of his glowering look. "Has he been wed to Lady Anna long?"

Emotion flared again in Radulf's black eyes; he was losing the tight clamp he had placed on his temper. He gripped Lily's hand painfully tight. "Come, lady, we are leaving. I have had enough of talk."

Their leave-takings were done in surprisingly short time. With William's good wishes and bawdy laughter ringing in their ears, Radulf and his new wife left to return to the inn.

Lily found the dark ride through York a far different affair from their journey to the castle. The quiet, cold streets were dreamlike, a scene from one of her mother's Norse stories. The white mist clung about the horses' hooves, stirring to their movement, lapping at the doors of the houses they passed.

Swaying, light-headed, Lily became aware of how weary she was. And how confused. What was this Lady Anna to Radulf? Why should he be so angry about something as simple as a borrowed gown? And what could the woman's hints and innuendos refer to?

They have been lovers.

Her inner voice scoffed at her stubborn refusal to see what must be clear to everyone else. Once Radulf had held Anna in his arms, kissed her wide mouth, and gazed into her golden eyes. And she had stroked that broad back and held him in the throes of love. According to Anna, Radulf's heart still belonged to her. Was that why he had not married until now? Because he could not have the woman he truly loved?

Lily shuddered, torn with a jealousy so great it was beyond description. Was that why he had been so angry with her, because she had reminded him of what he could not have? And Lord Kenton, did he know about Radulf and his beautiful wife? Was that why he spoke so strangely, firing little barbs at Radulf and trying to wound him?

It must be so.

Lily closed her eyes and felt the knife twist in her heart. The truth was, she wanted Radulf to be hers. Only hers.

The mist swirled, and she was cold despite her

warm cloak. Though Radulf's men rode silently about her and Radulf was a dark shadow at her side, Lily suddenly felt very much alone.

The inn was warm and stuffy, the air thick with woodsmoke. Una had decorated Lily's room with flowers, and there were fresh linens upon the bed. She had also set out a tray with warmed spiced wine and oatcakes. The fire was burning brightly, throwing wild shadows upon the walls.

It was a sanctuary, and yet Lily did not feel safe.

The girl served them silently, her bright smile quickly fading as she sensed the strained atmosphere between the couple. Beyond the closed door, Radulf's men laughed and cheered in celebration of their lord's nuptials, their noise accentuating the silence within the bedchamber.

Radulf drained his goblet, barely noticing what he drank. He was pale and there were hollows under his eyes from two nights with little sleep. He felt sick and wretched. "Take the gown off and I will have it returned immediately," he directed.

Lily touched the mellow, satiny cloth with one careful finger. It was unlikely she would ever wear such a garment again. Despite what Radulf had said, he would probably keep her in rags and chained to the wall of their bedchamber.

"I do not understand why my wearing it should displease you," she replied soberly.

He gave her a bleak look. "It is not a subject for this night. Take off the gown."

She was sorely tempted to refuse and see what he would do, but Lily was fairly sure that in his present mood he would strip it off her. She had more pride than to allow that. Widening her eyes to stop the tears, Lily undid the ties at either side of her waist, and with quick, jerky movements, loosened the gown so that she could slip it over her hips. She released first one arm and then the other, and the golden cloth fell in a pool at her feet. Beneath it she wore a chemise so fine it was barely more than being naked. The fire flared behind her, and she became aware that her body was clearly visible through the silken material.

She also became aware of Radulf's stillness.

He had caught his breath, and his eyes shone hot and black. Lily wavered, folding her arms across her breasts. She had opened her mouth to tell him to leave when the memory of Anna's seductive smile, the expression in those exquisite eyes, slipped unbidden into her mind.

How do you know that Radulf will not return the gown himself? that sly voice asked. *And that he will not stay to take wine with Lady Anna, and then to kiss her and fondle her? And before long they will be together, entwined, in Lady Anna's bed.*

Jealousy wrenched Lily again. *I am his wife now,* she reminded herself. *Why should I send him to another woman, when it is in my power to keep him with me?*

And it *was* in her power; she was almost sure of it. Whatever ill-feeling might exist between Radulf and herself, their bodies were perfectly in tune.

Slowly, her eyes fixed on his, Lily began to slip one sleeve of the chemise over one bare shoulder. That was all it took. In an instant he was on his feet and reaching for her. His hands twined in her hair, tipping her face up to his, and he plundered her mouth with the rough desperation of a man starving for kisses.

Was he pretending she was Anna?

No, he desired *her*, Lily, and had since the first moment they had seen each other. At least she had his lust, even if his heart was elsewhere.

Lily gasped as his hands smoothed over her back and hips, reacquainting himself with her soft curves, before closing on her rounded bottom. He pulled her closer against his body, until she felt the hard length of him jutting against her belly, and groaned. Lily felt a hot, melting joy. Radulf wanted her, just as much as she wanted him.

Lily's breasts were full and heavy, and now his hands were upon them through the gossamer cloth. He bent his head to scrape his teeth across her nipples, and Lily gave a soft cry, arching her body while her hands clung to his broad shoulders.

Radulf laid her down upon the bed, the scent of flowers and passion mingling in the air. He tugged impatiently at the laces of his breeches, shrugging them down over his heavily muscled legs before kicking them off. Lily slipped her hands up under his tunic and shirt, her cool fingers seeking and finding the many battle scars. He was a warrior feared by many, but tonight he was hers.

As impatient as he, Lily tugged his fine tunic up over his head, followed by his shirt, and then looked her full upon him. She would never tire of looking. The firm, curved muscles of his chest, the mighty shoulders and arms, the thick column of his neck. His belly was flat and hard, and lower surged the proud evidence of his manhood.

Lily ran her hands over him, unable to help herself, not wanting to stop. Bending, she began to ply her warm mouth to his chest, her long hair a silver waterfall, shielding her, tempting him.

Radulf bore her caresses until her tormenting tongue dipped lower and made him groan. Then he lifted her from him, dragging the flimsy chemise over her head and tossing it onto the floor. With a grunt of satisfaction, he leaned back to gaze upon her naked body. His face was taut and set with desire, his chest was rising and falling in hard, short pants. He looked up and met Lily's eyes.

The gray irises had darkened, and her eyelids were heavy. Her lips parted as her breath whispered out, and she trembled, little frissons passing over her heated skin. She was a mare ready for her stallion, and she saw him smile.

Slowly, torturously so, Radulf reached out one hand to her lips, his thumb rubbing over the soft flesh. Next he touched her breasts, carefully weighing each one, gently pinching the rigid nipples. Then his hands dipped lower, seeking out the curve of her waist, the soft warmth of her belly, the smooth length of her thigh. And with every touch he looked to her face, into her eyes, and read there the effect he was having upon her.

Lily could not hide her wild desire, so no wonder his smile grew. But she thought he had a right to smile. He was a god among ordinary men, he was her Thor.

By the time Radulf's attention had settled on the blond curls between her thighs, Lily was ready to burst into flames. When he slid his finger slowly inside her, she cried out involuntarily, so

sensitive was she, her body rippling and clench-
ing about him, her arms reaching to cling about
his neck.

Radulf lifted her, his big hands warm about her
hips, and sheathed himself fully inside her. Lily
gasped out his name, and then he was thrusting
deeply, his voice a low, husky chant. "You are
mine, lady. Mine."

Lily had thought herself beyond more pleasure,
but now a trembling began deep within her, dis-
solving skin and bone and sinew, causing her to
cry and moan into his shoulder. Radulf followed
her, his big body shuddering violently against
hers.

After a time their breathing slowed and their
bodies cooled. Radulf lay down, turning on his
side and pinning Lily to him. He dragged the furs
over them both. He knew he should pinch out the
flame in the horn lamp, but he was too comfortable to move. He also knew he should take the
cursed golden gown out to his men and send one
of them back with it.

The wild fury that had overcome him at the
feast threatened him again with sharp claws, but
he beat it down. Tomorrow. He would deal with
that tomorrow. Gradually, his body relaxed again.
He had Lily warm and compliant in his arms, and
he would enjoy her while he could. For who knew
what the future might bring?

As if she had heard his thoughts, Lily stirred,
her breasts brushing against the hair on his chest,
her long slim leg thrown over his hard-muscled
one. He thought her asleep, until her fingers
lightly tested the stubble on his chin before wandering up to the old wound near his left eye. She

moved her fingertips back and forth over the raised scar, again and again, as if somehow her touch could erase it.

Her gentle fingers soothed him, even as the touch of her body against his stirred awake the passion he thought sated. Radulf, monster of legend, had taken a beautiful wife. Perhaps she would yet turn him into a handsome prince.

"Am I truly yours?" Lily whispered, her breath sweet against the hollow of his throat. There was an urgency in her voice, a trace of fear.

He didn't know what she wanted. Was it reassurance or denial? He simply spoke what was in his heart.

"Aye."

Evidently she was happy with that, for soon her breathing slowed and he knew her to be asleep. Memories of the night returned to him: Anna's beautiful, evil face, and Kenton, that wordy fool. He had made Radulf seem like a brutal, fornicating monster, and although it was not so, Radulf had been afraid Lily might believe Kenton. Yet she did not seem to. When she had looked upon him just now it was as if she saw another man entirely, and it puzzled him, even frightened him a little. For what if one day the mist cleared from before her eyes and she saw the real Radulf, and he was every bit as brutal and despicable as the legends had claimed? What then?

Radulf shifted, settling his arms more comfortably about her and easing her head against his shoulder. Such thoughts were best left alone. Enjoy the here and now, and let the future remain hidden. Soon he would make love to her again. Already he felt that traitorous flesh between his thighs hardening as he dreamed of penetrating deep to her womb.

But first he would watch her sleep.

His wife.

The day seemed to resurrect all that had been put to rest in the night's darkness. At first light Radulf sent one of his men to return the dress to Lady Kenton, only to have it back again with her good wishes. Seething, blind with temper, he rent the priceless cloth with his bare hands and flung it into the fire while Lily watched, white-faced.

"You will never again wear anything of hers!" he shouted at her, his eyes reflecting the fury of the flames as they ate her golden wedding dress.

Lily's confidence and belief in herself had long ago been undermined by Vorgen's twisted cruelty. Instead of recognizing Radulf's anger as being against Lady Anna and himself, she believed that it was *she* he was displeased with. Did he think her unworthy of Lady Anna? Did he, despite last night, long to hold Anna in his arms? The burning of the dress could only be the frustration and misery of a man who loved a woman he could not have.

Without a word, Lily turned and fled back to her room. Radulf, furious with himself, strode outside, calling for some of his men to ride with him. There were many things to do if he were to return to Lily's lands in the north. *His* lands, he reminded himself. Building of the good Norman castle William had commanded be placed as sentinel in that wild country would need to begin very soon. Radulf wondered grimly how long it would take him to get the building started and stamp his fist upon those unruly lands. Maybe then he could safely return south to Crevitch, for a little time at least.

He wanted to take Lily to Crevitch. The thought of the two together brought a soft warmth to his chest. He would take her riding in the meadows along the river, and up onto the conical hill from the top of which he could see to every corner of his lands. The summer sunshine would turn her hair to silver fire, and her body would glow when he laid her down upon the green grass and loved her . . .

Radulf shook himself. As his father had loved his stepmother? he thought angrily. As his father had loved and been betrayed, and then died in misery? If he had any sense left, he would fight this sickness that was afflicting him. To allow any woman into his life was to open the way for torment and despair, but to give that privilege to Lily . . .

She would betray him. He might as well face that now. She had already lied to him and tried to run from him. How could he ever trust her?

He scrubbed an angry hand through his short hair, making it stand on end. His thoughts shifted, and he remembered Lily's face when he had burned the golden dress. She had suffered as if it were a living thing, not just cloth and thread. She had wanted it for herself, just like all women, and did not understand his extreme actions.

Radulf shrugged irritably. He did not see why he should explain himself to his wife. Such deep and painful memories were not to be prodded by anyone, and especially not by her. He had held them tightly for many a long year, and he was not about to relinquish his grip. And he could *never* lay down the burden he had carried for so long at the feet of a woman he was afraid to trust.

Radulf and Lily ate again at the castle. William made rough jests about their early departure the night before, until Lily's face was burning and Radulf's smile was a grimace. Beneath the shallow humor, Lily knew William trusted and liked Radulf; there was a bond between them.

Lily concentrated on her food and stayed close to Radulf's side. She had dreaded the thought of Lady Anna approaching her again, but if the golden-eyed woman was present, Lily did not see her. Just as well, for this time she wouldn't listen so passively to the woman's hints and innuendos. Gentle she might be, but she had a temper.

Although Lord Kenton smiled at her knowingly from beyond a group of motley mummers, he did not approach either, likely due to Radulf's grim demeanor. Lily was glad to be left alone; she still felt drained by what had happened. If Radulf still loved Anna so much, it was best they avoided her.

Misery swamped her.

With such gloomy thoughts to occupy her, Lily did not at first hear the tentative voice. "Lily? My lady? Do you not recognize me?"

Lily blinked and looked up. A young woman stood before her, her gown fashionably cut, her hair concealed by a delicate veil, except for two golden yellow curls that brushed her rounded shoulders. Indeed, she was rounded in every respect, and blessed with healthy apple-red cheeks and sparkling blue eyes.

"Alice?" Lily asked the question even as she

knew the answer. Rising to her feet, she took the hands held out to her, leaning dangerously across the table among the leftovers. The two woman smiled broadly at their good fortune.

"It is good to see you again, Lily. I heard of your . . . that is, I feared that you were in desperate trouble, and that I would have to rescue you. But my father would not let me. He sent me here instead, to visit my uncle and find a husband."

Lily laughed as she was meant to. "Have you found one yet?"

"No." Alice shook her head, her eyes dancing merrily. If her husbandless state concerned her, it was not evident. "I do not have your good fortune."

It was said jestingly, but there was a question in Alice's raised brows. Lily smoothed her skirts, trying to conceal her embarrassment. Everyone in York must know the circumstances of her marriage to Radulf.

"I do not know that I would wish my good fortune on you, Alice," she said at last, and her smile was awry. "But it is good to see you." There were not many friendly faces in King William's castle, and Alice's was very friendly indeed.

Alice slipped through a space in the trestle tables and stood close to Lily's side. She was shorter than Lily, though broader. Their basic coloring was similar, both with fair hair and light eyes, but placed together like this, the two women were very different. Alice was the sun and Lily the moon, the one bright and bubbly, the other cool and pale and mysterious.

"May I visit you on the morrow, Lily? Although life here in York is exciting, I cannot help but be a little homesick. I miss my father and my home at Rennoc, and I miss you. I have been worried about you."

Lily smiled. "I have been worried about myself."

"When I heard Vorgen had been killed I wanted to go to you, but my father declared it too dangerous. And then when we heard you were using my name . . . Oh Lily, I was most concerned. Are you really all right? Was Vorgen very cruel?"

Lily grimaced. "Vorgen was the worst sort of Norman."

"And the worst sort of husband," Alice added softly. "May I come to see you tomorrow?"

The girl was obviously dying to hear about Lily's troubles, and Lily did not believe there was anything other than genuine concern in her purpose. "Of course you may. Only . . . we do not as yet have a house here. I—"

Alice, sensing her awkwardness, waved a dismissive hand. "Furnish me with the address and I will find it, Lily. I know York very well by now. I have been shopping every day and have more new clothing than you can imagine. My uncle believes if I am to catch a fine husband, I must put on a fine show."

Self-conscious suddenly, Lily again smoothed her hands over her skirts as she gave Alice her address. It should not matter that she could not compete with Alice's new finery, Lily told herself impatiently. There were far more important things to think of. And yet she could not help but envy Alice, a little.

Alice had been chattering on, but suddenly she fell silent. Lily glanced up and saw that the other girl's smile had faltered and was trembling at the edges. Her already red cheeks had grown redder. Lily did not have to turn her head to know that Radulf had come quietly up behind her.

Alice gave a low, wobbly curtsy, disclosing a great deal of cleavage over the top of her blue gown. Radulf reached past Lily to take the girl's arm in a firm grip and help her rise. His glance to his wife was questioning but also amused. His mouth twitched.

"My lord," Lily said with as much cool hauteur as she could manage, "this is Alice of Rennoc."

His reaction didn't disappoint her, although she doubted anyone else would have noted his sudden brief stillness and the transient gleam that disturbed the matte black of his eyes. He turned back to Alice. "I have heard of you," he said in his low, husky tones.

Alice blinked, surprised by that seductive voice. "H-have you?" she managed. The girl was plainly in awe of the legendary Radulf, and Lily found herself looking at her husband through Alice's eyes. So big and powerful, he must be an intimidating sight, and yet she was not afraid of him—at least not in that way. What did frighten her was the power he had over her, and if he were ever to ascertain it, how he could twist her thoughts and feelings into knots.

Meanwhile, Radulf was nodding at the breathless utterances of his wife's friend. Alice, he had decided, was absolutely nothing like Lily. Her hair was too gold, her eyes too blue, her skin too pink and shiny.

His gaze, veiled by his lashes, slid over Alice's clothing. The blue gown she wore would have suited Lily very well. A man who rarely noticed women's attire, he had nevertheless noticed Lily's embarrassment at the state of her dress as he approached the two women, and he had overheard Alice's artless comment about her new wardrobe. It made him uncomfortable to think that a little provincial miss could outshine the wife of the great Radulf.

Perhaps it was time he did something about that.

Lily, aware of Radulf's eyes upon her, grew even cooler and haughtier than before. Behind her mask her pulse fluttered and her emotions dipped and dived, but Radulf would not know that. Alice, nervous enough in Radulf's presence, sensed Lily's tension and stumbled through another sentence. She rolled her gaze to Lily for help.

"Alice is coming to visit me tomorrow," Lily said, taking pity. "We have much to talk of."

"Not tomorrow morning," Radulf replied quickly, and bit back a laugh when Alice turned to stare at him with shocked dismay. "No, it is not that I forbid you the pleasure of each other's company. My wife will tell you, Alice, that I am not a husband to deny her her pleasures."

Lily's face colored delicately as she comprehended what "pleasures" he was alluding to.

Satisfied that his words had found their mark, Radulf went on. "You will have to postpone your visit. My lady wife has a very important matter to attend to tomorrow."

"Well," Alice glanced from Lily's flushed face to Radulf's impassive one. "This is all very mysterious, but I am sure another day will do just as well."

She had regained some of her spark and with it

her confidence. Radulf might still be an awe-inspiring sight, but there was something in his manner that made Alice believe he was no danger to her. Certainly he was nothing like Vorgen, whom she had hated on sight. Radulf's eyes were watchful but entirely lacking the inhuman coldness of Lily's first husband, and there was a warmth in them that made her feel quite breathless.

"Do you remain in York long, Lord Radulf?"

Instantly all the good points she had been gathering against Radulf's name were erased. He gave her a scowl that made her want to shudder in her pointy-toed shoes.

"I go north all too soon," he said tersely.

"Oh!" Alice swallowed. "I am sorry," she felt compelled to add. "I-I expect you will miss Lily."

Radulf raised his dark brows. He glanced down at Lily as if surprised by the thought and met her gray eyes gazing up at him. "Yes," he said softly. Lily's lips looked moist and sweet, and he wanted nothing so much as to bend his head and close his mouth on hers. To lose himself in her and to forget war and battles and the endless riding from one skirmish to another. Indeed, to forget everything but Lily and the mad, all-consuming need for her that had taken hold of him.

"Radulf!" The king's voice saved him from making a fool of himself. Abruptly Radulf straightened and turned in the direction of the shout. King William, taller than most of his court, was beckoning to him. Without a word, Radulf walked toward his king.

There was an uncomfortable silence. Alice, who had observed the telling moment between them, did not quite know what to say. Lily, still dazed by the burning look Radulf had fixed upon her, was struggling to find her voice. Alice's bubbly nature reasserted itself first.

"Oh Lily, he is very different from Vorgen!"

Lily frowned. "He is a man, just as Vorgen was."

"I suppose, although the stories I have heard have it otherwise. They say he is untouchable in battle. That a sword will glance off him rather than cut—" She stopped, shaking her head at her own lack of good sense. "I am sorry," she said softly, searching Lily's suddenly pale features. "You would care if he were hurt, wouldn't you? I did not think."

"As I said, Lord Radulf is but a man and can therefore be hurt like any other man." Lily's voice was cool though her heart was thumping.

"I do not think he is 'but a man' at all," Alice teased. "And though he may not be quite the ogre I thought him, he is still rather overwhelming. What do you think he means to do tomorrow, Lily?"

Lily allowed her gaze to find her husband's dark head, now close by the king's side, and rising above all others. "I do not know," she replied softly. "I really do not know." And then wondered at the speculative look Alice was giving her. "Do you know Lady Anna Kenton?" she asked abruptly.

Alice's smooth brow furrowed. "I believe so."

"What do you know of her?"

Alice shrugged. "She is here with her husband. He fed me honeyed sweets from his own plate one evening, and told me my eyes reminded him of summer." Alice grew a little pink. "I did not believe a word of it, of course, but it was pleasant to be spoken to in such a way. I do not like his wife so well. She was once a great beauty, but I find her sly. Why, Lily?"

"She gave me my wedding dress," Lily said. "I wondered what manner of woman she is, that is all."

Alice looked surprised. "Perhaps she is more generous than I thought."

"I don't know whether it was generosity which drove her."

Alice leaned closer, curious, and then jumped back with a squeak. "Your husband returns. Adieu, Lily, until I visit you soon." And with a quick kiss she disappeared into the press of people.

Radulf viewed her departure with raised brows, and the glance he gave Lily was weary and resigned.

A flare of protective anger lit her. Was he so used to people believing the stories told of him and fleeing whenever he approached? Could they not see, as she did, the man behind the tales? Lord Kenton had called him brutal, but Lily saw only a strong brave man who served his king, a man far from the mindless killing machine mothers described to frighten their children. He was intelligent, he inspired loyalty among his men and his people, and he found humor in the most unlikely situations. And he made love unselfishly and expertly, yet with a single-mindedness that made her believe that she was the only one. He had fascinated her, captured her like a wild creature in a snare. Besotted her.

And therein lay her problem.

* * *

When they left the castle that night, Lily was glad to return to the inn. The chill night and even the inn's ale-sodden air seemed comforting after the noisy heat of King William's court. Una had hurried to her side to help her remove her heavy cloak, and it was purely by chance that Lily happened to glance up at Radulf and spied the innkeeper handing him a letter.

Radulf inspected it, turned it over, and broke the seal. He read it swiftly, and his face tightened. As if suddenly becoming aware of her watching, he looked up and caught Lily's eyes upon him. His own eyes were blacker even than usual, but there was a glitter in them that shocked her. Was it anger she saw there, or something else?

Before she could decide, he slipped the letter inside his tunic. "Bring me some wine!" he shouted, and striding to the fire, held out his hands to the warmth with an uncontrollable shiver. When Jervois joined him, Radulf leaned close so that he could speak privately with his captain. Their voices were too low to be understood, but Jervois nodded unsmilingly, his flop of fair hair fringing his green eyes.

Lily sighed. Whoever had sent the letter would remain a mystery. There was nothing to be done but retire. Una followed Lily to her room and helped to brush out her hair until it shimmered in the firelight. Lily smiled and answered the girl's questions about the evening, but her mind was far away.

The letter was important to her; she sensed it. And Radulf did not mean to tell her whom it was from and what it contained. Otherwise he would have done so already. What if it was news of Hew and his rebellion? Lily knew she must find out for herself.

She had decided to pretend she was asleep when Radulf came to bed, but one touch of his hand and she found herself turning into his arms despite herself, her mouth hot and wanton on his. He responded as fiercely, rolling over and onto her, thrusting into her body as if he couldn't wait any longer. But she was ready; nowadays she seemed always to be ready. With a groan, Lily arched against him and heard his breath ragged against her cheek.

Does he think he's holding Anna?

The thought popped into her mind, and she wondered why she tormented herself with such questions. Wasn't it enough that they were wed and that he desired her? Did she seek love?

Instantly she denied it. Even if she were foolish enough to do so, love had little place in a Norman marriage. It was a contract drawn up for reasons of wealth and power, and the children who came from it were important for the same reasons.

Love was not for her and Radulf.

It was true that all her life Lily had hoped to find a man who would complement her heart and soul, as well as her mind, even though she knew it was foolish to long for what she could not have. But in many ways she was lucky. She had a husband who seemed to value her and who would rule her lands and her people with a strong hand—she only prayed he would also be just and that he might, sometimes, be guided by her.

There was no point in howling for the moon;

she must make the best of what she had. Maybe as the years passed the ache of longing would pass, too, and she would be content.

Radulf, as if sensing her lack of concentration, covered her mouth with his, his tongue seeking to tangle with hers. His manhood thrust into her, filling her completely. She forgot Anna and her fears and doubts as the tremors of pleasure grew stronger and the world dissolved into a hot, dangerous brilliance, leaving her stranded in Radulf's strong arms.

Afterward, he slept. Lily crept from the bed and found his clothing, scattered on the rushes by the door. Pretending to fold them, she slid her hand inside the tunic and found the letter.

The firelight was fading, but there was enough flickering light to read the single page.

Beloved, I will wait for you tomorrow at the old Chapel of St. Mary between Vespers and Compline.

Her fingers shook. There was no signature, no name, yet Lily knew who had sent the message. It was Lady Anna. She wanted to rekindle the passion she had once had with Radulf. She believed that the spark was still fresh enough to do so. That she only had to send word and he would fly to her . . .

Did Radulf believe that, too? Would he go to her between the prayers of Vespers and Compline, when the sky was darkening and the air was sweet and still?

Lily shuddered. With fingers that were suddenly nerveless, she pushed the letter back into the pile of clothing.

What she had feared had come to pass. Radulf was going to seek out his old love, and leave his new wife behind.

Chapter 13

The following morning, Lily woke blearily to the smell of fresh baked bread and Una's voice urging her to get up.

"Lady, lady, Lord Radulf has ordered you be ready this instant!"

Lily sat up, her loose hair tangled and hampering her movements. "Ready for what?" she demanded, her voice husky from sleep.

"Lord Radulf wouldn't say and I wouldn't dare to ask."

It had taken Lily a long time to get to sleep. She had kept thinking of the letter she had removed from Radulf's tunic. *Beloved.* She could no longer pretend her husband's strange behavior over Lady Anna Kenton was anything other than love.

She tried to rationalize it. Other husbands dallied with other women; it meant nothing. Powerful men often married with their heads and did not expect to find physical satisfaction with their wives, so they looked elsewhere. Why should she fret over such a commonplace event?

And yet this was different. Radulf and Lily found infinite physical satisfaction with each other. Lady Anna was not a lowbred whore, she was the wife of a rich and important lord. And Radulf, so strong and indefatigable, had seemed suddenly weak before her.

Lily did not doubt that he would go to St. Mary's Chapel. She shivered and pressed suddenly damp palms against the bedcoverings. Why was this happening? It was ridiculous; she had no time for it. She should be considering how, in her new position as Radulf's wife, she could best help her people. She needed to be as she once was: calm and cold, using her situation to maximum benefit. Why could she not turn herself back into the frozen woman she used to be when she was wed to Vorgen? Where had that woman gone?

Instead she had lain awake all night, tossing and turning and thinking of Radulf. She had raged and bitten back tears, all because the husband who had forced her into a marriage she swore she didn't want, had dared to love another!

She only knew that if he did turn to Lady Anna, she would not be able to bear it.

Lily had had to live alone for so long—there were her people, of course, but that was different. She had played Vorgen's cold wife, she had accepted Hew's perfidy. She had run for her life, hiding like a deer in the forest, and shivering with her loneliness. And then Radulf had found her.

He was like a huge, roaring fire in a room that had always previously been icy cold. The heat, the attraction drew her closer, despite her mind telling her it was wrong, that it was a trick, that the fire could be extinguished just as quickly as it had been lit. But instead of listening to good sense, she had held out her hands, she had crept nearer and nearer. The warmth flushed her face and softened her rigid limbs, she grew drowsy and unprepared. She cared only for the flames. She cared only for Radulf.

He had sapped her of her strength and purpose.

Now he was going to succeed where both Vorgen and Hew had failed.

He was going to break her.

"Lady!" Una was all but jumping up and down. "You must rise!"

Lily gave a deep, heartfelt sigh and reluctantly climbed out of her warm cocoon. Once again Una had worked miracles with her limited wardrobe, and her clothing was sponged and pressed. She splashed water on her face before dressing, then twisted her hair over one shoulder before opening the door into the common room.

As Una had forewarned her, Radulf was waiting.

As always, the sight of him burst upon her senses, no matter how prepared she had thought herself, bringing warm color to her cheeks and sending her pulses into a stuttering flurry. He was striding up and down the room, making his men nervous, but at the sound of the door opening he turned to face Lily. He gave her his blackest frown as he came toward her. She rearranged her face into an expression of calm disinterest.

It was not easy to appear disinterested when the man approaching her was so physically attractive. Those wide shoulders, that strong torso, the lean hips and long, well-muscled legs, those dark piercing eyes and the sensual mouth.

Inside, Lily trembled. Truly, she was besotted.

"Come, lady, do not tarry," Radulf growled.

"I am not tarrying, my lord," Lily retorted coldly. "Where do you take me?"

He must have read the flare of doubt in her eyes, although she tried hard to conceal it. There had been too many journeys of late, and none of them pleasant. His hand closed over her shoulder, fingers warm and firm and comforting. Lily resisted the urge to relax into his strength.

"Nay, lady, 'tis nothing to concern you. I intend to buy you materials for new clothing. The wife of the King's Sword should not feel shame in the presence of her inferiors."

Lily's eyes flashed. *"Feel shame?"* she bristled. " 'Tis not my fault if I am in rags, 'tis yours! You have harried me from one hiding place to another for weeks, and then dragged me across the countryside to York. Should I have had gowns of silk for such a life? It would be better I wore sackcloth!"

Radulf laughed, his dark eyes alight with humor.

"And when someone gives me a fine gown you burn it!"

The smile wiped from his face, Radulf glared down at her, pressing closer so that she smelled the clean, male scent of him and saw the dark shadow on his clean-shaven jaw. She began to feel breathless. Had she gone too far?

"Have a care, lady. I may change my mind about your new clothing."

Lily tossed her head, pretending not to care. "As you will, Radulf. If William the Conqueror asks why I am still wearing rags, I will tell him it's because Radulf mislikes my conversation."

He looked at her a moment longer and then snorted. "He is your king, too, lady, whether you will it or not. Best accept the defeat. The Normans rule here now."

Lily's eyes flared. "Oh, I accept defeat, Radulf. I will even persuade my people to accept their conquerors as their rulers. I can give you my mind, my powers of reason—but my heart is still my own, and in my heart the Normans will forever be interlopers in my father's land."

There was a silence so deep, it had a presence of its own. Radulf's men held their breath and awaited their leader's response. Again, he surprised her.

"Well said, lady. You are proud, and I will take what you offer." He reached for her hand, and all she could think was how well it fitted to his. "Come, now. The horses are waiting, and I have much to do."

York sparkled from an early morning shower. The streets were clean, washed free of their habitual dirt and refuse, and water ran through the lanes, draining away towards the swollen Ouse. By the time Radulf's party set out the rain clouds were already clearing, leaving a soft blue sky and a warm yellow sun. Builders were up and working about the city, constructing the stone edifices commissioned by the Normans.

The Normans were great builders, and they built to last. As well as William's two castles, a great church was taking shape, and with it, many smaller and less important buildings. There was a sense of change in the air; the Normans were there and they had come to stay. Radulf was right in that, thought Lily. She must accept; there was no going back.

York's narrow, twisting streets were filled with various tradesmen and those buying from them. The city had always been a port, and therefore much of its trade, and new citizens, arrived from other countries. York had swallowed them up without fuss. Many of those citizens turned now to stare at Lily and her entourage. She supposed some of them knew who she was; certainly many of them would know the great Radulf.

And fear him.

Lily glanced sideways and thought that he did look rather fearsome in his chain mail tunic, his great sword strapped at his side. Too little sleep gave his face a certain pallor and caused gray shadows in the hollows under his eyes, and he looked both grim and dangerous. Yes, Lily could see that many would fear him.

But to Lily he was the man who held her warm and safe in his arms at night, whose wonderful mouth made her sob with pleasure, and whose dark eyes evinced a hundred years of weary experience. Sometimes the need to reach out and soothe him was well nigh unstoppable.

In the beginning, Lily had prevented herself from doing so by remembering that Radulf was her enemy. Then, when he discovered her secret, she had been too angry. Now, she reminded herself that he loved another, and that although he welcomed her body, he would not want more from her.

Irritably, Lily thrust aside her unhappy

thoughts and found that Radulf had turned to look at her. He raised his brows when she simply stared back. "Is there something that catches your eye, lady?"

Lily shook her head. What could she say? Radulf had an appointment before Compline with someone else. Even if she wanted to, she would not risk her pride by revealing her softer feelings toward him.

Maybe pride was all she had left.

"This is the place." Radulf drew up, and his men surrounded them. The stout wooden building before them was of two stories: a storage area secured by heavy doors onto the street and living quarters above. There was a bulky cart drawn up to one side and several men unloading. One of them, a thin streak of a man, started toward Radulf and his party, his rich yellow tunic proclaiming him one of York's wealthy merchants and a Jew.

"Lord Radulf!" He bowed so low he threatened to scrape the ground. "You do me great honor!"

Radulf nodded somberly but amusement for the extravagant welcome made his eyes gleam.

"You have come to buy, my lord? I am Jacob, and you are in luck. This day a ship has arrived from Flanders with silks and linens and fine wools, our own good English wool made into cloth. What is it you wish to see?" His eyes were bright and eager, and Lily was certain they noted how his list of wares made her heart beat faster. It was long since she had chosen from fine cloth. Despite her determination to remain aloof, she gave Radulf a hungry glance.

"We wish to see everything," Radulf replied

mildly. "And my lady may have whatever pleases her."

Jacob's eyes popped. "You are generous indeed, Lord Radulf! My lady!" He gave Lily an equally low bow, his gaze sweeping over her on the way down and then again as he rose, taking in her coloring, size, and measurements. "My lady's beauty is beyond price," he said smoothly. "I doubt any of my wares could match it."

Radulf retorted with a hint of impatience. "Show us what you have anyway."

Determining Radulf had reached his limit where flattery was concerned, Jacob clapped his hands and the heavy wooden doors of his establishment were swung open. Radulf dismounted and lifted Lily to the ground beside him. "He considers me a fool now," he murmured in her ear. "No sensible man allows a woman to dictate the opening and closing of his purse."

Before Lily could answer, Jacob had returned, leading them inside.

The interior had an exotic scent, musky and heavy, like a foreign land. Jacob unfastened the shutters on his windows, letting in the sunlight. He began to choose bolts of cloth, unwrapping them from their protective coverings and rolling them out on the long tables set beneath the windows.

Wools in rich shades of blue, red, and green, and a roll of pure white, the most difficult of all to obtain. Linens, fine and soft to the touch, and silks that were shot through with a myriad of colors wherever the sun touched them. And then Jacob spread out a bolt of velvet in a red so deep and luscious, it made Lily gasp.

Vorgen had never cared what she wore, and certainly he had never bought her gifts. To him, her importance was in being the heiress to her father's lands and the daughter of a Viking princess.

It is just that Radulf does not want his wife to shame him by appearing in rags, Lily reminded herself.

"How many new gowns will I need, my lord?" she asked, struggling to keep her voice indifferent. "One, two, or three?"

Radulf was watching her, but his face was in shadow, hidden by the brilliance of the day framed by the open doors behind him. "As many as you wish," he said carelessly. "I am a wealthy man, Lady Wilfreda. Let our friend here decide for you. I can see he is well practiced at his craft. Only the rich of York can afford him, and he knows what is best for them."

Lily nodded slowly, her eyes very wide, hiding her confusion. Why was he being so generous? Did he feel guilty because of Lady Anna?

"Very well, my lord," she whispered. "I will be guided by him."

Jacob swallowed, but did not allow his shock to silence him for long. "The blue wool, certainly, my lady, and this fine linen to go beneath it."

He continued pointing to various rolls of cloth, and the list grew until he came to the red velvet, so deep it was almost purple. "My lady would look very fair in a gown of this," he said, a hint of uncertainty in his voice. Which meant, thought Lily, the price was exorbitant.

She began to shake her head, but Radulf spoke first. "Then we must have the red, Jacob." He laughed at the amazed look Lily threw him. "You will indeed look very fair, lady," he mocked. And then, leaning closer, his breath tickling her ear,

"Almost as fair as you do when I have you naked in my arms."

She turned her head sharply, finding his face almost touching hers. Briefly she felt herself to be drowning in the darkness of his eyes, and then one of York's church bells rang, loud and strident in the still, warm air, and the moment was gone.

The bell seemed to remind Radulf of other, more pressing matters. He shifted restlessly. "We have finished for now," he said. Arrangements were made for the materials to be delivered and Jacob was given the direction of the inn. Leaving the man goggle-eyed at his good fortune, Radulf strode outside where his men were gathered, his grip on Lily forcing her to quicken her pace.

Correctly reading his lord's expression, Jervois hurried to remount, calling to the others to make haste. The sun glinted off their chain mail and the puddles in the street. Radulf led them at a brisk pace, as though he had something to outrun. Or, thought Lily miserably, as if he had some urgent appointment.

The memory instantly spoiled her naive pleasure in her new garments. Of what use were lovely new clothes when the man she wanted to admire her, admired another?

Radulf was angry, and that anger was directed at himself. What had he hoped to achieve by heaping such generosity upon Lily? Did he think she would turn to him with dazzled eyes and fling herself into his arms? She already gave him her body willingly; what else did he want?

The question startled him, and he twitched his shoulders uncomfortably. *You are a fool, Radulf,* he thought bitterly. *You are your father all over again. You buy the girl pretty clothes, shower her with riches, and think that will endear you to her. Instead she will want more and more, and in the end, when you have no more to give her, she will betray you with another who can.*

She hates you, face the truth, and hates you all the more for enslaving her body to yours. She is a Viking temptress, a she-devil; she destroyed Vorgen. Beware!

But he couldn't quite believe it. There had been an expression in her eyes when he ordered the red velvet, as though she were touched beyond words. It had been enough to send his heart soaring, until reality crashed him back to earth. Did he really want a wife who valued him only for the pretty baubles he could give her?

When they reached the inn, Radulf swung Lily down without thinking. Her hair, which she had been unable to plait because of their earlier haste, spilled free from her cloak. Before he could stop himself, Radulf reached out and took a strand between his fingers and thumb, fascinated by the look and feel of it even as he despaired at his own weakness.

Lily cleared her throat, her hands clasped tightly together. "Thank you, my lord; you are very generous."

Radulf cocked an eyebrow, measuring her words. She appeared uneasy, as if gratitude was not something with which she was familiar. "A wealthy man does not lose much by being generous. You are my wife, Lily. Besides, I have not finished yet. I will take a house here in York, and you will choose your servants."

He had not called her Lily of late, preferring the

more formal Lady Wilfreda or lady. And it was this, as much as his statement about the house and servants, that undid her. Lily's heart gave an unexpected jolt, and a shudder ran through her. She would have turned away, but Radulf caught her chin in his strong fingers and forced it up again, so he could see into her eyes. They were glittering with unshed tears.

Some emotion lit his own eyes, surprise maybe, or suspicion. He frowned. "You are unhappy?" he demanded, his voice sharp.

Lily bit her trembling lip and shook her head, struggling to control her uncharacteristic display. "No, my lord," she replied huskily. "I am very happy."

He frowned a moment longer, trying to pierce the secrets in her stormy eyes. "We are wed now. We must both make the best of it." Impatience flared in his face. "Come. You are tired and this nonsense has made me hungry."

Suddenly Lily decided she would not sit idly by while Radulf went off to meet Lady Anna. She would follow him and watch, and then she would know exactly what she was up against. Surely that was only good sense? A soldier going into battle spied out the land on which he would fight, and the enemy he would face. So would she.

After their meal, each member of Radulf's party became immersed in his or her own affairs. For the men, there were weapons and equipment to inspect and clean and repair, as well as horses to groom. All those little matters upon which their lives might depend. Radulf and Jervois discussed at length the possible site for the northern castle they must build. Jervois was prepared to remain in the north and oversee the work after it had begun, which would allow Radulf to return to Crevitch for a brief time and check on matters there.

Lily found solace in borrowing needle and thread from Una and mending any item of clothing which required her attention. The mundane task allowed her to concentrate her thoughts. She had decided upon a plan for following Radulf, but it would require good luck and cunning in equal measure.

There was one thing of which she was certain: Radulf would never expect her to spy on him. Norman wives did not question their husbands, and as far as Radulf was concerned, the rebellious she-devil was now a Norman wife.

We are wed now. We must make the best of it.

Must they? Perhaps a Norman wife would sit back while her husband made love to another woman, but Lily was half Viking and half English, proud and determined. Following him was the sensible thing to do. In her precarious position, she could not afford to sit by and lose the only thing that bound Radulf to her; she could not afford to give that up to another woman. If she saw for herself, heard for herself, perhaps she could find a way to win him back to her side.

So Lily had spoken privately to Una soon after their return to the inn.

Una had been surprised at the request made of her and gave Lily a suspicious look.

"You say you want me to deliver a message to this Alice of Rennoc, lady? Why don't you ask your lord's men to deliver it? I do not have a horse to carry me or Lord Radulf's colors to see me past any obstacles."

Lily could not rely upon Radulf to see the urgency of the matter, and she did not want to stir his curiosity. "Please, Una, I will reward you well. All you have to do is go to Alice of Rennoc's uncle's house, and tell her that Lily wishes her to visit. Only it must seem as if it is her own idea, and she is to bring a horse and a manservant who knows the city well. Can you remember all that? Please, Una. You have been a friend to me during my difficult times; do this last thing."

Una shifted uneasily, but in truth she would have done whatever Lily asked of her. Since Radulf and his lady had come to her father's inn she had experienced life among the great ones, and her new knowledge was heady indeed. But she had also developed a true loyalty and affection for Lily.

"I'll deliver the message as you say, my lady."

Lily had sighed in relief. "That is good, Una. Thank you with all my heart."

God willing, her plan could now go ahead. It was simple enough: she would go to the meeting place and wait there. The difficult bit would be getting to the meeting place, and to pass unseen through the streets of York, she must assume another person's identity. If she was Lady Wilfreda, Jervois would not allow her out of the inn. She could play the part of Una, but she did not fancy traipsing on foot in the dark to a place she did not know. Besides, Una's lowly position made her vulnerable to Radulf's anger and possible punishment.

Alice of Rennoc would be better.

After Una had gone to do her bidding, Lily took a deep breath and tried to relax. Her fingers moved busily with her sewing; her head was bowed. To any watchers she must appear totally unthreatening. It would never do for Radulf to grow suspicious, and he seemed able to read her so well. She took another deep breath. It was as if his dark gaze could pierce her very soul . . .

"My lady, that is the fifth time you have sighed. Your thoughts must be heavy indeed."

Lily looked up, startled. Jervois gave her a questioning smile, and Lily hastily smiled in return. "If I really have sighed that many times, then it must indeed seem so. But I was only thinking of . . . of things past. There is sadness enough in such thoughts to make me sigh."

He nodded. Although he was clearly Radulf's man, Lily had always found Jervois approachable and sympathetic.

"Surely you have little to sigh over at present, lady. Lord Radulf has made that rogue Jacob a rich man with his attention to your attire."

Lily laughed in pure feminine delight. "I will be the envy of all other women!"

Jervois's eyes lit in appreciation. "And Lord Radulf will be the envy of all men."

Immediately her animation vanished, and the cool gray eyes surveyed him consideringly. "You are kind, Jervois, yet I do not believe I am quite what Radulf sought in a wife. Remember, he was ordered to marry me. There must be many women far prettier and far richer than I who would have climbed atop each other to become Radulf's wife."

Anna, for one. And tonight he goes to meet her. And

I will be there to see the truth. Aye, and I will sigh then . . .

Jervois looked evasive. He lowered his voice. "I think you wrong Radulf, lady, and undervalue yourself. King's order or no, Radulf would not have wed you if he did not want to. Radulf rarely does anything he does not want to do."

But Lily did not hear him.

She was looking past Jervois toward the door of the inn and the silhouette of the person who had just entered—Alice's small, curvy form. Jervois turned to see what she was looking at. For a moment he gazed wonderingly at those small but voluptuous curves. He had not forgotten Alice of Rennoc, and he straightened with a new alertness as the girl approached. Her hair was like summer wheat and her eyes as blue as the sky, a knowing twinkle in their depths.

Lily rose quickly to her feet and, with a happy smile of greeting, hurried to meet her friend. Jervois followed her slowly, almost against his will.

"I hope you have a good reason for luring me into the ogre's den," Alice murmured into her ear as she hugged Lily. In return Lily gave her a reassuring squeeze. Alice's gaze lifted beyond Lily, and her expression stilled.

Lily, surprised by the look on her face, turned to see Jervois bow his fair head. "This is Jervois, Alice, my lord's captain. Jervois, this is Alice of Rennoc."

Jervois's green eyes flared with rare humor. "We have met," he murmured, but his voice was strange.

"Yes." Color was further heightening Alice's already bright cheeks. She smoothed the skirts of the green gown she wore, and fiddled with the knot of her girdle, while Jervois fixed her with his serious stare and looked more than a little seasick.

Startled, Lily wondered if this was how she appeared when she was with Radulf. Jesu, she hoped not!

"Lady?" The familiar husky growl cleared all question of Jervois and Alice from Lily's mind. Taking Alice's warm hand in her own, she made her way unhurriedly toward the fireplace, where Radulf sat polishing the long, lethal blade of his sword.

He watched her come, his black eyes dancing with the flames. His face was impassive as Alice made her curtsy and stammered some excuse about passing and thinking Lily might be home.

"Do you often go about York on your own, lady?" he asked her mildly.

"I have one of my uncle's servants with me, my lord. He is outside tending my horse."

Radulf nodded and glanced to Lily, but as usual her eyes were cool and unreadable. He shrugged and turned back to his sword, his long fingers slow and thorough as he oiled the finely wrought steel.

"Come Alice," Lily said in a light voice. "We will go to my chamber, where we can speak in private. I am sure Lord Radulf and his men do not want to hear the frivolous chatter of women."

Radulf snorted a laugh, but Lily had already turned away, Alice close behind her. Lily shut the door to the bedchamber behind them and immediately felt better. As well as reducing the noise from so many men, it weakened the constant tension of Radulf's penetrating gaze.

She took a deep, calming breath.

"I hope you mean to tell me what this is all about," Alice said, plopping down onto the straw-filled mattress. "My uncle is from home or I would not have been able to come. Your servant was very mysterious, Lily."

Lily sat by Alice's side. The girl's color was still high, and now her blue eyes shone with curiosity.

"I am going to ask something of you," Lily began. "I will be honest. It may be dangerous and you may feel the might of Radulf's anger, and believe me, he can be very angry indeed. But mostly, if I am discovered, he will be angry with me. In fact he will probably forget about you altogether, Alice."

Alice's blue eyes had grown bigger and she leaned forward in breathless silence.

"I want to take your place when you leave the inn. I will become Alice of Rennoc and you will stay here in my bedchamber and pretend you are me. I've thought about it, and if you pretend to be unwell, then no one will interfere with you."

"Oh, Lily, do you mean to escape?" Alice cried out in dismay.

Startled, Lily pressed her fingers to her friend's lips and looked nervously to the door. In truth, escape had not entered her head. All she had thought of was Radulf and Lady Anna. Now that Alice had brought the subject up, she dismissed it. Where would she go? Who would hide her? And if she did run, what would become of her people?

Besides, how could she leave Radulf when all she wanted to do was stay?

"No, I don't mean to escape," Lily said, when it was clear no one had heard Alice's voice in the other room. "I need to follow Lord Radulf, and it has nothing to do with politics, Alice. It is a personal matter. He is going to meet someone and I wish to follow him and . . . and watch him."

Alice twitched her skirts. "I see," she said, and from the tone of her voice Lily sensed that she did. After a moment Alice covered her hand, squeezing it comfortingly.

"Radulf is a great lord, Lily. Great lords do not have to cleave to one woman. Even I know that, and I am still a maid. There is no place for jealousy in the lives of such as Radulf."

Lily's back stiffened. "I am not jealous," she retorted sharply. "I merely want to see the woman for myself, and read their feelings for each other by their actions. A wife needs to know these things if she is to survive in marriage, particularly if she is an English woman married to a Norman lord."

Alice's eyes softened with sympathy. "What you say is all very sensible, Lily, but when I met Lord Radulf at the castle he seemed more than fond of you. Why should he want another woman?"

Lily stared and then gave a high laugh. "Ah no, Alice, you are wrong. Radulf is a passionate and earthy man, and what you saw between us was but his lust. But you are a maid still and I will say no more."

Alice flushed and shrugged one shoulder. "Maybe I am ignorant, but it seemed he had an affection for you."

Lily dismissed her friend's comment as innocence and maybe wishful thinking. She rose to her feet and began to pace up and down the narrow room. Her heart was thudding anxiously inside her and she could no longer keep still. "I do not say these things lightly or to upset you, Alice. Please, will you help me?"

Alice hesitated and then gave an impish smile. "Yes, I will. But if Radulf finds out, have no doubt that I will lay the blame squarely on your head, Lily. Despite what you believe to be my 'ignorance,' I feel sure he will restrain himself with you, whereas he may well turn me over his knee!"

Lily laughed softly and reached out to take Alice's hand. "Thank you. I am in your debt. If there is ever anything I can do for you . . ."

Alice's smile wavered. "You can tell me why it is that all the men I like are unsuitable."

Lily frowned. "Do you mean Jervois, Alice?"

The girl flicked her a glance and then sighed. "He is rather nice, is he not?"

"He has always been so to me. He is the son of a mercenary, I believe; Radulf relies on him a great deal."

Alice's eyes brightened. "Well, Radulf is rich, so there is a start! I have to marry a rich man, Lily. My father and uncle would never agree to anything less, but all the wealthy men I have met, I do not like."

Lily clasped her friend's hand. There was little she could say in comfort. In all probability Alice would marry a man she merely tolerated, at best. Being practical, Alice would make the best of it. Perhaps that was better than the risk of being wed to a man you loved and who did not love you. At least then you would be spared the heartache.

Love—now *there* was a dangerous word. Lily shivered as if she was cold.

Radulf stared into the flames, a mug of ale in his hands. Soon he would leave for his assignation at St. Mary's Chapel—to meet the Lady Anna, that lovely viper. That very persuasive viper.

He wondered suddenly if Lord Kenton knew of the meeting, then dismissed the thought. Kenton might be jealous but he was a fool—he must be, to have wed Anna. Or perhaps he was in love with her as Radulf had once been. That blind, heedless love that concealed the beloved's faults behind a screen of sickly-sweet perfection.

Radulf blinked down at the ale mug and saw that his fingers were clamped so hard about it that his knuckles were white and the soft metal had dented. Carefully, methodically, he straightened his fingers one by one. This was not a good sign. If his very thoughts could arouse such anger, would he be able to keep his temper when he met her face to face?

He *would* keep his temper, because he had to. He would meet her and tell her that it was over. Tell her in a way that even someone as self-obsessed as she would understand and accept. For much of his adult life he had carried this guilt and pain within him, and half of it was rightly Anna's. He was tired of the burden.

Perhaps it was finally time to take it out, look at it, and then put it away forever.

Radulf transferred his fingers to his eyes, pressing at the ache behind them. His head throbbed and he did not want to go out in the chill night. He would much prefer to spend the evening in Lily's bedchamber. Her body welcomed him even if she did not, but one day, he vowed, he would slide under the shield of her cool gray gaze, and make her his captive.

He was already *her* captive, or near enough, though she didn't know it. He wanted her more now than he had in the beginning. God help him if she ever found out. The great Radulf, her slave! How she would despise him . . .

"My lord?" It was Jervois, his voice a respectful murmur. "The time approaches."

Radulf looked up. Jervois was in his confidence. His captain knew him as well as Lord Henry, maybe better, for they had spent more time together. They had fought together, seen each other's weaknesses and strengths. He had trusted Jervois with his life on more than one occasion.

"Where is my wife?"

Jervois showed no surprise at the sharpness of the question. "She is in her chamber with the servant girl. Do you wish me to bring her to you?"

"And the other . . . Alice. Where is she?"

"She has gone, my lord. She left with her servant a while ago."

Jervois had seen only Alice's back as she slipped through the door. Her veil had been wrapped modestly about her head and throat, her head had been bowed. He had called out a farewell to her, and then shaken his head impatiently when she didn't answer.

Had her heart, too, beat a little faster when their eyes met?

But what was the point in such thoughts? He

was a mercenary, to be bought and paid for. Alice of Rennoc would not consider such a man seriously. Women had always seemed like another country entirely to Jervois, and one he was far from certain he wished to explore. Now he had seen one that he liked, but she was not for him.

"I would I did not have to leave," Radulf began in a low, weary voice, "but I have no choice but to see an end to this matter once and for all. You will remain here to guard my lady."

That brought Jervois's head up with a jerk. "But my lord, you do not mean to go alone!"

"I do not fear a trick, but no, I will not go alone. I will take four of the men and they can wait for me nearby. Make your choice and tell them to be ready."

Jervois hovered uneasily. "You have many enemies, lord."

Radulf's eyes were full of grim humor. "That may well be so, Jervois, but I am immortal, am I not?"

Jervois refused to smile. "Others may believe the legends, but I know you are but a man, my lord, and a man can be killed. What would become of your lady wife then? The king would marry her to another, perhaps one not so inclined to cosset her as you do."

Radulf hesitated, and then nodded, clapping a hand on Jervois's shoulder. "Aye, you are right as always, my careful friend. I will take heed." He turned toward Lily's bedchamber, taking a couple of steps toward the door before stopping. No. It was better he say nothing to Lily. She had an uncanny knack of reading his moods and he did not want to answer her questions now. He would see her when he returned. Perhaps he would even explain to her what he had done.

Or perhaps not.

With a deep breath, Radulf turned away from the bedchamber and toward the inn door.

Chapter 14

⁓◟◞◟◞⁓

Seated upon Alice's docile gelding with her cloak wrapped tightly about her, Lily could have been any York housewife making her way home after staying too late at the house of a friend or relative. Or she might be taken for a foolish young maiden keeping a secret assignation. The last was not far from the truth, except that it was not *her* assignation.

It had been much easier than she thought. Alice's clothing fit her well enough, although Una had had to lower the hem, which left a narrow band of a deeper color. But the men didn't notice that; they rarely looked at a woman's feet. Jervois had called a farewell, but Lily had ignored him. Radulf had not spoken at all, and although she had been sure she felt two burning holes in her back where his eyes were fixed, everything had gone to plan.

A splatter of rain rattled upon the road and a

droplet splashed against her cheek. The servant, his tangled beard and long hair proclaiming his non-Norman origins, ran before her, perfectly comfortable in his role as guide. He had listened with eyes averted as Lily told him where he was to take her. "I know it, lady," he had assured her.

Lily had smiled her thanks and felt a stab of pity for the man. There was an ugly brand on his cheek, which had puckered the skin and scarred him badly. Such cruel marks were the Normans' way of accounting for their property.

If Radulf should discover her, she would *not* allow him to punish this poor man. This excursion was her idea and hers alone. Not that she expected to be caught. All she had to do was wait for Radulf, watch his meeting with Lady Anna, and then . . . Well, then she would most probably go back to the inn and sob herself to sleep. But at least she would *know*.

She shivered suddenly in the damp air. The warm day had stirred up a storm that brought early darkness. It still hung about the city, rumbling bad-temperedly, with the occasional flash of lightning. She might regain her bed tonight soaked to the skin, but at least the bad weather ensured the streets were empty . . . and safe. Lily and her servant met not a single soul as they traversed York.

Several times tonight, Lily had asked herself why she was doing this. Why was she putting herself, and possibly others, in danger of Radulf's retribution? The answer was simple and always the same: she had to know. Whatever the cost.

"Here 'tis, lady," the servant mumbled. He flicked a sideways glance toward a curving lane, its edges hidden by shadows. At the far end squatted a small building—the chapel. A providential flash of lightning showed a closed door and dark windows. All was still and silent. Lily turned the horse down the lane, just as thunder roared above them and the heavens opened in flood.

Lily bent forward to murmur soothing words to the gelding as she glanced quickly about, searching for a good vantage point. A deserted wooden cottage looked promising—there were many such places in York, left to rot by those fleeing from various waves of invaders. The rain poured down upon Lily and she wiped a hand across her eyes, blinking, blinded.

If she did not find shelter soon she would be drowned, she thought irritably. The servant had followed her, his thin shoes sinking in the mud, and now stood at her side, muttering English curses. Shielding her face, Lily dismounted and pulled the gelding through the cottage doorway. The air there was heavy with decay, the smell of abandoned hope. The roof thatch had partially fallen in and the rain hammered down.

Lily found what shelter she could, the servant huddling close by. His face was a white blur in the darkness, and although Lily was not afraid, he was. She felt his fear, acrid and cold, when he brushed against her shoulder in the confined space.

"You can go home now," she shouted above the rain. "Or better still, go back to the inn and find Una. She will feed you while you wait for my return. Then you may escort your lady home."

He hesitated, plainly torn between what he knew was his duty, and his terror at being in such a place and the consequences it might bring down upon him.

"Go," Lily insisted, touching his arm gently. "I do not need you now."

When the servant had gone, stumbling over some fallen timbers in his haste, Lily stood alone and listened to the rain. She was truly on her own now. Just as she had been on her own before Grimswade. Hiding, running, a vixen pursued by hounds; alone, abandoned, in a changing world. Standing there now in the summer storm, Lily felt as if nothing had really changed. Radulf might never have been. A dream, that was all it was.

Slowly the rain began to ease. It must be near Compline now, she decided, just as a frog started up a noisy song nearby. The gelding trembled, and as Lily reached to soothe him, she caught the sound of horses' hooves, coming closer.

Her heart pounding, she moved to peer through a dark split in the wall, but all she could see was the white cloud of her own breath. The horses had drawn to a halt at the head of the lane, and she could hear the faint shout of voices, of instructions given. And then a single horse clattered out of the streaky darkness, slowing as it approached the chapel. It circled cautiously as its rider surveyed his surroundings. He was tall, made bulky with his chain mail, and his head was otter sleek because of the steel helmet.

Radulf. Lily knew it by his spare, confident movements as much as by the size and shape of him. He was as familiar to her as herself. She pressed her palms against the damp wood on either side of her peephole, and heard the soft groan of unstable timbers. Alice's gelding, hearing and smelling the other horses, whickered softly.

"Hush," Lily murmured. "Soft now."

More sounds, more horses approaching, a sharp whinny. Lily stiffened and watched as Radulf turned to face the new arrivals. At the head of the lane there came the deadly scrape of swords leaving their scabbards, and then a female voice cried out, "Hold!" A moment later a lone rider passed Lily's cottage, moving to join Radulf.

That it was a woman was plain enough, despite the all-covering cloak and hood. As she reached Radulf she tossed back her hood and for a moment was lit up by a flicker of distant lightning. It was Anna, and she was smiling.

"Radulf!" she cried, her melodious voice shot through with triumph. Lady Anna's mount tossed its head uneasily, but she urged it closer to Radulf's stallion. "I knew you would come!"

"Aye, I am here." Radulf's husky voice was more difficult to hear.

Lily's eyes widened. He did not sound like a lover. There was anger in his voice, and steel. Something like hope stirred within Lily, her breath quickening as she pressed closer to the wall.

Lady Anna looked up at the sky, from which soft rain still fell. "Is the chapel open?"

"It appears not, but there will be shelter by the wall." Radulf dismounted, and reached up to help her down. She leaned into his arms, her body sliding against his as her feet touched ground. Radulf stepped back so quickly she all but fell, her hand going to his arm and fastening there.

She laughed. "You could not stay away, my

Radulf," she said, still supremely confident. "You remember, just as I do. I have never forgotten."

Radulf stared down at her, and Lily could see how stiff his shoulders had become, how straight his back. She ached with his tension, his pain. Did he struggle against the need to pull the Lady Anna into his arms? To kiss her fiercely and wildly and make up for all the years they had lost?

Hope dwindled once more.

"There is shelter over here," he said, and turned toward the chapel. Anna's hand slipped from his arm and hung a moment in space, irresolute; then she followed meekly to the place beneath the eaves. They moved together, the shadows joining them, concealing them. Their voices were now too low to be heard, for the rain had grown heavy again, drumming furiously on the roof.

Lily groaned in frustration. With all that she had done, now she could not hear what they were saying! Yet was there any need to hear, when Radulf leaned so close to Anna and her face was turned up to his, her body seeming to quiver with need?

They had been lovers and would be again. Lily's marriage would be an empty sham, just as it had been with Vorgen. But worse, because all she and Radulf had was desire, and when that desire began to fade—it might have done so already—Lily would have nothing. Anna held his heart and had no intention of releasing it.

After what seemed a long time, Lady Anna moved away from the wall. She walked toward her mount with a quick, hurrying step and even before Radulf could follow her, was reaching toward the saddle. He caught her up and tossed her easily into her seat. She clung there, head bowed, obviously under the influence of some great emotion.

"You say you have never forgotten," Radulf said, raising his voice above the rain. "I wish to God I could!"

There was agony in his words, and it twisted inside Lily. Her hands fell limp to her sides. If Radulf loved the woman so much, so unbearably, then there truly was no hope. She must accept that he would never be hers.

Anna lifted her head and stared at the man at her side, and then she snatched up the reins. She said something too low for Lily to hear. A vow perhaps, a promise for tomorrow? And then Radulf also spoke, but now the rain was much too heavy and his words were inaudible. He seemed to speak for a long time.

A tear slipped down Lily's cheek, tasting salty against her lips. She had reached up to wipe it away when Anna gave a single, almost inhuman cry. Shocked, shaking, Lily pressed her hands to her mouth, eyes fixed to the scene unfolding before her.

Anna dragged up the reins, forcing her horse onto its back legs. Lily gasped, thinking that the emotion had been too great for her and that she meant to ride wildly from the scene. But no, Anna gave another cry and dug her heels viciously into her horse's sides. It sprang forward, straight at Radulf.

He leaped to the side, probably saving his life, but the horse still knocked against his shoulder. He was spun around by the force, falling to the ground. Lily screamed and, stumbling over fallen debris and splashing through the downpour, ran out of the cottage.

Anna had wheeled her mount around. Another lightning flash showed her face. Her lips were drawn back, her jaw rigid. She clearly intended to set her horse at the prone man, to ride over the top of him.

"Radulf!" Lily cried as she picked up her skirts and sprinted.

Anna hesitated, looking around. The mounted men waiting at the head of the lane pounded to the rescue, muddying Lily as they passed. Before Anna could finish what she had begun, they had cut her off and surrounded her.

She was panting, cornered. "Let me go!" she screamed. "I am the wife of Lord Kenton and I demand you release me!"

The armed men hesitated, clearly not wanting to let her go after what they had witnessed. Then Radulf's voice rose from among them. He had struggled into a sitting position and stared up at the woman who had tried to kill him.

"Let her go. I have done with her."

Reluctantly, they released Lady Anna's reins. She took a moment to arrange her cloak. As she pulled up her hood she caught sight of Lily's bedraggled figure, standing just beyond the circle of armed men. When their eyes met, Lily had the impression that Anna might ride her down, too. Then she looked fixedly beyond Lily, her face shiny with rain and tears, and kicking the horse into a sedate trot, she rode past Lily as if she didn't exist.

"What do you here, girl?" A gruff voice spoke

in Lily's ear, a hard hand fastening on to her arm. Before she could tell him to release her, the man peered down into her face and recognized her. "Lady?" He gave voice to his bewilderment.

Lily was already shaking off his grip and brushed past him, hurrying toward where Radulf was hidden by his guard. Perhaps Anna had had some weapon! Perhaps she had struck at Radulf as she rode at him! Panicked, blinded, Lily moved the men by screaming, "Let me through!" when her fists made no impression.

They shuffled back and revealed their fallen leader.

He was still seated upon the wet ground, his back bent over awkwardly as he grasped his right shoulder with his left hand. His face shone with a pale sheen, sweat as well as rain. He was wounded. Radulf, the immortal warrior of legend, was hurt.

As Lily dropped to her knees beside him, she was more terrified than she had ever been before in her life. She wanted to touch him, to run her hands over his body, to heal him. But she was also afraid . . . afraid of what she might find.

Radulf lifted his head, his eyes dull in his pain-twisted face. He blinked, as if to clear his sight. "Lily?" he rasped. "What the devil do you here?"

Trembling, she reached out one hand and gently rested it upon his shoulder. He winced, but did not pull away. " 'Tis not like to kill me," he said with a hint of his old humor. "I've grown lax, and it serves me right. I had forgotten a woman could be as dangerous as any man."

"Is it broken?" Lily asked. Broken limbs could be mended, but often they were never as strong or straight again, and sometimes the patient took a fever or the flesh rotted inside, and death then followed. The lane seemed to swirl about her and she shivered violently.

"Lily," he murmured, and his voice seemed to come from a long way away, "what are you doing here?" Then, when she would not answer, "No, it is not broken. 'Tis out of its socket. Jervois can put it back in; he's done it twice before. 'Tis not a comfortable procedure, but I can bear it. Lily?" His voice grew anxious. "Catch her, someone, she faints!"

But Lily had no intention of fainting. "No, no, I am all right," she said, pushing away the eager hands. "I . . . we must see to Lord Radulf," she added, her voice growing more authoritative. "Help him onto his horse. We must return to the inn. But slowly, for the ride will be painful for him."

Radulf gave a laugh that turned into a groan as his men raised him to his feet. "I am used to a little discomfort, lady. I will not break."

But perhaps something in her eyes showed him what she had suffered when she saw him fall, because he gave her a long, searching look. "Did you ride here?" he asked, as if the thought had just occurred to him, and looked around him for a horse.

"Yes." She shook, bereft when he took his eyes from her. "In the cottage, hidden . . . It is Alice's."

A flare of anger lit his face, swiftly followed by resignation. "Fetch my lady's horse," he instructed, "and see her safely upon it. I do not wish to find her missing when we reach the inn. And as for you, my lady . . ." He paused, making her wait. "I will have an explanation very soon."

"You will soon be too feverish to hear it," Lily retorted with spirit.

The journey home was difficult, but no worse than many others Radulf had made in his life. And he had much to ponder. Tonight he had made a great change. He had finally opened that painful wound that he had merely prodded occasionally over the years. It had always been there, poisoning him, but tonight he had faced Anna, and the poison had spilled free.

Just now he felt too tired to be glad, but he had faced his past. It was done, over. Lady Anna was no viper, just a beautiful and selfish woman who had carelessly, heartlessly destroyed the lives of a father and his son. It was not her fault alone; Radulf accepted his portion of the blame. But soon he would be able to remember her without that familiar, grinding ache. And perhaps he would be able to remember his father without that final, shattering scene between them.

His shoulder jolted and the pain was so intense that it required all his concentration to stay in his saddle. When it had subsided and his vision had cleared, he noted Lily riding quietly at his side. She had not spoken since they began their journey. No doubt she was working at spinning a fine tale, lies tangled with just enough truth to make it plausible.

Radulf sighed. When he had first seen her standing in the rain he had thought she was a dream, some fancy of his tormented mind and throbbing body. And then he had seen that it really was Lily, and his heart had swelled with joy at the sight of her.

Until the doubts began.

Was she in league with Anna somehow? Two she-devils together? But that made no sense. Lily and Anna were not at all alike—the one so full of her own concerns and the other willing to sacrifice herself for her people. What then? And why, when she had escaped the vigilance of Jervois, had she not simply run north to the border, to her cousin Hew?

Of course, there was his threat to harm her people if she did not obey him. Lily would never abandon her people; she was not the sort of woman to abandon anyone who needed her.

Radulf shook his head. He was tired and in pain. His wife was by his side, and he did not want to think ill of her. This night's work had been for her sake as well as his own. He had wanted to free himself from his past, to face his future unfettered by those old chains.

"We will soon be there."

Her voice brought him up from the morass of his thoughts. Radulf gave a brusque nod, which made his shoulder ache again. He gritted his teeth and let the pain fill him, swallowing all else.

It was still raining gently when they reached the inn. Lily hurried to dismount, sending one of the men into the inn to fetch Jervois while she instructed the others. They did not really need instruction, but she was concerned that they would hurt Radulf and he would not say so. His face had grown paler and paler; she was sure that he would faint at any moment and was only remaining conscious because of stubborn masculine pride.

Radulf did feel dizzy and faint. His head spun

as he lowered himself from the saddle, and he had to lean heavily upon the shoulders of his men. He'd rather be drawn and quartered than faint in front of his wife. With a tremendous effort of will, Radulf pushed himself away from their support and, pulling himself up as straight as he could, walked into the inn.

The smoke made it difficult to see, and his nose twitched at the smells of confined living. It was hot, too, the fire blazing. Radulf wavered between continuing on to the wine jug he could see on a table or sinking onto the nearest bench. Jervois appeared beside him, looking almost as white and shocked as his lord.

"His shoulder has come out of its socket," Lily said briskly, before worse could be assumed. "Radulf says you have helped him with it before, Jervois."

Jervois reined in his moment of panic. "I have, lady." The words were out before it struck him that her presence in Radulf's party was wrong. "But . . . what do you outside? I . . . you were in your chamber."

Radulf shook with weak laughter. "Was she, Jervois?"

"Come, help me get him to bed," Lily cut in quickly. "Once you have dealt with him I do not think he will want to be moved again."

But the bedchamber door opened before they could reach it, and Alice's startled blue eyes peered out. When she saw Radulf supported between his men and Lily at his side, dripping and wet and white-faced, she gasped and scuttled back out of the way. Jervois shot her a furious glance as he passed but said nothing.

"Wine," Radulf gritted as he sank down onto the bed.

Jervois's tone was conspiratorial. "Best fetch it for him, lady. We have to remove his armor and clothing before I can tend his shoulder, and I fear it will hurt him a great deal."

She nodded and forced herself to turn away. Alice caught up with her at the doorway.

"What has happened? My servant said that you sent him away. How could you be so foolish, Lily?"

Lily waved one impatient hand. "There is no time for that now. Radulf is hurt."

"How was he hurt? You said it wasn't going to be dangerous."

"It wasn't . . . at least . . . I can't answer you now. I thank you, though, with all my heart. If I had not been there . . ." And she shuddered violently.

"Lily? Come, sit down. You are as much in need of wine as Radulf!"

"Lady?" Jervois said, looking less than his usual steady self. "The wine."

Lily took a breath and nodded. "Yes. I will fetch it immediately."

When she had gone, Jervois turned his green eyes on Alice. The girl pretended to be unaware, but there was a flush in her cheeks and her mouth was all pursed up. He knew he should be angry— he *was* angry—but something in her face made him want to take her in his arms and kiss her rather than rant at her.

"Lady Alice," he began in his sternest voice.

"Oh, all right." She turned and looked him straight in the eye. "Lily needed my help, and I gave it to her. I am sorry if I deceived you, Captain

Jervois, but it was not done with any intention of causing harm."

"And yet Lord Radulf is hurt and his lady was also in danger. They have enemies, a great many enemies, even here in York."

Alice appeared chastened but refused to drop her gaze. "I see that now, but Lily asked my help as a friend. What sort of friend would I be if I had refused her, or had run to tell you?"

Her answer placed him in a quandary. She had plainly acted foolishly, yet if she had been a man he would have applauded her stand. He wasn't used to hearing women speak in such terms; he had always thought honor was the prerogative of men. Was it possible that Alice of Rennoc understood the concept?

"I will send an escort home with you. It would not serve either of us if you were attacked by thieves on the streets of York."

"Thank you," Alice replied stiffly. "I am most grateful." She turned away.

"Alice . . ." The word was out before he could prevent it.

She turned and stared at him coldly. She wasn't going to help him, thought Jervois. She was going to make him work hard for every crumb.

"Alice, I would that I was a man with land and power, but I am nothing. A captain, that is all. I have nothing to offer you."

Her expression softened. "Have you not some prospects?" she asked eagerly. "I . . . if I do not name a man soon, my father will marry me to Sir Othric, and he is old. I know you do not know me, and I do not know you, but I *feel* as if I do, Jervois."

Jervois met her blue, blue eyes. "Sir Othric? The

old man with the . . . the warts, who was at Rennoc when I came?" He swallowed, holding back a shudder. "Well, he is rich at least. I cannot compete with such as he. Your father would laugh if I tried."

"Ask Lord Radulf to help," Alice replied briskly. "If he looked favorably upon us, then so would my father."

Jervois stiffened. "Ask Lord Radulf? I do not beg favors."

Alice grew cold. "You are lucky you do not need to!"

Jervois wondered why she could not see that it was no use. "I have to tend Lord Radulf," he went on in a more restrained voice. "And you must go home."

Alice spun on her heel and stalked toward the door. Angrily, Jervois bawled out orders, sending men scuttling after her. Women! He was better off without one.

When Lily returned with the wine, Radulf had been stripped of his chain mail, his tunic and undershirt. He sat bare-chested and dripping with sweat, black hair plastered to his head. He took the goblet she held out to him and drained it, then returned it for more. Lily poured, hands shaking. His shoulder appeared deformed and very swollen. She imagined that the longer it took for the deed to be done, the more painful it would be.

"Where is Jervois?" she demanded, her voice shrill with worry. "Jervois!"

"Here, lady." The grim-faced captain stepped forward. He watched Radulf down another goblet of wine. " 'Tis time," he said.

What followed made Lily feel sick, and Radulf

sicker. After one abortive try, Jervois popped his shoulder back into place. Everyone sighed with relief. Radulf was white-faced, his eyes squeezed shut and his lips a thin, pale line.

Jervois wiped his own dripping brow. "You must rest now, Lord Radulf," he said, as if Radulf could do else.

Radulf grunted. Then, rallying himself, he said, "My thanks yet again, my friend."

At the door, Lily placed a gentle hand on the captain's arm. "Thank you, Jervois."

Jervois managed a smile. "Keep him here, lady. If he moves that arm too rigorously too soon, it will slip out of its socket again. He might listen to you."

But would he? Lily asked herself wryly, as she closed the door. Even in his weakened state, Radulf was still Radulf. She felt immeasurably weary; her wet clothes hung heavy upon her and her tangled hair dripped. She wanted nothing more than to soak in a hot bath or crawl into bed and close her eyes. But there was still much to do, and no one to do it but she.

Radulf was hunched on the side of the bed. His head was bowed, and the bare expanse of his back gleamed in the firelight. Instantly Lily's own discomforts were swept away on a wave of longing. Her fingers itched to touch. Her cautious voice told her to restrain them, to hide her need, but she ignored it. Radulf had been hurt, and as his wife, she had the right to tend him. To touch him. Certainly she had more right than Lady Anna Kenton!

She drew closer. Just this once she would touch him, pretend that all was well between them. He was hurt and distracted. Perhaps he would not notice. Carefully, gently, Lily slid her hand down the long, smooth planes of his back.

Radulf started, a little jolt of movement. Lily stilled her hand but kept it where it was, waiting. He did not speak, and after a moment some of the tension eased out of him. Slowly, hesitantly, as if she were approaching a wild, untamed creature, Lily leaned closer. Wild and untamed he might be, but Radulf's body was everything she had ever dreamed of in her Norse god Thor. Powerful and graceful, and yet the skin so sleek over those hard, curving muscles. She cupped her other hand around the column of his neck, her fingers exerting some pressure as she began to rub the knots from rigid muscles.

Radulf closed his eyes with a grateful groan.

She stood behind him, yet he had never been more aware of her. The stroke of her fingers on his flesh had grown firmer, more insistent as she gained confidence. His body, bruised and battered, went limp. And still, that part that made him a man more than any other tightened with the desire that was never far away.

"Lily," he gasped.

She stopped. "Did I hurt you?"

Radulf shook his head. "No." Suddenly he moved, catching her about the waist with his good arm and tumbling her down into his lap. Lily cried out breathlessly, turning wide eyes upon him when her hip brushed against the hard ridge of his manhood.

He stared down at her, his chest rising and falling heavily. Her clothing was damp, but he did not notice; instead he felt the soft body beneath her garments and experienced the full power of those stormy gray eyes.

"Do not think to distract me. What were you doing at St. Mary's Chapel?" His tone was deceptively mild. When she didn't answer he leaned his face closer to hers, his breath warm and redolent of the wine with which he had fortified himself, his eyes glittering with determination and fever.

Fever!

Lily sat up straighter, touching her hand to his cheek. He turned his head slightly, so that he could press his lips into the hollow of her palm. Lily didn't notice. She was thinking how very warm his skin was, and how it had that parched quality that speaks of fever.

"You are unwell." She forced her voice to remain cool and firm, but her eyes betrayed her anxiety. "I will make you a soothing poultice for your shoulder and a drink that will help ease your fever. Let me up, Radulf."

He shook his head slowly from side to side, dark gaze never leaving gray. "Not yet. Not until you give me a truthful answer."

If Lily could have stamped her foot she would have, but her feet were dangling several inches above the floor. "You are *ill*, Radulf. Let me up!"

A smile twitched the corners of his mouth— even at such a time, he could find humor in the situation!

"It pleases me that you are concerned for my health, wife, but I want to know why you were out at night. And do not say you were at your prayers, because St. Mary's Chapel is abandoned. Come, Lily, what plot were you hatching? Tell me, before I become delirious."

Her eyes grew big and she gave a gasp of distress. "How can you jest about such a thing?"

"I am not jesting."

A moment longer she searched his eyes, and saw the implacability there. What was the use of lying to him? His imaginings were probably far worse than the truth—and she could tell him the truth in such a way as not to disclose the extent of her possessive feelings for him.

"I saw the letter." Lily lifted her chin. "I needed to know what sort of man I had for my husband. Whether he would take a wife in name and then spend his seed elsewhere. I have been a sham sort of wife already and I did not like it."

He went still, only his eyes moving as they searched her face. Whatever he found seemed to satisfy him, for at last he nodded tersely. "If you ever do such a thing again I will turn you over my knee and use my hand on you. Do you understand me, Lily?"

Lily had a sudden uncomfortable vision of her bare bottom beneath that broad, flat palm—uncomfortable because it was not entirely disagreeable. She flicked him an angry glance. "As you say," she murmured stiffly. "I won't follow you again . . . unless I feel I must."

Feel? thought Radulf. Why were women always following their feelings rather than their minds? Despite her cool gaze and proud demeanor, Lily was very much a woman, and her words softened his anger rather than adding fuel to it.

He forced a frown in case she might think he had forgiven her too easily. "You test me, wife. I will not spend each day worrying over whether you have decided to obey me. I ask your obedience for a reason. I need to know you are safe."

Lily blinked. This was no heavy-handed husband demanding that his wife jump to his slightest command. This was a man who was concerned for her safety.

It made a big difference.

As if taking a step in a new and untried direction, Lily replied, "And I need to know *you* are safe."

They gazed at each other in silence, hoping, and yet not daring to give voice to those hopes. Then Radulf nodded and, as if the strength had suddenly gone out of him, gave a deep, heartfelt sigh.

"Lie down." Lily slipped out of his arms. "I will fetch the drink and poultice."

When she had made him comfortable beneath the coverings, Lily went to see to her tasks. The ingredients she required were easily found in Una's kitchen, and when Una had stopped clicking her tongue and hinting that Lily would catch a cold if she didn't dry herself, she helped in stirring and heating and testing the brew. By the time Lily returned, she half expected to find Radulf sleeping, but he was still awake and watchful. With gentle fingers she applied the poultice, wrapping a clean binding about his shoulder and upper arm to hold it firm. The drink was bitter, but he swallowed it without complaint. When Lily went to rise again, however, his hand snaked out, fastening on her wrist and holding her with ease. Despite his weakened state, Radulf was still formidable.

"Wait," he said. "Come and lie beside me a moment. The feel of you soothes me."

For Radulf to admit to such a thing concerned her; was his fever worse than she had thought? With a grimace, she touched her skirts. "I am wet, Radulf."

Surprised, he caught a fold of the cloth, and felt the cool dampness for himself. "You take better care of me than of yourself, lady," he said, his voice low and deep. "Take off your clothes and climb under the covers with me. I will keep you warm. I have some things I want to say to you."

He expected her to argue, but after only a brief hesitation she nodded wearily. He watched her as she untied laces and peeled down the various garments that made up a woman's dress. Her body was alabaster, and she shivered as she stood at last naked, her arms folded before her breasts. Radulf held out his hand, moving more to one side to allow her room, groaning when the movement hurt his shoulder.

As if the sound spurred her on, Lily hurriedly slipped beneath the covers, gasping in pleasure at the sudden heat of his body when he reached out and hauled her against him. The hair on his chest rasped against her skin, and his strong hand molded over the curve of her hip, anchoring her in place. The hard jut of flesh against her belly reminded her that, hurt or not, Radulf was a passionate man.

"I have thought of what you said, the reason you followed me." He was resting his face against the top of her head, his voice a husky murmur. "You are right when you say a wife needs to trust her husband. Women do not see things as clear-cut as men do; they tend to weave their own feelings and imaginings into matters. I do not want you to spin fantasies where there are none, Lily. And I have grown tired of the stories they tell about me. For these reasons, I will explain to you why I went to meet her, and what passed between us."

Lily nodded, silent apart from her anxious breathing.

"But first, I forgot to thank you for saving my life. I do that now, Lily. I think Anna would have killed me tonight if she could, and perhaps I deserve to die. But not by her hand, and not yet. I have a great deal more to do before I face the grim reaper."

Lily tilted her head so that she could see his face. Her husband was more often than not a puzzle to her, but she sensed his honesty. Apart from the pain he must be feeling, there was a weary acceptance in his voice, as if he had come to the end of a journey and was simply glad it was over.

Words and questions fizzed in her head, but finally she elected to say simply what was in her heart.

"Tell me what it is that troubles you, my lord."

Chapter 15

"You asked me once about this scar." His voice was surprisingly strong.

"And you said it was given to you by a brave man," Lily replied, watching him closely.

Radulf smiled, but there was pain in the twist of his lips. " 'Twas my father who gave me that scar."

Startled, she sought for words while those black, gleaming eyes delved into hers. Judging her. Debating whether to open himself up to her.

"Were you not . . . close?" she managed at last.

Radulf shifted, as if to ease his shoulder. "Once. My mother died when I was but a child, and I looked to my father to supply both roles. He was a warrior like me, but there was a gentleness in him and great patience. Aye, we were close."

"Then why . . . ?"

"My father was a friend to King William's father, Duke Robert, and when Duke Robert set out on a pilgrimage to Jerusalem, my father promised to watch over young William. Duke Robert did not come back; he died far from home. I was a babe then, but as I grew from a child into a boy, I was often in William's company. We wrestled and trained together, and my father watched over us both. William was never a lusty lad when it came to girls. For me, it was different. I was already taller and stronger than my friends, and I was not so ugly then. The girls of the castle and the village began to follow me about. I tried to fix my mind on bold and brave deeds, like William, but my body told me differently. When I was fourteen I had my first girl. It was . . . pleasant, but it meant nothing."

Lily's mouth twitched. She could see the young Radulf training in the castle yard, stripped to the waist, black hair longer then, loose about his face. No wonder the girls watched him.

"And then I fell in love, and it was as if everything changed overnight."

Lily's heart gave a jolt. "You fell in love so young?"

"I was young in years, perhaps, but not in experience. At fourteen, boys like me are considered men. I already had the body of a man, but my heart and mind were innocent. I was . . . romantic. A dreamer with the face of a warrior. I fell hard in love. Sometimes it hurt me just to breathe."

Now Lily did smile. "First love is like that. When I thought myself in love with Hew, I believed I heard angels' voices."

Radulf stroked her hip, but did not smile in return. "Why did you stop loving him?"

She gave him a long, cool look. "He betrayed me."

Radulf nodded. He understood how that would kill love, no matter how strong. "Your Hew is a weak man. He abandoned you to Vorgen, then again when I defeated them in battle, and finally he left you at Trier. I would not have done that, *mignonne*. I do not abandon mine."

Something liquefied in her chest, trickling down into her stomach and her limbs. She had an unbearable urge to lean her head against him and give up all she had fought and struggled for and against. His strength was so great. Instead she took a shaky breath and reminded him, "You fell in love?"

He had read her confusion in her eyes, but he didn't pursue it.

"The woman—for she was no girl—was older than me. She was very beautiful—as you say, an angel, Lily. An angel of goodness, I thought." He laughed with bitter irony. "We struggled, but I think I always knew that was just part of the game. One night she came to my bed and said she could struggle no longer. After that, I was lost."

Lily read his reluctance. "It was Anna," she answered her own question.

"Yes, it was Anna."

"She was one of the women who lived at the castle?"

Shame brought color to his cheeks, and he bowed his head as though he were too embarrassed to meet her eyes. "Nay, Lily, she was my father's second wife. And the fact that each time I was with her, I was betraying him, did not stop me. I could not stop."

For an older, more sophisticated woman to seduce a boy was repugnant enough—it would be

like Lily taking Stephen the squire to her bed—
but that the woman was married to the boy's father was beyond disgrace. "She tricked you into
her bed," Lily said hopefully.

But honestly, reluctantly, Radulf shook his
head. "No, it was no trick. I was more than willing
to find my way there at every opportunity. I was a
young stag in rut, and she was my ever-willing
doe."

Lily felt sick with the bitter shame and regret
she read in his eyes, but there was also a stab of
jealousy. She did not want to think of that fine
young heart and body squandered on such a
woman.

"And then your father discovered you?" she
asked swiftly, to block out the pictures in her mind.

"He discovered both of us."

Radulf took a ragged breath and turned his face
away, so that Lily could see only the masculine
curve of his cheek with its line of uneven stubble,
and the white scar near his eye, a reminder of the
thing he had done.

His vulnerability was like an ache inside her,
and she had to bite her lip to prevent herself from
crying out at the injustice of what she knew he
was about to tell her.

"He found us together, indulging in our usual
carnality. We rarely spoke—there were no words
to say. If there had been a joining of minds as well
as bodies . . . But we were as animals." He shuddered, and Lily wondered if his fever was increasing. Gently, she brushed her fingers across his
brow, but he did not seem any hotter.

"Anna saw him first, over my shoulder, and
when I turned my head he was standing above us.

I got up off her. I was naked, and somehow that shamed me more than anything else, when he was fully clothed. My legs felt as weak as watered milk and I was stuttering my apologies, as if that could make it better."

He gave a soft laugh, a man looking back at the self-deceits of youth.

"He struck me. The heavy ring on his finger sliced open my face. I was fortunate he did not take out his dagger and cut me into ribbons, although I did not think myself fortunate at the time. I stood before him, blinded with my own blood, while she wept that it was my fault, that I had formed a calf-love for her and pestered her and, when she still wouldn't give in to me, that I had taken her by force."

"And he believed that?" Lily gasped. Despite Radulf's heated body close to hers, she felt cold. As if he sensed the change, Radulf pulled her closer.

"No. I don't think he did. I think he saw through her lies that time. He had been blind with love until then, so saturated with it that he showered her with an endless array of riches. Everything she asked for, he would find and give to her. He had doted on her, an old man's autumn madness for a much younger and beautiful woman. Maybe he thought if he gave her what she wanted she would dote on him in return. Now the scales had fallen from his eyes and he was confronted by a stark and terrible truth. And I think it was as much that truth as his son's faithlessness that destroyed him."

Outside the chamber, voices had risen in a friendly squabble. Jervois shouted for them to hush and remember their lord. When silence fell again, Radulf resumed his monologue.

"He told her to leave. He sent her back to her family—even then he could not bear to abandon her entirely. As for me . . . he turned from me without a word. He left and took sanctuary in a monastery in the north, and that was where he died six months later. We never spoke again, and I have no doubt he died cursing me."

Lily found her voice. "And what of Anna?"

"Oh, Anna would never have curled up and died of her shame. She remarried, first to some old French baron, and then last year to Lord Kenton. I followed William of Normandy and became his Sword, and have been rewarded for my loyalty. In truth, I have shown William more loyalty than I did my own father."

"So when you saw Lady Anna at the castle, you were not shaken by remembered love for her," Lily whispered, amazed. She had tormented herself with a fantasy of her own making.

" 'Remembered love'?" Radulf retorted angrily. "I hated her. I had heard from Lord Henry that she was asking after me, as if what we had done to my father was gone and forgotten! As if she believed I could touch her again without feeling sick to my stomach." He took a sharp breath and held it, steadying himself. Lily reached out to touch the back of his hand, and he turned it so that his fingers could tangle with hers. His grip hurt.

"I could see, after she sent her dress for you to wear, that she would not leave me alone. I had to make her see once and for all how I felt about her. That was why I agreed to her meeting at the chapel. And she came. She said that she had never forgotten me, that no one was like me. I told her that I wished to God I could forget her! She thought I didn't mean it. 'I couldn't live if I believed that,' she said. So I told her I hated her and that she had made my life unbearable, and that I lived constantly with the memories of what we had done to my father and that his dying words were probably a curse upon us both. This scar reminds me every day, even if I could forget."

Radulf's eyes were black hell in a face white and pinched with a pain and anger so deep, they went far beyond a priest's healing.

"She was his wife!" he burst out, and seemed to hover a moment on the brink of some dark abyss. Slowly, visibly, he pulled himself back. "I was his son," he went on, a little more calmly. "We betrayed him. There is no forgiveness, but she could not see that. So I told her that if she spoke to me or wrote to me or came close to me again, I would kill her and be glad of it."

"And that is why she tried to kill you?"

"Aye." He shuddered and was silent.

After a time, Lily said, "There is evil in the world, but that does not mean we should stop living."

Radulf gave a bitter, shaky laugh. "Aye, my sweet simpleton, but neither does it mean we should purposely seek that evil out."

"You have been scarred in more than your flesh, Radulf, but not every woman is an Anna."

He knew that—in his heart he knew that, but there were other factors to consider. His father's willing blindness, his doting, foolish love that made others laugh at him behind his back. There had been times since when Radulf wondered whether his father had known of their affair from the first, and had chosen not to see. Until the proof was pushed under his nose and he could no longer pretend.

How could a man cling to such a woman's love and be willing to give up his pride, his honor? It horrified Radulf. He was forever on the watch for similar traits in himself. And now he feared that in Lily, he had found his nemesis. Because he wanted her so much that he was willing to forgive and forget just about anything to keep her.

"You were young and hot-blooded," Lily was saying with cool good sense, rising up on her elbow so that she could gaze down into his face. "She was experienced in such matters, and did not care what harm she caused. She has shown that again tonight. You are grown now, Radulf, and wiser. Maybe your father did hate you then. Maybe he hated and loathed himself for loving such a wicked woman. But Radulf, I know he would be proud of the man you have become. You are a man to make any father proud."

Touched by her generosity, Radulf reached up and stroked her cheek. There were dark shadows under his eyes; his tale had drained him. Lily kissed his dry lips, a chaste kiss, and was surprised when his manhood twitched against her thigh. He reached out to grasp her head in his big hand, holding for longer, deeper kisses that were not so chaste.

"Radulf, your shoulder," she gasped, but he ignored her, reaching down to clasp her bottom and bring her sprawling over his hips. She wanted to protest more, but he had found the place between her thighs and knew she was ready for him. He smiled up at her with simple male pride.

"I can bear it if you can, *mignonne*."

Lily gasped softly as he thrust up into her, his body turned slightly to the side to protect his shoulder. They moved slowly, the need that drove them as intense as ever and yet subdued because of his shoulder and the story he had told. Lily arched in pleasure, feeling his hands on her breasts, her tangled hair a curtain about them.

Only a fine, strong man could rise from such a beginning without becoming twisted and weak. Like Vorgen, like Hew. Like Anna. Any woman would be proud to call such a man husband. To desire such a man, to love such a man . . .

I love you. The realization filled Lily with wonder. *I love you for who you are, and for what you are*. Radulf was the man she had dreamed of all her life.

The tremors pulsed through her body from the place where they joined, rippling upward and outward. Lily's senses were sharper, more attuned than ever before, as if the realization of her love had changed her in some fundamental way. The world she had known until now was spinning away from her, and there was only Radulf to cling to, and his hold upon her was strong and sure.

Somehow as she collapsed, Lily remembered to mind his shoulder and slide to his other side, a boneless tangle of hair and limbs.

Radulf slept almost immediately, and while he slept, Lily listened to him breathe. *He didn't love Anna*. The words formed a song in her mind, a lively jig for drum and whistle. It seemed frivolous to be so happy when he had told her a tale so sad. She had been warned that Radulf did not trust, and now she knew why. What man could believe in the basic goodness and honesty of women when he had been so callously betrayed by the first woman he'd ever loved?

He was a strong-willed man, but perhaps that will would work against his ever properly healing. He would hold a part of himself back, stop himself from trusting and loving completely, in case he, like his father, was betrayed.

It came to Lily then that, although he had opened himself up to her tonight, she might never win all of his trust. She and Radulf had come together in a hot flood of desire, and then he had learned that she was not who she said she was. She had tricked him, lied to him, although her reasons had been sound. But the similarities between Radulf and Anna, and Radulf and Lily, were there: the passionate beginning, the—in Radulf's eyes—betrayal . . .

Lily recalled his fury at Trier when he saw the hawk ring and established who she was. Then the forced marriage. The fact that she was no Anna, that she loved him, would make no difference. Oh, Radulf enjoyed her body, but that was all he would ever give her—his skill and his lust. Maybe it was all he could give any woman. The change in her feelings would not change his.

He did not want her love; her declaration of it would make him even more suspicious.

And yet Lily hugged her newfound knowledge to herself. She loved Radulf. True, she also had difficulty with trust because of Vorgen and Hew, but still, she loved him. And would continue do so, if necessarily secretly, forever.

Radulf's breathing soothed her. Lily dozed, and found herself in a gray place between sleeping and waking. She wandered, and for a time was back in Vorgen's stronghold, a cold unwilling wife, captive and afraid, longing above all else to be free. And then time moved on and she was running like a hare before the Norman hounds as they pursued her across what had been her land. She was free of Vorgen now, yet still a captive of her birth and Vorgen's machinations and the lies others told of her. Radulf chased her, riding his black stallion, and although Lily was terrified of capture, in her heart she longed for it.

The half-waking dreams shifted. She was in the rain and standing before the dark, abandoned bulk of St. Mary's Chapel. Radulf lay dead upon the ground, his blood leaching away, his face white and still, like her father when his body was carried home upon the makeshift bier. Lily screamed out in her loss and pain, running to Radulf's side. But the scene changed again, and Anna was there. She and Radulf stood together, arms entwined, heads close. As if sensing Lily's presence, they looked up at her. Anna was smiling with a savage mockery. "Did you really think I would let him go?" she asked Lily in that melodious voice. "He is my beloved. Forever."

"No!" cried Lily. "He is not! He is mine!"

And Radulf stood and smiled as they fought over him.

Lily woke with a start. Her heart was hammering very loudly, but even as it calmed and slowed, the noise went on. It was then she comprehended someone was banging upon the door.

Stiffly she rose, pulling one of the blankets about her nakedness, her toes curling against the cold floor. In the bed Radulf stirred, fumbling for his sword. He rose, cursing as he jarred his shoulder, and stood huge and naked behind her.

Lily met his eyes and, at his nod, called out, "Who is it?"

"Jervois. Lady, open the door."

Radulf frowned. "Jervois?"

Outside, Jervois's weary face loomed from the shadows. "Forgive me, my lord, lady, but . . . There is a messenger come from the king."

Lily pushed her hair out of her eyes with one hand, holding on to the blanket with the other. She tried to focus, her head still muzzy with dreams. Radulf had no such trouble. "What does he want?"

Jervois hesitated as if seeking the best way to answer, and then decided upon brevity. "Lady Anna Kenton is dead."

Lily shuddered. "Sweet Jesu."

Whatever Radulf had been expecting, it was not this. He was good at hiding his feelings, but this time he was not quick enough to disguise from Lily the shock and bewilderment.

"It is beyond belief," he whispered, and lifted his hands to cover his face, before shoving his fingers through his short black hair. "When did this happen?"

It was Jervois who answered. "After she left you. Her body was found near a candlemaker's shop. Lord Kenton had sent his men out to find

her when she did not return from her meeting
with you. He is saying now that her death is your
fault."

"He is blaming Radulf?" Lily gasped. Her blanket slipped, exposing the plump curve of one
breast. She didn't notice, though, wondering if
Radulf was to suffer Anna's lies even in death.
"Jervois, you must send the messenger back to say
Radulf had nothing to do with Lady Anna's
death!"

"Wait." Radulf came up behind her, his big hot
body pressing close. "Do you mean he is claiming
I killed her with my own hand?"

Jervois nodded. "That is what he means, sir,
though he has not said it so plainly as that. He
blames you. He says that you and his wife were
once . . . lovers." Color stole into Jervois's cheeks.
"Lord Kenton claimed that Lord Radulf had been
begging the Lady Anna to be his lover again. She
was considering it. She told Kenton that she was
going to meet you tonight, my lord, and give you
her answer."

Lily tried to think. "She said such things to him,
her husband? Did he not stop her? Why did he allow her to go?"

Radulf gave a brief bitter laugh. "You did not
know her, lady. She had Kenton twisted about her
finger. Maybe he killed her himself—she might
have twisted him too tightly."

Lily turned her head to look at him, causing the
blanket to slip again. Was Lord Kenton capable of
murder? Anna's face came to her then, the rigidity
of her expression as she rode past Lily in the rain.
She had been riding to her death and didn't know
it. Earlier Lily had celebrated the fact that Radulf

did not love Anna; now she felt a sting of guilt. No woman deserved to die alone, in the rain and the dark. But it was the living with whom Lily must now concern herself.

"Why does the king send this message to you, Radulf? Does he, too, believe you guilty of this crime? I had thought he was your friend."

Radulf looked down, meeting her eyes. His own were without expression, but Lily remembered the shock that had filled them a moment before.

"William is my friend," he said. "He has sent to warn me, for whatever outcome William might wish for, he knows there will be questions asked. Lord Kenton is a powerful man with many friends. The king cannot afford to dismiss his accusations without hearing them properly and fairly."

"I see." And she did see. A powerful man with a wanton wife, one upon whom he doted. Just as Radulf's father had doted upon that same woman. Would Lord Kenton accuse Radulf through jealousy, because in his grief he was determined someone must pay? Maybe he truly did believe Radulf had murdered his wife. Or had he killed her himself and was simply seeking a scapegoat?

Lily shifted uncomfortably, and the blanket slipped still further, catching on the very tip of her breast. Jervois stared over her head, pretending he hadn't noticed, while Radulf reached up to catch the cloth, tucking it more securely about her shoulders in a proprietary gesture.

"It is late," he said. "Tomorrow will come soon enough. Send a message back to the king saying that I thank him, Jervois, and will present myself before him tomorrow."

Jervois nodded and slipped back into the shadows, treading carefully between the bulky shapes of sleeping men. Radulf closed the door and, taking Lily's hand in his, led her back to bed.

Morning dawned bright, the smells of fresh bread and pies wafting through the inn. Radulf woke when Lily rose to wash her face. He stretched and then groaned when he moved his bruised and swollen shoulder, but the fever had abated, and he looked remarkably well compared to the evening before.

"You are up with the birds, lady," he murmured.

She turned to him, trying to hide her fears behind a smile, but he saw past the mask. His face grew still, watchful, and he sat up, wincing as the movement jarred his shoulder again.

"What is it? Tell me." Then, as she tried to find the words, "You have thought on what I told you last night and have decided you cannot live with such a man."

Lily stared at him in amazement. Could Radulf really believe himself so unworthy? Her heart ached for him as she shook her head. "No, Radulf, I have not decided any such thing, and I wonder at you for thinking so. I was thinking of the king's messenger and wondering what will happen today."

A gleam dispersed the dullness in his eyes.

"And I was wondering whether you mourn Lady Anna, despite what occurred between you."

Radulf raised a dark brow. "Mourn her?"

"You had only just begun to make your peace with the past."

"Aye, that is true." He thought a moment. "Although I felt only disgust for her and her manipulating ways, she should not have died like that. If Kenton killed her then he should pay."

"And if not?"

"Then the murderer will pay. William is a just man—England will be a law-abiding land under his rule."

"It was a law-abiding land before William invaded it," Lily retorted. As Radulf went to rise, she pressed her hand to his chest. "No."

He stopped, giving her a quizzical look. They both knew his obedience was an illusion. If he had wanted to rise he could easily have done so.

"I will bind your shoulder again before you go."

He nodded. "Not too bulky, in case I have to fight."

"Radulf, you cannot think you will be forced to defend yourself with a sword!"

He smiled and stretched, more carefully this time. His muscles rippled, and Lily had the impression of enormous strength held in check. "Probably not," he replied. "William will not see me punished for something I have not done, but neither can he appear to be one-sided. Lord Kenton has always supported him during the years of war, and he will be watching for bias. Now do what you must. I have to go."

Radulf watched her, enjoying the view. His wife's hair hung well past her hips, the ends tickling against her thighs. A silver screen for her modesty. Radulf's body tightened as he spied the soft curls between her legs and one jutting pink nipple.

At such a moment as this he should be thinking of what he would say to William and Lord Kenton, not how much he would like to toss his wife upon the bed and ride her until they were both breathless!

"Hurry, lady," he said in as stern a voice as he could manage.

Lily turned hastily toward the door.

"Lady?"

She turned with a sigh. "You told me to hurry. What is it now?"

Radulf gave her a slow, careful perusal. "If you go out into the other room like that, you'll have my entire garrison standing to attention."

Startled gray eyes met his, and then Lily gasped and quickly snatched up her shift and threw it over her head, tugging her hair impatiently out of the way. Radulf leaned back and watched her dress, enjoying the warm flush of her cheeks and the supple, smooth flesh of all those delectable curves.

Lily flung out of the room at last, and Radulf sighed as the door closed. He had thought to simplify things by meeting with Anna; instead, they were even more complicated. He shut his eyes and wondered how he would extract himself from the mess.

If only he were going into battle instead. Sometimes the sword was so much easier to wield than the tongue.

Lily found Una in the kitchen, sleeves rolled high as she dealt with a huge mound of dough. "Lady, there is ale and warm bread for Lord Radulf. If he is well enough to eat . . . ?"

Lily sniffed. "I believe he is well able to eat, Una." She began to gather together the items necessary for Radulf's breakfast and the changing of his bandage, placing them upon a tray. In the other room Jervois was giving the men their instructions. He gave Lily a polite greeting, looking so tired and serious that her ill-temper drained from her.

The matter *was* serious. Lord Kenton had as much as accused Radulf of murder. Radulf must defend himself, and without placing his king in a position where he must choose between his friend and Lord Kenton. Lily wondered if kings were really to be trusted in such a situation. They were just men, after all.

What would happen to Radulf if Kenton was believed? Would he be arrested and flung into a dungeon? Would he have to fight? Would he have to die? How could she bear such a thing now, when she had just discovered her love for him? Better that she had not known such wonderous feelings, than that they should be taken from her so soon!

She shivered and then readjusted her expression before she entered the bedchamber. It would not do for Radulf to realize how scared she was for him. Better that she bind his wound and feed him and send him off in good cheer.

Radulf gave her a lazy smile as she closed the door behind her. Lily set down the tray and handed him the mug of ale. He swallowed it all without pause. When he'd finished, Lily rested her fingers briefly against his cheek.

"The fever is gone," she said. "I can see why some think you more than mortal."

"Ah, but you know better, *mignonne.*"

Lily ignored him, unwrapping the bindings about his shoulder. The swelling about the joint had reduced but the flesh still appeared bruised and tender. Carefully, Lily smoothed more of her poultice upon it and rebound it, as he had requested, in a less bulky bandage. Meanwhile Radulf finished his bread and, after another mug of ale, swung his legs over the side of the bed.

"Go and get Jervois," he said. "I will wear my armor."

Lily's eyes widened in alarm. "Radulf, it will cause you agony!"

He shrugged, manipulating his shoulder carefully, circling it this way and then that. The eyes that turned to hers had lost all humor. "Better some discomfort than a blade through the heart, lady."

"Could it come to that?"

He shrugged, winced, and stood up. Naked, he somehow seemed larger than ever, with his thickly muscled legs and broad chest, the breadth of his shoulders. The giant of legend, the indestructible Radulf.

"I hope not. But if Kenton thinks I am to blame for his wife's death, he may take matters into his own hands." He reached for his breeches and paused, glancing at her sideways, almost slyly. "Would you care, Lily?"

Lily blinked, caught her breath and released it slowly, letting go of her sense of terror and loss. He did not want to hear such things. It was the cool Lily he wanted, the untouchable Viking princess. "What use is a dead husband to me?" she asked calmly. "The Conqueror will only find me another."

He laughed as if he had expected it of her, and

began to pull on the breeches. The curving muscles of his buttocks tightened with the movement. The skin of his broad back was scarred from battle but despite that, or maybe because of it, the urge to touch him was almost irresistible. Lily's fingers clenched to stop them from reaching out . . .

Abruptly she turned away.

"I will fetch Jervois," she said.

Jervois, when he was told, heaved the heavy chain mail into his arms and carried it into the bedchamber. By the time Lily returned, Radulf was completely dressed, his face impassive despite its pallor. If she had not known he was hurt, she could never have guessed it. Gone was the man who had held her in the night and spoken of his boyhood suffering; this was the King's Sword, and a stranger.

When they went out to the waiting men, there was a grim silence. No grins and jokes today, no grumbles or complaints about being so far from home. Everyone waited to hear what he would say.

"Jervois, you will remain here with Lady Wilfreda. If I am . . . detained, I will send word. If the matter is serious, you will take her south, to Crevitch. My people there will keep her safe, even from William."

Jervois bowed his head. "It will be as you say, Lord Radulf."

Lily stared at him, bewildered, her heart stuttering in her breast. Did he care so much, then? Did she mean so much that he would risk the king's displeasure to see her secure?

Despite the intensity of her gaze, Radulf kept his eyes fixed on Jervois. The next words, hastily manufactured to account for his great need to see her safe, slipped easily from his lips. "These are precautions, that is all. The lady may be carrying my child. My heir. Without an heir, all my wealth, all my estates will revert to the king. Therefore her value to me is beyond price."

Lily's heart grew quiet, the flame in her dying. "Of course," she murmured coolly. "I understand."

"Good." Radulf looked about him now. "I will take half of you with me. Jervois, see to it. And see that my orders are carried out. I rely on you."

Jervois did as he was bid, leaving Lily and Radulf briefly together. Radulf turned stiffly and took her hand. "If all is well I will return to you soon."

"And if all is not well?"

"Jervois will take care of you. Do not fear ill treatment at Crevitch, Lily. My people are loyal to me. I told you, I do not abandon mine."

"Your heir, you mean?" she asked quietly.

He hesitated. "Aye . . . that is what I mean."

He lifted her hand abruptly, pressing his lips to her limp fingers. "Lady."

"My lord," she whispered.

And he was gone. Lily listened to the sound of horses and men outside, and then the departing cacophony of hooves and weapons and armor as they rode away.

She wondered at the emptiness inside her, the sense of being bereft of something as urgent as air to breath or water to drink. Could Radulf really have become so important to her in so short a time? And what would happen to her if he didn't come back?

Had she discovered her one great love only to lose it forever?

Chapter 16

The lengths of cloth had arrived from Jacob. Beautiful wools and linens and silks, and the gorgeous red velvet that Radulf had insisted upon. Lily and Una unwrapped them, and while Una fell silent with breathless wonder, Lily tried listlessly to work up some enthusiasm.

"Lord Radulf must value you very highly, lady," Una whispered, eyes enormous. "Most Normans are too stingy to dress their wives in finery like this. Are you sure he is not English?"

Lily laughed. "Don't let him hear you say that, Una. Radulf is very proud of what he is. And Normans are always fond of show."

But her humor did not last long. Her mind was occupied with what was being said and done at William's court, and whether at any moment a messenger might come to a sudden halt in front of the inn, shouting that Radulf had been taken prisoner. If that happened, she had no doubt Jervois would bundle her upon her horse and race her south. To Crevitch.

Lily had thought to see Crevitch at his side. Not alone, running, mourning for her husband and lover, uncertain whether she would ever see him again . . .

Una was still speaking, and Lily realized she hadn't heard a single word. She must stop thinking such things. It wasn't like her to be maudlin and teary, yet her emotions had been so up and down since she met Radulf. Hoping Una had not noticed her abstraction, Lily bent to inspect the lengths of cloth with something of her old enthusiasm.

"I need sewing women," she said, reverently brushing one finger over the velvet. "It will take me forever otherwise, even if you were kind enough to help me, Una."

Una lowered her eyes uneasily. "I'm not much good with a needle, my lady."

Lily reached to touch the other girl's work-worn hand. "Perhaps the needle is not your skill, Una, but you make the best pastries in all of York."

Una smiled, pride shining in her eyes. "Aye, lady, I believe I do!"

The two women were still engrossed in the rainbow of materials spread across the bed when Alice of Rennoc peeped into the chamber, a little flushed from encountering Jervois in the other room. She was welcomed with open arms, and Alice knew of two households from which it would be possible to borrow sewing women for Lily's new wardrobe.

Una, with a regretful sigh, left them to go about her tasks.

" 'Tis the color of ripe berries in autumn," Alice breathed, when shown the red velvet. Afterward, however, Lily caught her friend giving her questioning glances. "I have heard the news about Lady Anna Kenton," Alice admitted.

"And no doubt heard that Radulf was responsible." Lily was angry. "Well, I was there and she was alive when we left her. And you saw Radulf when we brought him home. He was too sore to do injury to anyone. This talk is nothing but lies, concocted by men jealous of his wealth and power, to harm his friendship with the king."

Alice gazed at her in wonder. "You are very passionate, Lily! I was only going to say that I don't believe the things they are saying."

"Oh." Chastened, Lily grew quieter. "I am a little ragged, Alice. Forgive me."

Alice looked at her curiously. "You love him, don't you?"

Startled, Lily's eyes gazed at hers. If Alice could guess the truth so easily—

But again Alice put her mind at rest. "You disguise it well, Lily. Perhaps it is just that I have known you since we were children."

What was the point in denying it? She *did* love him, unwisely, irrationally, and with all her heart.

"Why don't you want him to know?"

Lily met Alice's curious gaze. "If I give up all my secrets to him, I will have nothing left to shield me. Even in marriage . . . especially in marriage, one needs a shield. I learned that with Vorgen."

"Radulf is certainly a formidable man." Alice was thoughtful. "But he seems honorable. He would not use your feelings against you, surely? You are his wife now."

There was no need for Alice to know of Radulf's past, his distrust of women.

"There is a difference between duty and love," Lily replied with finality. "If I do not speak of it to him, then the hurt will be less if he turns his back on me."

Alice fiddled with a length of water-green silk. "You know him better than I, and you must do as you think best. At least you have a husband, and one who is young enough to be lusty. I fear it is Sir Othric for me."

Lily shuddered. "Sir Othric, your father's friend? Oh no, Alice, he would not!"

"He has warned me that if I do not find someone in York, then Sir Othric it will be."

"But I thought . . . Jervois . . ." Lily glanced away. "I'm sorry. I saw you and him, and I just—"

"My father will see him as nothing more than a mercenary, and that is what he is. I want him as my husband and I think . . . I know, he wants me." She hesitated, seeking words. "Lily, if Radulf would speak for Jervois, and assure my father he looked favorably upon the marriage . . ."

Lily blinked. "Oh! I never thought . . . of course I can ask him! I forget sometimes he is not like Vorgen, who would refuse me something just for the pleasure of it. And I owe you far more than so small a favor, Alice. But why doesn't Jervois ask Radulf himself?"

Alice glowered, a difficult thing for her to manage. "He is a *man*, and he has his *pride*."

Lily winced with full understanding. She squeezed Alice's hand. "I will ask. You cannot marry Sir Othric. The man is so repulsive that the king should make a law that he remain unwed until his dying day."

Alice grinned. "Aye, and after that as well!"

Her hope restored, Alice shrugged off the somber mood they had fallen in to. "Come! Let us cut out one garment, at least! It will give us something to do, and take our minds off what is happening at the castle."

"What about this?" Alice lifted a fold of midnight blue wool. "And this for an undershift?" The linen was so fine that when she held it to the candlelight the cloth became almost invisible.

Lily smiled. "Perfect!"

She threw herself into the diversion. Anything to put Radulf from her mind, for a little time at least. Perhaps, when she allowed herself to remember, he would already be striding through the doorway.

Safe.

"What does Lord Radulf say to that?"

As he spoke, William leaned forward in his chair. His body was tense and still, and his very stillness was so uncharacteristic that it made the two men before him edgy. Lord Kenton, small and bejeweled, his narrow, handsome face gray with grief and fatigue. And Radulf, big, dressed for battle, his black eyes full of a cold anger that had already sent William's servants cowering.

The court fell mute as he answered, everyone straining to hear the low, husky voice.

"I say Lady Anna was nothing to me but a memory. Years ago she was wed to my father, but since then I have not seen her. Not until the night of my wedding, when she spoke to me and my wife."

"She was your whore." Kenton cut in angrily, his voice higher, shriller. "She told me so. She was your whore in the past, and when you came to York you wanted her again. She said you did not care for your wife—the marriage was forced upon you. You wanted my Anna."

" 'Your Anna' was lying." Radulf sounded unruffled, but the blood pounded through his head, making it throb. His shoulder was aching like the devil, but he dared not show the slightest weakness before these crows. It was his strength, and the legends of it, that kept him safe.

"Why should she lie?" Kenton's pale eyes were blazing. "She had nothing to gain from it."

"Your jealousy," Radulf replied mildly. "She played the same tricks upon my father, amusing herself by choosing favorites among the men of the household, driving him to greater and greater folly to please her. She wanted you to win her back, Kenton."

"Bah!" He waved a hand. The jewels on his fingers sparkled richly in the light of the tall candles.

"I have already told my story," Radulf went on calmly, speaking to the king. "I met with her because her behavior was upsetting my wife. I told her not to bother me again or I would go to her husband and disclose to him her faithlessness. I knew Kenton loved her and so did she, but she was not fool enough to believe he would keep forgiving her over and over. There comes a point where the wine of forgiveness is all drunk, and only dregs remain in the bottom of the cup.

Maybe she had reached that point. My father did."

"What do you know of—" Kenton began scathingly, but William held up his hand for silence. Reluctantly, twitching his richly embroidered tunic, Kenton held back the angry words bubbling in his throat.

William stroked his clean-shaven chin, eyes fixed upon the imposing figure of his Sword. "And Lady Anna took your advice in good part, Radulf?"

Radulf snorted a laugh. "No, sire, she did not! She was angry and rode off. I did not see her again. I was only glad that she had gone. I returned to the inn with my men."

Kenton spun to face him, unable to contain his fury a moment longer. "You followed her and slew her! Because she would not give in to your lustful demands! She loved you once, Radulf, and you could not let her go."

Radulf ground his teeth. "In God's name, you have seen my wife! If I have 'lustful demands,' do you not think she can more than adequately meet them?"

William smiled, bowing his head to hide it, but Lord Kenton saw. He glared savagely from one to the other. "I see I will get no fair hearing here. It is well known the king and Radulf are more like brothers than master and subject."

William stood up. His height, though not as great as Radulf's, was imposing enough. To his credit, Kenton stood his ground, although it was clear he was half regretting his outburst.

"I will forgive you those remarks," William

said softly, almost gently, his eyes steely. "I understand your grief, Kenton. I, too, have a wife I treasure. You have spoken what is in your heart and mind, and I have listened. Depend upon me, I will not rest until I have found your wife's murderer. However . . . I do not believe he is to be found here."

Lord Kenton shot Radulf a bitter and malevolent glance. Briefly, he struggled with words he knew were better left unsaid in the king's presence. When he spoke, his voice was harsh with strain. "I thank you, sire. You will understand if I continue to pursue my wife's destroyer in my own time . . . in my own way." Before the king could answer, he turned and walked quickly from the great hall.

William slapped a hand hard on the arm of his chair, and glared at Radulf's impassive face. "You have placed me in a difficult position, Radulf," he said softly. "I hope you appreciate it."

Radulf bowed his head. "I do, sire, and am grateful for your trust in me."

William nodded, watchful and a trifle sullen. "Kenton is a powerful man—almost as powerful as you, Radulf—and he has equally strong friends. England has only just found peace. I do not want two of my most important barons at each other's throats."

"I have no grievance against Lord Kenton."

William frowned, obviously unhappy with the situation. Suddenly, as if he had had as much gloom as he could bear, he challenged, "Come! I am tired of all this darkness. We will go down to the training yard, Radulf, and see who is the better swordsman!"

Radulf's heart sank. Weakness would be looked upon as a mark against him, especially when William had staunchly taken his side, so he dared not mention his shoulder. William would also know if he fought with less than his usual skill and vigor, and probably accuse him of currying favor by losing on purpose. So he must fight hard and for a good long time, long enough to satisfy William, and only then lose convincingly.

Still, this was a small thing when placed against the knowledge that he was safe again, warm in the favor of his king, free of Kenton's raging grief and Anna's lies, reaching out to him even from the grave. But despite all this, it was something more that gave a spring to his step as he followed William to what he knew would be an excruciatingly painful contest. Lily would not have to flee to Crevitch without him.

Soon he would return to her, knowing that she would be waiting, that she would lift her cool gray eyes to his. Call him a fool, but Radulf believed that hidden deep within that gray was a spark, an elusive promise, which spoke of better things.

A life, perhaps, such as he had only dreamed of. A warm, loving wife and children to follow where he led. A reason for doing what he did. A reason for being. Maybe that had been what his father sought, too.

A reason to *be*.

Alice had sent to her uncle's house for needles and thread and shears. They had measured Lily with narrow tapes, and after carefully cutting the cloth, had begun the task of sewing it.

Lily had forgotten how companionable sewing could be. When she was wed to Vorgen, she had been constantly tense with fear and worry. There had always been the fear that one of the women might carry tales to the Normans of what was said. She had forgotten the joy to be found in women gathered together. When Lily was younger, when her mother had been alive, there had been much gossip and laughter, and her mother's soft admonishments had in no way extinguished the twinkle in her eyes, as she listened to the hopes and dreams of those under her care.

Lily remembered now, and vowed that when she was settled in a proper home of her own, she would recreate those times. Surely Radulf would see the sense in the people beneath him being contented? Gudren, Lily recalled, had said that the inhabitants at Crevitch were strongly loyal to him because he kept them warm and well fed.

I do not abandon mine.

Well, it was only good sense to make certain one's people were well cared for, and not only because they were less likely to rebel against one. If they were happy then everything ran more smoothly, there were fewer problems. Vorgen had lived in bitter chaos. But Radulf, Lily thought with a little smile, might just be a man who preferred harmony.

It grew late and shadows filled the corners.

Alice was chatting but Lily had long ago ceased to pay attention. She was listening for Radulf, though she did not realize it until the sound of approaching horses struck through her like an axe through wood. Her head jerked up, the needle and thread slipping from her fingers. Alice continued to chatter on for a moment or two and then, noticing Lily's stillness, stopped in midsentence.

Heavy footsteps thudded into the inn, voices rising one over the other, Jervois's among them. Lily stood up, the piece of blue wool sliding to the floor. Alice caught it up, mindful of its value. She was startled by the white, waiting look on her friend's face. Lily had been calm, if abstracted, until now, but that veneer had crumbled, and her slim body seemed to vibrate.

"Alice," she whispered. "Will you go and see if Lord Radulf has returned?"

Alice flicked her an uncertain look, then rose and did as she was bid. The outer room was full of men, their armor and weapons cluttering up the low space. At first she could see nothing but sweaty faces and the dull gleam of chain mail, but she could hear Jervois. Alice pushed her way awkwardly toward him.

The captain stood by the fireplace, splashing wine from a jug into goblets. He turned, as if he sensed Alice's presence behind him. His green eyes grew arrested, admiring, and then wary. "Lady?"

Alice's gaze glanced off him; she had still not forgiven him. Instead she looked to the large figure slumped on the bench, silhouetted against the flames. Radulf definitely looked the worse for wear. His face was damp and grimy, there was a livid scratch across his jaw, and his black hair was sticking up on end, as though he had just removed his helmet. As he reached for his goblet it was obvious he was favoring one arm.

Despite all this he was grinning from ear to ear. "At last I see an end to the madness," he

growled to Jervois in a voice hoarse and scratchy.
"First we go north and oversee this cursed castle,
and then south. Home. To Crevitch!" he rasped,
raising his goblet.

The toast was taken up, ringing deafeningly
throughout the room.

Alice weaved her way back to the bedchamber.
She found Lily seated on the bed white-faced and
oddly calm.

"He is arrested," she said dully. "I am to go to
Crevitch. I heard them all say it. I must pack some
things."

She stood up, seemed to waver a moment, and
then without a word, Lily fainted.

Alice gave a small shriek and ran to her friend.
"Lily!" she cried. "No, no, he is here! He is outside, drinking wine and laughing. It is all right,
truly, Lily, it is fine."

In a little time Lily stirred, and with Alice's as-
sistance sat up. She listened, nodding, as Alice re-
assured her, and though her shoulders lost some
of their rigidity, she still did not smile. She sipped
the wine Alice poured her, the sour taste of it making her shudder. Lily thought then that she might
vomit. She subdued the urge, swallowing and
taking deep breaths until it, too, had passed.

"I am all right now," she replied to Alice's concerned questions. "I have sat inside this room for
far too long. I suppose I will get fresh air enough
when I ride with my lord to his lands in the
south." She tried to smile as she looked up at Alice, and then stopped, suddenly stricken, tears
gathering in her eyes. "Oh Alice, will I ever see
you again?"

Alice's own heart was tugged by the question,

but her nature was bubbly and resilient, and she smiled a reassuring smile. "Of course, why not? Radulf will need to oversee his northern lands . . . *your* lands. You will see me then. Or I could come to stay in the south, with you. I need a husband, remember? I am sure there are worthy examples to be found at Crevitch." *Jervois*, whispered her heart, but Alice ignored that impractical organ.

Lily smiled, as she was meant to. Her fingers clung to Alice's a moment longer, and then her eyes widened as a heavy step sounded. The doorway was filled completely with a man.

"My lord!"

He laughed at the look on her face. "No, lady, I have not been set upon. I have had some friendly sport with my king . . . though some may claim it is one and the same thing."

Alice rolled her eyes. Why did men think it a matter of pride to be bruised and battered?

Radulf limped into the bedchamber. Jervois began to remove the chain mail, trying not to hurt Radulf more than necessary. Lily moved to help, giving Alice a distracted smile as she bade her farewell. Her mind was filled with the joy of his being safe. She had been so afraid . . .

Radulf was in a lot of pain, and when they had finished, seemed content enough to lie back on the bed and let his wife bustle about him, tending to his hurts.

Radulf had never had anyone but a squire or a servant tend to him before. A wife, he decided, was infinitely better, particularly when that wife was Lily. Her care of him made the beating he'd received at William's hands almost worth it. Radulf all but purred beneath her ministrations, indulging himself as she sponged him clean and applied her medicines, and then tempted his appetite with cheeses and meats and red wine. When she had finally done, he lay watching her through half-closed eyes as she fussed about the chamber, folding clothing, tidying it away. Then she spent time combing the silver beauty of her hair before braiding it.

Radulf watched her long, nimble fingers and the cool, distant beauty of her face. He could not fault her care of him, yet now she was removed, shuttered against him. He might even have thought her afraid of the heat that lay between them; Lily, too, had her secrets. His eyes slipped over her rounded shoulder, to the breast hidden by the clothes she wore, and his gaze sharpened. Was that soft curve heavier, fuller?

He smiled. His beautiful Lily had put on some flesh now that she was safe. No more running and hiding, no more living like a wild animal in the thickets of the north. She would grow plump and contented at Crevitch.

"Come to bed," he said.

Her hands stilled at the sound of his voice, and he half expected her to refuse. Instead, she quickly finished with her hair, tugged off her clothing, and climbed under the covers beside him.

Her feet were cold; he caught them between his legs, warming them.

"You were worried for me, Lily?" he murmured, his voice even huskier than usual, his hand resting in its customary place on her hip.

She shifted restlessly, as though the question troubled her, but her eyes were cool. "Naturally I was worried for you. You are my husband,

Radulf. Without you I would once again be at the mercy of your king."

"Yes," he said quietly. "I had forgotten for a moment why it is you value me so."

There was a note in his voice Lily had not heard before—a sort of wry self-mockery—and it startled her. She gave him a suspicious look.

"What should I say?" she retaliated. "That I love you?"

Silence, as if they both held their breath. Lily's throat was dry; she licked her lips. Beneath Radulf's dark lashes, his eyes were gleaming black. He leaned closer, his mouth so close to hers that she felt the heat of it.

"Love was never a consideration," he said.

"Of course not," Lily whispered.

He kissed her, tongue thrusting hot, the palm of his hand filling with that fine, soft flesh he had just been admiring. She *was* bigger—the knowledge nearly drove him over the edge. Radulf rose above her, forgetting his aching body, only knowing he had to have her. But even as his manhood eased into the tight, welcoming sheath between her thighs, he knew to his delight and despair that it would never be enough.

After a time, when their breathing returned to normal, he said, "Sleep now," in a voice that was almost gentle.

Obediently Lily closed her eyes.

Radulf continued to watch her in silence. His head was so light with weariness, he felt as if he were floating. *Love was never a consideration.* He had taken her, married her, and it still wasn't enough. He wanted more, but with that "more" came the temptation to trust her, to place himself entirely in her hands. And Radulf doubted he could ever do that.

What would she do if he did? Despise him for his weakness, pity him? Or make his life a living hell, as Anna had made his father's?

It was better not to take the risk.

Lily listened to her husband's breathing steady and deepen. He slept so easily, and woke swiftly and completely refreshed. Like a child. Only he was no child; the pleasant ache between her legs reminded her of that. Lily wished her own thoughts were as easily stilled, but they gripped her vitals, making her feel hot and cold in turns.

She was going to have a babe.

For the past few days the question had been there, flitting about in her head like a bright, erratic butterfly, teasing and taunting her by turns. She had dismissed it—her monthly time was more than likely late because of the traumas she had suffered, both physical and emotional. And so what if she seemed to weep and worry more than usual? A great many women wept and worried—perhaps Lily was just becoming more womanly.

It was the fainting that convinced her. Lily's mother had fainted when she was carrying Lily. She had often said so during those companionable sewing afternoons, adding her story to the stories of other women who had borne their children safely and lived to tell the tale.

I am carrying Radulf's child.

The knowledge should give her joy, but all she could remember was how the thought of a child had caused Radulf to take extra care with her, when he feared he might be prevented from returning to her. He wanted an heir. Well, of course he did! Just like Vorgen had desperately wanted an heir, a son to step into his shoes as tyrant of the north.

And Radulf had far more to lose.

Lily closed her hand into a fist and pressed it to her belly. Somewhere deep within her there was a singing gladness—she loved a man and he had given her his child—but just now the sorrow and disappointment were greater.

She loved a man, and he did not love her.

Chapter 17

The house Radulf found them belonged to one of York's wealthier merchants, who was undertaking an extended trip to the East. The man was more than happy to vacate it and make way for the King's Sword. His servants remained, and all his linen and household goods, which meant there was little for Lily to do but give orders.

It was wonderful to have a house of their own after the cramped quarters at the inn. Still, Lily missed Una's friendly face and the less formal atmosphere of life with Radulf's band of men.

"Oh no, lady," Una had replied, when Lily asked her if she wished to come with them. "It's been like a dream, with you and Lord Radulf here, and one I'm not likely to forget. But it's time for me to wake up now. There's a boy who's been too afraid to come calling on me these past weeks. He'll be back now that you're leaving."

She smiled contentedly. "I thank you for asking

me, but my place is here, making the best pies in all of York."

Alice, however, visited constantly. She had purloined some sewing women, and Lily's wardrobe was moving ahead in giant leaps and bounds. Lily had worn the midnight-blue wool to court, and the water-green silk, and even King William had been struck dumb—briefly—by her beauty. As the King's Sword's wife she already had some reflected glory, but now she began to gather it in her own right.

On Alice's behalf, Lily had asked Radulf to look favorably upon a marriage between her friend and Jervois. At first Radulf had refused, still angry with Alice for helping Lily to follow him to the meeting with Anna, but Lily had persisted and eventually he promised to consider it.

"Perhaps Jervois does not want to wed the lady," he said mildly.

"And still look at her in such a way?" Lily retorted. "As if he will pounce on her and gobble her up?"

Radulf chuckled. "And how does Alice look at him?"

"As if she would be glad to be gobbled," Lily answered, as amused as he. "He is too proud to ask the favor of you, my lord."

"He is young," Radulf excused his captain. "He will learn."

"So you will agree to further this marriage?"

"I will agree to think about it."

Radulf's shoulder had healed slowly, though no one would have believed he had a sore shoulder at all from the way in which he "flung himself about," as Alice said. Only Jervois and Lily saw his pain.

Lily continued to rub her healing potions into his tender flesh at bedtime. She found such pleasure in touching him, in running her hands over that magnificent body, that sometimes she prolonged her ministrations just so that she could continue to stroke him. After she finished, it was Radulf's turn to watch her as she undressed and brushed her hair, braiding it sometimes, or sometimes climbing into bed beside him with the silken cloak loose about her.

By then he was always aroused, his hands reaching up to cup her firm breasts or between her legs, teasing her until she begged him to push that hard, velvet-covered flesh deep within her, and climb with her to that peak of pleasure.

The wonder never seemed to grow any less.

Lily didn't tell him about the baby. Although it was real to her now, not speaking of it allowed life to remain simple. Once Radulf knew, things would change, become complicated in ways she hardly dared imagine. She expected he would immediately send her south to Crevitch, where she would be watched over as carefully as his most precious broodmares. Perhaps he would even stop making love to her, fearing it would harm the child.

No, she was right to keep her secret from him. The longer she kept it, the more time they would have together.

Of course it couldn't last. She knew that. Every morning as she quelled her nausea, she knew there would come a time when she could no longer hide it from Radulf, and he would realize.

But every morning she promised herself one more day—and night—with him.

King William was leaving the north. As if to celebrate the fact, he increased his demands upon Radulf, bidding him here and there. Radulf wanted to start building his northern castle before the weather turned bleak—already summer was coming to its end, and soon the long golden days would fade, the trees turning red and orange with the colors of autumn. The wind was cooler, too, with a bite that spoke of darker days.

Lord Henry was to begin on the castle foundations, and Radulf sent him serfs and skilled men to do the work. "Though I cannot expect him to remain in the north doing my bidding, when he has lands of his own in the south, awaiting his return," Radulf told Lily. He stroked the scar near his eye, watching as she put the finishing touches to her costume.

In honor of the king's final evening in York, she was wearing the red velvet. Her skin and hair were so pale against the deep, rich color that they appeared almost translucent. Yet despite her unearthly air, there was a voluptuousness about her tonight, a flush on her cheeks and her lips, a glitter to her eyes, while beneath the smooth gown her body swelled full and opulent.

Radulf felt his pulse quicken, though he continued to speak as if it had not. "When I go north you will remain here in York. As soon as I return, we will go south, to Crevitch. I have been away too long."

Lily turned her head to look at him. She was

like an idol, he thought. Some Viking fertility goddess, luring him into lustful madness with her cool beauty. He felt his manhood twitch and almost groaned aloud. She would probably kill him with overuse, but he had no complaint. He was more than happy with the manner of death.

"I would rather come with you, lord," she said quietly.

Radulf blinked, trying to remember his words of a few moments ago. Crevitch, was that it?

"You *are* coming with me, *mignonne*."

"No, I don't mean to Crevitch. I mean north, to my lands, to my people. They need me. I thought that was why the king ordered us to marry, so that I could help bring peace to the north. I should be with you."

He frowned, his head clearing with a jolt. "Should you? Or do you want to run for the border and join Hew and his bloodthirsty Scots?" He spoke before he could stop himself, but the fear was real enough. He often wondered, in some dark corner of his mind, if she might try and run away from him again. Was all of this but an interlude, a pretty memory to take out and examine when he was an old, embittered man?

For a moment Lily looked as if he had struck her, then she was herself again. The ice queen, her gray Viking eyes daring him to show weakness.

"Why would I do that, Radulf? My running to Hew would not help my people. They will starve this winter if you do not see to food and shelter for them. I believe you will do that, if I can persuade them to trust you."

Radulf raised his eyebrows. "You are very sure they will listen to you."

Lily smiled, her red lips curving very slightly, her eyes downcast. Radulf clenched his hands on his thighs in case he grabbed her and kissed her to silence. A man of his stature, he thought irritably, should have more control.

She lifted her gaze and fixed it on his. "Oh, they will listen, Radulf. They have always listened. It was just that Vorgen would not allow me to speak."

He let his gaze run over her, slowly following the curve of her breasts, her narrow waist, the flare of her rounded hips. His eyes returned again to her face, the full moist swell of her bottom lip, the dark brows slanting above her pale eyes, the fairy-silver of her hair.

He could not risk losing her.

He shook his head.

"No, lady, I will not take you with me."

Something sparkled briefly in her eyes, but it was gone too swiftly for him to read. Sorrow? Anger? He could not tell. He did not care. The thought of his beautiful Lily in the harsh north, possibly in danger, possibly kidnapped by her cousin or tempted to run . . . No, everything in him rebelled.

"Come." He stood up and held out his hand. "It is time we went to say our goodbyes to the king."

Lily rose and placed her fingers obediently in his. He drew her to him, enjoying the feel of her body, the taste of her mouth. She softened against him, allowing him his pleasure, and yet . . . She was distant. It was nothing he could isolate, but she seemed to have removed a part of herself. Because he had refused her what she wanted.

It made him angry. As they rode off, he wanted

to spur his black horse into a gallop, but he restrained himself. He was Lord Radulf and therefore above such petty vengeance. If Lily thought
she could make him change his mind by sulk-
ing—which was what she was doing, more or
less—then she was sadly mistaken. Radulf
would travel north, but Lily would remain here
in York.

Safe.

The king eyed Radulf's wife appreciatively. "If
all the women in the north are like you, lady, I will
have no difficulty in fulfilling my command that
single men find English wives!"

Radulf smiled without humor. "Lily is unique,
sire. It is I who am fortunate."

Lily flicked him a look, the anger making her
eyes darker, stormier. He smiled to himself. Ah, so
the frigid distance was in danger of cracking already. Like ice under the warm sun.

"Well, Radulf, you and your men will soon be
able to put that to the test," the king went on,
shifting from foot to foot, as if he wanted to be doing something more than standing, talking. "A
rider has come from Lord Henry. He arrived an
hour since."

Radulf stilled. "An hour ago? Why wasn't I
told?"

William waved an impatient hand. "An hour
matters not, Radulf. Lord Henry sends word that
there is an army marching in his direction from
the southwest. I think you had best make haste to
meet it."

Lily gasped, the sound distracting Radulf briefly.

"Where is this messenger?" he demanded. "I would speak with him."

The king eyed him fondly. "All in good time, my friend."

"But . . . where does this army come from? I have dispersed the rebels, and the English have been quiet ever since. Apart from Hew—" He stopped, his brows coming down in a ferocious scowl.

"Lord Henry feels it may well be this Hew, and that he has found himself well-trained men this time, not just rabble. You will have a proper battle on your hands, Radulf. A contest worthy of the King's Sword," William added smugly.

Radulf was more interested in the details. "Where has this army of men come from?" he growled. "There were barely enough of Hew's supporters left to pour wine at our feast tonight! Are the Danes back? I thought you had paid them to go away. Has the Scottish king sent them? I thought Malcolm was cannier than that."

King William's eyes were hard and bright. "No, I fear Hew has found his army closer to home, Radulf. You have an enemy . . . remember?"

Radulf appeared uncomprehending, and then realization struck. "Kenton?" he breathed. "But surely, William, he would not commit treason to revenge himself upon me? For *her*?"

He had called the king by name in his shock and amazement, but either William didn't notice or chose not to.

"And yet, Radulf, it seems he has. My spies were too late to prevent it from happening, but they tell me that Lord Kenton went straight from here to Hew and offered him as many men as he wanted. Kenton's lands are close enough and the weather is good. It will not take them long to reach their destination.

"He hates you, Radulf. Although we have not yet found Lady Anna's murderer, Lord Kenton blames you. He wants to see you beaten and humiliated. He might really think he can win the north from you. Perhaps he will try to take your wife, as he believes you took his."

Radulf's jaw hardened. "I will stop him."

William nodded slowly. "Yes," he said, "you will."

Lily was frozen to the spot. Hew meant to make war again in the north. And Radulf would fight him.

For a moment the brightly decorated hall with its many candles seemed to waver and dance about her. With an immense effort of will, Lily prevented herself from fainting. Fainting, she thought furiously, would accomplish nothing. Words would.

"Hew thinks only of winning," she said loudly. "He does not care how many lives he destroys in the process. He will draw men and boys to him because he is English, and tells them he fights for their freedom and has their well-being at heart. He will lie."

Silence. Radulf was glaring at her as if he wanted her to be quiet. Lily ignored him. The king was listening, and that was all that mattered.

"If I go with Lord Radulf, and speak, those men and boys will listen to me. If *they* do not, then their wives and mothers will. Hew has the advantage of familiarity. Lord Radulf has not, except through the tales that are told about him, and they do not inspire confidence. How can frightened and starving people rally to a giant, or a warrior whose sword arm never tires, or a monster who eats their children? They will run from Radulf! But if I am there by his side, then they will question such tales. They will listen to me and see Radulf as he truly is rather than as he is portrayed in legend. Sire, I *must* go with Lord Radulf. We must prevent another long war in the north. My country, my people, cannot bear it."

King William was stroking his clean-shaven chin. "You speak sense, lady. This was, after all, why I married you to my Sword." A swift, mocking glance at Radulf. "If you are seen to support Radulf and encourage the obedience of your people to him, then many more will follow in your steps. Yes! You make good sense, lady. What say you, Radulf?"

Radulf looked as if he wanted to say a great deal. "No."

William blinked in surprise, then his expression quickly darkened. "You are overhasty, my lord. I like the idea. Your lady will go with you and see what she can do to help disperse any rebels tempted to join Lord Kenton's force. You will have your hands full defeating them as it is, without their army growing any greater. Do you not trust her?"

This last was spoken very softly, for Radulf and Lily alone. Radulf hesitated, and felt Lily stiffen at his side. "She is my wife," he said slowly. "I trust her as much as she trusts me."

William slapped his shoulder, a blow so hard that it shifted Radulf forward an inch or two. "Well, then! She goes with you. Peace, Radulf, that is what we need. Peace! First defeat Kenton's army, and then I will deal with the man himself."

When Radulf bowed, William clasped his hand. "I will not insult you by asking that you take care."

"Aye," sighed Radulf, "I am immortal, sire, remember?"

The king and Radulf had discussed how many men were available to fight at such short notice, and how many of the closer landowners would send troops. Because it had all happened so fast, Radulf's army would not be as large as he wished. Radulf had then spoken to Lord Henry's man, questioning him until he had extracted every ounce of information from him.

Now they were awaiting their horses outside William's castle, standing in the chill darkness while torches flared from sconces on the walls. The air smelled of the river and the sweet blossoms of some unseen tree.

"We will leave at first light," Radulf informed Jervois. "There will be no dallying on the journey this time. It appears Lord Henry is outnumbered, and even when we reach him, we may still be outnumbered—but that has never stopped us before."

His smile was savage; his eyes shone black in the firelight. Lily looked up at his big, tough body and understood why his name was the stuff of folklore.

"Aye, sir." Jervois chimed in with a bloodthirsty laugh. "We will finish them off once and

for all. This Hew's head would make a fine orna-
ment on the Bootham Gate."

Lily thought of Hew's pretty face and fine
blond hair and was neither sickened nor shocked.
He deserved to die. So many lives had already
been lost because of his lies and greed. Now her
plan for a peaceful and prosperous north was in
the balance. "As long as it is not your head upon
the gate, Radulf, or yours, Jervois, I do not care."

The two men looked at Lily in surprise. Jervois, she noticed, then became lost in thought.
After he had gone to hurry the grooms with the
horses, Radulf said, "You would not weep for
Hew?"

Lily shook her head. "No, I would not. If I
wanted him to win I wouldn't be coming north
with you."

Radulf shifted. She knew he was angry—she
could read it in his tight mouth and hard eyes—
but she reminded herself that his anger was unimportant when she had such an enormous task to
accomplish.

Radulf must fight a battle and Lily must save
her people. Right now, even the love she felt for
him was unimportant. And yet . . .

"You told the king you trusted me." The words
burst out of her.

"As much as you trust me," he reminded her.
"How much do you trust me, Lily?"

Her throat went dry. She trusted him more than
any other man she had known since her father's
death, but her streak of self-preservation was too
well developed for her to tell him so.

He spoke again when she didn't answer, his tone
deceptively mild and unconcerned. "I will take

you with me, and you will do what you promised to do. We will both obey the king and see this matter brought to an end. And then we will go home to Crevitch, and it will all be forgotten."

He was offering her a truce.

She smiled, her lips trembling. "Very well, my lord. The north, and then to Crevitch."

They were barely inside the house when Radulf began shouting orders and Lily began hurrying to pack. Jervois had felt dazed until then. He had been dazed since Lily said, in a strange sort of jest, that he might end up with his head upon Bootham Gate. As his horse had galloped through York's narrow streets he had been able to think of nothing else.

If he died, Alice would have to wed Sir Othric! He remembered the man well, a hideous figure with warts on his face. He might have been a creature of pity, only he was so full of his own importance it was impossible to feel sorry for him. Sir Othric would have found such a thing incomprehensible.

The fact of Alice marrying that repulsive old man hadn't seemed real until now. It had been a blur, but suddenly it took on a sharp and distinctive edge.

As Radulf strode toward the hall, Jervois stepped in front of him. "My lord."

Radulf halted, frowning down at him.

Jervois swallowed. "My lord, I . . . I beg you to . . . that is, I have a boon to ask of you." He was red; he felt the fire in his face.

Radulf watched him with some concern. "What is it, Jervois? Are you ill?"

"Alice of Rennoc," he got out, somehow.

Radulf's eyes lost their worried expression. A smile tugged at one corner of his mouth. "You want to gobble her up?"

Jervois stepped back a pace, green eyes blazing. "My lord!"

"Nay, calm yourself. 'Twas . . . a private jest." Radulf assumed a more serious demeanor. "Aye, Jervois, have her to wife if you want. We will find you some part of my estates to watch over. Go tell her uncle, in case he weds her to someone else while we are gone."

Jervois felt dizzy with relief, but he was not finished yet. "If I die in battle, my lord—"

Radulf frowned. "If you are slain then I will take care the girl does not wed against her will. My lady would probably be glad of her company at Crevitch. Worry not, my friend, all will be taken care of."

Jervois smiled. Without his habitual seriousness, his face looked suddenly young and transformed. "Thank you, Lord Radulf!" he said fervently.

Radulf shook his head as his captain hurried away to Alice of Rennoc's uncle. He had been thinking himself the only fool in the house; it was comforting to know there was another.

Lily straightened her spine, staring straight ahead. They had traveled hard and fast, and if she hadn't been young and strong and fit, she would have feared for her child. As it was, she was merely exhausted every night when she crawled under the furs inside Radulf's tent.

Sometimes he was very late coming to bed, re-

maining outside with his men and Jervois. But
when he did come, his arms were warm and iron
hard, and they held her safe. Often he caressed her
until she squirmed and pleaded, then he mounted
her and covered her mouth with his to take her
cries as she crested wave after wave of singing
pleasure. And every morning he woke her, laughing at her bleary eyes and tangled hair.

"Up, sleepyhead," he mocked. "You wanted to
come. Remember?"

Sometimes Lily thought she hated him . . .
when she wasn't loving him.

As they passed through the little villages and
settlements, Lily spoke to the people. She smiled
with them and sympathized with them, and she
told them about Radulf, her husband, and her
hopes for peace in the north. A peace they were
unlikely to have under Hew's rule.

Did they listen to her? She thought so, she
hoped so, but only time would tell.

As they drew closer to Grimswade and
Radulf's camp under the command of Lord
Henry, the countryside appeared quieter, sometimes deserted. Those who did remain watched
them suspiciously and when Lily tried to speak
with them, took to their heels or hid in the ruins of
their houses. Her heart ached for them.

She began so many sentences with, "If I could
only tell them!" that Radulf should have grown
tired of hearing it. But he was more patient than
she could have imagined. He listened to her, and
held her, and once when she wept with sorrow
over the burned bodies of a family trapped in a
farm cottage, he lifted her upon his lap and rocked
her, his lips warm and soft against her hair.

"You have done all you can," he comforted her. "Now it is up to me. Believe in me, *mignonne*. I am strong. I will win this battle, just as I have won all the rest."

She did believe in him, and yet the fear would not leave her. Was it because she loved him so much? Whatever the real reason for her deep anxiety, she admitted to herself that if Radulf were killed, then her own life would be over, as well as that of the child he did not even know existed. Many times Lily thought of telling him about the baby, but just as often she stopped herself. It wasn't because she didn't trust him, that inner voice insisted. Why should she add to his worries when he already had so many?

No, she justified to herself, it wasn't fair to tell him just now.

The camp at Grimswade hadn't changed. The tents stretched on endlessly, a haze of smoke hanging over them as the occupants cooked their meals and warmed their hands and feet. A scout had spotted the armed band, and upon recognizing Lord Radulf, could not prevent a grin of utter relief. He accompanied them jauntily through the cheering men, and once again Lily realized how popular Radulf was among his own people. If only her people could see such a scene as this, they would be begging to take up arms against Hew.

At last they reached the rise upon which sat Radulf's tent, and Lily gave it a fond, if somewhat exhausted, smile. Here she had been sent as Radulf's prisoner after he found her in the church, and here she had hidden, afraid of him and yet wildly attracted to him at the same time.

She remembered her turmoil now with some amusement. Resistance—though she had shown little enough of that!—had been useless. Radulf had had his way with her, although it had been no hardship for her to give in. Indeed, "giving in" had been a victory in itself, for Radulf was as much a slave of her body as she was of his.

She slid down off her horse and felt a warm arm curl about her waist, supporting her, setting her on her feet. Pale and shadow-eyed, Lily turned to thank her husband.

"You are tired, Lily," he murmured softly against her ear, his warm breath tingling in places she had forgotten for an hour or two. Amazingly, she felt desire pool in her belly and tighten her breasts, which had become so much more sensitive since her pregnancy.

"Rest," Radulf ordered. Then, "Stephen!"

"The squire appeared from nowhere, wide-eyed as he gazed up at his lord. "Lord Radulf?" he stammered.

"You are well, boy?" Radulf quizzed him. "Lord Henry has been treating you kindly?"

"Yes, my lord." Stephen's blue eyes were full of admiration.

"Where is Lord Henry?"

"He's with the workers at the castle, my lord. They've already made a beginning. Soon you won't have to live in a tent."

Radulf laughed. "Unfortunately, a good stone castle is not so quickly built, boy!"

Stephen caught Lily's eye and color stained his beardless cheeks, but she had expected him to be suspicious of her. The last time she had been there, Lily had been under guard, a possible threat to the Normans. Now everyone would know she was the she-devil, Vorgen's widow, and the wife Lord Radulf had been ordered by the king to wed.

"Bring food and drink to the tent for my lady, Stephen." Radulf spoke over his shoulder as he walked away. "And for me!"

Stephen bowed as low as he could. "This way, lady." He gestured toward the tent, as if she didn't know her own way. "Lord Henry moved when he had word Lord Radulf was returning to Grimswade. The tent is all yours."

"Thank you, Stephen."

The dim, airy interior was heavenly after her long, rough journey. Lily would have collapsed on the furs on the bed, but Stephen pointedly placed a stool by the table. Amused, Lily sat while the squire hurried to fetch the food and drink his master had commanded.

As she waited, Lily wrapped her new fur-lined cloak closer about her body. Summer was truly over here at Grimswade. As they had ridden north she had noticed the trees beginning to turn, their leaves a brilliant collage against the vast gray sky. The rocky crags and thick forests seemed more desolate, more lonely. This was not the soft south, where Radulf's heart dwelt. This was Lily's country, harsh and unforgiving. It had made her what she was.

Stephen returned and set down a goblet of wine and several platters of food. Lily summoned a smile, and chose a slice of apple and several plump blackberries. The latter were sweet and juicy against her tongue and, with the wine, helped to revive her.

"How is Grimswade, Stephen?"

"Until now, lady, it's been very quiet. Everyone who could has taken turns working on the castle. It is to stand upon the same hill where the she-dev—that is, where Vorgen had his keep . . . lady."

The color had once more flooded his face at the slip, but Lily pretended not to notice. "And Father Luc?"

Thoughts of the little priest had niggled at her while she was in York. She had wondered whether Lord Henry had discovered Father Luc's involvement with Hew and punished him for it. And of course, there had been the priest's masterly twisting of the truth where Lily's identity and whereabouts were concerned.

Stephen set her mind at rest.

"He left not long after you and Lord Radulf, lady. One of the villagers said he'd gone to a monastery on the coast. They say he was very fond of oysters," he added, with more than a hint of disapproval.

Lily laughed, more with relief at Father Luc's safety than Stephen's prejudices. But Stephen's fair skin pinkened for the third time.

"I'll leave you to rest now, my lady," he informed her with much wounded dignity.

Lily stretched and yawned. "Yes, Stephen, I am very tired. And Stephen . . . I'm glad your voice has stopped jumping about. It sounds very nice."

He bolted.

Lily chuckled to herself. She glanced longingly

over the platters but was just too weary to eat. Stumbling over to the bed, she climbed under the pile of furs and collapsed. She didn't even bother to undress. What did a few creases matter? Soon they would do battle with Hew and Lord Kenton.

Lily's head ached with thinking. She drew a deep breath, and promptly fell asleep.

And woke, disoriented.

It was as if the past had slipped forward, or Lily had slipped back. She was lying in Radulf's bed in his tent at Grimswade, just as she had before, and he was in the room with her. She sensed him, knew he was there even before she heard the sound of his low, husky voice.

Last time, she had been afraid—he had been her captor, and her future had been a frightening void. Now she was his wife, carrying his child, and they had come north to fight a last battle and start a new, peaceful reign in this troubled land.

"How can you know?"

The voice was familiar, though Lily needed a moment to place it. Yes, it was Lord Henry. Opening her eyes a mere slit, she saw that the two men were standing by the table, eating. Lord Henry appeared less smooth than he had when she had seen him last, his chestnut curls messy, his blue eyes snapping. Perhaps the time spent at Grimswade had taken its toll, or else Hew's approach had rattled him.

"How can you know?" he demanded again, his voice rising. His cherubic face was twisted with annoyance that did not sit well upon it. Maybe, thought Lily, he was not so handsome after all.

"I know." Radulf took a gulp of his wine, and poured more from the jug. He chewed and swallowed a piece of meat, following it with a handful of the juicy blackberries.

"You don't speak with your mind, Radulf, you speak with your cock!" Lord Henry snarled. "She has you by it, and all you care about is putting it in her. I saw that in your eyes when I came here. She had you even then, but I believed she might be good for you. I never thought you'd lose your head entirely over a woman! Jesu, the great Radulf! Turning into an old fool, just—"

He stopped then. Lily felt her own heart stutter, knowing what he had been about to say. *Just like his father.* Her gaze shifted to Radulf. His back was turned toward her, but she could see by the set of his shoulders, the tightening and bunching of the muscles in his upper arms, that he was very angry.

"You speak of what you don't understand," he said in a deceptively soft voice. "I will forgive you for it, because you have been my friend for so long, and I think it is concern which makes you so unlike your usual tactful self. Lily is my wife, and she has come with me by order of the king to speak to her people, to turn them to our side. I believe she will do this, Henry, because she cares deeply for their welfare. I have seen her ask after their children, I have seen her give them her own bread, and promise she will do all she can to help their lot. You wrong her, my friend."

But Henry was set on his course and meant to have his say. "You should have left her in York. She is dangerous, and you have brought her here where she can do the most damage. In God's name, Radulf, when I told you to enjoy her I did not know she was Vorgen's wife, and I did not know you meant to wed her!"

Radulf brought his fist down on the table, hard. On the bed, Lily jumped. On the table, the wine slopped, the platters jumped and spun, the food spilled onto the floor.

"She is not Anna!" Radulf rasped, his low voice infinitely more dangerous than Henry's shouts. "Can you believe me to be such a fool that I would marry another Anna?"

The words were hardly out of his mouth when Radulf knew they were the truth. The doubts he had been carrying with him ever since he learned Lily's true identity suddenly crumbled into dust. He was free, for perhaps the first time in his adult life.

Henry stared at him a moment more, and then heaved a heartfelt sigh. "Very well, Radulf. I am sorry for speaking so plainly. Sometimes friends need lies, and sometimes they need plain speaking. I have stated my fears and you have answered them. I will accept what you say. She is your wife, and if you trust her with your life . . . then so will I."

Radulf took the other man's outstretched hand in a firm clasp. The argument was forgotten, and soon they were discussing the approach of Hew's army and the battle they must win.

Lily's body gradually relaxed again as their words washed over her, and she must have slept. When she woke this time, Radulf was alone, seated by the table in his breeches and white linen shirt, his head bent over a parchment that he had spread across the table. Stephen must have come and tidied up the mess, for now only the wine remained.

Lily hesitated to disturb him, but his words still rang in her head. He had spoken up for her when he could just as easily have agreed with his friend. *You wrong her. She is not Anna.*

It was as if Radulf's rebuttal had freed something in her heart, some restriction that had been there since she read Anna's message.

Lily rose, her body still stiff and aching from the long journey. But at least the tiredness had gone. If necessary she could ride again, although she hoped she wouldn't have to do so. She walked quietly over to where Radulf sat, and rested her hand against his broad shoulder.

He must have heard her approach, because he didn't seem startled, only turned his head slightly to offer a weary smile. It was a map he had spread out before him, the cloth worn and tattered about the edges through much use. The candle had burned low, but Lily recognised Vorgen's keep and the hills surrounding it, as well as the countryside around Grimswade.

"This is where Hew is camped," he said. "And here is where we will draw him out."

Lily looked to where he pointed and nodded.

"We have two days at the most."

Lily stepped closer, leaning lightly against her husband. "Until you have to fight?"

"Until I have to win."

"You will." Lily bent to kiss his neck. He smelled of sweat and horse and man. "You are the King's Sword, the immortal Radulf; you always win."

He laughed softly. " 'Always,' Lily?"

"Always." She trailed her tongue across his ear, tickling, tantalizing. She slid her fingers through his hair, enjoying the silky feel of it against her skin. Earlier, Radulf had fought for her in another way. He had stood up for her honor when Lord Henry had tried to turn him against her.

Maybe he trusted her after all.

Maybe it is time you trusted him.

The thought startled her, frightened her.

Radulf turned his head just enough to catch her mouth with his. Their kiss deepened, until Lily's head spun dizzily and her legs lost their strength. His hands cupped her buttocks, drawing her closer, bringing her to stand between his thighs.

"Ah Lily," he murmured, nuzzling against her throat, her breasts. "So cool on the outside, but so hot within . . ."

She gasped as he found one of her nipples through the cloth of her gown, and held his face close. "Vorgen did not think me hot within," she managed, dragging the words out before she lost her wits entirely. Radulf's hands were on her thighs now, purposefully raising her skirts. "He thought me as cold as the ice that covers the streams in winter, as cold as the snow on the ground. Once, his soldiers brought news of a man who had become lost and died in the forest. His body was covered in snow, and it was frozen hard. Vorgen turned to me when he heard that story, and he said, 'That is you, lady. You are like that man.'"

Radulf had stopped, his hands gripping her thighs, his breath warm in the hollow at the base of her throat. His eyes had lost their dazed look.

Lily took a ragged breath and went on, before she lost her courage altogether. "He told me that it was my fault that he could not take me as a husband takes his wife; that my coldness shriveled his manhood whenever he came near me, whenever I touched him . . . there. He hated me for that. He swore to throw me to his men, and sometimes he wept because he could not do to me what he so wanted to do. He said it so many times that I believed him. I was cold. But you have thawed that ice, Radulf. You have turned me into a warm, living woman once more. I am alive again, because of you."

His eyes were fixed on her face now, taking in every movement, every emotion.

"He was lying to you. Give me your hand."

Slowly, Lily placed her fingers in his. He smiled, bending to kiss them. "You are no frozen woman, Lily. You are warm and desirable. Put aside what Vorgen said." His eyes narrowed, a flash of anger lighting them as he thought of what he would like to do to that particular Norman.

Instead, he gently pressed her hand against that ever-eager bulge between his thighs. "I have no difficulty in taking you as a husband takes his wife, and far from your touch shriveling this tireless piece of flesh . . . my dilemma is in resisting you, *mignonne*!"

Tears filled her eyes, blinding her. "I did believe him," she insisted. "He was very convincing. You have freed me of his evil."

He stroked her cheek, brushing aside the falling tears. Her lips trembled as he kissed them tenderly, a healing kiss. His heart was full to overflowing with what she had told him. He had guessed some of it, from knowing Vorgen and from her reactions, and from what she had said to him at Trier. Now he knew the whole truth, and he wanted to tear Vorgen to pieces. It was a shame that he was already dead. After what he had heard tonight, Radulf would have enjoyed killing him.

Chapter 18

◦◦◦◦◦

Throughout the following day, a constant trickle of men sought the safety of Radulf's army. Some of them came alone and expressed a desire to fight with the husband of Lady Wilfreda, others brought their families and set up camp, huddling dry-eyed and weary beneath the azure banner of the King's Sword.

As Radulf watched them come, and watched his wife go among them—with the bodyguard he had insisted upon—he understood at last that she had been right. Her people loved and trusted her, far more than they had ever trusted Hew or Vorgen. She had come north to give them hope of peace, and despite their instinctive distrust of the Norman conquerors, they believed in her enough to grasp at the opportunity she was giving them.

Hew was camped some five miles away. His army, mostly Kenton's men with a few rebels thrown in, had ruthlessly pillaged the surrounding countryside, making themselves even more hated than before. By joining Hew, Kenton's soldiers were doing as they had been ordered, but many of them didn't like it. They had fought at Hastings with the Normans they now faced as enemies. Deserters had already joined the trickle of Englishmen who were swelling Radulf's army.

He was well satisfied.

Lord Henry, too, had had to admit his mistake where Lily was concerned. Radulf had noticed, with amusement, his friend's attempts to charm his wife as only Henry could. He was even more amused to notice that, although she listened politely, Lily was not cajoled by his glib tongue. Had he once thought Henry could charm her away from him? She was not such a fool.

It was midday as Radulf stood, listening to Henry and Jervois argue about tactics, his eyes scanning the smoky camp with its many souls, all dependent upon him. He noticed his wife leave their tent. She paused a moment, breathing in the air, straightening her back as if preparing herself to face whatever obstacles might be set in her path.

Aye, she was a proud woman, and Radulf was proud of her and what she had done. A man could ask no more than to live with such a woman at his side. Her hair was bright and uncovered, like a young girl's, her gown a simple one, so as not to intimidate the common folk, and she wore no jewelry apart from the red-eyed hawk upon her thumb.

He watched her stretch again, as if her back ached. Something in the movement, something in the way her hands were folded so protectively across her belly, struck a discordant note in Radulf.

Puzzled, he watched her descend once more into the heart of the camp. Stephen was trailing behind her, and the boy shot wistful glances at the soldiers as they checked and sharpened their weapons, shouting bravado to hide their fear. Many of them would be dead tomorrow, but Stephen probably didn't think of that, Radulf thought wryly. He was dreaming of the glory.

Radulf had already decided that the battle would take place tomorrow, soon after first light. He would march his men in predawn darkness to the long, flat valley where Hew was encamped. Then they would attack. If Hew was unprepared, so much the better, but Radulf did not fool himself into thinking it would be an easy victory. Kenton's men were well trained; they were no rabble. No, it would be a hard fight, but one he had no intention of losing.

His gaze slipped back to Lily. She had reached Gudren and Olaf's tent, and seemed to be hesitating there. Even as she made to move on, Gudren's gray head popped out of the opening and her arms waved bossily, gesturing for Lily to enter. With a regal nod of her head, Lily did so, vanishing from his sight.

"I am glad to see you, my pretty one."

Gudren had not changed. She was as plump as ever, her face barely wrinkled, her pale eyes cunning.

"And you, mother." Lily smiled, answering her in her own tongue.

Gudren sighed. "It does my heart good to hear

the sound of Norway. I knew you were not who you said you were, lady. I told Olaf you were of Viking blood, but he scoffed and said I was getting old. Now see who is old!"

Lily smiled. "Olaf prepares for the battle?"

"He works all day and at night he sharpens his axe."

Lily hesitated. "He believes in a great victory, like Radulf?"

Gudren watched her thoughtfully, as if considering her question. "Radulf has a spell upon him. He cannot be defeated. That is what Olaf believes."

"Yes, I have heard such things myself."

"But you do not believe them," Gudren answered for her. "You doubt, because you are afraid for him. We always fear losing what we love most, pretty one. But Radulf is strong and clever. He will not take risks with his life. You will see. He will return to you and your babe."

When Lily stared at her, eyes wide, Gudren laughed in delight.

"You thought I would not know! Me, Gudren, who has borne five babies and helped to birth many, many more? You have a look, my pretty, a softness. I am never wrong."

Lily swallowed, pressing her hands over the slight rounding of her belly. "No, mother, you are not wrong."

"You have told him?"

"No." Lily gave the other woman an appealing look. "I thought he had enough to worry about. Will you keep my secret, Gudren? Just for now."

Gudren smiled and patted her hand. "Sometimes it is better to wait . . . to see how things turn out. I understand that. But Radulf will not be pleased when he learns you have kept this from him. He will see it as betrayal. And he has known much betrayal."

Gudren was watching her expectantly, so Lily nodded. "I know about Anna," she said quietly. "He told me."

Gudren beamed. "That is good! That means he begins to trust you, my pretty one. Do not put that trust at risk, even if it is . . . easier to do so."

Lily closed her eyes against the smoky haze in the tent. "Yes, mother," she agreed reluctantly, "but I fear he will send me to York. I need to be here."

Gudren leaned forward. "Tell him, lady, before it is too late. Lay all that you are open to him. It is the only way."

Lily felt an instinctive rejection. Let Radulf search with that knowing black gaze into every corner and crevice of her heart and mind? How could she bear for him to know all there was to know about her when, like Hew or Vorgen, he might use her weakness against her?

Lily had spent too many years keeping herself safe behind barriers. Radulf had already broached them at some points, and weakened them at others, but she had not opened those gates to him of her own free will. Not yet.

Lily looked up, doubts on her lips, but Gudren appeared to have gone to sleep.

There was much preparation for the morrow's fighting. Lily glimpsed Radulf now and again, usually at a distance, overseeing some detail large or small. Gudren was wrong, Lily decided. Radulf had enough to do without his wife running after him, tugging at his arm, demanding attention.

She did not allow herself to question the relief that filled her at her decision.

But as darkness swept down over the camp, and silence fell, her doubts returned. She heard an occasional raised voice, a woman weeping, a child laughing, but mostly there was silence and hushed voices. Everyone was aware of the importance of the battle in the morning, and although Radulf had made certain there was enough ale for a drink or two, that was all he would allow. Too many soldiers spent the night before a battle in a drunken stupor and then found it impossible to fight. If there was drinking to be done, then it would be to celebrate their victory rather than preempt it.

All knew that many would die. Radulf's force was still smaller than Hew's, but that did not seem to give them pause. His men trusted Radulf to get as many of them as possible home to Crevitch.

Trust, thought Lily irritably. There was that word again. She paced about the tent, her mind agitated, her body tense. If only tomorrow were over!

And still Lily waited.

She knew he had much to do. She knew how his men looked to him. But Lily wanted to speak with him, hold him, kiss him. She wanted to give him a respite from his heavy burden as leader, she wanted him to be *her* Radulf, just for a short time, before he stole some well-deserved sleep. There was an aching longing in her heart that would not be satisfied until he was there.

He came to her at last, but Jervois and Lord Henry followed. They talked as they ate the food and wine Stephen brought, plotting and planning, discussing the merits of this tactic and that, dredging up other battles and skirmishes to prove their point.

Lily had sent Stephen to bed. Though the boy would have liked to remain listening to the men talk, he was asleep on his feet.

"We need to take the hills to the north of the valley." Radulf chewed as he spoke. "Remember at Hastings, how Harold held the ridge and we had to fight uphill? We were fortunate to win the day."

Jervois nodded, remembering. "We lost many good men."

"And many good horses." Henry stretched and yawned.

Radulf poured more wine, and gave Henry a fond glance. "You didn't have a mark on you. I remember thinking that the blood and dirt must have rolled off you rather than spoil your new armor."

Henry grimaced. "I pray the same happens tomorrow, Radulf. Get your Viking wife to cast her runes." He stopped, suddenly aware of Lily's still form in the shadows. "I beg pardon, lady," he said contritely, "but I did not speak in jest. If you can protect us with a spell, I, for one, would be grateful!"

Lily stepped forward, a slender figure in her blue wool gown, her silver braid spearing down her back. "I wish I knew one," she replied coolly.

Radulf glanced from one to the other and gave a jaw-cracking yawn. "I can't think anymore. Enough. We have done all we can tonight."

The other two men rose promptly, bowing to

Lily as they took their leave, and at last she and
Radulf were alone. He held out his hand toward
her, and she didn't hesitate, tumbling onto his lap
and into the warm strength of his arms.

"How long before you must leave?" she murmured, her face pressed to his neck.

"Three hours, maybe."

Shocked, she started to rise. "You should sleep!
Lie down, Radulf."

He looked down at her, his eyes dark with emotion. "Three hours may be all we have, *mignonne*. I
won't waste them in sleeping."

"Radulf . . . you will win. I *know* that you will
win."

He laughed softly. "Aye, I'll win. Now, kiss
your husband."

His sensual mouth plundered hers and she
moaned, pressing closer, her arms clinging about
his neck. She wouldn't allow herself to imagine
life without him; she wouldn't!

He was hard against her thigh, and when she
reached to caress him, he groaned. "I want you,"
he whispered. "I always want you. Come, Lily."

Radulf led her to the bed. With slow, gentle fingers, she removed his clothing, supplementing
kisses with licks from her tongue, until he captured her against him, mouth hot and demanding,
sapping what strength she had left.

It was his turn then, and he took full advantage,
exploring her body, his tongue lapping at her
breasts, then sucking on her nipples until she
arched toward him with delight. He leaned over
her, blocking out the candlelight, and without a
word drove deep inside.

Lily cried out, for with each thrust he seemed to

go deeper than ever before. His breath came fast, the perspiration damp on his brow, while Lily gasped and gripped him with her legs.

"You are mine," he said, deep and low. "If I die tomorrow, you will always be mine."

Tears shone in her eyes, but he kept thrusting slowly, so deeply, taking her with him. He began to move faster, plunging into her again and again, as if he would make her a part of him.

"Radulf . . ." she gasped, the choppy waves of pleasure beginning to peak. Only this time they simply grew and grew, tossing her about as he controlled her rise. She cried out and the pleasure broke over her, tumbling her headlong while she struggled to gain the surface.

Drowning in love.

They lay for a long time, bodies drained of strength, until the world steadied about them. Replete, calm, Lily could not think of a single reason that she should not trust Radulf with her heart. He already held her life in his hands, and had done so since their first meeting.

She would tell him about the babe soon. Maybe she would even tell him how much she loved him.

Radulf raised himself up on one elbow. He stroked her, curving his hand over her breasts, down to her belly. Her skin was so fine, so delicate, that his fingers felt big and rough against it. Her breasts rose and fell with each breath, her eyes closed, the lashes dark against the flush in her cheeks.

Gradually he became aware of a cold sliver of doubt in his mind—the same unease that had come to him when he watched her earlier that day. Like the prick of a splinter in soft flesh, it niggled and teased. He remembered Lily stretching her back outside the tent, and the way she held her hands across her belly. He remembered, too, her pallor and her lack of appetite before they left York. Suddenly, frowning, his gaze slid over her body once more, searching . . . Her breasts were lusher than ever, her skin glowing as if the moonlight shone down on her, while her hair gleamed. The hand he had left resting on her belly pressed gently, as though sensing what lay beneath . . .

He went cold. She was having his child and she hadn't told him.

She hadn't told him.

"Radulf?" Lily had noticed his stillness and turned her head lazily, gray eyes searching. The sated expression on her face vanished as her wits sharpened into watchfulness. If he hadn't known then, he would have guessed now. He met her eyes and knew what she would see there, but he didn't care. She had hurt him beyond bearing.

"You are with child." He didn't speak accusingly or angrily; it was a statement of fact. She was frightened, he could smell it, sense it. He knew enough about death to be well acquainted with fear.

"Yes." It was so soft he could hardly hear her.

"How long have you known?" But he didn't really need to ask; he knew the answer.

"I—"

"How long!"

Lily's throat was dry and raw. There was a drip, drip of ice in her heart. From nowhere, Gudren's voice said, *Tell him, lady, before it is too late.* Something in his stillness, his anger, made her wonder if it already was.

"I knew in York. I didn't tell you because I knew you wouldn't let me come with you!" She rushed the words out quickly, not knowing when he might stop them. "I had to come with you, Radulf, for the sake of my lands and my people. The king agreed with me—"

"You lie," he bit out. "You knew before I was to come north." His anger trembled in his arms and his voice, it shone in his black eyes and flushed his cheeks high upon the cheekbones.

"I . . . maybe I did know, but I was afraid to tell you. I thought . . . I . . ." Her voice drifted off. She thought he would love her only for the children she could give him, and she had wanted more than that. Now, starkly, she saw that by not telling him, she had not trusted him—and that was the way he would see it, also.

"You were afraid," he mocked. "The she-devil, the Viking witch, was afraid? What were you afraid of, Lily? That I might kill you with kindness? That I might lavish even more of my kisses on you than I do already?"

He rolled over onto his back and stared at the ceiling.

Outside in the darkness, an owl called. Lily trembled. Her Viking mother would have said the owl was a sign, an ill omen. Lily refused to believe it. An owl was a night bird, that was all. It meant nothing. And yet the childhood superstition slipped under her guard, taunting her with possibilities.

"I thought of telling you when we reached Grimswade—every day I thought of it, but I didn't want to add to your burden." She moved a little, trying to see his face where it was turned from her. "Radulf? If I have wounded you, then I'm sorry."

The Viking ice queen had gone, and in her place was a frightened girl.

"I have opened my heart to you," he said quietly, "and you have taken what I gave and kept your own counsel. You were wrong, Lily. You should have told me."

"Radulf, please—" Her voice broke and she couldn't go on.

"Was that story about Vorgen true? Yes, I see it was. I already knew most of it, but it kept me happy, didn't it? Kept me from wanting more. With it, you drew me down even deeper. I am drowning, Lily, and you won't even hold out your hand to save me."

"That's not true! I have tended you when you were hurt, I have seen that you are fed and have wine to drink, I have—"

"These are things any woman could have done. A servant could have tended my wounds and seen me fed. I wanted a wife, Lily. I wanted more . . . I *want* more. I treasured you." He glanced at her swiftly, as if the words shamed him now. "Like my father, I am a fool for a pretty face, and like him I will suffer. Maybe I will forget what has happened between us. Probably I will forget . . . he always did. But not now, not yet."

"Radulf," she whispered. "I . . . I have had to guard my heart to survive. It is . . . difficult for me to open it after so long, to offer to you freely that which has been locked away."

He drew a deep, shaken breath and touched her hair, lightly, so that she barely felt it. "Perhaps it is as you say. Maybe I have been as guilty as you, lady. I will try to forgive you, but just now that is hard for me. Perhaps you should sleep. We will talk tomorrow, when all this is over . . ." Then, remembering that he might not be alive to speak to anyone, he added, "In the morning I will consult with Lord Henry. If anything happens to me, you and the child will be safe. Lord Henry will probably marry you himself."

"No!" she gasped in horror, but Radulf didn't look at her. He had turned away again, his eyes closed, and she could see by the hard line of his mouth that he had no intention of debating the matter further.

I treasured you.

The realization made her dizzy. She had been a coward, safe behind her barricades. She had found excuses not to take the final step and open up her heart to him. What could he have done, after all? Laugh? He would never have hurt her; he was not that sort of man. But she had remembered Vorgen, and Hew, and she could not take the chance.

So now she would be sorry.

Lily turned away, curling herself up tightly, as if she could disappear into nothing. Gudren had been right. She should have told him, no matter what else was happening, no matter how much she feared his reaction. She should have shown him her trust, and then he would have forgiven her.

Quietly, still proud enough to hope he couldn't hear her, Lily cried herself to sleep.

The birds woke Lily. Not an owl this time, but blackbirds singing their melodious song. She sat up, knowing even before she found her feet and stumbled to the door of the tent, that he would be gone. The light was still very faint, creeping across the deserted camp. The blink and flicker of lanterns and campfires shone in the half dark.

Lily stood barefoot and swaying in the chilly gray predawn. She had wept for a long time, and at last, exhausted, had slept deeply. Radulf had risen, donned his armor, strapped his sword to his side, taken up his shield, and left to fight Hew. He had not even awakened her to say goodbye.

"Oh, Radulf," she whispered.

A tiny child ran by on shaky legs, and was caught by its young mother. That was all that remained in the camp now: women and children, and the men who were either too old or too infirm to fight. And Lily.

Somehow she had to find her way to Radulf. She had seen the map; she knew which way to go. Filled with determination, Lily ran back into the tent and donned her shift and gown, tossing her hair over one shoulder, not caring how she looked. She slipped on her stockings and shoes, and then her cloak, grateful for the enveloping warmth.

"Stephen!"

Would the boy be there, or had he gone with the soldiers? As she waited, she snatched up a few blackberries left from the morning repast and sipped a half-filled mug of milk.

"Lady?"

He sounded and looked sullen; he had clearly been instructed to remain there with her while the others went to fight. Despite the tenseness of the moment, she hid a smile.

"Stephen, I must find Lord Radulf. Will you come with me?"

He stared at her as if she had gone mad. "L-lady?"

"You heard me. Is my mare still here, or has she been taken to the fighting?"

He shook his head, still watching her carefully. "No, lady, your mare is still here."

"Good. Then the sooner you fetch her, the sooner we can go to Lord Radulf."

He stared at her a moment more and then quickly turned away, but Lily noticed a jaunty little skip to his step as he hurried to where the horses were stabled.

The mare was all that remained. The other animals, no matter how old or hobbled, had gone to be used by the cavalry, or to carry the wounded home again at the end of the day. Lily's mare had been left, perhaps because she *was* Lily's.

Whatever the reason, she was grateful. She must find Radulf and speak with him before he went into battle. He treasured her; he had said so. Surely, even in his anger, he would be pleased to know that she loved him?

Or would he?

Memories of his face and his voice and his words last night returned to deflate her. Was she better off keeping her feelings safely contained? Should she cling to those last shreds of her dignity, and deny him? Lily rejected the safe course. This time she would say what was in her heart, even if it killed her. What if it was her last chance?

"They've probably started already," Stephen grumbled, as he brought the mare and helped her to mount.

"It is not yet dawn," Lily retorted. "Hurry up! Climb up behind me, Stephen, and hold on."

The boy did as she asked, and Lily kicked the mare into a trot, then a gallop, and turned her head toward the valley where the battle was to take place.

She prayed that she would make it in time.

Jervois leaned forward over his galloping horse's neck, cursing under his breath, the cold wind stinging color into his face and tears into his eyes. He had not wanted to return to camp; he was ready to fight. But neither was he a man to disobey his lord, especially after that lord's generosity in regard to Alice of Rennoc.

"Bring my lady here," Radulf had told him, his voice harsh with some tightly contained emotion. "I believe her Englishmen will fight better if they see her beside me."

"Lord Radulf—" Jervois had begun, but one glance from Radulf had stopped his protest in his throat.

"Bring her here," he repeated the order. "Now go, quickly!"

There was nothing for him to do but obey. He had climbed upon the fastest horse he could find and set out to fetch Radulf's wife.

" 'Fight better if they see her beside me,' " he muttered under his breath. "Aye, my lord, and pigs might fly! You want her with you, that is what it is. You rode off without her, and now you are heartsick."

He spurred the horse, taking a low rise and starting down the other side. That was when he saw the other riders coming toward him, two upon the one mount. He slowed and halted his horse.

"Good, lady! You have saved me much time!" He wiped a hand across his brow, sweat dripping down his face beneath the helmet.

Lily gave him a bewildered look. She was as white as her breath in the cold light.

"Lord Radulf has sent me to fetch you. He says the English will fight better if you are there."

"I was just now going to Lord Radulf. I was thinking the very same thing."

Jervois nodded soberly, as if he believed her. "Make haste, lady. Lord Radulf may be able to persuade the king to do his will where you are concerned, but I doubt he can prevent the enemy from attacking."

Lily urged her horse forward. There was bitterness in her voice when she spoke. "When has Lord Radulf ever persuaded the king to do his will where I was concerned, Jervois? I remember him arguing with the king on a number of occasions, but it was never to please me."

Jervois gave her a look of astonishment. "Why, lady, what about when Lord Radulf persuaded the king to agree to your marriage? He knew who you were then, and knew that King William could well have him arrested for treason, but still he laid claim to you. Has he not told you this?"

Lily shook her head, staring at him as if he had grown horns and a tail. Her mare plodded to a stop. "That can't be. The king *ordered* Radulf to marry me. I was there; I heard."

It had not occurred to Jervois that Radulf would not tell his wife what had transpired that day at William's court. "Perhaps it is not for me to say," he began, but Lily would have none of that.

"Tell me. Please, Jervois. I swear I won't come with you unless you do."

There was desperation in her face, in her eyes, which Jervois had never seen before. Here was not the cold creature of rumor, but a warm, living woman, a woman who was suffering.

"Very well, lady, but we must ride swiftly as I speak, or the battle will commence before we reach Lord Radulf!"

Chapter 19

❧ ⟋⟍ ❧

Radulf had been watching the sky grow lighter. Hew's army occupied a goodly portion of the upper valley. The number of Englishmen had dwindled to only a handful, but there were archers and foot soldiers, as well as a heavy contingent of horse soldiers, tough men who had fought at Hastings for Lord Kenton—my lord was safe elsewhere, the harsh reality of the battlefield was not his to taste.

Hew sat upon his horse, his long, fair hair, the glory of an English noble, as yet uncovered by a helmet. His gaze often turned to Radulf's position. Radulf tucked his own helmet under his arm, his black hair stirred by the cold wind that swirled up the rise upon which he stood.

If Hew could read his mind, he thought, he would be even more confident. For who could fear a man who was as sick with longing as he?

Radulf had awakened that morning, the rage

still pounding in his head, to find Lily tucked against him, her hand upon his chest, her cheek nestled into his shoulder. Her face was pale and still puffy from the tears she had shed. He could have gathered her closer and kissed her, but he didn't.

The anger had gripped him again. He remembered how he had grown weak with the want of her, squandering his wealth by buying her clothes and searching out a fine house to suit her. And all the while she had held herself cool and distant, and taken what he gave. No, he did not want to forgive her deceit. In God's name, was he not Radulf, the King's Sword?

So he had risen from the bed, washed, dressed, and eaten, and left her to Stephen. It had seemed fitting, and when his anger eventually cooled, he could tell himself he had done it for her own good, that she was tired and needed her rest.

It wasn't until Radulf was halfway to reaching the rebel army that he began to regret what he had done, to wish that he had awakened her and kissed her. What if he never saw her again? What if he were struck down in battle by a sword or a spear or an arrow? What if he lay on the green valley floor with the life pumping from him and the sky growing dimmer, remembering only that they had parted in bitterness?

Furiously, he had tried to set his madness aside, organizing his men, sending orders for their placement, bolstering their courage. But the picture in his mind wouldn't go away, and he finally couldn't bear it any longer, and had sent Jervois to do his bidding.

Poor Jervois; he had been down that road before!

It was more than possible Lily would not reach him before the order was given to commence the fighting. Perhaps she would refuse to come. He could not blame her for refusing; he had been cruel to her when he could have shown a little more kindness, a little more understanding. It was not as if he didn't have his faults, and he had admired her cold pride and her bravery in standing up to him, when so many others feared him for the tales that were told about him.

I am not afraid of you. She had said that to him more than once, gazing up with her brave gray eyes even as her mouth tightened to stop it trembling.

But these memories did not alter the fact that Lily had hurt him deeply by keeping the secret of the babe from him. He had given her all that he could, protected her with all that he had, lavished his body upon her like one starved; and she had stood like the cursed English at Hastings, with their shields held up before them, defending themselves from the enemy.

"Sir!" A voice rose above the noise.

Radulf yanked himself back from his daydream and found the man, who was pointing. Radulf turned his head and shaded his eyes against the rising sun. There were a couple of riders coming toward them. Jervois was one of them, and the other . . .

"Stand firm!" Radulf cried. "Hold a little while longer." Faces turned toward him, white and strained, shaking hands gripping spears or bows. The foot soldiers and cavalry would wait until the archers had had their turn, and then they would sweep down the valley. Beside Radulf, Olaf held his great battle-axe delicately in one hand, as if it were not capable of removing a man's head with a single blow.

"Odin shield me." The amorer muttered his pagan prayers under his breath. "Mighty Thor, strongest and most virile of all the gods, protect me . . ."

"My lord, I have the lady," Jervois panted as he arrived.

Radulf nodded, his eyes sliding past his captain to where Lily was dismounting with Stephen's help.

"Thank you, Jervois," he said quietly. "I will remember this."

Lily's cloak had blown back, and Radulf saw that she wore the dark blue gown, the wool cloth molding her slender body. Her hair was loose about her, tangling in the wind so that she had to hold it back from her eyes. She was staring at him, her white face ablaze with some powerful emotion.

Anger, he supposed. What had he expected? He bit back his frustration. It couldn't be helped; he must go ahead with his plan. And hope that Lily would not revenge herself upon him by refusing to obey him. The reason he had given for fetching her had been partially the truth; her presence would make a difference to the English contingent of his army.

The other reason . . . How could Lord Radulf, the monster of legend, admit that he wished to feel his wife's softness against his body, and smell the scent of her hair, to take with him into the terror of battle?

He was a weak fool. He had sent Jervois to bring

him the woman who, after last night, had every reason to hate him more than ever, and who was capable of turning half of his army against him.

A woman he mistrusted.

Radulf was frowning as he came toward her, but Lily forestalled him. She held up her hand, and he halted. Her gaze flicked over him, so large and formidable in his armor, his expression still angry and somehow expectant. This was the man she loved, without whom her life would be nothing. What did it matter if he did not love her? She would *make* him love her, she thought fiercely. In a few minutes he would fight Hew, and if he were killed . . .

Lily swallowed hard. She had guarded her heart for too long. It was time she opened it to all the joy, and maybe the pain, of which she was capable.

She stretched her arm against the lightening sky and cried out, as loudly as she could, in English and then in French:

"Hear me! Oh, good Englishmen and Normans, hear me!"

Gradually the noise began to drop away as, one after another, the men of the army became aware that something was happening. Radulf was standing unmoving, hardly seeming to breathe.

"I wish Lord Radulf luck today in his fight against the rebel Hew. I know that he will win back the north, and we will have peace here at last. Those of you who have families here, who live here, must long for peace as much as I do."

Lily stepped forward, tugging at the ring on her thumb—the red-eyed hawk that had been her father's symbol of power. The black enamel inscription caught her eye: "I give thee my heart." It seemed particularly apt.

"Lord Radulf, I give you this," she said in stirring tones, and held the ring high, so that the hawk's ruby eye caught the sun and glinted like blood. There was a muffled cheer from those who understood its significance.

Lily took the steps that brought her face to face with him and, trembling, reached to grasp his hand. She heard his hiss of breath, and then his hand lay acquiescent in hers, the flesh warm and callused. She did not dare think of those fingers touching her, loving her. She did not dare meet those dark eyes, which she knew were watching her every move. If she allowed herself to think or to look, she might not be able to finish what she had begun.

Lily managed to push the ring onto Radulf's little finger, at least as far as the second knuckle, and there it stuck.

She drew in a deep breath and proclaimed to all, "Lord Radulf, I give you this ring, and with it . . . all that is mine!" And raising his hand to her lips, she pressed a fervent kiss against the roughened skin.

Only then did she look up, into his eyes, her own shimmering with tears, her face naked, vulnerable, and laid open for him.

She meant it. With growing wonder, Radulf understood what she had just given him. He had feared the worst and instead she had given him the very best. There was no longer any reason to mistrust her, to fear that if he admitted to loving her, she would use it as a weapon and destroy him. She had had her chance, and instead of his destruction, given her own heart into his keeping.

Aye, he loved her! He spoke the words in his head, and liked the sound of them. A huge smile split Radulf's face. He caught Lily up in his arms, lifting her feet off the ground. She gasped, her arms twining about his neck, and he fastened his mouth on hers in a long, soul-wrenching kiss.

The shouts and cheers rose headily about them as the great Radulf kissed his wife, and their army celebrated the joining of Norman and English, and the victory they were about to have.

"I will win today, my Lily," Radulf murmured huskily in her ear. "I will win for you."

"Just come back to me," she said, and tilted her head so that she could gaze deep into his coal-black eyes. "I love you, Radulf. I think I have loved you from our first meeting in Grimswade church. I dream about your wonderful mouth and your strong body, moving inside mine . . . Radulf, you are my Thor."

Thor? Olaf's prayer came back to Radulf, and he gave her a slow and satisfied grin. "Keep dreaming that, *mignonne*. Soon I will make it come true."

Farther up the valley, Hew's horse was stamping, sensing its master's fury, as Hew stared white-faced at the scene being enacted before him. Radulf and Lily! He felt sick with bitter disappointment. Well, they would see who were the victors there today . . .

Hew raised his gauntlet, and screamed out the command to do battle.

* * *

Lily's arms felt cold, empty. Radulf had gone, riding with his men down into the valley. She held her breath, gazing over the distance until her eyes ached and stung, unable to do more than shake her head when Stephen asked her if she wanted wine, or to take shelter in the tent since it was lightly drizzling.

She was nothing, an empty shell, and she would not live again until Radulf returned.

He loved her. He had not said it aloud—maybe he never would—but there had been no mistaking the expression in his eyes, the fiery longing in his kisses. Last night he had said he treasured her, but this morning she knew he loved her.

The azure banner fluttered below, its brilliance catching Lily's gaze. She watched it move back and forth among the seething mass of men. *Radulf's banner.* At first it had shown her where his army was situated, but now the fighting was so intense, there were no clear demarcation lines. Radulf's men could be anywhere within that unwieldy killing machine. The noise was deafening.

But where was Radulf? Lily scanned the battlefield, and finally found him—she had not realized she had stopped breathing until she gulped in a mouthful of cold, rain-laden air. He was fighting from his black destrier, his mighty sword arm swinging back and forth. Lily had never quite realized before how attuned her lord's body was to fighting, how superbly strong and fit he was. Now, even in her terror, she admired him.

A fair-haired giant caught her eye. Olaf. He was pushing his way through the enemy, the great battle-axe rising and falling. He appeared to be set on a particular destination, and although the foes

threw themselves into his path, he dispatched
them with hardly a pause. Lily lifted her gaze beyond Olaf and saw that the enemy was still strong
to the left of the field. A horseman, slender even in
his armor, fought furiously, urging his men to
push forward.

It was Hew.

His horse reared and turned, and briefly Lily
thought he was about to run. But Hew forced the
animal back around, facing his opponent, just as
the blond giant rose up beside his saddle. The battle-axe sang through the rain, and took Hew's
head from his body.

There was a collective groan from the enemy
ranks.

"Now we will win!" Stephen's whisper was
hoarse, his throat raw from shouting.

The azure banner flapped, moving through the
field. Hew's men held a moment longer, and then
began to retreat. First one or two, and then more,
stumbling and running, pursued up the slope by
Radulf's forces.

Radulf himself rode forward, and was suddenly surrounded by Hew's men. No, Kenton's
men—tough, battle-hardened Normans determined to battle to the end for their absent master.
Rigid with fear, Lily watched Radulf fight first
one, and then another, his sword slashing and
jabbing. Oh God, he was desperately outnumbered . . .

Thunder rumbled across the hills, the dark
clouds moving in as though to signal an end. Another crack of thunder and the rain came down, a
deluge. And now Lily could not see a thing.

"Where is he?" she whimpered, and began to

pray. There were glimpses of color, the green of
the grass and the brown of the churned earth,
men's armor and clothing, and men's blood. Even
the noise of the battle had faded beneath the roar
of the rain.

Stephen gripped Lily's hand, pulling her toward the shelter of a tent. When they stood dripping within its walls, she turned to him frantically.

"Did you see Radulf? At the last, did you see
him?"

Stephen stared back at her. She could see the
lies forming in his eyes, but in the end he offered
her the uncomfortable truth. "No, lady, I did not
see him."

Was he dead, then? Fallen upon the battlefield?
He had been surrounded, overwhelmed. She had
seen how easily Hew's head had been parted from
his body . . . If it had not been for her babe, Lily
would have run from the tent to search for him.
What was her life without Radulf? Had she given
him her heart, only to have it smashed? Lily's
tears mingled with the rain . . .

A rough, ragged cheer floated across the valley.
The rain was easing, the thunder's growl drifting
away. Lily blinked, wiping the moisture from her
lashes and gripping the tent doorway with a trembling hand. There was the sound of horses approaching; a voice—Jervois?—rose in tired
laughter. Lily edged forward on shaky legs. A
huge, dark shape was approaching her, taking
form through the white shield of the rain. She
heard the clomp of horse's hooves, and then
Radulf's destrier was suddenly before her.

With a gasping sob, Lily began to run toward
him. The stallion whinnied, already unsettled by

the fighting, and reared up dangerously.

"My lady!" Stephen cried and, sprinting after her, held her back.

The destrier snorted irritably, settling to the soft murmur of Radulf's voice. A groom ran up as Radulf dismounted, leading the stallion away.

Radulf reached up and removed his helmet. His face was grimy, his hair plastered to his head with sweat; he tilted his face to the rain and let it wash him clean. Of all the battles he had ever fought, today's was the most important. Because he wasn't just fighting for the king, but for Lily and himself, and their future together.

When he straightened again she was standing before him.

"Radulf." Lily's voice trembled. "My lord."

She was soaked through, her hair dripping, her skirts clinging to her legs, her face without color. He could see in her gray eyes the suffering she had endured while she watched him fight. Radulf put out his hand, and then seeing the state of it, pulled back with a grimace.

"You won?"

A weary smile tugged at his lips. "Aye, Lily, we won. Now we can go home to Crevitch."

Lily did not remind him that, to her, this place had always been home. The truth was, it was only home if he was there.

"You are hurt?"

He shook his head. "No, Lily, I am whole. A scratch or two, but nothing to concern you." His wonderful mouth curved into a smile. "You will heal me with your salve, *mignonne*?"

He is safe, he is alive!

With a glad cry, Lily flung herself into his arms. He caught her, half laughing, half wincing. "Lady," he murmured against her hair, "I am not fit . . ."

"You are here with me," she replied fiercely, "and that is all that matters."

He gave in and rested his cheek upon her damp hair, stroking the silver strands. She was soft and sweet, and it mattered not that he was neither. They would bathe together, wash the dirt and sorrow of this place away, and turn their thoughts to a better future. The red gleam of the hawk's-eye ring caught his tired gaze.

I give thee my heart.

Lily would never betray him, he knew that now with solid certainty, and if he did not declare his trust of her, then they could never be truly free of Anna or Vorgen.

"You gave me much before the battle," he said softly. "In return, I give you all that I am. I give you my wealth and my estates, I give you my might and my sword—and I give you my heart, Lily, for now and all time."

She lifted her head, her gray eyes swimming with tears. "Your heart will be safe with me, my lord."

He bent to kiss her, and just as he did, the rain stopped and the sun shone out. Around them, the weary army cheered. Aye, thought Radulf, here was an omen.

Lily, glancing up from the shelter of his arms, found herself the center of attention of a great many muddy, weary men. "Radulf," she whispered, "can we not go somewhere more private?"

With a laugh, Radulf swung her up into his arms. "Your pardon, men! My lady requests privacy to give her thanks . . . properly." And with Lily's flushed face pressed to his heart, and the amused shouts of his men in his ears, Radulf carried his wife from the field of battle.

Epilogue

The following year

Crevitch Castle, usually such a lively place, was surprisingly hushed. Radulf stood alone in the great hall, staring into the fire, two hounds lying at his feet. No one had approached him since breakfast, when he had almost bitten Jervois's head off for offering him a mug of ale.

He hadn't meant it, and Jervois, pale and shaken, had accepted his apologies, even offering his heartfelt sympathies to his lord. Jervois knew exactly what Radulf was going through—Alice was also with child.

Radulf ground his teeth. Sympathy just made it worse. He should be rejoicing; his wife was giving birth to their first child. So why was he not rejoicing?

Because he was sick with worry, that was why.

Radulf sighed. He loved the lady too much. She

was his joy, his heart, his life itself. If anything should happen to her, if she should be taken from him . . .

This was all beyond his experience, beyond his control. Radulf was used to giving orders and seeing a thing instantly done, but he could not order a babe not to hurt its mother, and he could not order Lily not to scream. Frustrated and powerless, Radulf could do nothing at all.

Apart from wait.

It was the waiting that was driving him to despair.

Suddenly there was whispering behind him in the doorway. Radulf's hands clenched on the mantel, fear raking through him. Was it bad news? Were they choosing straws to see which of them would tell him? His stomach threatened to spill the ale he had swallowed hours since. These past few months at Crevitch with Lily had been beyond happiness. Were they all he was ever to have?

"My lord? Lord Radulf!"

Radulf spun around, white-faced. Alice of Rennoc. She had come up silently behind him, her little rounded form even more rounded these days, as Jervois's child swelled within her. Her bright eyes appeared sympathetic, though shadowed with weariness. Radulf searched her expression for clues to his wife's well-being but could find none.

Alice wasn't smiling; did that mean something? But then Radulf was well aware that he had always made Alice nervous, and at this moment he was a sight to frighten the smile off braver faces than hers. He had been up for many hours, slumped outside their bedchamber, listening to Lily's pain. Until he could bear it no more, and had retreated down there, to be alone with his terror.

"Lady Lily is ready for you now, Lord Radulf."

Ready for him? That had an ominous ring to it.

But before he could ask her what she meant, Alice had turned, and Radulf followed her with unsteady feet and a pounding heart. A shudder rent him. If she was dead . . . but his thoughts could get no further than that. There *was* nothing beyond that. Life for him would simply cease to exist.

Alice had slipped through the door into the bedchamber, and Radulf hesitated. Was he brave enough to face what was in there? He straightened his broad shoulders and took a deep breath for courage. There was nowhere else to go. Radulf followed her in.

The room was warm and scented with herbs. Compared to the rest of the castle, it was a pleasantly cheery place. Radulf swayed, disoriented, as if he had entered a dream.

Lily was propped up in bed, her hair combed like a silken shawl about her, while Gudren sat, smug as a well-fed cat, by the fire. Alice was smiling down at the bundle she held carefully in her arms. Lily turned at his entrance, her face pale but radiant, and her gray eyes filled with tears. Her voice trembled with happiness.

"Oh, Radulf, you have a daughter!"

Radulf stared at her a moment, bewildered by the sight of her so much alive when he had been imagining her cold and dead. Then, with a groan, he stumbled to the bedside and fell to his knees.

His dark head dropped to her breast, and he breathed in the familiar scent of her with a great shudder of joy.

Startled, Lily cried out softly as he jolted her aching body, and then, feeling him shaking, her own discomforts were forgotten as she gathered her husband into her arms. "Radulf? My love, what is it? You are unwell?" In between her words, she was covering his face with frantic little kisses, her hands touching him, stroking him, searching to heal his hurt.

Radulf shook his head, only gripping one of her hands with his and pressing it hard to his lips. She was warm and alive; he felt her heart beating, her breast rising and falling with each breath she took. His Lily was alive. Suddenly the dark clouds lifted from him, as they had done the day of the battle with Hew, and the sun shone warm and cheering.

Radulf raised his head and, hollow-eyed, met her worried gaze. With shaking fingers, he touched her beautiful face. His voice was so soft it was almost a whisper.

"If you had died, lady, there would have been no point to living."

Her gray eyes widened, and one tear spilled over her lashes as he leaned forward and pressed his lips tenderly to hers.

"I am the King's Sword," he went on, more firmly. "Give me a battle to fight and I will fight it; send me to win a war, and so I will. But *mignonne*, I cannot bear your pain. I would rather die myself than stand by while you suffer."

Lily's expression softened. Gently, she smoothed back his dark hair. "Radulf, I will not break. I am strong. And the pain is gone now. Come, look at your daughter. She will think you do not want her, if you ignore her."

Alice stepped forward, and handed Lily the bundle in her arms. At his wife's urging, Radulf dropped his gaze to the face of the sleeping babe. It was round and sweet, with a pale fuzz of hair, dark lashes, and a pouting little mouth. One look, that was all he needed, and any resentment in his heart melted. Instinctively he put out his finger, and then hesitated, glancing at Lily.

"Go on," she urged him again. "She will not break either."

Radulf stroked his daughter's cheek and, when she stirred, allowed her to take his large finger in her tiny hand.

"You see," Lily whispered, blinking back more tears at the sight of Radulf, the great warrior, and this little babe. "You have a daughter, my love."

His daughter . . . Lily's daughter. Suddenly it made their love more real, more lasting. For how could it ever die, if their daughter was there to carry it on?

Radulf leaned closer, his lips seeking his wife's, and said, "No, Lily, my love—*we* have a daughter."